cargo of orchids

THE NATIONAL BESTSELLER

ALSO BY SUSAN MUSGRAVE

Fiction
The Charcoal Burners
The Dancing Chicken

Poetry
Songs of the Sea-Witch
Entrance of the Celebrant
Grave-Dirt and Selected Strawberries
The Impstone
Kiskatinaw (with Seán Virgo)
Selected Strawberries and Other Poems
Becky Swan's Book
A Man to Marry, a Man to Bury
Tarts and Muggers: Poems New and Selected
Cocktails at the Mausoleum
The Embalmer's Art: Poems New and Selected
Forcing the Narcissus
Things That Keep and Do Not Change
What the Small Day Cannot Hold: Collected Poems 1970–1985

Children's
Gullband
Hag Head
Kestrel and Leonardo
Dreams Are More Real Than Bathtubs

Non-Fiction
Great Musgrave
Musgrave Landing: Musings on the Writing Life

Compiled and Edited
Clear-Cut Words: Writers for Clayoquot
Because You Loved Being a Stranger:
55 Poets Celebrate Patrick Lane

cargo of orchids

S U S A N   M U S G R A V E

VINTAGE CANADA

A Division of Random House of Canada Limited

NATIONAL LIBRARY OF CANADA CATALOGUING IN PUBLICATION DATA

Musgrave, Susan, 1951–
Cargo of orchids

ISBN 0-676-97308-6

I. Title.

PS8576.U7C37 2001   C813'.54   C2001-901548-8
PR9199.3.M88C37 2001

www.randomhouse.ca

Printed and bound in the United States of America

2 4 6 8 9 7 5 3 1

This story is true.

La verdad es una puta y hay que pagar.
(Truth is a whore and you must pay for her.)
— Colombian saying

To the Virgin of Mercy,
the patron of prisoners

And to prisoners the world over:
No tenemos que pedir permiso para ser libres

contents

editor's note

Though this story is true, some names have been changed. Otherwise there have been few alterations.

The writer intended both the Spanish and her translations into English to be included in the text, but in most cases the Spanish has been dropped for the sake of expediency. A few words and phrases and colloquialisms have been retained for flavour, and she would like to thank Paul Oscar Nelson for his input. Also Gustavo Gomez, for his fine-tuning.

It is the writer's wish that her name appear nowhere in the book.

part one / valentine's day in jail

Stop and imagine for an instant a world where someone is grateful for something.

—Bret Easton Ellis,
American Psycho

chapter one

Death Clinic, Heaven Valley State Facility for Women

If you are a new inmate only recently sentenced by the courts,
this will probably be an entirely new experience for you.
—*Inmate Information Handbook*

When you find yourself listening to their keys and
owning none, you will come close to understanding the
white terror of the soul that comes with being banished
from all commerce with mankind.
—Pat Conroy, *Prince of Tides*

When a reporter asked Rainy to compare being given the death sentence to being hit by a train, she said, "The train was quicker, the train was softer."

I've lived next door to Rainy for ten years, on the Condemned Row. They call it the Death Clinic—as if it's a place you go to get treatment for a terminal disease. You can't cure death, but while you wait for it, they make life impossible.

In many cases death-row inmates are not allowed to write anything longer than a one-page letter, double-spaced. That they permit me to write this story is not a right, they remind me every chance they get, it's a privilege. If I write gossip, to spread rumours that might end up embarrassing the staff, this privilege will be revoked. So I do as I am told, and "confine all writings to inside the lines." If you ignore the lines, you are considered "out of bounds without authorization and subject to disciplinary action."

When I write the word *lines*, I think of cocaine. My care and treatment counsellor, Mrs. Dykstra, would say the word *lines* is a trigger, a connection to my former "drug-seeking ways." Not to mention *connection*.

La Reina de la Cocaína is what they called me in the papers after my arrest: the Cocaine Queen. They gave me other names, too. La Madre Sin Corazón. The Mother without a Heart. When I told one reporter I wished I'd been called Oriana Fallachi, a name that sounds like you're having sex without doing it, he said he could understand why a woman like me would want to change her identity.

Rainy says I shouldn't take it personally, what they say about me in the press. They always end up bad-mouthing mothers who kill their kids.

———

Frenchy, my only other neighbour at the moment, is suing the railway. When the train passes the prison at 2:16 every afternoon, it whistles and wakes her up.

Rainy says, what does she expect? She sleeps all day.

Every day is a gift, I say. Who can blame her for not wanting to get out of bed?

Each Christmas Eve we are issued a new calendar so we can start X-ing off the days — until *next* Christmas or our date certain, whichever comes first. But aside from the barbed-wire sculpture meant to symbolize a Christmas tree in one corner of the chow hall, and the matron who has a "negativity scene"—what Rainy calls it—on her desk, Christmas is like any other day on the Condemned Row. The Salvation Army used to donate a poinsettia for our common room, until one year a girl made a salad out of the leaves.

This morning in the shower, Rainy started singing, "Deck the halls with marijuana, fa-la-la-la-la-la la la la." She would have gone on, but Frenchy, who doesn't have the Christmas spirit, told her to shut up. The rule here is that if someone *asks* you to shut up, you shut up. Because they're not asking for a debate, and they're not asking again.

Rainy says she and Frenchy are the two best friends I could "hope to never have." She also insists that if anyone reads this book, they will want to know what my best friends *look* like; she doesn't understand when I tell her I don't care about appearances. Rainy's expressions, actions and thoughts count for more in this story than the fact that she is so thin her elbows and knees look like they're going to slice through her clothing, or that her eyes are empty because she's cried all the colour away, or that she has no chest at all and a mouth that turns down from the way things have gone.

Despite the freight of anger she carries, Rainy seems so frail it is hard to imagine her giving birth to anything heavier than tears. Rainy gave birth to twins, and six months later left them on the railway tracks. She claims it prejudiced the jury. If she'd smothered them or driven them off a pier, it would have been more socially acceptable. She might have been able to cut a deal, had her sentence commuted to life. She could have gone on "Oprah" and become a celebrity, maybe even a role model for women who are child-free by choice.

The train was quicker, the train was softer. But abandoning your kids on the tracks wasn't in fashion. She wishes now she'd gone out drinking for the evening instead, but she didn't have enough money to hire a babysitter *and* pay for the beer.

I can hear Rainy singing, under her breath as she leaves the shower room, "'Tis the season to be jolly." In prison, time does not progress, it goes round and round in a spiral of endless pain. I want to say, Rainy, there are no seasons in prison—only time.

Frenchy has a little peacock-like crest of hair shooting from the white bandanna she says she wears "to keep my brains wrapped up in." There's a male heaviness about her face: her broad nose, brown eyes, a mouth made for smiling and for grief. Her most distinguishing feature, though, is the white, heart-shaped mark, shining like a beauty spot in reverse, on her cheek. Frenchy calls it her "ugly spot."

Frenchy's here because she killed her sixteen-year-old son. "The two of us was just fooling around, you know. Robbing a bank. I've made a few mistakes in life I probably shouldn't have made. *And* we was doing more drinking than we probably should have, considering we was both on probation. *And* I was high at the time. So I think I might have overpanicked when those alarms went off, but I don't recall shooting anyone on purpose.

"We got away from the bank, even though he couldn't run fast and had to drop most of the money and got blood all over the rest. I was pretty hot about that. I left him by the river, thinking I could go back and find a doctor when things cooled off. The whole town was looking for us, so I stayed at Laverne's getting high for a week. When Laverne and me went back for him, some animals had eaten on him and there was bugs everywhere, and Laverne shot his teeth out. She told me she done it so that his dental records couldn't be used against me. That's what I loved best about Laverne—you could count on her to take care of the details.

"The shooting his mouth part, that made it look bad, but I kept my own mouth shut and never gave up Laverne to the cops, even though I could have got a deal if I did." Frenchy's got a few good qualities like that—loyalty. And hindsight. She sees now she made some bad choices, but Frenchy didn't have a lot of positive influences when she was growing up. She still likes to shock people by telling them, "I was so young when I started sucking cocks, I had to be burped afterwards."

Her father was "good part Cajun, mostly bad part black"; her mother, who gave birth to her in a mental institution, Crow—you can see it in Frenchy's bones. She's got one finger missing—she gave the finger to her father when he boxed her one time; sliced it off right in front of him. Frenchy has no regrets. Nine fingers, she says, gets you a discount at the manicurist's.

After Laverne shot her boy's teeth out, Frenchy told me they went on a road trip, stealing a Grand Prix, refuelling with hot credit cards. Laverne made one more mistake, Frenchy said, when she paid for a Diet Coke with a gold American Express card at a Holiday Inn. Then when the card came up invalid, she pretended she didn't speak English and left Frenchy holding the bag. When she went to trial, Frenchy asked Laverne for a character reference, "because Laverne, whatever else she might screw up, wouldn't screw up my character."

I found one book in the library that says there are five ways to die, all of them painful. Even when you die in your sleep, it hurts. Those five painful ways don't include the choices I've been presented with under the state's new pro-choice with a twist policy. Pro-choice means the freedom to choose which form of capital punishment is best suited to your personality—lethal injection, gas chamber, electric chair, hanging or the firing-squad. If you can't make up your own mind, they choose for you. "Dead if you do, dead if you don't," says Rainy.

Unlike those whom society invests with authority, most people who live on the Row have learned that killing people is wrong. When I write that the death penalty is an unambiguous disgrace to civilized humanity, I suppose there are people who say that's because I have an axe to grind. I do, and it's blunt from being ground down over the ten years I've lived waiting to die in prison.

Another book I read says the key to understanding capital punishment is to be found in its ritual element. Many cultures have made ritual sacrifices—the Aztecs, for instance, spread their victim on a stone altar, cut open his chest with an obsidian blade, then ripped his heart out. State-sanctioned murder should be, in theory, no more curious than that.

Rainy has come with me to the library to see what I do with myself all day. When I describe how poor Aztec children were sold to priests by their parents, who couldn't afford to keep them, she wants to know if those children got their hearts torn out, too. Not unless the priests wanted it to rain, I say; they believed the rain god favoured little children's tears. Rainy says those kids were lucky if getting sacrificed was the worst thing that ever happened to them in their lives.

Rainy never learned to read or write; she thinks a sentence is something you have to serve. She's never been in a library before, and didn't know God had created that many books. The one book she recognizes is the Bible. I tell her parts of it were written in prison, and that capital punishment, like feeling guilty about having sex, has all its roots in religion.

Rainy thinks about this, then says *she* hasn't had sex for so long she is afraid her parts have healed shut, like a pierced ear you don't wear a post in.

I sign out *The Rituals of Human Sacrifice* to save Frenchy the trouble of stealing it for me. Frenchy prides herself on her ability to steal, but where books are concerned, I've had to tone her down.

When we were back in the general population, I caught her tearing the last page out of a mystery I'd been on the waiting list to read. She claimed to have "edited" hundreds of books this way; if she was going to die, she said, she wanted to make sure those left behind would remember her. I said I'd pay her a bale of tobacco for every book she could steal for me that came *with* an ending. Before long I had to put a limit on the number. It was easier for Frenchy to pinch books than it was for me to find places to hide them, and soon I was paying her to steal books *back* to the library.

When I told my mother I was writing a book, she begged me to write it under a pseudonym. I've never heard of a person writing her memoirs under an alias; if anyone reading this wonders why I've left my name out of this story, one reason is to make my mother proud of me. When I asked her not to visit me here, I think she was relieved. She toured a dungeon once, in the Azores, and found it "stuffy."

I write to her once a week, but I'm careful about what I say. She'd only worry if she knew I lay awake at night thinking up ways to short-circuit the electric chair, or calculating how long I'd be able to hold my breath in the gas chamber.

In her most recent letter, she told me she was going to the Caribbean, "to some island where they speak English, I hope." She will be wearing the watch passed down from her great-great-grandmother, with its diamonds and sapphires "worth more than my house." She wears it because she's afraid she'll lose it otherwise. There's logic.

If anything happens to her, and she doesn't make it back in one piece, she says, I should be sure to file a claim. I don't remind her where I live, or that I won't be able to spend her insurance money where I'm going, but I do warn her that if she flaunts the watch, some cracked-out desperado might hack off her whole arm with a rusty machete. That might not be such a bad thing. A lost arm would provide her with a permanent conversation piece now that my father is gone, or, at the very least, give her something new to talk about besides the unreliable lamp in her life.

Last night I dreamed I buried my face in my father's nut-brown jacket, reaching for the smell of him in the old corduroy. I could smell his pipe tobacco, the kind I used to catch a whiff of on the street, like sugared leather dipped in wildflower honey mixed with dust. My mother still keeps his jacket over the back of his chair, as if she expects him to walk in from the garden with a handful of the Chinese tea roses he bred. In my dream, the roses smelled like tea leaves when you bruise them.

When I first came to the Row, they made me sign forms saying that in the event of death or injury sustained during my incarceration, I would not hold the institution responsible. I can't say they haven't been taking care of me.

When they escort me to the chow hall, they attach a trip chain to my leg shackles so the guard behind me, holding the chain, can pull my feet out from under me if I make a break for it and try to vault the seventeen-foot-high fence of electrified wire—assuming I make it through all six electronically controlled doors and across six hundred feet of open yard first. My wrists are handcuffed too, although they undo the cuffs to let me eat. Then they just watch me extra hard.

I have been classified as an escape risk, among other things. It doesn't take them long to classify you. They read your file, look you over, ask your age, race and religion, and then write down whatever Representation of Female Evil they figure you most closely represent.

> a) Cold Calculators: Women who ruthlessly kill their husband(s) or loved one(s) for financial gain.

> b) Black Widows: Serial murderers of husbands, male lovers and next of kin. Some killings seemingly have no motive. Most common *modus operandi* is poisoning.

> c) Depraved Partners: Highly charged, (hetero)-sexual, violence-loving young women who link up with an evil, murderous male partner to commit serial murders, often involving the kidnapping and torture of young white women.

> d) Explosive Avengers: Manlike or lesbian women. Premeditation is far from clear.

e) Robber Predators: Women who murder while committing or covering up financial-gain felonies.

My classification officer got excited when I asked her to read again the definition of an Explosive Avenger. When she reread it, watching my face this time, I asked for clarification on "Premeditation is far from clear." She said "premeditation" meant you had planned your crime in advance; it wasn't just something you did because you lost control of your reason in a moment of passion. I said I understood what the word meant, but I didn't understand the meaning of "Premeditation is far from clear." Did that mean it was unclear whether the crime was premeditated, or that the premeditation itself was not very well thought out? My CO looked at the words, frowned, then admitted it must be a mistake, that the line ought to read "Motivation is far from clear."

I went back to my house, feeling I had made one small step for Female Evil. However, nothing changed. My CO wrote that I probably had a "lesbian-type affiliation" with Consuelo de Corazón, which is why I maintained the illusion I was being held hostage. In her opinion, I had clearly murdered my child, "though premeditation is far from clear."

Rainy says that if it is any consolation, she too has been classified as an Explosive Avenger/Cold Calculator, even though she never made one dime from killing her twins.

Everyone here gets classified as a Something-American.

Rainy. Age: 32; Mexican-American; Explosive Avenger/Cold Calculator.

Frenchy. Age: 35; African-American; Robber-Predator.

Yours Truly. Age: 47; Canadian-American; Explosive Avenger/Cold Calculator.

I appealed my classification, saying I did *not* have U.S. citizenship, but the classification officers who reviewed my case could not conceive of a nationality that wasn't at least half American. "Everybody's got to have *some* good in them," they said.

Once you have been classified, that's what you have become. And you go to your grave here with your classification papers stuffed in your hand like a diploma.

My husband (more about him later) hired a lawyer to represent me—Ferdinand Pile, Jr.—the self-acclaimed "Cadillac of lawyers." As soon as I heard his name, I figured Vernal must have a million-dollar insurance policy on my life.

Even though I don't think Pile, Jr.—who promised he'd get me out of prison if it took him the rest of his life—had ever defended a murder case, I'm not blaming him for the fact I got the death sentence. I want it to go on record that I take full responsibility for what I did. That's one reason I'm writing this book.

It's so easy to get sidetracked in here. To lose my train. Alone in my house I open *The Rituals of Human Sacrifice*, and turn to a section of photographs. A child's shoe in the grass—this one makes me saddest. I think how much of a story that shoe, with the mindless persistence of objects, has to tell. I imagine slipping my baby's narrow foot into it, tickling his sole when he curls up his toes, the way he always did.

I fed my child; I did what I could. But even in my dreams he is always hungry, and no matter how much I feed him, it's never enough. He sucks his thumb and pulls out his eyelashes with his fingers. Sometimes he dips the eyelashes into honey, or something else sweet, like treacle or molasses, then plays with them between his teeth. I honestly think he swallows them, though by that point the dream is usually over.

I can only guess what he might have become. Sorrow is nourishment forever.

chapter two

In books, people meet on tropical islands or in high-class restaurants or when they're both doing something danger- ous in a foreign country and are thrown together because they narrowly escape stepping on the same land mine; I met Vernal in a public washroom. Both of us were so embar- rassed that we never could remember afterwards which one of us had been in the wrong place. We both remember apol- ogizing, each one tripping over the other, as we Canadians do, to apologize first.

It was April 1985. I'd just turned thirty, and I'd been flown to New York to attend the launch of a book I'd trans- lated from Spanish into English. I had majored in languages, and had a job freelancing for a publishing house with offices in Vancouver (where I lived), New York and Bogotá.

My assignment had been to translate the memoirs of a woman who was connected, by marriage, to one of the major Colombian drug cartels. Carmen María de Corazón had been kidnapped by a narco-terrorist guerrilla group called Las Blancas (The White Ladies), who had taken to abducting wealthy foreigners and nationals alike, using ransom monies to finance their drug-smuggling operations and the recruiting and training of young *guerrilleras*. Carmen had been released once a ransom of six million dollars had been paid by "undisclosed sources." Kidnapping had become so prevalent in Colombia that a new law had been passed: when a national was abducted, his or her bank account was automatically frozen, to prevent ransom payments being withdrawn.

Carmen's orange-haired bodyguard, who introduced herself only as Bret, met me at JFK. It was my first time in New York, and I was there because Carmen had insisted— all expenses paid. On the way into town, Bret gave me an envelope full of cash, including a hundred-dollar bill "for the mugger." She advised me, too, not to walk through Central Park "with that pack." The Canadian flag, with its bull's-eye maple leaf, was an open invitation.

When the cab let us out at the Ritz ("Carmen María wants you to feel at home"), Bret pointed me to one of the overstuffed chairs in the lobby while she checked me in. There was a problem with the room, in that they didn't have one, but I was quietly upgraded to the honeymoon suite, and given a complimentary bowl of fruit and a bottle of chilled champagne—just the sort of treatment I would have expected at the Ritz.

As we went up in the elevator, I told Bret the Ritz had always been part of our family mythology. Every summer, from the time I was ten years old, we'd spent two weeks "getting away from it all" in the Kootenays. I resented the leech-infested lake, the pack rat that stole my mood ring, the outhouse with its "If You Sprinkle When You Tinkle, Be a Sweetie and Wipe the Seatie" sign and the fact that there were no boys within fifty miles, boys being the "it" from which my parents were intent on getting me away. I'd be picking the scabs off my mosquito bites and the mouse droppings out of the butter, and complaining that I couldn't just go to bed and sleep for two weeks because my mattress had no springs in it, when my father would say, "What do you think this is, the Ritz?"

Bret looked at me as if I came from Canada, and when we got to my suite, asked if I liked Chinese. I said yes, assuming she meant food (I had been warned not to take anything at face value in the Big Apple), and she rolled her eyes again and said she'd be back to pick me up at five-thirty.

My suite took up two floors: there were three television screens, a computer and a fax machine, and a king-size bed with a mirror on the ceiling that made me feel a pang for the crab fisherman from Prince Rupert I'd been seeing in the off-season. I had a seashell-shaped bathtub made of green marble, with gold faucets, and a toilet that flushed soundlessly. The glass cases, antique, were filled with clay figurines. I examined these closely before getting undressed and wondered if anyone else had noticed that the rain god had a double-headed penis, or that the child lying on his back holding up his heart to the rain god had a hollow place in his chest, a bowl to catch his tears.

I tried to nap, but then gave up, got dressed again in my jeans and T-shirt and duffel coat with two toggles missing, and went for a walk—without my pack. Halfway across the park I got tired and sat to rest on the only empty bench I could find, one with a used tampon and a dead rat lying beneath it. I returned to the hotel, took a long bath and dressed for the third time that day in the same clothes I'd been wearing since I'd picked them out of the dirty laundry before leaving Vancouver. It was either that or go to the launch in my pyjamas. I'd forgotten to pack anything fancy.

When Bret, who had even changed her hair colour for the evening (to match her boa constrictor pantsuit), arrived, we took a death-defying cab ride through the potholes of New York to Philippe's Chopsticks Restaurant. "Don't order the Strange Taste Chicken," Bret advised when a tiny waitperson brought us a menu thicker than Carmen María's book, *Rescate* (Ransom). "It doesn't taste like any bird you'll ever eat." Bret was an expert on everything from Chinese beer to firm-textured tofu; she knew the caloric content of every dish I considered ordering, and when I couldn't make up my mind, she told me the only thing you could be sure had no calories was sex. One teaspoon of spermatozoa contained thirty-two different substances, including vitamin C, vitamin B12, fructose, sulphur, zinc, copper, magnesium, potassium, calcium and many anti–free radicals, she explained. She figured she could even give up eating if she could find a man to have oral sex with once a day. "But not for the sex, just for the health part. I stopped going to bed—with men—centuries ago. All they were ever interested in was, you know, spreading their gene pool around."

I drank three Tsing-Tao's in a row and left most of my WorWonton untouched. I didn't say this to Bret, but I wished I could meet *one* man who wanted to procreate. There'd been men in my life—but either they already had children and didn't want the prospect of more child support, or they were too young and didn't want the commitment, or they were away from home with their work too often, or they worked at home and didn't want to share the playroom. I'd always wanted babies, and the life that went with them, everything from the environmentally friendly diaper service to the folding stroller. Well, at least *one* baby. Someone to love, who would love me back, forever.

That kind of forever didn't seem to be in the offing. Even my fortune cookie advised, "Romance is iffy." Bret snorted when I showed it to her, and said Margaret Trudeau was the only person she'd ever heard of who got lucky in New York, "if you can call giving Jack Nicholson head in the back seat of a stretch getting lucky."

After she'd paid the bill and flagged down another cab, we endured a second near-death experience all the way to The Purple Reign; Carmen María's husband had shares in the fashionable nightclub, now owned by "the Asians." After briefing the doorman to ensure I would have no problems getting in (they had a no-jeans policy, she explained), Bret said she was abandoning me because she had a coming-out party to attend; a friend of hers had just done nine

months, and they were going out celebrating. Bret kissed me
on both cheeks and said she regretted not having the
chance to get to know me better. In retrospect, I felt I had
barely escaped from an iffy situation: when she embraced
me, it felt like being hugged by a knife drawer.

Inside the club I climbed the purple-and-gold-carpeted
steps to a landing where a woman barely dressed in a gold
lamé gown informed me I would have to check my handguns
at the door. I checked my duffel coat instead, glancing
around the room trying not to appear as nervous as I felt, and
when I saw no familiar faces, helped myself to a tray of soggy
canapés. A man in a white suit introduced himself, saying he
was looking forward to hearing me recite from . . . his voice
trailed off, and I filled in the name of the book for him . . .
which would be in half an hour or so, after a few drinks.

A Cuban waiter tried to tempt me with one of his mini
sausage rolls as I sipped a cautious new wine from the
Niagara region, which, I was sure, Carmen had had import-
ed especially for me. The Chinese beer I'd had earlier, and
the canapé mixed with the wine, started, suddenly, to have
an unexpected effect, and I asked a man in a mauve tux,
who looked like he ought to know, where the ladies' was. I
pushed open the heavy doors he pointed me to and had
ensconced myself in the cubicle furthest from the door (the
toilet that has the least germs, according to an article I read;
the one in the middle has the most, and it was occupied),
thinking I would stay there until I threw up or it was time
to give my reading, when I heard the person in the middle
stall clearing his throat. Then, with the hint of a question
in his voice, he spoke my name.

I got to my feet, flushed the toilet, even though it wasn't necessary, and pushed open the door, certain now I was in the wrong washroom. He came out of *his* stall and that's when we both began apologizing. With his wind-blown blond hair and blue eyes that looked as if they were more suited to picking rocks on the beach than picking weenies off toothpicks, he looked attractively out of place, not just in this washroom but in the clothes he wore too: he was the only person—besides me—who had not dressed formally. He met my gaze, smiled as if he had been caught, then looked away. The scar on his cheek, just below his right eye, made him look dangerous.

Our hands touched as we both reached for the brass door handle. Once we were on neutral ground, I asked him how he'd known it was me in that cubicle next to him.

"Only someone from Vancouver would wear hiking boots to a nightclub in New York," he said, smiling. He pointed: his own boots were the same make as mine.

Back in the crowded room, Carmen brought us each a glass of champagne and kissed Vernal on the cheek. "I wondered who'd kidnapped you," she said. She looked exotic— her red hair, sullen, scarlet lips and black-painted fingernails embedded with emeralds like cut stars. Her eyes were the light green of a parrot's wings, and her body smelled faintly of nutmeg.

Carmen and I had spent hours together on the telephone when I was translating her book. At first I didn't know why I had been asked to take on the work—New York must have been full of Spanish-into-English translators—but I soon learned that nobody south of the border would even *look* at the manuscript for fear of reprisals, of being kidnapped themselves or having their families threatened. I'd learned a lot more from Carmen María than just the Spanish colloquialisms for *bribe* and *assassin*.

"Vernal is *canadiense, mijita,* just like you!" Carmen exclaimed. "He lawyer." She pronounced *lawyer* "liar," and when I looked at Vernal he pushed his hair out of his face and gave me a what-can-I-say kind of smile. Carmen told him to bring us some more drinks.

I ran my thumb over my own chewed fingernails as Carmen dabbed at her mouth with a paper napkin covered with small blue fleurs-de-lys, her way of showing off the emerald ring, worth ten times what I'd been paid for translating her book. I raised my eyebrows, and she waved her hand dismissively.

"A gift from my husband. He is in prison again today, or else he would be here with us, celebrating. What can I tell you? At least he remembered my birthday."

When Vernal came back with our drinks, Carmen turned to speak to a group of women dressed as if they were going on a safari to Tiffany's. Vernal had a copy of *Rescate* but couldn't decide whether it was the right thing to do, to ask the translator to autograph it; he kept flipping through the book instead, the way people do when they haven't read it yet and don't know what to say.

"I look forward to reading it . . . very much," he said finally. He looked down at the floor, and it seemed to me he blushed. "That goes without saying, I suppose—I mean, that I look forward to reading it. What else are you supposed to do with a book?"

"You could put it on your head," I said, trying to make him feel at ease. "It's an exercise they used to make us do . . . at charm school. Walk across the room with a book on your head, to improve your posture. I grew up thinking books were instruments of torture."

He was still looking at his feet. "*Writing* must be torture for you then. Is it?"

"Translating is very different from writing," I said. Vernal downed his second glass of champagne rather too quickly. I straightened my shoulders. "Do you read . . . many books?" I asked.

He stared into his empty glass, turning it round in his hand. "I hate to confess, but only what puts me to sleep. Which means I like very dull books. *Burke on the Law of Recision in Contracts*, for example. I don't think I've ever got to the end of the first paragraph."

I laughed, trying to sound impressed.

"I hope Carmen María's book doesn't put you to sleep *that* quickly," I said.

"It won't. Of course it won't. Not if the cover is anything to go by. And I'm sure you . . . your translation will keep me awake. If nothing else does."

After an awkward pause, where we tried not to make eye contact, I asked Vernal how he knew Carmen. "I know her husband," Vernal said. "He's been to Vancouver . . . on several occasions. In the past." He dropped his voice as he looked around the room. "He's a client of mine."

"And vice versa," said Carmen. She apologized for butting in on our conversation, but said she wanted to excuse herself—she needed to compose herself before her reading.

I watched two men in white jackets setting up chairs, another filling goblets with ice water from a cut-glass pitcher. Shortly afterwards, the man who had introduced himself to me earlier cleared his voice in the microphone and, when he had the crowd's attention, said that—he hesitated, and I prayed he would at least remember *her* name—Carmen María would read first and her translator would follow. Those who didn't have glasses in their hands clapped, so the applause sounded a bit thin and I began to wish I was safe under the covers in my round bed back at the Ritz.

Carmen had not warned me what part of her memoir she would be reading. Not everyone in the audience understood Spanish, but all listened attentively, picking up, no doubt, on the emotional intensity in her voice. Halfway through her performance her voice suddenly broke, and she collapsed on the floor and had to be taken upstairs to recuperate. I assumed Vernal had gone with her, because I looked for him when I got up to read but couldn't find him in the audience.

I explained to the crowd that this had been the most difficult part of the book for me to translate, and how brave I thought Carmen María was for having written about such a brutal and offensive act. I took a deep breath and read that Carmen María had been eight months pregnant at the time she was taken hostage, that she had been kept tied up in a dirty underground cell until she was ready to give birth. Even when she went into labour, her captors wouldn't loosen the ropes around her ankles or her wrists so she could bear down properly, and when the baby came out they wouldn't let her hold him, but took him to another room where she couldn't see him, only hear his cries. When she heard her baby cry, her milk would come in. She could not feed him and his cries grew weaker every day. She thought her breasts, and her heart, would burst.

I signed thirty books, and when Carmen reappeared we both signed more. Vernal told me he'd been watching me read on a closed-circuit television, and that he could have listened to me all night, despite the subject matter. He asked where I was staying, and I told him the Ritz. He said he had a room there also, then asked if I'd like to share a taxi back to the hotel.

Vernal asked Carmen to come too, which, I secretly hoped, meant he didn't trust himself to be alone with me. The doorman called a cab for us. I felt a strong attraction to Vernal; I also felt that, in my nervousness, I must have drunk more than I ought to have, because I sat close to him and didn't pull away every time his arm brushed my breast.

Halfway to the hotel, Carmen lit a cigar and Vernal rolled down the window. Carmen kept complaining the potholes in New York were caused by bad taxi drivers, and Vernal kept saying, "Shhhhh," to which Carmen would reply that she lived there, what was the driver going to do, shoot us?

Vernal sighed through his nose. When we stopped at a red light, a man wearing nothing but a burned-out television set around his waist approached our car.

"Tell him you've only got Canadian," Carmen said. Vernal patted his jacket, as if to say he'd left his wallet at home, locked the door and leaned back in his seat, resignedly. The man hurled an empty bottle at the cab, shouting, "I have no shoes, I have no shoes," as the light turned green and we sped off.

"He is fortunate he still has feet," Carmen said.

Vernal sighed again. "New York, New York. They liked it so much they named it twice."

At the Ritz he ordered a bottle of brandy, and after I'd had too much to drink, I found myself telling the story of dinner with Carmen María's bodyguard and the caloric content of a mouthful of come. Carmen, who was by now so drunk she could hardly lift her snifter to her lips, put her head in Vernal's lap and went to sleep. Vernal gave me his card and asked me to call him when I got back to Vancouver. I wrote my phone number for him on the back of a cocktail napkin. We said good night, and I rode the elevator alone to the hotel's top floor.

My rooms seemed bigger and lonelier than ever. I put on the top half of my pyjamas and climbed between the heavily starched sheets. Then I remembered I'd forgotten to bolt the door, and was on my way downstairs to secure it when I heard a key turn in the lock. For a moment, I thought my crab fisherman from Rupert had tracked me down.

"Who is it?" I called when I heard the door rebounding off the door stopper and the sound of someone breathing unevenly.

"I beg your pardon? Who is *this?*" came a familiar voice. Vernal stepped into the room with Carmen over his shoulder. When he saw me, half-naked on the stairs, his mouth made a perfect O.

"There must be a mistake," he said, glancing at the key in his hand.

I laughed and invited him to come in anyway while we got it straightened out. Vernal carried Carmen upstairs and laid her down on the far side of the king-size bed, and we both reached for the telephone at the same time to call the front desk. It was their mistake, I was informed, and if I could please bear with them they would send a bellman for my luggage and find me alternative accommodation.

As Vernal uncorked my complimentary bottle of champagne and ate the squashed Godiva chocolate I hadn't spotted on my pillow, I started getting dressed. Vernal said there was plenty of room for all of us, that he could always stretch out on the love seat downstairs if the idea of a *ménage à trois* didn't appeal to me. We both started laughing, and with Carmen still soundly sleeping, Vernal undressed, put on the bottom half of my pyjamas and cut out four lines of cocaine, two for each of us, with a gold razor-blade he took from his wallet.

"It keeps me honest," he said when I raised my eyebrows at the Criminal Code, the book he said he *always* used to cut his lines on. He asked if I had a bill, and I dug in the pocket of my jeans for the hundred-dollar note Bret had given me for the mugger.

I had never snorted cocaine before. Two minutes after I had inhaled both white lines, I told Vernal I thought I'd just lost my virginity.

Vernal smiled and asked me if I'd like to repeat the experience.

"Maybe," I said, "later." When you first do cocaine, you don't need much. A couple of lines and you're good for the evening—not like after ten years, when one line is too many and a kilo isn't enough.

Vernal said he liked the way I looked at him when I was high. I got edgy all of a sudden, and talkative, and before I knew it I was asking him how he got his scar.

"I cut myself shaving," he said, adding that I was the first person who'd noticed how dangerous he really was. I laughed and said, "You liar!" imitating Carmen's accent.

"Criminal liar," said Vernal, and seemed pleased. He chopped out more lines, and I did them anyway, even though I'd said I'd wait, just to keep him company. After we'd sucked up everything he had in his sandwich-sized baggy, after he had scraped the baggy clean with the gold blade, I asked him if there was more where that came from.

Vernal produced a planning diary from his carry-on bag and opened it to a map of the western hemisphere. He put a finger on a tiny dot in the southwest corner of the Caribbean Sea, an island five hundred miles off the coast of the southern continent, called Tranquilandia.

"You're not planning a trip there in the near future?" I asked hopefully.

He laughed and shook his head. "Not me," he said, "but I wish I knew someone who was."

chapter three

The slightest thought of him—a letter in the mail, a phone message, the mention of his name—was enough to send a tsunami of exhilaration through my brain. I quit eating, lost weight, got pimples (I *know* it's true love when my face breaks out). I woke up each day delirious, gregarious, in an optimistic, euphoric, stuttering, agonizing, blissful, *adjectivey* state. Love, I felt in my blood, was to die for. There could be nothing better, nothing hotter or holier on this earth.

Vernal and I lived for nine months, in sin and a single-bedroom apartment, in Vancouver's Kitsilano. "Who will ever marry her now?" my father asked.

I was the one who proposed. My brain couldn't go on for-ever in a heightened state of etherized romantic bliss, and when the excitement began to subside I suppose I thought marriage might be some kind of a solution.

My father fought back tears when it came time to give me away. We had to wait outside the church for Vernal, who arrived late. That was Vernal. Late and hung-over. He never changed. Whenever I tried to talk to him about drinking, he'd say, "The graveyard is full of sober men."

There were a lot of things I didn't know about Vernal when I married him. I didn't want to know. All knowledge is loss, I know now, when it comes to love or being married to someone.

We flew to Mexico for our honeymoon. (Like Frenchy, I've made a few mistakes in life I probably shouldn't have, and marrying Vernal was definitely one of them. *And* Vernal and I were both snorting more cocaine than we probably should have at the time.) I took a copy of Malcolm Lowry's *Under the Volcano* to read on the train from Mexico City to Mérida. Vernal read as far as the title. "I won't be taking you anywhere like *that*," he promised.

When we got back from our honeymoon and neither one of us had proposed divorce, I felt there might be hope for our marriage. We decided to stay together "because of the kids"—the kids, I believed then, we both wished desperately to have. We gave notice on our apartment and bought a 4,000-square-foot mock-Georgian manorhouse in the walled community of Astoria, twenty minutes from downtown Vancouver, because Vernal wanted a safe place for our kids to grow up. At the entrance to what I nicknamed the Walled-Off Astoria, we had a gatehouse manned twenty-four hours by two security guards. Our house had an eight-foot-high decorative stone wall built around it, and when you drove through the electronically controlled, floodlit gate you looked straight into the big brotherly eye of a surveillance camera.

I had my own office overlooking our heart-shaped swimming pool. I worked, every morning, translating a book by a Colombian sociologist about growing up homeless, eating shoe leather and whatever else he could scrounge from the dump. Vernal was dead against my making the trip to South America my publisher had planned—he said I'd be taken hostage and he'd have to cash in our entire RRSP to buy me back, or I'd contract an incurable tropical disease and he'd have to keep me on life-support, next to his filing cabinet, for the rest of my natural life. More likely—and I knew this was his worst scenario—I'd fall in love with my bodyguard and give birth to his love-child in some bug-infested jungle guest-house, then bring the baby home and expect him to take care of it. Vernal had begun to blame himself for my inability to bear his children.

When, after eighteen months of trying, we still hadn't conceived, Vernal went to a breeder and paid $3,800 for a dog. Brutus turned out to have a heart condition and had to be driven to Saskatchewan to have a pacemaker installed.

Our first heated argument, about something other than the prospect of my infidelity or Vernal's continued drinking, was over the swimming pool. Vernal wanted to hire staff to maintain it. I said there were children starving right in our own city—how could he justify spending money on having someone retrieve Brutus's sticks from the deep end?

From our balcony on a clear night, you could see into the heart of the city. Our third Christmas together, Vernal gave me a telescope so I would still be able to see how the poor people lived.

One night when Vernal and Brutus were still in Saskatchewan, I got a call. Carmen María said she couldn't speak on the phone, but that she would be coming to Vancouver at the end of the week, and would need Vernal's help. She'd also need a room in a hotel—a single room, she added.

From the silence that followed, she must have assumed I knew more than I did. But Vernal read the newspaper for me, selectively, and I knew nothing of the trouble that brought Carmen back into my life. She was coming, she explained, because her husband and his two brothers were being held in custody there without bail.

"What are they in prison for . . . ?" I didn't add "this time," but Carmen knew how I thought.

"For getting caught," she said.

I found the press clippings on Vernal's desk, studied the photographs of the three Corazóns—Carmen's husband, Gustavo, and his brothers, Angel and Mugre. The caption below Angel's photograph read, "At sixteen exchanged a modestly successful career as assassin for chance to make millions as trafficker in drugs." In the picture his long black hair was tied back in a ponytail. A scar shaped like an exclamation mark bisected his cheek. He didn't have the eyes of a man who would cut himself shaving.

The *Vancouver Sun* carried a front-page story describing the brothers as "ruthless drug tycoons" who had negotiated for eighty tonnes of marijuana in the middle of a Colombian jungle and had had the bales dropped from a plane onto a freighter waiting off the Tranquilandian coast. The bales were loaded into the *Byzantium*'s hold. The crew headed north with its cargo.

The article included a sidebar on the disputed territory of Tranquilandia, described as being strategically situated between the major drug producers and the U.S., "where the refined end-product was snorted up by airplane-load," and for this reason claimed by the Colombian, Venezuelan, Panamanian and American governments.

La Ciudad de las Orquídeas (the City of Orchids), "a sprawling, predatory seaport at the island's northern tip," was known to be populated by thieves, assassins, cocaine queens, money laundresses and others attracted by the rich pickings to be had from the port's thriving import-export business.

The journalist, who had been commissioned to write an exposé of Tranquilandia's drug trade, had lived over a series of low-life bars and in hotels not included in any of the tourist guides. A *viejo*, an old man, a resident of the Hotel Viper, told him that this outlaw territory had been named Tranquilandia by a dark-skinned woman pirate of the Caribbean who was executed in the late 1800s. Chocolata was so revered by the islanders that they had built a shrine in her honour on top of the island's highest peak. For years, devout drug lords had sent their couriers up the mountain to beseech her image to bless their bullets, render their crops bountiful, and to seek her guidance in customs and immigration affairs. Resident islanders and visitors from both continents gave thanks to her for drug-related employment, hospitals, orphanages, schools and community centres, all endowed by drug barons.

These days, Tranquilandia was still controlled by a woman, the Black Widow, the spiritual leader of Las Blancas, the same narco-terrorist group responsible for Carmen María's kidnapping. Carmen had, in fact, been lucky to survive. "They treat hostages like Dixie Cups," she'd told me. "Use them once and throw them away."

I read every article I could find about the Corazóns. One paper said their boat had broken down off the west coast of Vancouver Island, and the crew found a remote fiord where they could make repairs. Another reported that the *Byzantium* ran aground and the smugglers had to offload the cargo, which had shifted, so the boat could float again. One story credited a Royal Canadian Mounted Police undercover operation with the bust; another said it was the combined forces of the Federal Bureau of Investigation and the U.S. Drug Enforcement Administration, assisted by the Canadian navy and the U.S. Coast Guard, tipped off by a pair of German kayakers.

I found myself searching for references, in particular, to Angel Corazón.

The trial lasted three months; I went to court with Carmen every day, at first because she wanted me to be there, and because Vernal liked me to watch him perform—and then for my own reasons. The Corazón brothers sat shackled together in the prisoner's box, and Carmen held my hand, digging her long fingernails into my palm each time the prosecutor got up to object. Gustavo, the oldest of the three, with eyes like thimblefuls of black coffee and curly black hair misted with grey, nodded to Carmen when he came into court at the beginning of each day, but kept his eyes trained on the judge after that.

For the first week, I stayed only for the morning sessions. But when I saw Angel looking for me in the crowded gallery, and smiling when he picked me out, I started staying for the afternoon sessions as well. He had a smile bittersweet as a love pill for the sick at heart, a pair of lips you wanted to lick under a moustache that would keep you from getting close enough, and fucky brown eyes. But I think it was his smell that attracted me most: even from the gallery I could smell him—like the air before a storm, long before there is any visible sign of it.

And then there was Mugre Corazón, who had the same hair and regulation outlaw moustache as Angel, only his moustache was grey and stained with nicotine and his skin was a darker shade of brown. He was thinner, too, than either of his older brothers. *Mugre* meant "dirt." You didn't need to speak Spanish to see he came by his name honestly.

I don't think even Vernal was surprised when the Corazóns were convicted (their Mexican deckhands had all pled guilty and been sent to the penitentiary). It was the eighties, after all, and we were supposed to be saying no to drugs, and an emphatic "No, no!" to foreigners who smuggled drugs by the tons. Vernal, at sentencing, tried to argue that

Gustavo Corazón had brought stability to Tranquilandia, a measure of prosperity to an otherwise impoverished Third World country, by financing low-cost housing, hospitals, community centres, roller-skating rinks and banks.

Angel Corazón had sponsored a rehab clinic where drug addicts went to recuperate. While he recognized that Angel had made a lot of money by exporting narcotics, Vernal said a clinic to treat drug addiction allowed him to "give something back."

His Honour had a different view of Carmen María's better half and his brothers. He noted that Mugre Corazón had been responsible for the executions of at least six members of the judiciary prior to the expulsion of the police force from Tranquilandia, and that the "rehabilitation centres" Angel Corazón had built were nothing more than five-star hotels with all kinds of facilities for "drugs and orgy parties." Gustavo Corazón Gaviria was wanted in the U.S., Venezuela, Jamaica, Costa Rica, Mexico and Bolivia in connection with the biggest busts those countries had ever made. The judge said life imprisonment wasn't long enough these days for drug traffickers, who looked upon doing time as an occupational hazard.

Afterwards, Vernal was photographed on the steps of the courthouse, holding his Criminal Code. He told reporters it would be more fair to bring back the death penalty than to send men like the Corazón brothers to jail for twenty-five years. "They should kill you before burying you," he said.

Carmen and I went back to her hotel and had a few drinks in the bar. I asked her what she was going to do now that her husband had been sentenced to stay in Canada.

"Go back to work," Carmen said. She was running out of money. "And you? What are *you* going to do with your life?"

I hadn't realized it until that moment, but ever since Angel had met my gaze, I'd felt a hot, secret tugging—to be somewhere else. I couldn't remember the last time Vernal and I had danced, or confided in one another, made love, or made anything but small talk. We weren't doing well, in the marrow of things.

I told Carmen that sometimes I thought I wanted a different life. Carmen dipped her knife into her Caesar and swirled it twice.

I should have tossed the visitor's application form in the recycling box, but instead I completed it the same day Carmen brought it home to me. I checked "No" beside most of the questions: no criminal record, no outstanding warrants, no communicable diseases, no plans to smuggle contraband (weapons, drugs or books) into the prison. Under "Marital Status" I left a blank.

Fourteen days later, I was approved to visit Angel Corazón Gaviria. Carmen suggested I come with her to the Valentine's Day social; I knew I could get away without Vernal asking any questions, because he had his own plans—to go sailing and dry out in Desolation Sound with two of his partners. I told him February wasn't the best time of year for boating, and he reminded me I'd said the same thing about August.

Vernal didn't own a car (he claimed he'd rather drink than drive), and mine was too small to transport Carmen and her entourage to the prison. Carmen said her new friend Thurma, who had moved to Vancouver to make sure her incarcerated boyfriend "stayed out of trouble," would find us a ride.

Thurma, dressed in an African-style tent dress imprinted with stampeding giraffes and flying monkeys, picked us up at the apartment Carmen had rented in the west end. Thurma could have been Frenchy's double, but I didn't know Frenchy back then. At every red light she opened her purse—scarlet leather, black onyx clasp—and brought out a tube of Day-Glo orange lipstick, which she reapplied to her lips. By the time we stopped at the Pay 'n' Save to gas up, my own lips were drained.

Thurma ground the gears as we jerked away from the gas station in the VW van the colour of her lipstick. She confessed she'd never stolen anything with a gearshift before, but that she'd found the van idling in front of a bank. "I loves to steal," she said. "I *looovvveeees* to steal."

This is something else Frenchy has in common with Thurma. Frenchy would steal your last tampon. I know.

Carmen said it didn't count as stealing if the owner left his keys in the ignition, but that didn't make me feel any better. At that time, I wasn't used to stealing as a lifestyle. I slunk lower into my seat, afraid we would be arrested; Vernal had taken a five-day weekend, and I'd have to wait until Thursday for him to bail me out.

We pulled into a lane behind a high-rise apartment building, and the van sputtered to a stop. Thurma leaned on the horn until a tall, delicately built Native woman, with black hair so long she could tie it in a knot and still sit on it, pushed open the Emergency Exit Only door carrying a canvas bag that said "Born to Shop" and a bundle that turned out to be a baby.

Bonnie climbed in the back beside me, clucking to the bundle, whom she addressed as Little Shit Shit, and who was dressed in a beaded deerskin jacket and pants and moccasins decorated with porcupine quills. I held tight to Bonnie's arm to keep her from crushing Little Shit Shit against the door as Thurma jerked back onto the road.

"Baby likes your bracelet," Bonnie said, clucking her approval of the silver band with a frog design. Vernal had taken it from a client, in lieu of a retainer, and given it to me on my birthday.

Baby sneezed, without letting go of the bottle stuck between his lips, and his eyes watered. "She misses her dad," Bonnie said. *She?* I took another look as Bonnie wiped the baby's nose with a Popsicle wrapper she found in her purse.

She kissed Baby's nose. "You better give up that bottle soon or you'll end up just *like* your dad."

I didn't ask what Little Shit Shit took in her bottle. Bonnie said Little Shit Shit was the nickname Baby's father, Treat, had given her, that Baby's real name was Kingfisher Sky. In the old days, she said, it had been the custom in her village for a woman to name her baby after the first thing she saw when she opened her eyes upon giving birth, like Salal Berry or Raven or Stones Being Pulled Back by Water on the Beach. She too was trying to follow the old ways, even though she'd given birth by Caesarean at the hospital in Rupert. She'd looked up to see sun coming through the skylight in the birthing room, and then when she turned her head, she saw the tiny blue irises her sisters had left for her. They looked like baby kingfishers.

Thurma, having scraped her way into second gear, was driving full out now. After two near misses (a school bus and a cyclist club), we roared onto the freeway. She ignored my offer to take the wheel and opened her purse again, fishing around. I watched as she unscrewed a bottle cap with her teeth. "You want to feel good back there? Get in the mood for a good visit?" she said.

"No. Thanks, I feel fine," I said, as we zipped under an overpass where someone had spray-painted the message "See You at the Alter Beefy."

"Treat and me are getting married for sure this time," said Bonnie. "Not like the last times; he never even turned up at the church or paid for the rings. I just hope he doesn't stand me up again."

Thurma laughed as she emptied a bottle of black pills into her palm, and then proceeded to eat them, as if they were Reece's Pieces. "Hope to die if I knows where we is headed!"

"Straight ahead, bullhead," said Bonnie.

I was going to tell Bonnie I figured there were three things certain in life—death, taxes and that if you married a man in maximum security he would be waiting for you at the altar—but I suddenly felt as if to say such a thing would be tempting fate.

"When we get married, we can have trailer visits," Bonnie said. "The way normal people live. Watch TV."

The valley, once lush and green, stretched before us, a wasteland of leeched soil, used-car lots and trailer parks with names like Chuck 'n' Flo's RV Heaven. Thurma stopped at a rest area and for takeout coffee at the Instant Café outside the small town of Agassiz, half an hour from the prison. It took her longer, each time we stopped, to get the van started again, and she swore next time she wouldn't steal something that coughed blood every time you turned the key in it.

Mountjoy Penitentiary, which had been completed the previous summer and opened its six-hundred-pound doors in time for Remembrance Day, squatted like a concrete womb at the northern end of the valley. Referred to as the Joy, by convicts and prison staff alike, the institution was cut off from the world by mountains on three sides, their western flanks cloaked in blue shadow. Thurma parked her stolen van in the Visitor's Only lot, facing a fence topped with razor-wire that surrounded the near-empty tract of land set aside for the prison cemetery.

I got out of the van, stretched and stood staring at the two lonely white crosses, each with a black number stencilled on it, no name.

"No one wanted them when they were alive and now *nobody* wants them," said Thurma, following my gaze. "I told my old man, You die on me in here, I'm going to bury you in leg-irons. Just so's you don't go to hell and try stepping out on me before I get there!"

I looked at my watch: 12:45 p.m. and the sun still hadn't made it over the top of the imposing Mount Joy Mountains (so imposing they named them twice, Vernal would say). Carmen held Little Shit Shit while Bonnie opened a soft drink labelled "Freedom of Choice: Big Gulp Brand" and topped up her bottle. The four of us joined the line of visitors waiting to be buzzed in the front gate at one o'clock.

"It's busy today," Thurma said. "A lot of people come when there's a social. The food's good. Better than those machines in the visiting room."

I eavesdropped while we waited: one woman bragged she'd been partying all week because a judge had reduced her husband's sentence to two "lifes" instead of four.

"Don't say fuck. You're not old enough to say fuck," another admonished her adolescent son; her younger one, in a stroller, kept pointing at the razor-wire glinting in the sun, saying, "Pri-ttee, pritt-ee, pri-ttee."

Two bikers joined the end of the line and talked about a party over the weekend at Scutz Falls. One of them kept leering at Carmen, the other, wearing a T-shirt that said, "I May Not Go Down in History, But I May Go Down on Your Daughter," asked Bonnie how old the baby was.

"Old enough to know better," said Bonnie.

Carmen ignored the bikers and explained the visiting procedure to me in Spanish. Some guards would let visitors in early, give them time to store their purses or wallets in a locker and be scanned by the metal detectors, but there were others, like the one on duty today, she said—the one she'd nicknamed Roll-Over—who believed rules were not meant for bending. Sure enough, it wasn't until one o'clock sharp that Roll-Over rose with a yawn, belched, stretched, adjusted the thin belt that held his fat belly from sagging any further and buzzed us in.

I let Bonnie and Baby go ahead of me in the line because I needed to use a washroom, but both the men's and the ladies' in the identification area had out-of-order signs on the doors.

"It's to prevent you from flushing anything at the last minute, in case they decide to search you," Carmen explained.

I watched Bonnie walk through the metal detector, and then saw Roll-Over pointing her towards a door marked No Entry Staff Only.

"It's because of that Treat," Thurma said when I asked what was happening. Bonnie was about to be "skin-searched," she said, which meant she'd have to take off all her clothes, squat over a mirror and cough. If the man you were visiting had been causing problems inside, or was a gang member like Treat, you would more than likely be subjected to an internal search.

"They know she ain't packing," said Thurma. "It's a humiliation score. They hurt you, it hurt your old man more. That's the way they play it around here. You can tell who's been stirring up shit inside by who gets to squat, spread their cheeks and crack a smile out here. They do it to her every time."

Suddenly I had an urge to flee from this place, from the company of these women for whom life meant stealing cars, squatting over mirrors, swallowing uppers and downers by the fistful, wiping their baby's noses with Popsicle wrappings: I felt, as my mother would say, out of my element.

"Whom are you here to see?" Roll-Over asked when it came my turn to sign in.

"Angel Corazón," I said, scribbling my name. I wrote "None" beside the space reserved for "Relationship to Visitor".

Roll-Over's fat eyes glanced from the visitor's book to his computer and back again. I crossed out "None" and wrote "Friend's husband's brother," but this still didn't seem to satisfy him. When I said this was my first visit, a wary smile cut into his face like a knife mark in bread dough waiting to be punched down. He asked me to remove my jewellery and said I'd have to leave my comb in a locker (the sharp end, he said, could be used as a weapon). After I walked through the metal detector, he tugged at my hair to make sure I wasn't wearing a wig and asked me to remove my footwear (his fancy word for shoes), which he bent back and forth to make sure nothing was stashed in the soles. He seemed almost disappointed they were not filled with drugs, and handed me a sheet of yellow paper, the visiting room regulations.

Bonnie and Little Shit Shit were still in the special room reserved for those who were visiting troublemakers inside. As I waited for the others in front of the electronic grill, the matron appeared.

"You can get dressed now," she said, over her shoulder, to Bonnie and the baby. "Have a nice social."

We had to walk outside again, up a concrete path to the front door of the prison; I shivered in the cold wind funnelling down from the mountain. Thurma, who'd had to leave her comb in a locker also, said she wasn't going to be able to face her old man with her hair looking like a tornado in a steel-wool factory. Carmen said lots of people paid good money to have their hair look like that.

Another guard, who didn't get up from the chair he sat in by the entrance, pushed a button to admit us to the visiting room. Here we had to wait for the visitors and correspondence officer to escort us to the gymnasium, where the social was being held.

Behind a wall of glass adjoining the visiting room, the officer sat, eyeing the clock on the wall and eating Hershey Kisses out of a paper bag. There was nowhere left to sit, so I leaned against the Coke machine ("Use at Own Risk"), reading the list of rules Roll-Over had given me. *A kiss and embrace are permitted at the beginning and at the end of the visiting period. Necking, petting, fondling, embracing, tickling, slapping, pinching or biting is PROHIBITED. No running, shouting, excessive laughing, standing on chairs, swearing, cursing or use of unnecessary language.*

An empty yoghurt container with a note taped to it had been placed on the floor next to the Coke machine. "Cigarette foils, please. Jim's cat chases them. Thanks." Whoever Jim was, he had collected quite a few foils. Smoking was one of the few pleasures allowed in this room, and it looked like everyone took advantage of it.

One of the bikers had given Bonnie his chair. The other, explaining to Thurma how he'd earned the black-and-green wings he wore pinned to his sleeveless Levi's jacket by going down on a venereally diseased black woman, bounced Little Shit Shit on his knee.

"Those Latino broads are nice, very nice," the first biker said to Bonnie, grinning again at Carmen, who pretended not to understand. "They really turn me on. But you know what the men are like. You fuck with the sister, you also get fucked by a bunch of mafioso assassins."

Another baby in the room began to wail.

"You never hear an Indian baby cry," said Bonnie, wiping Baby's sticky face with one of Jim's foils.

Little Shit Shit, clutching her empty bottle, had gone to sleep.

chapter four

The V&C officer wore a black plastic badge with his name, J. Saygrover, in gold lettering; he ushered us into a corridor smelling of turpentine and fresh paint. The walls were an avocado green, the ceiling a chocolate brown and the floor a dirty rust. Whoever wrote "Stone walls do not a prison make/ Nor iron bars a cage," couldn't have been much of an interior decorator.

Mr. Saygrover stopped us at an iron-barred gate. He nodded at the younger guard in the control bubble. I watched the heavy steel doors parting on their runners. We passed through five more identical gates before reaching the gymnasium. I wondered what would happen if anyone had to leave this place in a hurry.

Vernal once told me that prisons exist for one purpose:

locking people away from life's good things, most often *other people's* good things. Up ahead, behind the last gate, I saw a crowd of men who looked as if they had been locked away from other people's things for a number of very *good* reasons, each one craning his neck to see us as we approached. On either side of the gate, the air throbbed with expectancy. All of a sudden I missed Vernal, pictured him tacking towards Desolation Sound, the *Manchester Guardian* open on his lap, a bottle of near-beer in one hand and a Gitane burning in the other.

The gymnasium had been decorated with red balloons and white streamers, which were affixed from corner to corner and had lost their elasticity. A giant heart, made of papier mâché, encased in barbed wire, had been inscribed with the words "For Life."

I stayed close to Carmen, who told me that every social was sponsored by a different inmate group. This one was being hosted by the Lifer's Committee, which meant it would be done properly, the implication being they had the most time on their hands. We worked our way through the riot of bodies, across the room to a banquet-sized table laden with bottles of soft drinks and plates of food—sandwiches, fruit, cookies, a heart-shaped cake that had been hacked into pieces—where her husband and his brothers sat in a cloud of cigarette smoke under a Thank You for Not Smoking sign.

The men rose to shake hands with me, and when it was Angel's turn, I couldn't meet his eyes and my face began to burn. Far away up the valley I heard the whistle of a train, and deeper inside, the deafening rat-a-tat-tat of machine-gun fire in my heart.

Mugre, who looked even thinner than I remembered him from court, addressed me (or more accurately, undressed me) in rapid-fire Spanish.

"Pay no attention to him," said Gustavo. "He is very ill-mannered. We have all been to the same reform schools, but Mugre has never graduated."

Carmen said her husband was making a joke. The three of them had spent most of their life in prison, but that was no excuse for bad manners.

The coffee machine percolating at the back of the room sounded like someone vomiting. Mugre got up from the table and went to join a group of men who looked as if they had ridden down from the hills with Emiliano Zapata and gone on a shopping spree at K-Mart.

"Our crew," said Angel, nodding at the group of Mexicans. "*Campesinos. Indios.*" He shook his head sadly. "My brother Mugre belongs with them. We get a visitor, and what does he do? He runs away." He looked at me again; I felt my heart knocking on the back of my front teeth as he pulled out a chair for me. I sat, hoping I didn't tip over in my nervousness.

Carmen took an orange and an oatmeal cookie from a platter and broke the cookie in half. Gustavo took the other half from her hands; I watched it shrink under his moustache. I wondered if it was proper prison etiquette to help oneself to the food, and was just going to ask Angel, when I felt someone tap my shoulder. I turned and saw Thurma, standing behind a man wearing jeans, a Mickey Mouse T-shirt and bright yellow headphones, sitting in a wheelchair.

"This here is Chandler," Thurma said. "The one I told you about?" The boyfriend she was determined to keep out of trouble had a grin that turned his mouth into an accordion being played by a drunken acrobat.

I tried to shake his hand.

"He's got no control over himself," said Thurma. "That's why I worry; he's got no control over *nothing* no more."

When Thurma had wheeled him away, Carmen said Chandler's face hadn't always been that way. "His mouth is the only part on him that moves any more, and *still* she doesn't trust him." Carmen said Thurma's biggest worry was whether her boyfriend would be faithful to her for the duration of his life sentence, and whether he would continue being faithful to her if he ever got out.

Angel said he knew one way to tell if a person was faithful, and asked to see my hand. With his middle finger, he began tracing one of the lines on my palm to where it disappeared at the base of my ring finger, then he turned my wedding ring until the gold heart, clasped in a pair of hands, faced up at him. He nodded, then smiled, as if he now knew some dark secret about me.

"My brother sees that you are a married woman, and I know him, I know what he thinks," said Gustavo, chuckling. "That whoever has given you the ring must trust you very much to let you come alone to visit a place full of men who have been deprived of the company of women, some of them for a long time." I told Gustavo my husband had every reason to trust me.

Angel turned the ring again, so the heart was no longer visible.

"My brother's wife trusts him," Gustavo went on. "If she didn't, you can be sure he would have been dead a long time ago."

Carmen had said nothing about Angel having a wife. I didn't know why it bothered me.

"She must miss you," I said. I looked away from him to the gymnasium doors.

"She hasn't had much of a husband to miss," he said. "I worry about her. Some nights." He must have felt my whole body pulling away, because he let go of my hand. I hadn't even realized he was still holding it.

He moved his chair in close, edged his hand around the back of my chair and rested his thumb on my shoulder blade.

"And you, you have how many children?" The question slammed into me.

"Oh, no. None. I mean, a dog is all. He's like a child; he's like ten children, sometimes. Only I doubt he'll ever grow up. He's my husband's dog, actually. My husband sleeps with him. I mean, he sleeps with him on the futon."

I felt embarrassed to be babbling on about Vernal like this, painting a sorry picture of my married life, but the way Angel looked at me he didn't have to say what kind of a man would sleep with a dog when he had a woman like you waiting for him in bed?

"I hope you never regret coming to visit me today" is what he *did* say, after a bit.

I stared at the Mount Joy Mountain range, a deep sea green in the late-afternoon light, which I could still glimpse through the gymnasium doors, then at the clock on the wall. I had less than an hour left. I didn't want to leave. Part of me, at least, wished all of me could stay here with Angel.

"I like it here," I said.

Angel reached for my hand again. My palm felt sweaty. I had seen Bonnie and Little Shit Shit, and presumably the father whom Baby missed—a small, muscular man with a tense face, wearing a red bandanna, and a black T-shirt with the words "Narrow Gauge Posse" on the back—going outside; I said I'd like to go for a walk, too.

Angel stayed close beside me as we made our way around the tables towards the gymnasium doors. Every time we brushed against one another, I felt a shiver of something lost stirring inside.

We walked in the same direction, around and around the yard. He said he'd never wanted children, but since coming to prison this time he had changed his mind. "It's easy to think you don't want a family until you know you are not having one," he said.

I remember listening to him, thinking finally I had found a man, the right man for what I wanted—which was to have a child—and where did I find him? In a maximum-security penitentiary.

We made five circuits of the yard before the cold wind sent us scurrying back inside. Angel returned to our table. Carmen, who had been to the chapel, the only room off the gymnasium that wasn't kept locked during a prison social, steered me towards the washroom. We had to squeeze past Bonnie and another woman, who were trying to reapply their makeup in the chrome of the condom machine, from which a sign hung saying, "Sorry. Out of Order." (The word *sorry* had been crossed out.) The other woman, wearing a red leather mini-skirt the size of a heating pad and a T-Shirt with two fried eggs on the front, tried to wipe the smudged mascara off Bonnie's face.

"If you're going to hang around a man who makes you cry, you should at least buy waterproof mascara," Carmen told her.

She ran a comb through her hair. "So," she said, turning back to me, "what do you think of my brother?"

"He's nothing like I expected," I said. That was a lie. He was everything I'd imagined him to be, and more.

Carmen turned to me. "Spit on a bean," she said, her green eyes shining. "That's how polished his face grows when he looks at you."

Vernal came home a day early, saying Desolation Sound had been aptly named. There was no liquor store within a hundred and fifty miles.

He was catching up on a forest of newspapers in front of the living-room fire, nursing a cold and a tumbler of malt whisky. He looked up when I brought in a tray of cookies, picked out a chocolate chip and fed it to Brutus, who lay at his feet sipping occasionally from his bowl.

"Listen to this," Vernal said. One of his habits was to read aloud, everything from the grammatical errors on milk cartons ("old-fashion taste"—*what* is the world coming to?—old-*fashioned* taste, please!") to the list of ingredients in Brutus's healthy dog biscuits. "'Dogs Find Dead Body in Shallow Grave.' 'Dead body' is an oxymoron when the body is found in a grave." He paused. "You know, I've always thought your cookies ought to be a controlled substance."

He fed Brutus another chocolate chip.

"Don't," I said. "He'll get spots." I lay on my stomach on the carpet, flipping through a magazine. Brutus had been diagnosed with canine acne, a stress-related disorder, according to his pet-care provider at the K-9 Holistic Health Centre.

Vernal put his paper aside to light a joint.

"'Would you rather die before dessert, when you still have dessert to look forward to, or after you've eaten dessert?'" I read.

"It depends." He paused and threw a third chocolate chip up in the air; Brutus caught it before it hit the floor. "What's for dessert?"

"Just answer the question. It's a quiz. To see if we're compatible."

"It's a bit late now. You should have asked me that two years ago."

"I did."

"And . . . ?" he asked, inhaling and holding his breath.

"You were reading the newspaper." I took hold of his left foot and began massaging it.

"I need another drink," Vernal said, exhaling as he spoke, trying to extricate his foot.

"Drink to me only with thine eyes." I held on tight, rubbing in between his crooked big toe and the next one.

"That won't cure cotton mouth," he said, pulling away and going to the cabinet for another Scotch.

We'd snorted a few lines together, then attempted to have sex, when he got off the boat. I always knew when Vernal had been with another woman, even before he got his clothes off and came to bed. He smelled different. And when he touched me, I knew the rest.

But this time *I'd* felt different too. Whatever part of me had been drawn to Angel—so much so that I even fantasized about having his child—made me feel I was betraying him by lying naked beneath a man I'd been married to for almost two years. And when Vernal began thrusting deeper, I sank my teeth in his neck and my fingernails in his back, wanting to hurt him for not sensing the distance in me. He'd stopped, rolled off me and looked away through my eyes.

"Don't mark me," he'd said.

I closed my magazine, sat up and hugged my knees, looking out over the lawns and formal gardens to the stone wall while Vernal opened a pack of cigarettes and found something else in the paper he thought would be of interest to me. "Listen to this: 'Wife Who Smashed Television Gets Jail.'" He always began by saying, "Listen to this," followed it by the headline, and then let me suffer until he decided whether to read me the rest of the article—another of his habits.

"'Carrotty Nell Kelly—where *do* they get these names?— came home and found her husband, Seamus, peacefully watching a wrestling match. When she suggested he turn the television off immediately, and he didn't comply, Mrs. Kelly smashed the screen with a toaster oven and went back to the bar,'" Vernal read.

Vernal tossed Brutus a cookie without any chocolate chips left in it; Brutus sniffed it and turned his head away, looking miffed.

"'The judge said that any woman who preferred drinking to watching family television was not only a threat to the family unit, but a menace to our society,'" he continued. "'Furthermore, women who expressed their preferences in a violent manner did not belong in the home—jail was the only place for them.'"

As Vernal read to me, I pictured Angel lying on his bunk, staring up at the dull green institutional gloss on his ceiling. I thought of lying on top of him, then underneath him, and then I thought, jail might not be such a bad place for a woman like me either.

I had gone back to the kitchen to get a bag of jalapeño-cheese-flavoured tortilla chips—of all things Latin, Vernal liked only tortilla chips and cocaine—when I heard the doorbell ring. Vernal yelled, "Got it!" and when I went back to the living room, I-5 was there, sweating in the *sarape* he had just purchased "somewhere high in the Andes." I could think of only one reason he'd be wearing a *ruana* (*sarape* in Mexico, *ruana* in South America, but I didn't bother correcting him) in the house. Like most of Vernal's coke dealers, this one was another right-wing expatriate.

He was living off the land again, he told Vernal—which, I assumed, meant he'd sold the timber rights on his property, as well as the mineral rights. He'd built a "pine shack" on the outskirts of the city, no running water, no mod cons.

"What do you heat with?" Vernal asked.

"A .44 Magnum, man," I-5 said, patting the bulge his *ruana* covered, making a snorting sound in his throat before cutting out a dozen lines for us to sample on Vernal's Criminal Code. I-5 got his name because he was famous for laying out lines as long and straight as the interstate highway that ran the length of Florida. I did my share, then went back to the kitchen to reheat the Chicken Quito Ecuador I'd made from the Time-Life series.

I heard Vernal laugh, then the rustling of newspapers. I-5 snorted through his throat again, a constant irritating habit of his. "Shallow grave! What's this friggin' guy talking about? I spent an hour digging in that friggin' hard scrabble. Look at these blisters! I oughta put that reporter in a shallow grave. Makes me look like a friggin' amateur." He left soon after, saying he had an appointment with a landscape artist, but by that time neither Vernal nor I had an appetite for Chicken Quito Ecuador.

I lit a fire in the bedroom fireplace and went to bed early while Vernal played Frisbee in the kitchen with Brutus (his K-9 heart specialist said this would prevent "misdirected energy") then went for his evening jog. Later he came to bed with *Under the Volcano*, which he opened to the middle, not the best place to begin in this sort of book. But when he started reading it upside down, I knew something was wrong. After a while he closed the book on his chest, crossed his hands over it and stared up at our ceiling, as if somebody close to him had died: I couldn't imagine who it would be, because Brutus was dozing on his futon and I-5 had left the house looking healthier than either of us.

"Something's the matter," I said to Vernal. It took time, but I finally weasled it out of him. Vernal felt it would be compromising my integrity to expect me to be faithful to him. He said he should have told me before we were married, but he didn't want to lose me then. We weren't going to have a family, he said. He'd had a vasectomy.

I was engrossed in a mystery—Vernal had complained since our honeymoon that I preferred mysteries to him—and waited until I got to the end of a paragraph before I turned to him. "Is there something else you are trying not to tell me?" I said.

Brutus, who had only been feigning sleep, opened one nosy eye. Vernal said yes, that he'd been seeing a lot of his secretary. I said it made sense, since they worked in the same office.

"Oh, you know what I mean," he said glumly. "She came sailing with me and . . . I can't go on living like this. She feels guilty about it, too; I'm the one to blame, really . . ."

I grabbed the book from his hands and threw it in the fire. It didn't burn, just lay there growing thickly black. Then I switched out the light. I heard Brutus sigh, and after a few minutes Vernal got out of bed and joined him on the futon. I thought of Vernal saying, "Don't mark me," and knew now it had nothing to do with him not wanting to appear in the Court of Appeal with a love bite. Vernal didn't want his secretary to know he still had relations with his wife.

For better or worse, mostly worse. Till death us do part. I should have parted his cranium right then with the Steuben paperweight he kept next to his bed, covering his greasy little wad of phone numbers. When I saw Carmen the next day, she said she knew a trustworthy person who'd kill your best friend for a hundred dollars. As far as I was concerned, I told her, Vernal was not a friend.

part two / no parking for the wedding

Set the foot down with distrust on
the crust of the world—it is thin.

—*Author Unknown*

chapter five

Death Clinic, Heaven Valley State Facility for Women

*Clear conduct, excellent sanitation and positive adjustment
will be the basis for television viewing. No items will be
stored on top of the television except for a religious book.*
—*Inmate Information Handbook*

*Kill one man and you are a murderer. Kill millions and you
are a conqueror. Kill all and you are a God.*
—Jean Rostand

Rainy's hobbies are shopping and crying. The papers said
she'd never wanted children, that she killed her twins
because they'd prevented her from having a life. Nothing
could be further from the truth, she swears. From the day

her twins were born, they never stopped her from doing anything she wanted to do. "If I want to go to the mall, I just strap them in their car seats and take them to the mall with me," she says.

You don't get to do a lot of shopping in here, but old habits die hard; that's why Rainy still speaks in the present tense. Your chances of staying sane are much better if you have somewhere you can go, to get away to—in your head. Rainy gets out of bed every morning, changes her sheets, has six cups of coffee, locks the kids in the trunk of the car and then goes shopping.

Rainy wears a T-shirt that says "Property of Jesus Christ." She talks to God twice a day in the interfaith chapel and says He can save Frenchy and me too, as if God were a form of oxygen mask or a life-jacket. Frenchy, who swears she won't go down on her knees for any dead man on a cross, says next time Rainy talks to God she should tell him to drop the capital *H* when it comes to words like *He* and *Him* because it looks like God thinks he's a whole lot holier than the rest of us. I've made it clear I'm not about to be converted, either.

I used to blame my parents for the spiritual vacuum in which I've spent most of my life. They didn't make me go to church. I had no friends who *weren't* forced to go, and one Sunday morning I was playing in the ditch when two kids from down the street walked past, dressed in their party clothes. I asked what they did all morning at Sunday school; I thought I might be missing something.

"We learn about Jesus Christ," the boy said.

I was impressed. "*You* get to study a swear word!" I said.

At that point my parents decided it was time I had some religious instruction. I attended Sunday school for two weeks, learned that "Eve made a bad choice" and then dropped out.

I have a history of dropping out. I dropped out of kindergarten the first morning, after nearly hanging myself in the playground. My father threatened to sue; he said that in designing the equipment, the architects had resorted to the aesthetics of the torture chamber. My school claimed the equipment had been designed by a child psychologist.

My care and treatment counsellor here at HV says I have the wrong attitude: I've always believed that's the only kind to have. Mrs. Dykstra says I am glib; I don't take life seriously. How can she expect a person who is told she is going to be executed on such-and-such a day at such-and-such a time to take *anything* seriously, least of all life?

When you arrive on the Row, you are given your clothing issue: 3 Jumpsuits; 5 Pairs of Socks, useful for padding your 3 Brassieres (White), which look like the mailbags they're always busy making back in the general population; 1 Jacket; 7 Pairs of Underpants (Coloured); 5 T-shirts; 1 Pair of Shoes (no laces). The same intake officer who hands you those Extra-Large Jumpsuits will give you underpants too extra-tiny for a kid going through toilet-training. You wear a different coloured pair of underwear for each day of the week (i.e., Red Monday, Blue Tuesday, Yellow Wednesday and so on). It took me a few weeks to figure out the colour code is their way of making sure you put on clean underwear every day, in case you are "differently motivated."

If a guard catches you wearing yellow underwear on Monday or red on Thursday, it is considered an infraction of prison rules and you are subject to disciplinary action. My red underwear fell into some bleach by accident (Rainy was sterilizing her needle) and became orange, and I tried to explain this to Officer Gluckman (the only guard who bothers to check). My excuse wasn't good enough for her. She said there would be no exceptions to the rule that all Death Clinic inmates were to wear red on Monday, and as a result of my failure to comply with prison regulations, I would be forced to relinquish my television-viewing privileges until she had conducted a further investigation.

As well as new clothing, you are also given your own television, and the freedom to watch whichever religious or educational programs they choose, at any hour of the day or night. When my counsellor asked me what I liked to watch, I made a mistake by saying I preferred *not* to watch television. Mrs. Dykstra said my failure to take advantage of my viewing privileges demonstrated that I had a negative attitude, to which she hoped I would make a positive adjustment, so she could write a more favourable psychological report.

Officer Gluckman must have conducted her investigation by reading Mrs. Dykstra's files, because one morning my punishment changed. After that, I was unable to turn my television *off*, and when I tried to cover it with my towel, they cranked the volume up. It was, for me, a no-win situation. If they turned the volume down, I said, I promised I would watch the television. I always have to pretend I'm watching it when Officer Gluckman's on shift.

———

My mother, while waiting to board her ship for the Caribbean island, had to spend the night at a Miami Beach motel. The motel had been recommended by her travel agent, and it turned out to be the choice of the local prostitutes also. All night long, men kept banging on my mother's door, imploring "Fuckface" to "open up." My mother, who was "out of her element," spent the whole night searching for a place to hide her watch. The "rude men" at her door, the rasp of the palm fronds against the window all night—it was a holiday made in hell, she told me; she wished she'd never left home.

But, she says, East Oyster, the town thirty miles north of Vancouver where I was born and raised, is almost as foreign to her these days. She no longer recognizes faces on the street. A sign on the outskirts of town is a constant irritation to her. East Oyster. Population 276, and Still Growing.

That's one thing about Heaven—I recognize everybody's mug. Some faces get *too* familiar, sometimes. Over the past ten years the population has declined, though at the moment it has stabilized and there are just three of us. After reading my mother's letter and birthday card (I turned forty-seven on March 12, 2000), I thought of putting up a sign: Death Row. Population 3, and Still Shrinking.

My mother's card was shaped like a wedge of Swiss cheese. "Happy Birthday," it read. "Another year shot to hell." We got such a kick out of it that Rainy and I decided to make our own line of death-row greeting cards, available in time for Christmas next year, by mail order.

Rainy was responsible for the graphics. For her first effort, she drew a bunch of turkeys getting decapitated by an axe-wielding Santa. When you opened the card there was Santa Claus, strapped in the electric chair. I had to think up a message. I penned, "Hope you get a charge out of this."

She drew another picture, same theme—only this time it was Jesus in the hot seat, trying to blow out a life's worth of time on the birthday cake in his lap. I wrote, "More power to you."

Then Rainy went a bit too far, I thought, and drew Mrs. Claus being ambushed by a firing-squad disguised as a party of carollers. I wrote *The Executioner's Carol* across the cover of the book Mrs. Claus died reading.

But what kept me awake at night was trying to think of words to go with Rainy's depiction of lethal injection. She drew Santa lying on the gurney while the guards tried to find a vein for the IV drip. Rainy says the hospital gurney they strap you to is shaped like the gingerbread-man cookie cutter her mother used to use. Her mother made gingerbread men every Christmas, and she let Rainy decorate them. Rainy gave them eyes and noses, and before she was old enough to spell her own name, she began giving them erections. Her mother wanted to know where she was getting her "ideas." From her father, Rainy said.

I wrote, "Run, run as fast as you can. You can't catch me, I'm the gingerbread man."

Rainy didn't make the connection. She says I have to think the way someone buying a card would think—whatever that means.

This was one business venture doomed from the start.

———

When it comes to choosing the form of capital punishment that best suits your personality, there's no book in the library to consult. So I devised a guide for those who can't make up their minds, or people with multiple or non-existent personalities. I wrote it after I heard a psychologist being interviewed about the idea that we all have a personality. He said most of what people think of as their "own personalities" are "absurdist idiosyncrasies" at cross-purposes with their lives and happiness.

In my *Guide to Capital Endings*, the personality description would come first, followed by an appropriate Final Solution:

> 1) You're very committed—to work, friends and relationships; when the going gets tough you're *always* there: hanging.

> 2) You're aggressive, crave adventure, live for the moment: electric chair.

> 3) You're a little unsure of yourself, never quite certain what you're looking for: lethal injection.

> 4) You've got a big heart, love everything on earth that lives and breathes: gas chamber.

> 5) You're nurturing, impulsive, a little preachy, but get a bang out of everything: firing-squad.

Methods of torture and killing people have evolved, like everything else, to keep abreast of the times. (I've left out other antiquated methods of capital punishment—the guillotine, beheading with an axe, gibbeting, breaking at the wheel, stoning, pressing, drawing and quartering, crucifixion.) For instance, one modern form of torture used by guerrilla terrorists in repressive Third World regimes is to force a starving rat into a woman's vagina, then to stitch up her labia so the rat will have to gnaw his way out through her stomach if he wants fresh air. In one case I read about, the woman happened to be pregnant. They waited until she went into labour before proceeding with the questioning.

All these methods were devised (surprise! says Rainy) by men. Rainy's let a childhood of being sodomized, an adolescence of being forced to have sex with dogs and an adulthood of being beaten with wire coat hangers colour her attitude. The only reason she has accepted Christ is because she wants at least one sympathetic male figure in her life.

Here I am getting a touch preachy. My rule is there's no room for preachiness on the Condemned Row. Frenchy admonishes me. "Rules are for breaking. What else would anyone make them for?"

But don't get too attached to Frenchy. She doesn't make it to the end of this book. Hardly even to the middle. She chose the firing-squad. The first time.

The prison chaplain, the guards, your classification officer, your care and treatment counsellor—all work on you to choose the firing-squad, or hanging, so that your organs won't be damaged. They distribute all these pamphlets urging you to "Be an Organ Donor."

When you choose the firing-squad, they tie you to a chair and pin a red tissue-paper heart to your chest. (I guess they must figure the heart doesn't count as an organ, or that people needing a transplant would rather die than go on living with the heart of a condemned criminal.) The guards stand behind a screen with a slit in it, facing you. If any one (or all) of those five guards likes you, or even feels sorry for you, she'll aim as far away from the bull's-eye as she can get without missing you and getting a demotion for gunnery. This could mean four bullet holes in the right side of your chest (one of the rifles has a blank in it) and you bleeding to death, slowly, while everyone reloads.

Gary Mark Gilmore, who helped revive capital punishment, donated his eyes. Something else I know about him—he ordered pizza for his last meal and then couldn't finish it. (His eyes must have been bigger than his stomach, Rainy says.) I always wondered who got his eyes. When you stop at Pizza Hut for your pepperoni and pineapple two-for-one special, is that pimply faced boy taking your order looking out at you through Gary Gilmore's eyes?

His last words were "Let's do it." No muss, no fuss, no bleeding to death before getting executed properly. When they did it, the four shots overlapped in the centre of the bull's-eye, like a four-leafed clover, without the luck usually associated with four-leafed clovers.

Rainy's chosen "legal injection." She figures it gives her a chance; Rainy's been a drug user all her life—there's hardly a vein in her body that hasn't dried up or collapsed from the constant barrage of dope. The only usable blood vessel left is under her tongue, she says, and she doubts whether anyone will find it.

Lethal injection is made to look like an everyday medical procedure. They even swab your forearm with a disinfectant before trying the most likely vein, as if you have a medical future. Two people sit in different rooms and each presses a button: one cocktail goes into your vein through an IV drip, the other down a drain. This means the person pushing the button never really knows if she is the one doing the killing. The executioner can always console herself: "Maybe I did, maybe I didn't."

That's how I console myself too. I know I screwed up at the trial by saying I would have done *anything* to save my baby. I didn't mean it literally. *Anything* didn't include killing him. I was just telling the truth.

That was another mistake: telling the truth. Hindsight, as Frenchy would say, is 30-30. Frenchy used a .30-30 on her boy in that bank. She should know about hindsight.

Rainy is looking forward to having her execution televised. She hopes it will deter other people from killing their kids. She tells Officer Freedman that she should buy stock in the network doing the televising, that her execution—the instant replays and summer reruns—will make investors a ton of money.

Executions began being televised when the state of California went pro-choice in 1995, five years after I moved to the Row. I figured that in a culture as show-business oriented as ours, executions, when they wound up being a continuing series, and a repetitive series at that, would lose their appeal and be cancelled for poor ratings. When people could turn on their TV sets any night of the week and see daycare centres being blown apart by bombs, or schoolchildren gunning each other down outside the classroom, I didn't think they'd be too likely to have a continuing interest in the executions of convicted murderers. I was wrong. "Executions Live!" continues to get better ratings than "Larry King Live" or even the Super Bowl.

Widely reported press conferences are held every day with notorious death-row inmates; every week we see televised images of ambulances bearing away the bodies of executed men and women. The papers flash news photos of mourning friends and relatives outside the prison on the night before the execution, and the local Nazis, or Klansmen, always gets a lot of coverage, with placards saying, "Fry Gay Preverts [sic]" and "Gas: A Sure Cure for Black Crime."

There may be X number of days left until next Christmas, but when you live under a sentence of death, you never know if there will be a next year. Any one of us could be history by then. That's not soon enough for Officer Freedman. She'd like us to die laughing in the meantime.

She calls it "having a sense of humour": who but a moron would think "No noose is good noose" a joke? We call it guard humour. Their jokes harass me more than Frenchy's train, but I'd never let Frenchy know that.

Another year shot to hell. There's a *real* joke for you. I can still see my mother standing in Jonesy's Book and Stationery in East Oyster, trying to find the right greeting card to send her birthday girl on death row.

I admire my mother—she's got guts. And a sense of humour. A lot of mothers would have nothing more to do with a daughter who did some of the things people say I've done.

My mother never knew my baby, but she knows how much I loved him, through the letters I've written to her since coming to prison. She knows how much he changed me, insofar as one person is capable of being changed.

Insofar as. I am starting to sound like Vernal. He sent me a memo for my birthday, and a twenty-dollar bill (Canadian). The memo said he was celebrating fourteen days of sobriety. These weren't consecutive days, he wrote, but a ballpark figure for the nineties.

Frenchy's got her "last meal" order in already. She's requested steak and onions and pie à la mode. "At least I don't have to worry about it repeating on me," she says.

After questioning Frenchy at some length, I'd discovered that she thought "à la mode" was a flavour, like lemon meringue or cherry. We heard she finished her last meal, leaving a wedge of pie "for later."

chapter six

I moved into an unfurnished apartment in the same building as Carmen. Vernal worked late the day I went back to
the house to pack up my life, most of which I decided to
leave behind. I didn't want the memories, or the reminders.
I took a few cookbooks, some pots and pans, and—I needed something to sleep on—Brutus's futon. I figured with me
out of the house, Brutus would be moving onto our Beauty
Rest anyway. Later that week, Vernal phoned to say two of
his Time-Life cookbooks were missing. I sent them back to
him in a cab.

In the weeks that followed, I got a series of memos, by
courier, signed from Brutus, saying how much he missed me
and how he wished I would come home to bake cookies,
with the odd P.S. from Vernal saying Brutus's cognitive
therapist was worried about the effect our separation was

having upon him, that dogs from broken homes were more likely to think less highly of themselves than other dogs. The day Vernal fired his secretary and sent me a memo begging me to come with him to Mexico, where we could "relive our honeymoon all over again," we ended up having another row: I called him and said it was redundant to say "reliving all over again"; it was almost as bad as "old-fashion taste." He said he didn't want to sleep with someone who corrected his grammar, and I said, is that what Brutus is doing these days, correcting your grammar?

Carmen, Bonnie, Little Shit Shit and I rode with Thurma out to the prison every Saturday morning most of that spring (I'd sold my car because I couldn't afford the insurance now), and for two hours we sat, always at the same small square table in a corner of the visiting room, played cards and drank bad coffee from the machine. Once a month, a social would be held in the gymnasium, often with entertainment for the visitors—a movie, a skit put on by the prisoners, music or a comedy routine. I saw little of Mugre, who spent all his time rehearsing. Mugre was going to play a prison guard in a production staged for the Halloween social in November, Angel said.

I became Angel and Gustavo's unofficial translator, rendering everything from prison regulations and lawyer jokes into English, and translating the guards' demands into Spanish also.

Counts and Accountability
12:20 a.m. . . . Counted in your assigned bed

3:00 a.m. . . . Counted in your assigned bed
5:00 a.m. . . . Counted in your assigned bed
4:00 p.m. . . . Standing count in your assigned cell
9:15 p.m. . . . Counted in your assigned cell

Memo from Corrections Services Canada to Inmate Gustavo Corazón Gaviria: *"There will not be any kicking of the volleyballs or basketballs. If you come to the recreation yard wearing a jumpsuit, it will remain on."*

Memo from Corrections Services Canada to Inmate Angel Corazón Gaviria: *"Authorized items may be considered contraband when found in excessive quantities or altered in any manner. Possession of unauthorized contraband [sic] is subject to disciplinary action.*
    The following Food Services–issued food items are allowed for possession by inmates at any one time:
2 chocolate bars
15 packets of sugar."

Memo from Corrections Services Canada to Mugre Corazón Gaviria: *"It is against the rules to tie a knot in a handkerchief and throw that around."*

On the last weekend in June, the Native Brotherhood sponsored a social. Thurma couldn't find a car, so she and Carmen and I travelled to Agassiz by bus. We were about to phone for a cab to take us the rest of the way to the prison when a car pulled up at the curb. Bonnie rolled down the window, and I was hit with a cloying pine-forest smell coming from the green Christmas tree dangling from the mirror. "Climb in," she said.

The passenger doors were riddled with bullet holes and rusted shut; Bonnie had meant it literally when she told us to "climb in." I struggled through the window, across the laps of the women packed in the back. The front of the car was empty except for the driver, a big man with two braids and a beaded headband. He didn't look at us. "This in Kono, my brother," Bonnie said. His name meant "a tree squirrel biting through the centre of a pine nut," she explained.

Little Shit Shit, dressed in the same deerskin jacket and pants she'd worn since the first time I'd met her, lay sprawled on Bonnie's lap. She snatched my purse and began chewing on the strap.

"She sure likes your bag," Bonnie said, as the woman next to the window reached over and offered me a toke. I said no thanks, and tried to get my purse back before Little Shit Shit took an interest in my credit cards as well.

Bonnie said she would be sending out her wedding invitations soon. "All we need now is permission from the attorney general," she said.

Kono began speaking, choosing his words as if measuring each one for its impact. "Why should you ask the attorney general for anything. He is not *our* attorney general."

I nodded. Best to remain neutral, especially when someone is giving you a ride, though judging by the noises coming from under the hood, and the smell of the fumes, I was surprised when the car made it as far as the prison. Kono parked, and we piled out into a cloud of blue smoke the same moment as two patrol vehicles drew up on either side of the lot, eyeing us.

The process of signing in, getting scanned and stamped, waiting for Jack Saygrover to lead us from the visiting room to the gymnasium was beginning to feel too familiar—the men standing behind the barrier waiting and waving, and the women approaching, awkwardly, like girls at a junior high sock hop.

Gustavo came over to greet us. The doors to the yard were wide open and I could see a group of Native men, including Treat and Kono, standing in the doorway, holding drums.

I looked around for Angel; he saw me at the same time and waved me over to where he stood talking to Mugre.

"Those drums are giving me a pain," Mugre said. "It is like being in the jungle, that noise. All night I couldn't sleep."

Angel told him he was going to get himself in trouble with the Posse if he didn't keep his complaints to himself. Mugre made as if to spit on the ground, then glared at the group of Natives.

"That one there, he insulted my brother," Angel said to me, pointing to Treat. "He said to him, 'What kind of Indian *are* you, anyway?' Where we come from, to call someone an Indian is a sign of disrespect. It is like calling him *malparido*—which means 'born from a really bad place'."

This time Mugre spat. *"Hijo de la chingada!"*

Angel and I went outside and walked in circles around the big yard. Angel said his brother was starting to talk like a Mexican—*"hijo de la chingada"* was the worst thing one man could call another in Mexico. The Indian women had been raped and carried off by the Spanish invaders, and to this day Mexicans of Spanish descent still refered to *los indios* as *"hijos de las chingadas"*—sons of fucked mothers.

I watched the convicts keep as close to the perimeter fence as they could get without being out of bounds. Angel told me he missed me every time I left, the way he missed the stars at night. In prison, he said, you couldn't see stars because of the glare from the sodium lights on the yard. "Someday I would like to take you to Tranquilandia—the stars there, they keep you awake with their brightness."

To some extent I had always romanticized South America—the last frontier! And when Angel spoke to me the way he did, I conjured up images of afternoon sex under slow-moving fans in the shade of jagged bluish mountains swept by light breezes from the Central Cordilleras. Of evening sex, and morning sex, too. I looked at him and saw, in the gleam of his shadowy eyes, a depth of wanting that promised heaven.

Months later, I realized the desire must have been my own reflected back, that the promise I thought I saw had been nothing more than the neglected spirit of my own lust.

My life took another twisted turn the day Carmen called to say Angel's wife would be coming in the fall to visit him.

I was curious to learn as much as I could about Consuelo de Corazón, the wife Angel had said he worried about at night; but from what Carmen told me, he had nothing to worry about except his own mortality. Angel was Consuelo's third husband.

Nothing had stopped Consuelo since the time she picked her first pocket, Carmen said. She graduated to stealing tombstones from cemeteries, chipping off the names of the deceased and selling them back to their families. By thirteen she had become a courier, sewing drugs into the ribs of a line of underwear she'd designed herself, making weekly runs to Miami and Los Angeles. When she met her first husband, Don Mario, he wanted a more traditional stay-at-home wife, and so he set her up in a new business, Hits for Hire, which meant she didn't have to travel. Because the city was crawling with "confidence tricksters"—gangs of teenaged boys posing as *sicarios*, assassins—it was acceptable for customers to require a *muerto de prueba*, a test killing, which could be of anybody, for as little as fifty dollars. Consuelo was a good businesswoman and before long had several hundred women on her payroll, and two years later she claimed responsibility for wiping out a rival crime family to gain control of its trafficking network. This, Carmen said, led to more problems at home.

When Don Mario himself was assassinated, Consuelo relocated to Tranquilandia and immediately remarried—this time a *contrabandista* from Medellín. Her second marriage ended abruptly when she shot her husband because he said no to her—no, he didn't want another drink—in the bar of the Hotel Viper shortly after he had presented her with an emerald choker.

Consuelo had told Carmen that she felt, in retrospect, it had been a senseless thing to do, one killing that could have been avoided if they both hadn't had so much to drink. She had always been a fast learner, and unlike many of her countrymen, she quickly learned that killing people had unpleasant side-effects. For one thing, Carmen said, she had to sell the choker to pay her lawyer's costs.

"She got bored with smuggling," Carmen said. "She wanted to retire from the business. That's when she opened *Cositas Ricas* (Tasty Little Things), the boutique she'd always dreamed of." She specialized in intimate apparel, Carmen said, and used her shop to recruit cover girls— women paid to pose as tourists on small planes loaded with cargoes of cocaine destined for southern Florida. One day, Angel Corazón wandered into the boutique and took her to a party at the Hotel Viper, where three hundred guests munched quail eggs dipped in wildflower honey and drank the best champagne. "It used to be a respectable hotel, back then," Carmen said.

The next day, Consuelo put a Closed for Stock-Taking sign on the door of her boutique, picked up Angel and flew him to New York, where they rented an apartment together. They kept a limousine parked outside, with a driver who stood at attention beside it at all times. Angel bought her white orchids and sweet oranges and gold buttons. He bought her jewellery and flew her to Hong Kong to see the one man in the world he could trust to polish the hole that held the cord to her pendants. Angel's heart at that time,

Carmen said, was "as big as the Rock of Gibraltar": he bought Consuelo a different-coloured Mercedes for every day of the week.

Carmen paused and looked at the sky, as if Consuelo might descend at any moment to pick up where she'd left off in her love story. "She has been parted from Angel before. The last time Consuelo smuggled a grenade in her *choca* [vagina] into the prison where they were keeping him, in Medellín. They say no one escapes from El Zancudo, not even a mosquito. Forty people died trying to stop them from getting away.

"But now," Carmen continued, "she has decided to become a nurse. I told her, *amor, killing* is your business. You don't know *how* to do anything else."

I saw Angel only once during the summer; my own work—deadlines—not to mention my mixed feelings about his wife's impending visit, kept me from travelling out to the Joy as frequently as I had in the past. Relations had grown more strained between the Posse and the Tranquilandians, which meant Carmen didn't feel comfortable driving to the prison with Bonnie and Baby Shit Shit and Thurma every week. Carmen said it was not likely that the two groups would reconcile. "Gustavo always says forgiveness is for people who lack an adequate form of revenge."

The day Consuelo de Corazón landed, in her Lear jet, in Vancouver, Carmen rented a car to pick up her sister-in-law at the airport. She invited me to drive with them to the Prison Justice social. Angel'd had little to say about his wife's visit. "She likes to drop in on me once in a while. But at least she lets me know when she's coming. Back home we have an expression: *It is a sin to be surprised.*"

Consuelo de Corazón had a steamy, smouldering way of carrying herself, as if she might have been conceived in a strange greenhouse, then raised wild. The second thing you noticed were her lips—like razor nicks—but what she lacked, she made up for in lipstick so fierce and thick that it almost sucked your eyes out of your head. A small, dark-skinned woman, with black hair falling in waves to her waist, she sat in the front of the rented car, next to Carmen, who tried to introduce me. Consuelo took no more notice of me than she might have of her bodyguards riding in the back of her car on Tranquilandia, though she showed more interest when Carmen told her Angel had been trying to persuade me to take a holiday on Tranquilandia. "Price-wise, a woman like her could be worth quite a lot," Consuelo said, as if she had read Angel's mind.

I leaned forward and, in her language, said that from what I had been told about Tranquilandia, no one could expect to be accepted socially in the best circles until they had survived at least two kidnappings. Consuelo, who didn't seem fazed, said it was true, the crime page and the society page were the same thing in the City of Orchids newspaper—but a single, pro forma kidnapping for a foreigner like me would be enough to open a few doors.

When we got to the prison, Consuelo disappeared to the chapel. I sat with Carmen and Gustavo and Mugre, who drummed on a metal plate with the back of a stainless-steel spoon. If you ever needed to find Mugre, Gustavo said, you waited until it got close to meal time. You could always find him at the chow-hall door twenty minutes before a meal.

"He wants to be first at *something*," Gustavo said, and Mugre brought the spoon down on the back of his brother's hand and tried to grind it into his flesh.

Carmen sighed and said why did men want to be *first* at everything? Why did they insist on having virgin snow they could cut up with their skis, and virgin forests they could cut down? Mugre might be the first one in line for dinner, but he was the only one of the bunch who hadn't gained weight since they'd arrived in Canada, she added. Even though the food was better here, and there was more of it than most people got at home, Mugre's illness had left him without an appetite.

I watched Mugre picking at a running sore on his hand. He had not been himself since he got out of prison the last time, Carmen said. She'd gone to El Zancudo with Gustavo to pick him up and had found him passed out on the floor next to a thin broth of rotten horse meat he'd cooked up in his cell, his arms around the whore they called Salsa Picante.

"I've always said it was that soup, not the whore, that gave him the virus," said Gustavo.

I waved to Bonnie and Thurma when I saw them sitting together on the other side of the room, and made a face for Little Shit Shit. When Angel and Consuelo joined us, Angel didn't look at me. He sat close to his wife, with his arm around the back of her chair, the way he usually sat with me. I heard Consuelo tell Carmen that they had jimmied the lock on the chapel's folding doors, behind which the prison chaplain stored his chalices, paraphernalia and prayer books, and that she and Angel had gone in there to have a private visit. It wasn't what she would call intimate, she said, kneeling beneath an organ under the eyes of the Blessed Virgin.

A group of inmates began erecting a makeshift stage in the centre of the gymnasium, and Mugre left the table. "I think he has stage fright," Angel said when Consuelo said she'd never seen Mugre look so pale.

We sat back in our chairs as the lights dimmed. A spotlight came up on one of the Mexican crew members who was dressed as a priest—the play we were about to see was called *Rehabilitation*, he said in broken English; it had been written and produced by the prison writing group. I was looking forward to the entertainment. For one thing, it meant I wouldn't have to make small talk with Angel and his wife.

Mugre and Treat stepped onto the stage, Treat wearing the same red bandanna he always wore and the black T-shirt with "Narrow Gauge Posse" on the back, and Mugre in a guard's jacket and hat, carrying a very realistic-looking baseball bat. Treat, I thought, had either studied method acting or was on drugs: he moved warily and uneasily. The prisoners in the audience began whispering to one another. Mugre thumped his bat on the floor for silence.

When that didn't get everybody's attention, Mugre swung the bat and connected with Treat's skull. We all gasped as Treat fell to his knees, clutching his bleeding head. Only Angel and Gustavo sat still, their faces expressionless.

"That's not in the script, not to fucken kill me, man," Treat cried.

He looked dazed, and blood trickled from between his fingers.

Mugre scowled and looked at the priest, who held up a crucifix and cried, "Show time!"

Treat tried to stand up but only made it as far as one knee. He looked around for help, his face contorted with confusion, as if Mugre had forgotten his lines or who he was supposed to be. "You been rehabilitating me for the wrong job," he managed to whisper, as if sticking to his script, when all else failed, might save him. "All you teach me to do is mail-bag repair, and they don't do that nowhere except in here."

The men in the audience began whispering again. Mugre slugged Treat with the bat a second time, knocking him off his knee.

The real guards, who had been standing in an uncomfortable silence, muttered to one another. I buried my head in my hands, wondering how I would make it out of here to safety, wishing I understood what was happening.

"Now—when you get out, where do you go to get a job?" the priest shouted. There was blood everywhere, and Treat had curled into a ball on the floor. Mugre spat on him and kicked him in the ribs.

"Back to prison," Treat moaned.

Mugre struck him once more. "Now you are getting with the program," the priest cried.

The warden appeared by the door marked Emergency Exit. It was clear to me by now that Treat was badly injured, and yet the Tranquilandians and the Mexican crew were applauding, stamping their feet. The priest lurched onto the stage, turned Treat over with the toe of his foot and crossed his arms over his chest.

"This prisoner has been rehabilitated," said the priest, placing a paper lily in his hands.

A siren went off and a voice came over a bullhorn. "ALL INMATES TO LINE UP! THE WALL!" Guards rushed the stage; Mugre raised his bat and the guards began to swing their batons, beating him back. Most of the audience looked lost, the visitors not knowing what to do. The guards put Mugre on the floor, handcuffed him; the whole incident seemed to be contained, then one of the guards brought the butt of his stick down on Mugre's head.

I tried to get out of the way, but got knocked down on the floor as Angel and Gustavo pushed a row of chairs aside and scrambled towards Mugre, who was being dragged out of the gymnasium by his feet, tangled in balloons and streamers. Then everyone in the gym froze—all the convicts had left their visitors and formed a circle around the guards. The loudspeaker blared out repeatedly, "CLEAR THE GYM, RETURN TO YOUR UNITS, CLEAR THE GYM, RETURN TO YOUR UNITS," and the siren screamed in our ears. Consuelo de Corazón bent down, took me by the hand and pulled me towards the door. Carmen was right behind me. When I looked back over my shoulder, I saw the prisoners keeping the six guards surrounded and moving in on them, inch by inch.

Then, as we reached the exit, the loudspeaker went dead.

I saw the warden give a signal to the control centre as the gate slammed open. A wave of uniforms poured into the gym—*Star Wars* figures with Plexiglas face shields, helmets, padded gloves, black leather boots. Tear gas exploded; I heard the swish, the sickening thud of flesh being pounded down, as riot sticks filled the air.

Consuelo still had me by the hand; we pressed ourselves against the wall, inching towards the barrier. I tried to find Angel, and at the same time as I saw him coming towards us, I saw Little Shit Shit on the floor, smiling and waving her bottle at the crowd of rioting men. Angel scooped her up, delivered her into my arms. I stayed long enough to see him catch a baton across the shoulders and then go down; I fled through the gates as more guards arrived in the gymnasium.

Jack Saygrover met us in the hall and hustled us through the remaining barriers. I waited in the visiting room with Carmen and Consuelo, and when Bonnie finally arrived, she looked as bruised and beaten as Treat had been. I started to ask her what had gone wrong, but she grabbed Little Shit Shit, gave Carmen and Consuelo a look of contempt, and didn't say a word to any of us. We were all held for another half-hour, and they searched us, one by one, as we left the prison building.

chapter seven

On October 29, Vernal and I had dinner together. He came to pick me up in a taxi, and arrived early for once. I asked him to wait in the living room while I took a shower.

"Listen to this," he shouted so I could hear over the hiss of the water. I'd already read last weekend's news, so for once I knew what was coming.

"'Inmates surrounded and attacked six guards after a riot broke out during a play, in what CSC officials are calling a race-type riot.' What's a race-*type* riot, as opposed to a *race riot*, know what I mean? Anyway, it looks like one of Gustavo's bad brothers took a baseball bat to a Native . . . because the Native had insulted him by calling *him* an Indian."

I finished showering and then went into my bedroom wrapped in a towel. "What do you mean, 'one of his *bad* brothers'?"

Vernal followed me in and sat on the edge of the bed. He didn't answer my question. "Here's a woman who says she went to the Prison Justice social looking for "Mr. Right" and got tear-gassed instead. It amazes me how many squirrelly women there are out there. There are 750 men in that prison. Each one of them has a dick *and* an imagination."

He put the paper down and lit a Gitane. I asked him not to smoke in my bedroom. "That place has been open less than a year and already it's nothing but trouble," Vernal said, pointing to an aerial photo of Mountjoy Penitentiary on the front page of the newspaper. "Harder to get into than all the other country clubs put together," he added, meaning, I supposed, you had to be pretty hard-core to be sent there.

"A lot of those men probably haven't done anything worse than you or I have ever done," I said.

Vernal gave me an odd look. "I never raped a retarded child and bucked him up with a chain-saw afterwards. Like that Chandler? The one the cops beat so badly he'll never walk again? You said you'd leave me if I even *considered* defending him. I hear he's got some woman chasing after his wheelchair now. Wanting to marry him. Some women think love can change anything," Vernal said, "even homosexuality."

I was sitting on the opposite side of the bed, still wrapped in my towel, waiting for him to leave the room so I could put my clothes on. He leaned over and kissed me and tousled my hair. "But then again," he said, "so do some men."

I asked him to leave, then got dressed, wondering how much Thurma knew about her boyfriend's past—she had met him through an ad he'd placed in a magazine, looking for penpals. I thought, as I slipped on my black stockings and hooked them to my garters, how little we know of *anyone*, especially the person we go to bed with every night, who is also the one most likely, statistically, to kill us. I wondered, too, if I would end up in bed with Vernal before the end of *this* night.

Even though we'd obtained a legal separation, Vernal had insisted we celebrate our anniversary, "for old time's sake." Over drinks—tequila served in hollowed-out sections of cucumber with chili salt around the rim—we reminisced about our honeymoon. How innocent we had seemed back then, arriving in Mexico City in the midst of the Day of the Dead celebrations. I didn't think it was a good omen when our welcoming drinks at the Hotel Geneva were brought to us in fragile skull-shaped pottery goblets, or when we walked through the streets at dusk and lampoons illustrated with skeletons, natural or clothed, going about the business of the living—getting married, making love, giving birth and dying—were being circulated. At midnight there were fireworks and prayers and a hymn of welcome to the *angelitos*, the children of the family who had died.

That was then. Now Vernal couldn't finish his meal—unusual for him—and he finally confessed that he'd been seeing a doctor. Vernal never got sick, except from drinking, and he had a home remedy for that affliction: a double single malt. I'd never known him to see a doctor.

I took his hand and said, oh God, Vernal, I hope it's nothing serious. He hung his head, bit his lower lip. Not that serious, he said, he'd only seen her half a dozen times in the past month and was already thinking of breaking it off. He'd really like to start seeing *me* again. I picked up my knife and brought it down hard on the back of his hand.

When he started bleeding, I suggested taking him to emergency, mostly because I didn't want to get charged and go to jail. It was, he protested, only a minor flesh wound, but he made a big production of wrapping his hand in the Hermés scarf he had given me for an anniversary present. He said he would now be able to show the world the scars of his marriage.

Neither of us spoke. Like the knife, the unresolved issue of his infidelity had come between us. Then Vernal asked me if I had ever considered having sex with someone I didn't know very well.

"What kind of a question is that?" I asked. He glanced towards the door of the restaurant, then took my hand and pulled me to my feet. Outside, standing alone in the slanting rain, our bodies pressed up against the north wall of the building, I hugged him hard, as if I could squeeze his other lovers, as if I could squeeze the past, out of him. I kissed him. He kissed me back, brushing my eyes just as I was opening them to see the expression on his face.

We kissed again and again, kissing as if to seal our fate, to finish a life together we hadn't even begun. We kissed as if kissing could save us.

———

I might not have gone back to visit Angel again, but the day after my anniversary dinner with Vernal, I met Carmen for lunch. She'd called saying she had a letter for me. *"When Carmen first described you, I thought, already I want to make sin with this woman in my heart. Waiting for you to come back has become my way of getting through the days, and if you ever decide to return to this place, I will still be waiting. I have already made sin with you in my heart; it won't be long before I am walking in your veins."*

There was more. He said he had reserved the chapel for us. He wanted to be alone with me, he said.

Four days later, I met Carmen at the bus depot. The Halloween social was being held on November 2, to coincide with the Latin holiday of El Día de los Muertos.

Thurma had had her visits chopped (she'd been suspected of packing drugs and had refused a strip search)—I was glad, in a way, because without Thurma, Chandler would be unlikely to turn up at the social and I wouldn't have to face my complex range of emotions about his situation. Bonnie wouldn't be going to the Halloween social either, because Treat was still in the infirmary.

I'd seen Bonnie once since Mugre's attack; she was still planning on getting married. "Even if he's on life-support and I have to unplug him to get him to the chapel, we're going to go through with it." Bonnie had chosen a dress in red satin, with suede high heels to match, but the bridal consultant had talked her into something more traditional. "Married in white, you have chosen all right. Married in red, you will wish yourself dead," the consultant had cautioned.

On the bus out to Agassiz, I told Carmen about stabbing Vernal. I said I didn't know what men wanted.

"We never try to kill each other any more, Gustavo and me," Carmen said. "Those days are over for us. We fight sometimes . . . but it's *corazón*. You never fight unless it's for heart. Consuelo taught me that."

Angel kissed me when we arrived; I felt his moustache, smelling of the red-hot cinnamon hearts he sucked—to hide the scent of the dark tobacco on his breath—scouring my upper lip. He kissed me for so long I started getting self-conscious. *A kiss and embrace are permitted at the beginning and at the end of the visiting period.* I pulled away from him. I felt his eyes, like the guns in the guard towers, holding me in their sights.

"You worry too much. No one's looking at us. On Tranquilandia, we have another saying: Don't worry, at least not until they start shooting. And even then, you shouldn't worry. Don't start worrying until they hit you, because then they might catch you."

Angel asked me to walk with him in the rain. My coat was not waterproof (Vernal says I am the only person born and raised on the West Coast who has never owned proper rain gear), and I felt my dress sticking to me. I felt, too, Angel's hand warming my waist, moving up until it brushed over my breast, and then down again to rest on my belly. All of him washed over me, like the mystery of wind.

But I sensed a distance in him that day, as we walked up to a doe and her two fawns, browsing on the thick grasses next to the perimeter fence. The three bolted for the woods when the patrol truck slowed as it passed. Angel said if any wild animal ever came this close to civilization in his country, it would be shot dead on the spot, or taken to a zoo, where it would be tortured over the years.

"We had one polar bear in La Ciudad, in the zoo. He was very peaceful and shy until someone threw a stone at him and drew blood. Then he would rear on his hind legs and roar; he'd attack the flies that tried to land on him."

The black bear at the zoo, though mangy and bad-tempered, was never a target for the stone-throwing boys, he said. Angel believed people liked to provoke the polar bear because of the colour of his fur.

"People like to see blood," he said. "Lots of it."

The Day of the Dead looked like any other day in prison, with the exception of the food. Every table held plates of sugar cookies shaped like skulls, with the names of inmates who had died in prison during the past year inscribed on the foreheads. Bowls of candy skulls and chocolate leg bones and fingers and ribs, and the traditional "bread of the dead" (decorated with shin-bones made of flour and eggs), were spread out on each table on a carpet of yellow flowers: marigolds, daisies, carnations, black-eyed Susans.

Angel took off his jacket and placed it around my shoulders. I asked where everyone had gone: Gustavo was in the kitchen and Mugre had been put in segregation, Angel said.

"My brother needs a woman in his life," Angel said, "to keep him in line. It's been a long time since Mugre's been interested in anyone but himself." He paused and tried to pull his jacket around me and button it up. "He's always said you might as well take a razor to your . . . *cojones* . . . as let a woman in your heart. That's his philosophy."

"That's going a bit too far," I said.

Angel took my hand. "My brother believes 'far' is the only place worth going." He raised my fingers to his lips.

I pulled my hand away on the pretence of adjusting my dress. "You always smell so clean," he said. He put his hand on my knee. "I like that."

Immanuel Kant says the hands are the only visible part of the brain. I sat staring at Angel's hands as if they might provide a clue as to what he was thinking, not knowing how to tell him what I desperately wanted to do, looking out through the open gymnasium doors, past the guard towers to the mountains.

Then I put my hand on his hand. I could feel the heat coming from his skin too, mixed with the smell of my own excitement.

Carmen, sitting across from me, raised one eyebrow and nodded, and I didn't need any more encouragement. I got up, quickly, from the table, and pulled Angel to his feet. I flicked my eyes in the direction of the chapel.

It was everything Angel had promised in his letter: the Day of the Dead committee had jimmied the folding doors and made up a bed for us on a weight-room mat—two green blankets and a pillow, upon which had been placed a yellow rose. I turned the statue of the Blessed Virgin away from us to face the wall, and began to unbutton Angel's shirt. He didn't stop me until I got to the hollow place in his chest. It looked as if his heart had been excavated.

He took my hand, curled it into a fist and placed it in the little hollow. "My mother used to say it would fill up with the tears she would shed for me during her lifetime," he whispered.

My mouth felt dry. Then (the smell of him!) he was beside me, kissing me all over my face and head, sniffing my hair along the part line.

I laid my head back on the pillow as Angel picked apart the rose. I shut my eyes; he placed the creamy petals on my eyelids. He pressed his nose in my armpit, edging one finger under the elastic of my bra. My arm was going to sleep; I shook the petals away and shifted my position.

Angel put his arms around me, settling his body alongside mine. "You're not like any woman I've ever known," he said to me.

I leaned over and kissed him, for a long time. It didn't matter that on the other side of the folding doors, a few feet from the door of the chapel, there was a world of men and women eating and laughing. We were alone with one another, and nothing could intrude upon this new world of the flesh we were both, at the same time, discovering.

He took my hand and guided it. Erotic texts from ancient India claim there is a definite relationship between the size of an erect penis and the destiny of its owner. The possessors of thin penises would be very lucky; those with long ones were fated to be poor; those with short ones could become rulers of the land; and males with thick penises were doomed always to be unhappy.

For now, I would try to make Angel happy. When I looked up at his face, across the nut brown expanse of his body, he smiled back, that slow smile. "I'm going to die," he said.

Then he pulled me up, so I lay next to him, and reached inside my panties. I nuzzled up to his hand the way a horse's soft mouth does when you offer it a lump of sugar. I arched my back, spreading my legs wider as he moved down over my body and began licking me, slowly, teasingly, moving in small circles with his lips and tongue, his kisses falling on me, gentle as the scent of rain.

I didn't want to come, not yet. I sat up and pulled him down on top of me.

"I don't have any protection," he said.

There are some exquisite moments from which we are not meant to be protected. I slid him inside me, achingly. I had never had anything so hard inside me. I held my breath as he kept pushing into me; we were both breathing and then not breathing, and I brought his hand up to my mouth to cover it, suppress any sound, and then I began sucking his fingers, one at a time, then two at a time, then three. His fingers tasted of salt, and of my own juices.

He pushed into me, harder still, as if by trying he could disappear up inside me and escape forever into the orchid darkness of my womb. When he came, his whole body stiffened, as if it hurt him to come so hard. We lay that way, me underneath and he still inside me, until he moved down on me and began licking me again, making me come with his tongue, his lips and his fingertips. I cried when I came and doubled up, curling into myself. He began kissing me, from my toes up along my legs and the insides of my thighs, over my belly and breasts, up my neck and onto my face and in my hair.

Afterwards, as I lay on a bed of bruised petals, licking the drops of sweat that had rolled down his chest and collected in the hollow above his heart, he said coming inside me was like coming on velvet rails.

chapter eight

Tension between the Tranquilandians and the Posse had escalated even further after the Halloween social, and Angel and Gustavo had also been moved to segregation. Four and a half months passed before I was to see Angel again, on Good Friday, the day Bonnie and Treat were finally to marry.

The Friday before Good Friday, Bonnie was called with bad news. She wept from the time she handed Little Shit Shit over to Thurma at the bus depot and we boarded the bus in Vancouver to the moment we pulled into Agassiz, blowing her nose, over and over again, into a sodden handkerchief.

A light snow had begun falling. I called the only taxi company, and when the cab arrived, the driver said he didn't know if we would make it as far as the prison, "the way she was coming down."

He asked if we minded if he smoked, then lit one anyway. He had an opinion on everything from Native land claims to capital punishment. He believed all men in prison were queer. He said all he'd ever wanted was a warm girl in his bed every night, and all he'd ever been was disappointed.

He rubbed the blue shadow of his beard. He said he wanted a girl with pride and femininity too. The last girl he'd taken a shine to admired women older than herself.

"That shows great intelligence," he said, "admiring a woman older than yourself." He accelerated as we passed a sign saying Slow Children Playing.

"She liked my beard; she thought it looked masculine," he said. "She was a real intelligent girl."

He swerved, trying to hit a reserve dog slinking across the road. "Now you take Sean Connery. *He's* masculine. James Coburn. John Wayne. They wouldn't do the dishes either."

Bonnie let out a sob from the back seat.

"I say something?" the driver asked.

I didn't answer. Bonnie buried her face in her hands. The snow had turned to freezing rain, and a fierce wind tugged at the car, nearly pulling us off the road. Our driver kept his eyes on the road the rest of the way, then let us off in the parking lot, as close as he could get to the front gate.

Bonnie's throat was raw from crying. I explained to Roll-Over, when he finally buzzed us in, that we had come to pick up Treat's effects. Roll-Over told us to sign the book while he called the Admissions and Discharges officer.

"Got two for Discharge, sir. No paperwork on it."

He paused and looked at us. "One of you . . . relative to the body?"

I nodded towards Bonnie. "They were going to get married. He's . . . he was the father of her child."

Roll-Over half turned his back on us as he spoke into the phone. "No relation. That's right—that's what I've got too." He looked back at Bonnie. "Computer says here he's got no next of kin. I can't let you in. I'm sorry, ma'am. Them's the rules. I don't make 'em. I don't break 'em either. That's why I only work here; I don't live here."

I could picture us standing this way forever. I asked Roll-Over if he could do us one favour and call Mr. Saygrover, who might be able to straighten out the problem. To my surprise, I watched Roll-Over look at the phone, as if he were about to do something he'd never before attempted to do on his own: make a decision. He picked the phone up, dialled, then, after a brief conversation, shook his head and looked at us.

"If you say so, Jack. Will do. Right away, sir. Yes, sir. I'm aware of that now, sir."

Roll-Over went through my purse, taking apart my fountain pen and getting ink all over his hands before putting it back together again. I was allowed to take a tube of liquid foundation, but not the tampon I'd always kept, just in case, in a pink plastic holder in a zippered pocket of my purse. Roll-Over handed me a key so I could leave the tampon in a locker. "Safety measure," he said. "Inmate could suicide himself by choking on one."

I passed through the metal detector and then waited while Bonnie went into the room marked No Entry Staff

Only. Surely they weren't accusing Treat of making any more trouble? When Bonnie reappeared, the matron popped her head out of her office and handed me a Kotex maxi-pad, to replace the contraband tampon, I guessed. No inmate, evidently, would try suiciding himself with a sanitary napkin.

The snow fell harder as we walked between buildings. Mr. Saygrover saw Bonnie and waved us through the glass doors into his office, where a notice read, "Tomorrow has been cancelled due to lack of interest." A leaning tower of files stamped Classified was stacked on his gunmetal desk.

"Feeling bad just isn't good enough for some people—they got to make everyone else feel bad too." He indicated the files. "They send me all this from the warden's office . . . all these complaints. This one's toast is too hard. That one's toilet paper's not soft enough. This one's mattress has teeth marks on it. I tell you."

Mr. Saygrover shuffled through his paperwork until he found what he was looking for: release forms in triplicate for Bonnie to sign.

Bonnie began crying again, and Mr. Saygrover looked embarrassed. He patted her on the back, offered her a fresh piece of Kleenex. He looked at me, helplessly.

I said I was going to get a cup of coffee from the machine.

"Get one for me too. Extra sugar and whitener, if you don't mind." Mr. Saygrover reached in his pocket and pulled out a handful of change. "Here you go. It's on me."

When I returned with the coffee, Bonnie had gone to the washroom. Mr. Saygrover told me no one "higher up" had given permission for the body to be released, so Treat would be laid to rest in the prison cemetery. "That way, we can keep an eye on him." He winked at me.

I asked if it would be possible to arrange to have his body flown back to his last address, which was Bella Bella.

Mr. Saygrover shook his head. "Too late now. You got to plan ahead."

Mr. Saygrover sniffed his coffee, then asked if I wanted to see the autopsy report. I nodded, and he handed me a file marked Confidential. He hadn't started out as a visitor's and correspondence officer, he told me—years ago he'd taken a St. John's Ambulance course at the YMCA, which had qualified him to work on the daily sick line. He'd wired more jaws, sewn more torn anuses, he said, than you could shake a stick at. But never, in all his years at the infirmary, had he seen anything as sick as this.

"I'd like to get my hands on the individual that did this." No charges had yet been laid, Mr. Saygrover said— the "incident" was under investigation.

Treat, who had been discharged from the infirmary at the beginning of March, shortly after the Corazóns had been let out of segregation and back into the population, had received a wedding gift: a stainless-steel cutlery set, pilfered from the prison kitchen. Knives, forks, even the dessert spoons had been driven into his flesh. His rectum had first been carved out with a knife to permit the entry of "an object larger than the normal man," though the report didn't specify what kind of object, or what part of a normal man.

I held the photograph in my hands, thinking Treat looked like a piece of performance art with all that cutlery sticking out of him. I was ashamed of myself, too, for want-ing to laugh. Looking back, I believe I was anaesthetized by shock. I told Mr. Saygrover I didn't think Bonnie needed to see the report, or the photograph; he put it away in a file before she came back into his office.

All Treat's worldly goods fit in the shoebox on Mr. Saygrover's desk: a key chain with no keys, $2.36 in change, a toothbrush, a rosary and an unopened bag of Cheetos. Mr. Saygrover emptied onto the desk a brown paper bag containing the clothes Treat had been wearing when he'd been discharged from the infirmary, the red ban-danna, the black T-shirt.

"I hope he gets a clean shirt to wear," I said, folding the T-shirt and laying it in the shoebox with his other belongings.

"Sally Ann donates us a suit," said Mr. Saygrover. "I think they found one that would fit him. He won't be get-ting any heavier, that's for sure . . . " His voice trailed off.

Bonnie had washed the streaks of mascara off her face, but her eyes looked even blacker now with grief. Mr. Saygrover patted her on the back again and handed her the whole box of Kleenex. "Keep it," he said. "It's the least I can do."

Before I returned to my apartment after picking up Treat's effects, I kept another appointment—at the hospital. That evening, I made a pot of tea and sat watching the day grow dark, a jasmine-scented candle filling the room with its hot-night fragrance. Outside I could hear the howling March wind bowling the day's litter of bad news down the alleyway.

I called Carmen and asked her to come. I switched the radio on, but the reception was no good. I sat with the fuzzy ultrasound photograph in my hands, listening to a woman sing a love song through the static.

I'd had the blood work done when I first suspected I was pregnant, and now the ultrasound the doctor recommended because of my age. "Women want to find out whether they are carrying a child with birth defects, one they may choose to abort." Having any baby, but especially one that required more attention because it was born with Down's syndrome, or with fins instead of feet, would be hard. But since when had I turned my back on anything the moment life became hard?

I turned the black-and-white photograph over in my hands. The fetus, half-fish, half-human being, rubbed its eyes as if trying to shield its face from the probing camera. Ten fingers, ten toes. What had given birth in my heart now kicked in the womb, small enough, still, to fit inside a tear.

Carmen opened a bottle of non-alcoholic champagne and poured us each a glass. She asked if I had thought of a name: even though the ultrasound hadn't indicated the sex of the baby, Carmen felt sure it would be a boy, because that's what Angel wanted most of all, a son. I tried explaining to her I didn't want to raise a child who thought going to prison to see his father was a normal way of life. I didn't want *my* son's diapers examined or his tiny orifices probed in the name of security, I said. I didn't want him growing up thinking razor-wire was "pretty." Besides, Angel had a wife, one who smuggled grenades. What might she do to a woman like me? I wanted this baby, I said, but I wasn't going to see Angel again.

Carmen said Consuelo was not a *big* problem, but insisted that Angel would want his son to be part of his life. She poured more champagne, put on Pachelbel's Canon over the sound of a heartbeat, as recorded from inside the uterus, and waltzed around the room caressing her belly. "Sweet Baby Dreams," the tape was called. I envied my friend, how she could spin about the room and laugh without effort, or carry on a conversation without having to close her eyes mid-sentence. I was too tired to walk as far as the bathroom to brush my teeth, or to the kitchen for a glass of flat ginger ale and a couple of soda crackers—the only breakfast I wouldn't lose. Most days, I simply curled up on the couch in a floor-length flannelette nightgown and furry sleepers, with a strip of Scotch Magic tape between my eyes to prevent frowning wrinkles.

The funeral was held on Good Friday, Bonnie's wedding day. The chapel had been reserved anyway, she said. She pinned a corsage to my lapel—one that complemented her bouquet of orchids—before we set out in the rain for Agassiz. Bonnie had ordered the flowers for their wedding; she said there was no point cancelling the order—people appreciated flowers at their funerals also.

Carmen, who had insisted on coming to the funeral— to pay her respects, and for Bonnie's sake, she said; it was not *their* fight, she maintained, but the men's—said it was just as well Bonnie wasn't getting married today, because it was raining so hard that it would have been an unlucky wedding. "Lady Unluck has the rain for her train," she said to us.

The smell of the orchids filled our rented car, and when the windows began steaming up, I almost convinced myself I was driving through some tropical rain forest, not the Fraser Valley. Torrential rains had washed out a bridge on Highway 1, and we had to take a back road through the mountains. Grey moss overhead, a ghostly presence in the pervasive green, trailed from tree to tree, reaching for the ground or the surface of the water in the overflowing creeks. Bonnie, sniffing and dabbing at her tears, told us what the tree moss meant to her people. A girl was killed by an enemy tribe during her wedding ceremony, and her mother cut off her daughter's hair and spread it on the limbs of the spruce tree where they buried her. Her hair blew from tree to tree, eventually turning grey, enduring as a tribute to those who are not destined to live out their love.

Neither Carmen nor I had an unhappy ending to top that one. We drove on in silence, encountering holdups even along the alternate route—two minor accidents and a police roadblock warning us of the possibility of landslides. I had never known it to rain so hard as when we pulled into the Visitors Only lot, where a sign read No Parking for the Wedding. Perhaps the same official who had tried to prevent Bonnie from entering the prison because she wasn't Treat's blood relation had unwittingly posted the sign. Feeling frustrated and angry, I dropped Bonnie and Carmen at the front gate.

I parked on the road and walked the quarter-mile back. We had to stand outside in the rain, waiting, until the big hand on the clock inside gave its single-digit salute to the sky and Roll-Over buzzed us in. Our clothes were soaked through, and Bonnie's hair hung in bedraggled ropes around her shoulders.

"Wet enough for you out there?" said Roll-Over as he went through Bonnie's purse. He sniffed her bouquet, held it upside down and shook it.

"Check with the matron before you go through," he said, pointing Bonnie towards the body-search cubicle. I told Carmen I hoped to God they would give it a pass today, but Carmen said she doubted they made any concessions in this place, not even for grieving brides.

The guard at the main doors buzzed us through and waved us into the visiting room, where Mr. Saygrover sat with his feet up on his desk.

"My breakfast," he said, disgruntledly picking another french fry out of a pond of gravy. "Don't like to waste, not with all the famine and lack of food in the world today. I'm supposed to be on a diet, mind you. The wife's idea. Not mine. What the heck, is my attitude. Life's short enough without her always telling me to push away from the gravy."

I saw Bonnie stiffen, and Mr. Saygrover looked at me, embarrassed. "I've put my mouth in it again," he said. "Me and my big foot."

He looked from Bonnie to the clock on the wall above the soft-drinks machine. "We'd better mosey on down the hall," he said.

I never knew whether Jack Saygrover's lopsided walk was a result of injuries or the weight of the keys at his waist, but I felt myself unconsciously imitating him as I walked behind. The floors were freshly mopped and the corridor reeked of disinfectant, and Mr. Saygrover told us to watch our step because he didn't want any more casualties.

He nodded to the guard in control of the iron-barred gate, and the heavy steel doors slid back on their runners. We crossed the five further barriers before reaching the gymnasium and the chapel.

Mr. Saygrover looked at his watch and said, "Count's going to happen in the middle of the proceedings if they don't get the show on the road. This is as far as I go. You girls are on your own from now on."

He shook each of our hands. I'd noticed how Jack Saygrover always seemed to take a paternal interest in both Bonnie and Carmen. Carmen could look as if she needed protection. I pitied the man who ever thought fingernails were something women grew long to make their hands look feminine.

Suddenly Bonnie reached up, put her arms around his neck and kissed him on the cheek. "Thank you for everything you have done to help," she said.

She kissed his other cheek, and Mr. Saygrover blushed. The creases in his neck stayed white, but everything else above his collar turned the colour of a cardinal bird I'd once seen run over on a California road.

"I don't know how long it's been since anyone around here said anything they meant sincerely," he said. He shook her hand again, then turned back towards the steel barrier that opened to let him pass.

Daddy Lord, the only man licensed to perform funerals and weddings inside maximum security, welcomed us at the chapel door, his breath smelling of last night's Old Grouse. He looked more like an exhausted bus driver than a man of God, with his Expo pin in his lapel and a calculator dangling from his belt. In an aqua plastic insert above his heart, he carried an array of pens, and in his hands, a copy of *Good News for Modern Man*.

Treat got a full house. I saw the wedding cake Bonnie had ordered from the prison kitchen and forgotten to cancel, and an officer standing guard over the cake knife. Floating above the cake was a bunch of pink and white heart-shaped balloons. Daddy Lord began apologizing for the mix-up and said funerals were like weddings—administrative nightmares. "Paperwork till it's coming out your yin-yang. Myself, I'd rather see a funeral than a wedding any day. At the funeral, at least you know a person's troubles are over."

Bonnie said it didn't matter about the cake; it was all for looks and made of Styrofoam anyway. She could take the balloons home to Baby.

The prison-issue coffin Treat was to be buried in lay beneath the organ and the statue of the Blessed Virgin. She still faced the wall: no one had turned her back around since the Halloween social. I leaned against the wall, staring out through the bars of the chapel window, as Daddy Lord negotiated his way to the front of the room and stood to the right of the coffin. In the silence that fell, I could

hear the hum of a generator outside and men playing bas-
ketball in the gymnasium, even the internal workings of my
own body—the churning in my stomach, the rush of my
blood—and my eyelids opening and closing like a moth's
wings brushing against silk. I thought, too, I could hear my
baby's heartbeat.

Daddy Lord opened his prayer book. He had sweat running down the sides of his cheeks. He pulled a wrinkled
handkerchief from his pocket, mopped his brow and began
quoting the words of the Holy Writ, as found in St. Luke:
"Be ye also ready, for at what hour you think not, the Son
of Man will come." These words, he said, were as applica-
ble to the inmates within the walls of Mountjoy
Penitentiary as they were to any other men. He then turned
the service over to Bonnie's brother, Kono, who said Treat
would not want any of us to pray for him. "The only time I
heard *him* pray was when he found out someone had a contract out on him because of a drug deal that got fucked up.
He prayed to the Virgin because she is the Mother of God,
and his mother was the most sacred thing to him.

"You can only have one mother, he'd say, but your
father could be any son of a bitch."

Everyone laughed, which seemed to release some of the
tension in the room. When it grew quiet again, Kono continued. "He was a believer, but he only went to church for
one reason. Whenever he ran out of rolling papers, he
would go get a copy of the New Testament. He believed the
New Testament had the best paper for smoking up."

Daddy Lord thanked Kono for his remarks. "Nothing so
nearly touches man as his mortality," he said, taking over

again at the front of the room. "Daily he meets with objects and situations that remind him of the frailty of his existence here on earth, and from time to time the Angel of Death makes his periodical visit to our midst, in order to remind us that 'it is appointed for men once to die, and after this, judgment.' Our brother Treat has been called to give account of his stewardship before the throne of the Eternal judge of the living and the dead. Let us pray that death, the grim officer of God, will not invade our ranks for the remainder of the month."

Even though he wasn't in the room, I felt Angel's breath slip into my ear, whispering its way through the fine hairs on the back of my neck.

Just as Daddy Lord was inviting everyone to congregate in the gymnasium for lunch after noon count, I heard thumping and loud voices outside the chapel door. The lights went out and alarms began going off in the building. Daddy Lord pleaded with us to stay calm.

I heard a familiar voice shouting, "Chapel! Chapel!" from the gym, and Daddy Lord fumbled to get the door open. Mugre, holding a zip gun made from a length of pipe, pushed Mr. Saygrover into the chapel; he almost knocked me down. "Now look here, you fellows know . . ." Daddy Lord began, starting towards Mugre.

"Stand back," Mugre said—I'd never heard him sound so level—"or I will kill you. We're going out." He passed off the zip gun to Angel, who had appeared with Gustavo out of nowhere, grabbed my arms and pinned them behind my back. Mr. Saygrover charged, Gustavo grappled him and they toppled together, upsetting the table that held the wedding cake. Mugre scooped the cake knife from the floor. Then I heard, above the pandemonium, the staccato beat of a helicopter overhead, a throaty *thwap-thwap-thwapping* out of the skies.

Mugre dragged me towards the chapel door, holding the cake knife at my throat. He told the security guards who were backing off into the gymnasium that if anyone else made an attempt to take me, I would die too. Outside I could hear the clatter of automatic-weapon fire, the muffled thud of helicopter rotors and a voice over the loudspeaker calling, "Clear the yard! Clear the yard!" The machine-gun fire, from this distance, made a hissing, sputtering sound, like sparklers on a birthday cake. Mugre shoved me towards the gymnasium doors. Carmen, Angel and Gustavo were close behind.

The guard standing in the darkness by the door had a flashlight in one hand and a truncheon in the other. He looked young and scared. Mugre kept me in front of him like a shield, making a sawing motion back and forth across my throat.

"We don't want to have to hurt anyone; we want to leave here in peace," Angel said.

The guard might not have understood Angel's words, but there was no mistaking Mugre's gesture. I glanced up at the control tower, where the prison arsenal was kept; I could see the guards lined up at the window, levelling their guns at us. They could easily open fire and prevent the escape from going any further. I looked away again, and the young guard's eyes met mine.

Mugre pressed the blade on my dress into my neck. "If any one fires, we all die. You shoot first and she . . . like this!" He drew the knife first across my throat, and then across my belly. Outside, I could hear the metallic *pop-pop-pop* of machine-gun fire.

"Open the door! We're going through," Mugre said, straining his voice over the thud of helicopter rotors overhead and the machine-gun chatter.

The young guard stood his ground, switching his flashlight on and off again in our faces. "Surrender your weapons and let the hostage go. Don't do anything you might regret later." He nodded at Mugre. "Sir."

The "sir" was a concession, I supposed, to the knife making a deep indentation in my belly. And then, as I prepared to die, the warden's voice came over the bullhorn, a voice welcome as morphine. "What are your demands? Tell us what you want, and we will do whatever we can to assist you. But first, let the hostage go."

The three men grew silent, looked at each other and then at me for an explanation. I tried to translate what the warden had said. The young guard stood, feet apart, flashlight going on-off at his hip.

"We want access to the yard," Angel said quietly. "Then we will release the hostage unharmed."

I translated his demand. The guard continued playing with his flashlight.

And as I waited, and kissed an imaginary pair of dice and tossed them high, the doors opened and the warden came on the bullhorn again, saying, "*No one gets hurt. Let the hostage pass.*" The guard stepped aside, shaking his head.

I could smell smoke as Mugre pulled me out the door; a shot from one of the guard towers shattered the wall beside us, and I saw Gustavo fall. I heard more sirens and gunfire as Mugre pushed me ahead of him, still using me as a shield, out across the grass towards a helicopter hovering over the yard like an outlaw dragonfly, firing on all guard towers.

Angel fell. Mugre stopped and turned to help him. But then Carmen got hit too: she lurched forward and to one side, doubled over and clutched her bloodied shoulder. Mugre let go of Angel, pushed me towards the helicopter, dragging Carmen after him. An arm reached down from the cockpit to pull us up; looking back in terror, I saw Angel rise and stagger towards us. I heard another shot and saw him sink to his knees. The guards kept firing; his body jerked with each shot, then lay unmoving in the dirt, curled in the foetal position.

We rose to meet the sky. I sat numbly watching the blood flow down Carmen's back, and listening to Mugre getting sick in the seat behind me.

The pilot's face was concealed by a kind of balaclava made from the leg of a pair of sweatpants, with holes cut for the eyes and mouth. But it didn't hide the black hair that fell in waves to her waist; for one blind moment, I thought of trying to jump out of the helicopter as it angled into the wind.

part three / the hostage

*It is difficult to understand those
whom one does not hate, for then one
is unarmed, one has nothing with
which to penetrate into their being.*

—*Pär Lagerkvist*, The Dwarf

chapter nine

Death Clinic, Heaven Valley State Facility for Women

Should you desire a personal mirror, you may purchase one from the commissary. When not in use, it should be set down in an appropriate place where you will not be distracted by looking at it.
—Inmate Information Handbook

There is never enough time, unless you're serving it.
—Malcolm Forbes

I sent a kite to the warden, saying they should bring back burning at the stake. It would make great television, the flames raging out of Heaven, the eyes popping out of heads.

The warden thinks it's because I crave the spotlight, but it's not. I didn't ask for the publicity I've been getting; it's just that I keep insisting that if they're going to kill me tomorrow, they might as well kill me right now. I would have been out of here long ago, feet first in a Styrofoam coffin, if the Women's Empowerment Coalition hadn't taken up my cause. Most men on death row who insist upon being executed are allowed to die, but we still don't grant women the same right to self-determination. The group fighting on my behalf says that after everything that has happened to me, I am not capable of making the right decision. American law forbids the execution of a person who is insane, and any woman who *wants* to die is not sane enough for execution. If *I* won't apply for clemency, they will keep doing it for me.

Pile, Jr. has a brilliant theory about why so many women are being executed: the state is correcting a previous gender imbalance. You don't even have to commit murder these days to get the book thrown at you.

In one so-called civilized country, a kindergarten teacher was sentenced to death for the "counter-revolutionary" offence of possessing manuscripts critical of the government. I read that she'd been electrocuted with the organ-transplant doctor standing by.

The story got out because the woman had not died immediately. She was kept alive, in fact, by the doctor who later came forward with details. He couldn't live with himself, he said, and described how he had removed both her kidneys while she was still living, and how her liver had been "too hot to handle."

"Is demand influencing supply?" read the headline in the *New York Times* after the doctor made his disclosure. "Is the free world executing prisoners to feed a clandestine transplant trade?" The country had a thriving business that relied on prisoners' organs for raw materials, but this business also fed an insatiable state killing machine that led to more and more executions every year.

Frenchy's life, on the other hand, was *saved* by politics. The guards had been staging wildcat strikes for better working conditions, and when those who'd volunteered for the firing-squad were told they had to go ahead with the execution or replacements would be called in, they went to work but deliberately missed their target, and then refused to reload. It was the first time in the state's penal history this had happened: each of the five guards put down her gun and walked off the job.

Rainy asked Frenchy what was the first thing she'd done after not dying. Frenchy said she'd sat down and scarfed that last piece of pie she'd been saving "for later."

Rainy is always asking me, "Have you got a date yet?" It's like being back at high school, having her around. She makes it sound like we're all going to a dance. No, I don't have a date. Yet. I'd like to say, on that particular night, I won't be going out.

On her next date, Frenchy says, *she's* going to dance. Rainy tries to persuade her to go on a diet: she's heard that if you weigh less than 112 pounds, you won't be heavy enough to hang. A life-saving last meal, for example, might be an undressed garden salad and a Diet Coke.

Rainy says she wants suckiyaki for her last supper. She waits for us to ask.

"It's when you have a mouthful of chop suey and a guy sticks his dick in your mouth."

After Frenchy stops laughing, Rainy says what she really wants is the regular fare served to all other death-house inmates, so she can tell herself she's going to wake up in hell the next morning with the same indigestion as the rest of us stuck here in Heaven.

The Women's Empowerment Coalition would be opposed to it, of course, the idea of women burning at the stake. They send me their literature on "Capital Punishment and Sex Discrimination." Back in the fourteenth century, when they stopped boiling people alive, they substituted public hanging as a far more humane execution. "With one glaring exception," the pamphlet read. "A woman convicted of a capital crime was not to be hanged, 'as decency due to the fairer sex precludes the exposing and publicly mangling of their bodies,' but to be bound to a stake, and there, fully clothed, to be burnt alive. In the name of decency women endured a far more painful death than did men."

"I've got a joke for you," says Officer Freedman. "There are three women, an African-American, a Mexican-American and a Canadian-American, lined up in a courtyard, waiting to be executed." She paused, looking at me, as if the joke was on me because I had appealed my classification and lost. "As the guards raise their rifles, the African-American shouts out, 'Earthquake!' The guards drop their guns and run. The African-American escapes.

"Next morning, there's just the Mexican-American and the Canadian-American. As the guards raise their rifles, the Mexican-American shouts out, 'Flood!' and, same as yesterday, the guards drop their guns and run away. The Mexican-American takes off too.

"On the third morning, the Canadian-American is there all alone. When the guards raise their guns, the Canadian-American shouts, 'Fire!'"

I can see why it came to be called gallows humour. You laugh in the face of death, knowing death gets the last laugh every time. They can take everything away—they can make us beg and cry and puke—but when we still laugh at ourselves begging, crying and puking, they have to know theirs is a hollow victory.

My mother writes asking me to describe a typical day in Heaven. She'd like to think it's a place full of angels eating angel food cake and playing harps on clouds. I don't tell her we live on tinned spaghetti and mystery meat sandwiches. I make the meals served in Heaven sound just as tempting as the gourmet Meals-on-Wheels she's been helping distribute to shut-ins. I don't tell her how I am ordered to bend over every time I leave the chow hall, and that a trusty, another prisoner, examines me for contraband—it will remind her of her own holiday from hell.

"I'll never go back," she writes. "Everybody leaving that dreadful island was detained." Before boarding a plane that would carry her back to "civilization," my mother, who is in her late eighties, had been called into a little room, where she'd seen a policewoman pulling on a pair of white gloves. My mother convinced herself that the police were going to strangle her and steal her watch, and that the policewoman was putting on gloves so she wouldn't leave fingerprints.

And she was worried sick about me the whole time. "Are you getting enough sleep?" she asks. "In that article I read on the plane you had bags under your eyes."

I don't tell her how I have to sleep with some part of my anatomy showing, that when the guard on night shift comes by with her flashlight she must be able "to see flesh." A 250-watt bulb, "extra-long life," burns from the ceiling, so I never sleep deeply. It adds insult to injury to know there's a good chance I'll be outlived by a light bulb.

I don't mention how much I miss doorknobs, or toilets with seats, or especially light switches. If I mention light switches, it will get my mother going again on *her* lamp, the one that works intermittently. She's going to have to return it, but she's been putting off going downtown because of the parking. She wonders if she is going to live long enough to get her money back, or if she'll die knowing that Aladdin's Wonderful Lamps owes her $49.75 plus tax.

As far as worrying about my appearance goes, I'm in no position to check to see if I have bags under my eyes, because my "personal mirror" was confiscated after I got caught looking in it instead of watching TV.

Rainy made a drawing of me with three eyes in my head. I'm weeping from the third eye, which is in the middle of my forehead.

I show it to Frenchy. "It's a very flattering picture," Frenchy says, "except for the three eyes in your head."

After the article in *Newsmakers*, the same one my mother read, I got a fan letter. "Your visage is quite arresting, with crooked teeth interesting in the extreme," wrote Helmut Bender, who had also seen me on one or two TV clips, "though I'd of still written to you even if you were plain." Helmut turned out to be a prison guard engaged in writing his memoirs also, "tentatively titled *We're All Here 'Cause We're Not All There: Memoirs of a Good Screw.*" If I could fix him up with a publisher, he'd put me in touch with an orthodontist in Philadelphia.

I sent Helmut a note asking how much of his book he had completed. "Only the title, so far," he replied. "The wife says I've already written too many words—you can tell a good book, she says, because there's only one word in the title. She wants me to write that kind of book. The kind of book people can read."

It's a lonely life. And lonelier for all the people in it.

I've digressed again. I was about to describe a typical day in Heaven when I got sidetracked. Got to keep my train on its tracks.

I have seen what happens to most women in prison. They take drugs, then sleep their lives away, like Frenchy, or find God and drug themselves, like Rainy. Or they get themselves killed. I suppose that's going to happen to all of us, sooner or later, but meanwhile, we can sleep, pray, get high or, like me, write about it.

One time I wrote to my mother that each morning I

wake to a day already stale, controlled, a thin mattress, a pillow watermarked with tears. She wrote back, "There is only one thing to do when you are bored—learn something." She would be pleased to know I've learned many new tricks.

I've learned to "front," to hoard, to be distrustful, to "mask"—to cover up, put everything on the outside and cry on the inside. And how to confine all my letters to one double-spaced page. The guards monitor our mail, and as far as they are concerned, the shorter the sweeter.

To "front" means it doesn't matter whether you're rock hard or sullen soft, you've got to be *about* something and stand up for yourself and rip a girl's arm off if you have to. When I was first in the general population, before I got sentenced and hardly knew anybody by name, this girl said to me, "I'd like to lick your clitoris." Rainy took me aside and said I had two seconds to set up a confrontation with her or else I'd end up being walked all over by every dyke in the joint. I waited until there was a crowd in the shower room and then accused her of stealing my last tampon. She denied it, but I sucker-punched her full in the face, if not exactly breaking her nose, doing a little blood work in the area. I got put in a punishment cell for two weeks (I got an extra week tacked on for saying, "Aren't all cells punishment cells?"), with a pissy mattress on the floor, one pair of baby-doll pyjamas made of a thick quilted material not unlike packing blankets, and one puke green blanket to serve as anything you'd want to use it for—a sheet, a pillow or just something to hide your face under, and nothing to read but improperly spelled graffiti: "Loopy is a necofilliac"; "Fuke the World."

The hole was another not-so-happy learning experience, but when I got out I had one thing coming: respect. Frenchy, whose nose was still a bit swollen, never threatened to lay her tongue on me again, and we became friends.

Rainy's the one who taught me to hoard. She used to work in the chow hall. Every night after she'd cleaned up, she emptied three quarters of each of the sugar containers down the front of her shirt, into her 42D bra (there are few things more humiliating for a woman than having to wear a bra that is way too big, though in Rainy's case it came in handy), and smuggled the sugar back to her house. You never knew when you would need a sugar fix, she said, and you couldn't exactly raid the kitchen here when you felt like stuffing your face at midnight. I couldn't see hoarding bread and peanut butter—my kind of comfort food—down the front of my shirt, so I learned to do without, hoarding my own emptiness.

What else did I say I'd learned? Trust? There's no such word in here, it's all about *dis*trust. Take any good word and in Heaven you learn to prefix it with *dis*. *Dis*respect. *Dis*regard. *Dis*engage. *Dis*illusion. *Dis*integrate. *Dis*appoint. *Dis*allow. But especially *dis*trust.

Rainy doesn't even trust anyone to give her the time. Rainy, I say, that's all we've got. She'll ask me for the *exact* time, and I'll tell her: 5:33 p.m. Then I'll hear her getting a second opinion from Frenchy.

"Still half past nuttin' last time I cared," Frenchy will tell her. You can either do the time or the time will do you. *Prison time is chicken bones. Something to be sucked clean.*

"Do your own time." "Don't let anyone mess with your mind." "Keep to yourself." "Don't let friends choose you. You do the choosing." Prisoners learn to hide their true feelings, to create a mask. You may present yourself as a tough bitch or tell huge lies about your former life—you may act crazy so the prison pests will leave you alone. Eventually, though, switching between your mask and your true face gets more and more difficult.

chapter ten

At my trial, the prosecuting attorney made it sound as if I'd conspired with Las Blancas from the start. What kind of woman would risk sex with a convicted felon *in a maximum-security penitentiary*? Had I ever once tried to escape when I was a hostage? No, the prosecutor said. Hadn't I had plenty of opportunities? Why did I stay? Why didn't I try to get away and go to the authorities? Because I had wanted to be *one of them*, the prosecutor said. She said I was an *unfit mother*, that right from the start my baby never stood a chance.

She got all her information from the diary I'd kept during my captivity. Consuelo had given me the stub of a pencil and a lined notebook with two cartoon ducks embracing on the cover beneath the words *Contigo soy feliz* (With you I am happy). Consuelo let me know she was not happy with the account Carmen had given of the treatment she'd received from Las Blancas in her book, *Rescate*. She let me know, too, that I was being given a second chance—to undo the damage Carmen had done; I was to write only the truth about Las Blancas, about their dedication to freedom, to *los derechos humanos*, human rights.

In my first days as a hostage, I wrote that I was about as pampered as a prisoner could expect to be, that I was being fed gourmet meals and considered myself very lucky to have such a unique opportunity to practise speaking Spanish. My prosecutor had, apparently, never heard of *irony*. I'd also written, she said, that my captor was not a criminal at all, but a person in need of sympathy and understanding. What was I supposed to have written?

When I was arrested, they took my diary, so I've had to reconstruct most of this story from memory. I remember the helicopter, being forced to kneel on the floor, my head pressed between Mugre's knees, and having difficulty breathing. And, after we landed, being pulled across a field towards a car—black or dark blue—and seeing mountains all around. But then I was blindfolded and my hands were tied behind my back, and I was squeezed onto the floor of the car. I heard Consuelo telling Carmen to lie down in the back. Mugre covered me with a jacket and sat with his feet on me. More than the fear and the discomfort, I remember the smell of Mugre on that jacket.

I recall being thirsty, and after we'd driven for—I don't know—an hour maybe, the car stopped and I was given some warm, very sweet orangey drink and a plastic container of apricot (or peach?) yoghurt. I asked Mugre to untie my hands so I could eat, but he removed my blindfold instead so I could see what he was feeding me. He let me out of the car, then helped Consuelo move Carmen onto a bed of moss and spruce needles. We were parked beside a dirt landing strip that had been bulldozed out of the forest; there was a shed used to store drums of aviation fuel and other supplies, and a plane, a twin-engine Cessna, covered by a camouflaged tarpaulin. Mugre made me stand in a dark corner of the shed while he and Consuelo rummaged through boxes containing semi-automatic rifles, Uzi machine guns, cases of grenades, riot shotguns, military-style M16s and rounds of ammunition. Consuelo opened one marked "First-Aid Emergency." I looked out through the dirty window and glimpsed the sun trying to bleed through the fingers of two fist-shaped clouds.

I was taken back outside; Mugre went behind the shed, where I heard him throwing up again while Consuelo gave Carmen a shot of morphine. She tried to clean her wound, saying Carmen had much to be thankful for, at least she wasn't being eaten alive by fire ants.

"Strike a match on Consuelo's soul, it won't make her flinch," Mugre said to me under his reeking breath.

I tried hard to find a tiny hint of human weakness in Consuelo, something she might dislike in herself, which would explain her cold-blooded nature as an attempt to camouflage this "flaw." But the only time I ever saw her soften was when she talked about Angel. Even then, all she said was that talk of love wasn't for people like them, that revolutionaries could not descend with small doses of daily affection to the terrain where ordinary people put their love into practice.

Angel was dead, she was sure of it. Gustavo too. Carmen had told Consuelo I was pregnant. "And when I told Angel, he knew, more than anything in his life," Consuelo said, "he wanted to have this child."

The sun had been squeezed out again as the fists joined and became one defiant hand. I felt cold and wanted to move around to get warm; I asked Consuelo if I had to be tied up all the time. Lines from Carmen's book kept coming back to me, how her kidnappers had had rules, and those rules had been harsher than those of any prison. Starting with the first day, harsh treatment was the method used to demoralize a hostage.

"It's for your own good," Consuelo said. She wanted to know if I'd ever been taken hostage before, and when I didn't answer, she said to consider myself lucky, because very few *norteamericanos* ever got an opportunity to live with the *guerrilleras*, share their dreams and their hardships.

My wrists felt raw from where the rope had cut into them. The slow burn spread up my arms, across my breasts, over my neck and face. "You hurt people," I said. "I don't want anything to do with you . . . or your cause. You talk about freedom, your dedication to human rights. Well, what about *my* rights? Don't I have any?"

Her face darkened. "Only the dead cannot be judged," she said.

I considered myself warned. I knew that by showing what I felt, I had violated the first rule when it came to dealing with kidnappers, (one I'd learned from Carmen): Do not show pity or contempt for their ways. I tried to drop the contempt from my voice when I said kidnapping pregnant women wasn't high on the list of Canadians' favourite pastimes. She seemed curiously disappointed. Did *canadienses* place such little value on maternity? A pregnant hostage in her country seldom had to be killed, because the father or the grandparents would pay anything to get the victim back.

I remembered another of Consuelo's warnings: "A woman like you could be worth a lot of money." I reminded her that my husband and I were estranged—why did she think he would pay to get me back?

She looked at me as if I were stupid. "It is *you* who will pay," she said. "Eventually."

Outside, the snow was coming down. A green van pulled out of the loading-dock area and made its way up across the prison parking lot. It pulled over by the gates to the cemetery.

The gates opened and the van drove through. I watched a coffin being lifted from the back of the van by four corrections officers who were soon out of breath, struggling with their load. I watched the snow settling on the fake-fur trim of the guards' brown winter jackets as they lowered Angel into the earth.

I woke up shivering, not knowing where I was, feeling something kicking me; then the world came into focus, sadly, the way desire takes shape sometimes. I lay rocking, coaxing my baby back to sleep, trying to recall how I'd come to be lying on the cold, hard floor of the Cessna. The last thing I remember, we had been climbing into the clouds, and now we were on the ground again and, judging by the sounds I heard, the plane was being refuelled. I could see nothing in the darkness; I wondered if I would live to see daylight. The baby kicked me a second time, hard, as if to stop me from having these kinds of thoughts—ones that wreck with their futility.

I curled up on the floor, closed my eyes and vowed not to open them. I dozed, but when I woke it was always to the same agony, the same emptiness. I felt nothing but dread.

Carmen lay next to me, her breath making a gurgling sound. Eventually, the evil-smelling jacket was thrown over my head, and then I heard the plane door being shut and felt the plane shuddering into the air again.

The next time we put down, Consuelo let me off the plane. I didn't want to get up and walk as far as the stairs, but I remembered another rule: Never say no to a hostage taker. There was nowhere to go—not a building in sight, no welcoming farm or convenience store or gas station on a distant horizon. Nothing but high moraine wheat fields and dirt roads that stretched on in silence to little hills.

A lightning storm struck the benchland to the west. Consuelo told Mugre they had *un trabajito*, a little job to do, at a drop site in the bayou, and she estimated we would be arriving there shortly after dusk. From what little I overheard, I gained that the two men employed by Las Blancas had also been working as informers for the DEA. They were the ones responsible for the bust that had put the Corazón brothers behind bars. Even the DEA treated these men as disposables: they had code-named them Walking Death I and Walking Death II. WD1 and WD2 for short, but not for long, Consuelo said.

We took off again, and I felt lonelier than I'd ever been before, looking down at the prairie, blowing and grey. The sky was so big a cloud would have to pack a suitcase to travel from one horizon to the other.

Gradually the continent below us began to grow dark again; above us the distant galaxies shone like dust. Our moon looked close enough to touch, flirting behind the milky sails of clouds and stars dangling in the wind.

Mugre had fallen asleep in the co-pilot's seat, and was *honk-shooooing* over the engine drone in the back. Consuelo shook him awake and said, "I'm bringing her down. Now."

She reached under her seat and brought out a sawed-off shotgun. "They were expecting us an hour ago," she said. "Cover me when we land." Consuelo banked to the left as we lost more altitude. We levelled out again, the plane's nose dropped, the engine went quiet and Consuelo glided towards a narrow runway.

Mugre slid his side window open and aimed the gun into the blackness. Both barrels were loaded. He pulled back the hammers.

There was silence after Consuelo cut the engines, then a couple of shots rang out. Mugre swore into the darkness. I heard more shots; I rolled over next to Carmen and tried to flatten myself to the floor as the plane tipped to one side. We'd been hit.

Consuelo grabbed the shotgun, pushed Mugre out of the way, kicked open the airplane's door and fired into the night.

Through the doorway I saw a flashlight beam slice the dark and two men creeping towards the plane. One carried a pistol, the other a light submachine gun. Consuelo threw the shotgun out the door and stood, largely, in the spotlight.

"*Estas tarde, amiga*," said the smaller of the two, holding the machine gun. "*Es la tarde, ahora.*" He said Consuelo had told him she would be arriving in the afternoon, and now it was already evening.

Consuelo climbed down from the plane, wrenched the machine gun out of the man's hands, pushed past him and began haranguing the other. She said she had more important things to do with her life than get killed by some *hijueputa* (son of a whore) who couldn't tell the difference between a plane and a bird. And now, because of their incompetence, she had an even worse problem. She pointed over her shoulder at our wounded aircraft. A hole in her fuel tank: how did they expect her to get the plane back up in the air and keep it there?

Walking Death I, as if trying to buy time, produced a bottle from inside his coat. He unscrewed the cap, threw his head back and drank. I could see his throat muscles working. When he offered the bottle to Consuelo, she shook her head, stared straight ahead into the darkness. "Not when I have work to do," she said.

I spent another night trying to get comfortable on a cold metal floor, listening to the sounds issuing from Carmen's body and Mugre muttering in his sleep. I heard him get up twice during the night and leave the plane, to be sick.

When sunlight cut through the canopy of buds and branches and tapped on the window beside my head, I looked around and saw that I was alone—except for Carmen, who hadn't moved since we'd landed. I sat up and sneaked a glance out the window. Our plane lay in a clearing surrounded by a black-water swamp. The snaky roots of tupelo and bald cypress, their branches depressed by Spanish moss, held up soft, spongy banks on either side of a sunken road leading away through the swamp.

When Consuelo came to check on us, she took Carmen's pulse and looked worried. She told her they were going to move her to a bed inside as soon as they had taken care of business. I thought I heard Carmen groan. In some ways, it was a blessing she was too sick to know what was happening. I figured she was better off dead than knowing she'd been kidnapped by Las Blancas again, and that her sister-in-law was a major player in this guerilla organization.

Consuelo got off the plane again, signalling me to come with her. There was a smell in the air of spring, of life born again out of decay and rot. In the woods all around, the red buds and white blossoms of dogwood fought for light under the evergreen canopy. The slow swamp water moved darkly, full of rank and eggy life. And as we walked towards the shack I hadn't seen from the plane's window, I could smell meat frying, bacon smoked with sweet maple or hickory perhaps. A shiny red pickup was parked outside, and a yellow dog with runny eyes, locked inside the cab, snarled at us, his spit icing the rear window.

I could hear Mugre inside the shack, coughing. Consuelo pushed open the door and told me to watch my step. She pointed to Walking Death I lying on the floor, but paid no attention to him after that, other than to complain about the dirty flies that lifted from his staring eyes as she stepped over him.

Even though sunlight filtered through the cracks between the rough planks, the room appeared cold and threatening, like a dark jail cell with luminescent bars for walls. I stumbled over WD1's leg, which jutted at an unnatural angle from his body, then drew back when I saw Walking Death II slumped over a plywood table, one arm bound by a frayed nylon rope to the chair behind him, the other stretched out straight and ending in a garbage bag. I took in the cleaver, the table's surface a pond of blood so clear you could see your face in it.

Mugre stood over a propane burner, an egg-lifter in one hand, a fat reefer in the other. He took a long toke, exhaled, then passed the joint to the hand turning black and crisp in the frying pan.

"You snitched us off," Mugre said to the hand, snatching the joint back out of the fingers as if he had decided not to share after all. "Wheelchair dope," he said to himself, offering Consuelo a toke. Consuelo said she'd never seen the point in smoking anything that made you paralyzed. Mugre said he kept hoping it would paralyze his intestines so he wouldn't throw up anymore.

"Did you get the key to the truck?" Consuelo asked.

Mugre grunted. "I had to chop off his whole fucking hand."

He turned the shrivelled hand in the frying pan, then handed Consuelo the key to the pickup truck. I watched the fingers curl in the greasy heat. Mugre flipped the hand back into the centre of the pan, where the heat was the most intense. After a few minutes, he turned the burner off, slipped the hand onto an aluminium pie dish and set it on the table in front of WD2's swollen lips. He scooped the hand up with the egg-lifter and held it under the man's nose.

WD2's eyes rolled up into his head. Consuelo tried prying his mouth open, putting one hand under his chin and then pushing down on the top of his head, but he passed out again and she let him fall forward, the hand wedged obscenely between the table and his chin.

"It's too late," Consuelo said. "He's not going to talk." She picked a plum from a white bowl on the counter, squeezed it, put it back and chose a riper one. She told Mugre we'd wait outside until he'd cleaned up, then led me back over WD1's body in the doorway to the far side of the truck, where we stood listening to the spitting dog. I wanted to throw up, but there was nothing in my stomach and I ended up retching in some bushes. Consuelo said I was getting as bad as her brother-in-law; she would have to give us something that would settle both our stomachs for good; she sucked the meat out of the plum and spit the pit at the spitting dog. It stuck to the truck's rear window and further enraged the animal. "I hope you will write about this in your book. It might make the next *hijueputas* think twice before crossing us."

Later that afternoon, after the bodies had been disposed of, Mugre and Consuelo carried Carmen into the shack. They laid her down on a mattress in a corner of the room. She seemed barely alive.

Mugre, who hadn't been sick for a while, insisted on cooking a meal. Consuelo hovered over him, telling him how to do everything, even how to boil water to make coffee. I watched as she took a bullet from her pocket, removed the lead and emptied the gunpowder into the coffee pot.

"*Hermanito*, for you," she said, "This will calm your stomach *and* steady your nerves." She poured a cup of her brew for me also.

Mugre made a face. "You're going to kill someone one day with your quackery," he said as he spooned a gruel made of oatmeal and pasta, with a tin of sardines mixed in, onto each of our plates.

I picked through my food, trying to avoid eye contact with the greasy sardine floating in the greyish milk, then set it aside with the coffee smelling of death and metal. Consuelo asked for my opinion of Mugre's concoction; I wanted to say that short of lowering my naked foot into the weeds at the bottom of that black-water swamp, I could think of nothing more revolting. Instead I said I had never thought of making soup from porridge and sardines before, and Mugre seemed to take that as a compliment. Consuelo said she had never understood why people thought it was all right to eat every part of the sardine—bones, guts and excrement—just because it was so small.

Mugre looked hurt. "*Algo es algo; peor es nada,*" he muttered. Something is something; nothing is worse. Then he went around the side of the house to be sick again. Consuelo looked discouraged. The gunpowder hadn't taken effect. "Remind me not to waste any more bullets on my brother-in-law," she said.

Later, Mugre ransacked the shack and found more drugs; he sat with a butane torch in the corner, on the mattress beside Carmen, smoking *basuco* (a derivative of coca, adulterated with lead and sulphuric acid, lethally addictive to all who smoke it, and leading to a very early grave), which, Consuelo said, fuelled the craziness of even the most normal people. Mugre tried to rouse Carmen, to give her a hit of *basuco*. He glared at us when Consuelo told him to mind his own business, then went outside to tease the dog, holding the dead man's charred hand up to the window, pretending to gnaw at it himself.

Consuelo pushed back from the table, saying she'd had enough of Mugre's depravity. She grabbed the key and went outside to unlock the truck. Instead of leaping for Mugre's throat, the way I think Consuelo had hoped the dog would do, he stood cowering, his tail between his legs, sniffing the air as if the air were a woman into whose warm crotch he could nuzzle and disappear. Then he lay down and started snapping at his testicles.

"There's something unnormal about that dog," Consuelo said, as Mugre, who'd pinned himself against the side of the truck, began edging his way back towards the shack. "He does not act like any other dog I've met."

Just as she spoke, the dog saw Mugre out of the corner of his eye and charged, knocking him over—almost all in one motion. He lunged for his master's charred hand and bounded up the road, the hand dangling from his mouth. He ran flat out, his skinny flanks rising and falling in the furrows.

Consuelo swore at Mugre. It was sloppy work, she said, to leave bits of evidence behind. Mugre picked himself up and ran after the dog before Consuelo had a chance to go inside the shack and get her gun. I believe she would have wasted no time shooting Mugre right then.

Under the canopy of the tupelo and bald cypress trees, I sat and waited for the day to stumble to a close. After an hour had gone by and Mugre still hadn't returned, Consuelo went looking for him. She didn't tie me up this time but took away my shoes so I couldn't go far. The moment she was out of sight, I did precisely what the prosecutor said I'd never tried to do: I tried to get away.

I crept through the bush behind the shack and came out on a dirt track running parallel to the road. I started running, clutching my heavy body; hot and sticky, the oven air seemed to hum. My imagination, too, grew legs and began to run flat out in front of me, as if on a reconnaissance all of its own, so that when I rounded a bend where the remains of a high metal gate swung on its rusted hinges and a sign saying Keep Out Unprotected Territory Not Subject to State Law had been tossed at the side of the road, I envisioned my own body lying in the ditch, unprotected from the laws of nature, to be discovered by hikers ten years hence: the perfect skeleton of a woman with the skeleton of a baby imprisoned in the cage of her bones.

I had not gone far before I heard Consuelo shouting— and I dove into a tangle of blackjack. My mouth was dry and my scalp tingled. I smelled fear in the damp earth under me and in the clouds that moved over me.

I waited for my heart to slow down. It was getting dark, and the insects had come out to feed in the cooler air. I decided I should stay well away from the road, and began crawling on all fours through salt-poisoned grass, skirting a dead lake dotted with dead cypress, keeping the most colourful part of the sky, violet slashed with crimson streaks, to the east, over my right shoulder.

A sudden wind banged into my face, a hot wind carrying with it sand from the dunes and pine needles and flying insects. When I opened my mouth to catch a deeper breath, a small bug flew into my throat and caused a coughing spasm. I lay down, covering my head with my arms, trying to muffle the sound.

As I lay there, trying to suppress my cough, I felt my face being pushed into the sand, a hand on the back of my neck pinning me down. When the hand released me, I rolled over and looked into Consuelo's .38. Her eyes, the blade of swamp grass between her teeth, it was all I could do to keep a blank face and not let my fear of her be any more plain.

She spat out the blade of grass. She said she'd heard my coughing, and decided to rescue me before the alligators had me for their for dinner. She said I had much to thank my baby for, then led me back towards the clearing.

My feet were cut and bleeding. When we reached the shack Consuelo pushed open the door, and I could see Mugre lying naked next to Carmen's body, grinning awkwardly, as if Consuelo should have had the decency to stay away a little longer.

A pillow covered Carmen's face. My first thought was that Mugre had placed it there out of some twisted sense of decency—so Carmen would not have to look into his face —but that was naive of me: he must have smothered her.

The dark closed in around me, and silence drew me in like a sucking undertow. I felt dizzy, unsure of my footing. The world seemed to be sloping away.

I watched Consuelo remove the pillow from Carmen's face. Then she pulled out her gun and turned to where her brother-in-law lay, the sound of his laughter like water lapping at the holes in a shipwreck's hull.

The silencer made the shot sound no louder than a sigh.

chapter eleven

Carmen's body had a smell to it that lodged itself in my throat, crabbed and small, and threatened to choke me when I breathed. The smell reminded me of the hunting trip I'd taken with my father when I was small, butchering the doe in the bathtub at home, what it felt like to cut open a body with a knife and plunge your hands into the guts of something that had once been beautiful. The smell of rain falling on the summer dust, the warm stink of the dead foetus inside the deer's body as we emptied her out: how quickly beauty could be transformed into something else.

Before it got dark, Consuelo had made me go with her as she dragged Mugre's body up the road, away from the shack. I followed, struggling up a bank, hanging on by the roots of the high, ancient trees, until I stood on a ledge overlooking the swamp. Phallic shoots of plants gave off a musky, post-coital odour. Consuela pushed his body into the black water. I felt dirty just being there—the kind of dirty you can't wash away.

On the afternoon of the second day, it began raining, not the misty rain I had grown up with in the Northwest, but a dingy, obscuring rain that dropped straight from the sky. Consuelo stood naked in the rain, a few feet from the door of the shack. She was soaping her breasts, holding them up to the sky, then letting the water slide down off her nipples. I remembered as a child standing in the rain and lifting my face, opening my mouth wide to catch the water that trickled down my hair onto my waiting tongue. I remembered the taste of the rain after it had washed through my hair. I wondered why it had been so long since I'd stood in one place long enough to let the rain soak me through to the skin. All my adult life I'd tried to keep dry, taking shelter whenever it rained, staying inside. Back then, the driving rain had hammered into me a kind of joy; both madness and divinity had been introduced to me by the rain.

By mid-afternoon, the rain had stopped and the sun was a chip of fire in an otherwise colourless sky. Consuelo went inside the shack and poured diesel fuel on Carmen's body. Then she came out and sat with me.

She had prepared many bodies for death, she said, "ever since the day me and my youngest sister, Magdalena, were selling lottery tickets on the street and the guerrilla heroes came.

"They drove past in a shining red truck like that one parked over there," she said. "They invited all the kids in the neighbourhood to join their camps. A lot of us went along, because it was something to do. They promised us a better life—so it didn't take much to convince me to go with them. I learned how to handle guns, to make explosives, to organize military operations. But then the police raided our camps and there were shoot-outs with the army, and the guerrillas took off to the hills."

Her brothers started their own self-defence group in the neighbourhood, she told me as she rolled a cigarette, where other gangs had already grown up and were spreading terror. One Saturday, Magdalena, who was pregnant with her first child, was coming home from work, and four *pelados* (kids who at twelve or thirteen are already learning how to assassinate people) wearing black hoods, followed her, dragged her into the middle of the street, raped her and shot her in the face. "They did it because she was my mother's daughter, because any child of hers would grow up to be more trouble for their gang, and they wanted control of our neighbourhood," Consuelo said, striking a match, lighting her cigarette. "Where I come from, it is considered more hygienic and effective to kill *guerrilleras* while they are in the womb than in the mountains or the streets."

Magdalena's body was taken to the morgue. Consuelo said she spent the next day making her dead sister's hair look beautiful. Then she organized a wake.

"The whole family and everyone in the *barrio* came to pray for her and offer their condolences. Then around midnight, the *pelados* burst in with their revolvers and made us all kneel in a straight line against a wall. They ripped the flowers and palm branches off the coffin and smashed the candelabra, started breaking up the furniture in the room. Everyone was screaming. The intruders were still aiming their guns at us; they tipped over the coffin, and my sister fell out on the floor. When my brother tried to straighten the hem of her dress—it had ridden up to her knees—they tied him up, too, and beat him, and then they put two more shots in our sister's head. All that time fixing her hair—for nothing."

Consuelo got up, closed the door tight and circled the shack, leaving a trail of diesel behind her as she walked. She lit another match and tossed it into the grass. We climbed into the red pickup as tongues of black smoke licked the air.

She didn't speak again until we reached the paved road.

"Things like that happened every day in our neighbourhood. You learn not to care about it. You look after your back, because no one else is going to.

"Over the years I've watched dozens of people die—friends, relatives. It's not the same thing when you are the one doing the killing. If I have to kill someone, I don't think about it. All I think is: too bad for him; he crossed my path. If his back is to me, I tell him to turn around first, to make sure I have the right person. I only pray I don't kill the wrong person by mistake. If I'm going to kill, there should be a good reason."

Consuelo had said to me only the dead cannot be judged. I wonder if she believed, too, the dead would not judge her.

There were no other vehicles, not even a road sign to indicate how far we were from the nearest town or highway. We passed a trickle of a creek where a turkey buzzard fed upon the carcass of a dead cow. On a solitary oak tree, someone had carved a heart and the words "Stella Loves Bill Bob Forever," with an arrow piercing the heart, and I looked ahead up the empty road, hating my loneliness, the sadness I had come to at the edges of my life.

Years ago, in high school, my boyfriend had climbed to the top of a cliff to paint our names inside a giant heart. When we broke up, six months later, I demanded he climb back up and paint them over, but he wouldn't. He said whenever I drove by that cliff with a new love, I would look up and see my name—and his; in this small way, I would belong to him forever.

A black man with little clouds of white at his temples stood in the dust at the side of the road and tried to flag us down as we rounded a corner. Consuelo slowed, came to a stop and waved out the window to the man. I watched him approach in the rear-view mirror, sticking his tongue in and out through the gap where his front teeth were missing. He carried a metal washtub with a mop handle protruding from it, which he tossed in the back of the pickup. Then he climbed in beside me.

His name was Junius, and he smelled of the road. His clothes were shabby; he'd lost all the buttons on his shirt but wore it pinned together down the front. He said he was one lucky man to have a couple of beautiful ladies stop for him; he had been overheating at the side of the road all morning; he always appreciated the company of ladies. He told us he had been married once, and that everything about his lady had been beautiful too, even her name—Antoinette. He told us his stomach had always bothered him. He told us he had thirteen brothers and sisters, and that one of his brothers ran a concession stand at Max Allen's Reptile Gardens, which we would have seen if we'd ever driven south on Highway 54. I was reminded, again, of the willingness of strangers to divulge their life story to other strangers when thrust together by a common journey, for as long as it lasted.

Consuelo looked bored and restless; she didn't understand what he was saying. Junius told us he'd planned on having a big family, but that Antoinette had barricaded herself in a room when their first son was born, then smashed the baby's head against the bedpost and thrown him up to the ceiling, where he hit the fan before starting down. He told me he'd had to wash the blood off everything, including the doorknob. He said he'd never forget how it felt to hold a doorknob wet with his first son's blood. He said when he turned the doorknob, it had opened up the place inside him where he locked his grief.

I listened to him talk, peering through a window smudged with sunlight and dirt, the live oak trees at the side of the road full of mockingbirds and screeching blue jays. After that incident, Junius continued, his crazy wife took blankets and stuffed them under her skirts, pretending there was another child, as if she could fool him. Every Saturday, she took the blankets out and waded into the flooded cypress trees and stood on one leg like a great blue heron. Then she would beat on the blankets with a stick, until one day she got sick and dried up inside. He took the blankets away and washed them, then rolled her up in them and buried her next to the body of his son.

Junius mopped his brow with a oily handkerchief and asked Consuelo if she might happen to be driving all the way to Lafayette, which he pronounced "Laughyet," where he was going to hunt for a job on the gut bucket. I translated for him. Consuelo told me to ask him how much further it was to Lafayette, and he said that all depended on how long they took to get there. Consuelo wanted to know if we would arrive before dark, and Junius said maybe yes, maybe no, depended on if she kept driving the way old people made love. I told her what he'd said, and immediately regretted it; Consuelo drew her .38 out of her waistband and asked him if he thought he'd get there faster if he got out and walked. She pointed her gun at Junius's feet; no translation was necessary. Junius started lifting his feet one at a time, as if dancing. His tongue lodged itself permanently between the gap in his teeth.

I told him Consuelo wasn't going to hurt him as long as he co-operated. Consuelo cursed. Junius, who seemed to have become more shadow than flesh, began to moan and rock back and forth in his seat. His face had ballooned with fear, and his jaw was working overtime; he seemed to be chewing air and swallowing it. He had spit coming out at the corners of his mouth. I half shut my eyes against the glare from the road, wishing the world could be another kind of place.

Then—I couldn't help it—I told Consuelo to leave the man alone. It was the wrong thing to say; I had once again showed contempt for her ways. I could see it in her eyes, the triumph of one who has gained dangerous power over another.

The air inside the cab felt dense and wet. Consuelo drove, avoiding potholes, avoiding conversation, still holding her .38, which rested on the steering wheel. I kept my eyes on her hands as she drove, trying to read my future. I already knew what was going to happen to Junius.

She took everything he had, except his undershorts, and left him, the sun teetering over the tips of the pines, at the edge of a wood bordering a sandy red track that cut through an endless pecan field.

"Don't think he wouldn't have robbed *us* if we'd given him half a chance," she said.

The sky to the south trembled with dry lightning. Consuelo pulled into the oyster-shell parking lot of the first motel with a Vacancy sign and parked between two rain barrels full of empty Jax bottles. When she opened my door, the truck filled with the smell of creosote and burnt diesel fuel from the railway tracks across the road, where a Southern Pacific freight car was on fire. The fire seemed to draw the night sky down around it, enveloping two men with flashlights who stood a short distance from the wreck, trying to contain the flames.

When I translated for Consuelo what the motel manager had said, that the nearest accommodation was a mile up the road, that he wasn't looking for more business tonight, Consuelo told me to ask him to reconsider. She left a hundred-dollar bill on the counter, then went to get a Coke from the machine. The manager, who smelled of nicotine and a franchise chicken dinner, said the Coke machine was on the blink and the ice machine was broken too. As far as he was concerned, he said, ice was for Eskimos.

"You girls travelling alone?" he asked me, toying with his moustache.

"Help me," I tried to whisper. "Help me get away from her. Call the police."

He looked at me sideways, lit a cigarette and sucked the smoke in through teeth that were stained as yellow as his moustache.

I pushed the smoke away with my hand, and tried to communicate, by using sign language, that I was desperate. He nodded his head, trying to appease me, as if to say he would agree with anything just to keep me happy until the men in white jackets arrived. He stubbed out his cigarette in an ashtray filled with nail clippings, then covered the ashtray with a wad of invoices stamped Overdue.

"She got some kind of problem?" he asked Consuelo when she came back to the counter. He nodded towards me, then looked at Consuelo and raised his eyebrows. "I don't need any trouble here," he said. "I have to call the police, it will only bring more."

Consuelo narrowed her eyes at him, and then at me. If she didn't understand the words he spoke, she must have understood my intentions. Behind him, on the wall, I could see rows of room keys hanging on hooks. I thought of what had happened to the last man who hadn't surrendered his key. The manager stared at us, not moving, but Consuelo had a way without words. He shook his head, then tossed her the key to Room 0.

"Leave it in the room when you check out," he said. "I don't do mornings."

The night air felt cooler when we went back outside, and a light rain washed over me as I lifted my face, exhaling the unpleasant fumes of the day—the stale air, cigarette smoke and chicken grease. As we crossed the parking lot, through glazed pools of yellow light from the street lamps, the blue neon Vacancy under the Pair-A-Dice Motel sign, I sensed a new loneliness taking shape around me, and I wanted to run out onto the highway leading down into darkness in both directions and wait for the ride that would take me away from myself.

Then the lights went off inside, and the word Sorry replaced the neon Vacancy. Consuelo pushed me across the shell parking lot into the blackness.

Consuelo tied me to the bed, saying that if I was going to behave like a *loca*, she would start treating me like one. I said I was her hostage, that I would be crazy if I *didn't* try to get away. She reminded me again that the only reason she wasn't going to hurt me was because of the baby. I said she had hurt me enough, keeping me tied up, giving me food I wouldn't have fed a dog. She replied that I had much to learn, and left me lying there on my back while she sat flicking through the channels on the television. I caught snippets from a world I felt further away from than ever before: ". . . more people are alive today than have died in all of . . ."; ". . . over and touch your toes, now count . . ."; "Before me, she was vegetarian . . ."; "In seahorses, it is the male who gives . . ." and "1,250 prisoners on death row have gone on a hunger strike . . ." She didn't switch right away from the Spanish-speaking news channel, and I heard that a woman from Tranquilandia had been arrested for smuggling, that customs officers, "aroused by the unusual shape of her buttocks," had conducted a search revealing two eight-inch-long incisions in her buttocks stuffed with bags of cocaine. The newscaster called the incident, in English, a "bust bummer." Consuelo asked me what this meant, and when I didn't reply she turned off the television.

In the middle of the night, I was awakened by the sound of gunfire and glass breaking. The room was bright, lit by a full moon that had bullied its way through the clouds. The sound of guns going off had become so familiar to me that I almost rolled over and went back to my dream. I had followed a glass bird into a forest, where it fed on small white seeds of moonlight as I watched: inside the bird a transparent egg, and inside the egg an unborn bird whose cut-crystal wings were splinters of glass. Consuelo, as she stood before the window, blending with the moonlight, looked like the bird I had followed deeper and deeper into the night, and now I couldn't remember my way back. I lay on the bed, lost, trying to remember where I belonged, as she peered out at the sultry darkness, the dirty lace curtains enveloping her.

There was a breeze smelling faintly of ozone, dust from the shell parking lot, and gun-metal. I could hear a motor running. Consuelo backed away from the window and stood beside my bed, motioning for me to keep quiet. I heard a man shouting, "Sireena, SI-REEEN-A! If you won't fuck me, FUCK YOU!" and a car door slamming shut. I heard the squeal of tires across crushed beer cans and oyster shells, and then peace again, except for the sound of my own heart beating. I lay back, waiting for the black heavens to close around the moon and leave me in darkness. I lay that way for the rest of the night, brooding, like a small idea in a disturbed mind.

Consuelo untied my hands as soon as we had daylight, but kept a grip on my arm as she steered me towards the truck. Neither of us spoke as she headed south down the highway.

I thought of the woman called Sireena, waking in a room with a broken window and no way out. Sireena with her hotbox heart, splashing cold water on her face, bringing the swelling down. The crackling radio playing inside her head, *Sireena, Sireena, why can't you be true?* Sireena wearing dark glasses in the sanctuary of the shower, singing off-key and aching.

By now the sun was threatening to rise, bleeding rusty streaks across the sky, and I could make out the silhouettes of clapboard beer joints, brick warehouses and tumbledown paintless houses built along railway spurs, as if they might suddenly decide to pack it in and hop a freight train out of there.

We drove through the morning, heading towards the coast, past distant islands of sawgrass, dead bald cypress trees twisted like peppermint sticks, fishing shacks built up on stilts above flooded woods, pirogues tied to cabin pilings, herons lifting on extended wings to the strains of "La Jolie Blonde" on the truck radio.

At noon, Consuelo pulled in to a ramshackle restaurant called Ida's Home Cooking and Live Bait Shop. She took the keys and tied my hands to the wheel, but halfway to the door of the restaurant she changed her mind. I could come in with her, she said, as long as I didn't open my mouth except to eat.

A harried Ida, wearing a white T-shirt with "Live Bait" across her chest and flamingo-pink stretch pants, pointed us to take any one of the unoccupied driftwood tables, held together by rusty spikes and littered with crab shells. I couldn't tell if the shells were part of the decor or if Ida hadn't got round to cleaning them up. We ate boiled shrimp and blue-point crab with *sauce piquante*, and piled our shells on top of the others. Consuelo ordered iced tea, which came in tall blue glasses with cracked ice and mint leaves. I watched her pop a sprig of mint into her mouth, chew it, then swallow.

Consuelo wanted to know what *live bait* meant. I said it meant Ida was in the hostage-taking business too.

Early that evening, we drew up outside the gates to an above-ground cemetery on the outskirts of a small town called Jean Batista. Consuelo let me out of the truck but told me to stay by the gates while she went across the road to make a phone call. I had a chance to read the glassed-in directory map of the cemetery, which showed where the town's VIPs were buried, including the smuggler and priva-teer after whom the town had been named.

When Consuelo had made her call, we walked up Jesus Steet to Business. The graveyard, which turned out to be a perfect replica of the town its residents had relocated from, had streets and avenues, some of them tree-lined, others littered with garbage. Most of the more well-to-do dead were housed in miniature replicas of the plantations or white-pillared mansions they'd left behind. The less well off had been crowded into six-storey blocks of coffin-sized apartments.

Planters full of Holy Ghost orchids surrounded the Cattle family's real estate. "Here Lies Major Desiard Cattle, Erected by His Wife," I read when we stopped in front of the major's resting place. I was trying to explain to Consuelo why this was amusing, when she pointed to a plot I hadn't noticed, a simple stone with the name Tiny Cattle inscribed on it, his birth date, then a dash and the year he had died. "He should be here soon," she said, and sure enough, shortly afterwards, Tiny Cattle arrived, wearing a wide-brimmed straw hat without a crown; his long white hair, tied in a top knot, spilled out over the hat's rim. His face was a translucent white; he wore dark glasses and an AA medallion around his neck. His once-white shirt was half tucked into his wrinkled khaki trousers. One of the largest men I'd ever seen, he was also barefooted.

He wiped his sweaty palms on the sides of his trousers before shaking hands with Consuelo. He didn't look at me; I suspected she had told him that where I was concerned, he was to mind his own business. He kept looking at the sky instead, as if he expected someone else to join us.

When Consuelo asked him about the headstone, Tiny looked embarrassed and said there'd been a sale on tombstones and a bunch of his buddies got together and bought one for him, thinking he was going to drink himself to death that year. "I fooled everyone," he said. Though he admitted he was looking forward to joining the rest of the family, "the most executed family in Luzianne," starting with his great-grandad, Desiard Cattle, who grew loonified in his twilight years, robbed the Merchants and Farmers Bank in Nakitish with a pair of pearl-handled duelling pistols and got hanged for crimes against property.

"I'm the last—and the worst—of my line," Tiny said; he spoke Spanish with a distinct southern accent. "My old man's over there; cops shot him. I buried him with his pager and a roll of quarters. So's he can keep in touch."

Consuelo, I could tell, was not interested in Tiny's geneology. "When can you get us out of here?" she asked.

Tiny wiped his brow and adjusted his hat. "You're free, white and twenty-one. You can walk right out of here any old time."

Consuelo shot him the look. Tiny checked himself. "No problemo. I can get you out tomorrow night. Where you all headed?"

"Tranquilandia," said Consuelo.

Tiny scratched at his face, pulled his ear, then began twisting his medallion as he pulled a flask from his hip pocket and took a drink. He said he could think of only one good thing to say about Tranquilandia, and that was that no one on the island owed him any money. "Last time I flew down, I got shot at," he said. "The only law they got in that place is the law of gravity, and even that don't work most of the time . . ."

Consuelo waited until his words trailed off. "Tonight. Can you get us out of here this evening?"

She walked Tiny back to the road where our trucks were parked. "*Mañana, por la tarde*," he said. "Tomorrow evening, soon's it's dark."

A bumper sticker on Tiny Cattle's truck said "Easy Does It, Jesus." He raised the flask to his lips and had another swig. Consuelo took the flask, sniffed it and made a face.

"Come and pick us up in the morning. Nine o'clock. We will wait for you. Don't be late."

Tiny's relaxed demeanour, his style of walking and talking, had changed since Consuelo mentioned Tranquilandia.

"Where can we get a room and something to eat?" she said.

Tiny adjusted his straw hat again, so it shielded his face from hers. "Hotel Eden down on Canal Street. Got a good diner. Reasonable rates, too."

Her face didn't soften.

"It would be on me," he said. "No problemo."

Problema came out "problem-o." Consuelo said she had the payment for the plane; they discussed a price. Tiny would take *plata de polvo*, powder money.

"*Hasta mañana*," Consuelo said. "And if it's later than *la mañana de mañana*, you can start digging your own grave under that bargain-basement stone."

We left Tiny standing at the entrance to the graveyard. I watched him disappear in the rear-view mirror as we pulled onto a yellow dirt road, the windows rolled down, the smell of the bayou and burned chitterlings filling the evening air. The road twisted beneath a canopy of vine-choked oaks. Further on, where the river became hidden by the levee, we passed a row of shotgun houses—each identical, imitation brick tarpaper on the outside. Compared to the cemetery, everything here had an air of melancholy and decay. In one garden, where someone had beaten a path through the weeds to the door, a bulky oak had lifted the rusty iron fence with its bulbous roots. Empty Milk of Magnesia bottles had been strung up in the tree's branches. I heard a tinkling sound as we passed, the dark blue bottles colliding with the roofing nails that had been lashed together to form sharp silver crosses.

Further along, the posts of a falling-down fence were crowned with the sightless heads of dolls. A woman armed with a toilet plunger sat in a rocking chair at the side of the road, guarding her mailbox. Behind her, a copper-coloured pool of stagnant water stretched across her lawn, where a half-submerged Armed Response sign greeted anyone foolish enough to try to deliver a parcel to her door. Consuelo said the plunger was probably loaded.

She reached under her arm, then slipped her .38 back in her belt. "There's something unnatural about that Tiny," she said. Then, after a pause, "My mother taught us a prickly palm belongs to a man who does not always tell the truth. He means to, perhaps, but he can't. That's Tiny. He wants to tell the truth, but he doesn't know how."

By the time we reached town, the sun had torched the western sky and was hovering above the horizon. Consuelo turned up Gun Hill Road, past a row of attached houses where women leaned over their balconies—small jungles of potted geraniums and banana leaves—blowing kisses to the men below.

Consuelo drove on, slowly, in the heat. The sky had darkened and a warm jasmine-scented rain pocked the sidewalk. I expected to see lightning soon, as I'd seen every night, in the foreboding sky to the south.

chapter twelve

An illuminated plastic palm tree at the entrance to the Hotel Eden advertised all you can eat for $5.95 in the adjoining Rib Room. Consuelo had dinner sent up to our suite.

That night I dreamed I had filed for divorce. I sat at the back of a courtroom, waiting, the last on the list for the day. A woman in a T-shirt saying "I'm Not Fat, I'm Pregnant" pushed away from the man who sat bowed on the seat next to her and limped to the witness box.

Angel held my hand as I waited in the courtroom; Vernal refused to be present.

When our names were called, two newspaper reporters lifted their heads. The walk to the witness box seemed longer than the walk up the aisle the day I got married.

"Do you swear to tell the truth, the whole truth and nothing but the truth?" the judge asked.

"I do," I said, though the last time I'd said "I do," things hadn't worked out.

"Any chance of a reconciliation?" she said, frowning over the top of her wire-rimmed glasses.

There was, I believed, always a chance. "No chance of a reconciliation, Your Honour." My lawyer had instructed me to answer no to all the judge's questions. It would be quicker that way.

The judge looked at me suspiciously. "One of these days, someone is going to surprise me by saying yes," she said.

It wasn't too late, I thought. I could still change my mind.

"She's asking for nothing, Your Honour," my lawyer was concluding.

The judge shuffled her papers. "Then that's all she's going to get."

My lawyer had to help me out of the witness box. Matrimony is one thing, but no one leaves a divorce court feeling holy.

Angel led me to the elevator. The woman who was not fat but pregnant got in with us and said, "My old man had to come to court, the jerk!" and Angel and I got off on the third floor because I had to go to the bathroom. There was only one toilet, and it looked as though someone had miscarried in it. I sat there, over a great purple jellyfish of blood, reading the graffiti on the cubicle door ("Live Life Like a Dick: When It Gets Hard, Fuck It") and weeping for the way things might have been, for myself, for Vernal. I wept for the dead shapeless child in the toilet, whose brief appearance on earth had to end this way.

Afterwards, Angel disappeared and I had lunch with Vernal and we tried to celebrate. I asked Vernal, finally, if he was happy, and he said, "Yes, but I like *you.*"

We took Brutus for a last walk along the waterfront. Her canine acne was getting worse. When Vernal dropped me off at my apartment, he said he wondered how things would have turned out if I'd got pregnant with him instead of Angel, and I said I just didn't know, but if he and I ever got together again, would he mind looking after someone else's baby?

"Oh, I suppose not," said Vernal.

We had breakfast in our room while we waited for Tiny Cattle. Consuelo paced while I stood at the open window, looking out over the town square. Facing our hotel was a bail-bond office, a tattoo parlour with a Confederate flag painted on the broken glass of the window and the Negro Grocery Store.

The square was full of people. Consuelo came to the window to see what I was looking at. "Drug addicts," she said disgustedly, pointing to a black man with a wooden leg begging for change. "To them, everything is simple. You snort a few lines, you forget to eat. You smoke a few lines, you forget to live."

I asked her what made her say the crippled man was a drug addict.

"What else could he be?" she said.

She didn't think his injury was "legitimate" either. "Some parents, they mutilate their children so they can get them into the begging business before they are old enough to eat from a spoon," she went on matter-of-factly. "He is lucky he misses only one leg. We have a man in La Ciudad, he has nothing. A torso only. He is propped up outside the bar one day, the bank the next. For fifty centavos, you can butt out your cigarette on one of his stumps. For a peso, he'll eat the stub afterwards. I refuse to give him money because I know his father—the one who did this to him—will get every cent of it."

Strike a match on Consuelo's soul . . .

The man with the wooden leg had joined two women in chenille dressing gowns. "I change my mind," Consuelo said. "That *cojo* (cripple) is a pimp."

. . . she wouldn't flinch.

The one-legged man and the two women bought green ice cream cones and sat on an iron-scrolled bench in the square, letting the ice cream drip onto their hands. I said I didn't care who they were, I envied them the freedom to do something as simple as buying an ice cream cone and letting it melt all over themselves.

"To free yourself is nothing," Consuelo said, lowering the blind so I couldn't see out any more. "The real problem is to know what to do with your freedom."

Tiny Cattle arrived in the late afternoon, looking morose and jittery. He was late, he said, because he had an appointment he'd forgotten about, and by the time he remembered it the doctor was in surgery.

"*Es tarde, amigo. Es la tarde, ahora,*" Consuelo said.

Tiny pulled a prescription from his back pocket. "I'm not so *tarde*," he said, speaking English now and aiming his words at no one in particular. "It's your fucking Spanish day that takes place so *tarde*. I told you I'd be here *en la tarde*, the evening, comprehendo? Now you tell me your *"tarde"* means afternoon *or* it means evening *or* it means we're late. It's not my fucking problemo. You say *"mañana,"* you mean this morning or tomorrow or the day after that. But I got a worse problemo now." He broke into Spanish again. "I can't wear shoes. I get foot itch."

Consuelo looked disgusted. "You kept me waiting because of a foot?"

"Feet. It's disaffected both of them." He took a wad of bills from the same back pocket. "I imagine you'll be checking out right about now?"

"You *imagine?*" said Consuelo. Her eyes grew blacker than the storm clouds I'd seen gathering over the gulf.

Tiny pushed his hair out of his eyes and tried to tuck it up under the brim of his hat. "You sure you all want to take the trip in weather?" he asked. "There's a system over the Gulf, means a storm, big one. I still got to fill this prescript . . ."

His voice trailed off as Consuelo stabbed him with her look. *"No me mames gallo,"* she said (literally, "Don't make me suck clit," but used to mean "Don't waste my time," "Don't be running a game on me"). "If the storm comes, that will be your problem."

I had given up trying to find logic in Consuelo's reasoning. Perhaps she believed that if Tiny's plane didn't make it through the storm, it would be none of *our* business, and only he would die in the wreck. She told him to wait for her outside while she took care of our bill.

"No problemo," said Tiny.

He was sweating, even though the air outside felt cool, tossing his hat high in the air and catching it behind his back when we met him later in the parking lot. He glanced at our bug-encrusted vehicle and swiped the sweat from his forehead with the palm of his hand. I felt a strong gust of wind from the south, before the rain began spitting down on our heads.

"Storm's coming in all right," Tiny said. And then, looking at Consuelo's face, "Heard it on the news."

The sky overhead had turned solid and cold, like a stopped heart. Consuelo ordered Tiny to drive, and abandoned our red truck in the parking lot. On the outskirts of town we passed another graveyard, where a young couple arranged flowers on a freshly dug grave. Further down the road, a pair of lollipop-white panties drooped from a mailbox; a man with skin the colour of burnt cork urinated beside a crêpe myrtle.

We passed another row of shotguns, white-shingled houses with deep front porches, and yards full of pecan trees, vegetable patches, chicken coops and rabbit hutches. Tiny braked as a cow ambled across the road, leaving a train of manure behind her.

When we reached the small airstrip, he parked his truck and pointed across the tarmac. "That's her, the *Fat Lady*. She ain't much on the outside, but she's full of guts. I interior-decorated her myself." The small plane had fire-engine red flames along its cowling. The paint had run, making it look like a nosebleed.

We crossed the tarmac, fighting the wind, and climbed

aboard the *Fat Lady*. The interior had been gutted, and most of the cabin space was taken up with wooden crates marked Danger Explosives, and This Way Up (they weren't). Tiny said the *Fat Lady* had always carried more weight than she was built for.

His "interior decorating" consisted of a human head. It was that of a woman, her eyes closed peacefully as though in thoughtful sleep. Her lips had been sewn together with a white fibre of some sort, but had come undone, as if the force of her words, of trying to tell her story, had torn the stitches from their fleshy hold. I couldn't tell how old she had been, or how scared; I hadn't known it was possible to shrink a human head until it was the size of a Christmas orange, an ear to the size of a burnt almond. The sight of it, and the fumes from Tiny Cattle's auxiliary fuel tank (a mixture of smells—oil and beer and fuel) was making my stomach turn.

Until this stage of my life, I had flown only on aircraft where you were assigned your own seat, one bolted to the floor, an aircraft where the lavatory had a door that told you whether it was Occupied or Vacant. I had felt a sense of security (probably a false one) knowing that these regulated airlines spent a million dollars a day on maintenance.

Tiny's idea of maintenance was to twist himself into the pilot's seat and blow the dust off the instrument panel, which consisted of a series of circular holes with most of the instruments missing. He told Consuelo he'd learned the hard way, that no one left instruments "lying around" in a plane like this one, which often sat for days on remote jungle airstrips. People were not trustworthy any more, and would steal anything, "even your shadow, if you happen to turn your back," not like in the old days of *la movida*. "A marijuana deal used to be done with a handshake," he said, "but a coke deal is done with a gun."

He told us each to grab a seat, and he meant it literally. I carried mine, which looked as if it had been salvaged from a bus that had tumbled off a mountainside in Mexico, to the front of the plane and set it down by a window. The dirty maroon plastic had been ripped open, and I had to depress the broken springs before sitting on them. I kicked a space for my feet amongst oil cans and empty Jax bottles.

Tiny blew a kiss to the shrunken head, and then struck himself on the forehead. "My goggles," he said. "I forgot my goggles. I bring you anything? A twenty-sixer?"

"*No me mames gallo,*" Consuelo repeated.

I watched him scuttle back over the runway to the truck. Tiny's father had taught him to fly without lights at night, Consuelo explained as he disappeared from sight. He left him a pair of special night-vision goggles—ones that magnified the light from the stars and moon more than fifty thousand times.

"His father was an *hombre de negocios*, one of the best," she said. He had spent years studying the testimonies in all the big drug cases, learning from other people's mistakes, and by doing so had created a nearly fail-safe system. He taught Tiny how to fly his plane through "windows" in Panamanian airspace, when, at prearranged times, the military looked the other way, for a *mordida*, a bite, a pay-off.

He taught Tiny how to fly back into U.S. airspace, too, without being detected. You flew low, and slow, so that on radar screens your plane looked like a helicopter coming ashore from an oil rig in the Gulf. When you reached land, you flew over a radio checkpoint, and if the spotter on the ground figured your plane was being tracked, you aborted your mission. If you had no tail, your plane followed VFRs to drop sites, like the one we'd left behind, in remote parts of the Louisiana bayou. "At one time, he and Tiny parachuted hundreds of children (a code-name, I learned, for kilos of cocaine) into that swamp every week," she said, "until he lost his nerve." She nodded at the shrunken head but didn't elaborate.

By the time Tiny Cattle returned, it had begun to grow dark and the storm was gathering strength under cover of darkness. As the engines spluttered, then roared into life, Tiny tapped the fuel gauge, which read empty.

"Let's hope the gauge is inaccurate in our favour," he said. "I got back-up anyway. See that wire poking out of the gas tank . . . over there, up front to the right?"

Consuelo nodded.

"It's connected to a cork. We start running out, the cork sinks."

I knew, as we putted onto the runway, my life was in the hands of some far greater power than Tiny Cattle. I took a deep breath and kept my eye on the bobbing wire that was attached to the cork as the Piper thundered fatly down the runway and laboured into the air. A red light warning Engine Fire Push came on. Tiny kicked it and it went off. My lungs hurt.

"My truck back home, the brake light comes on too," he said. "I'll get it fixed one of these centuries."

We stumbled against the southern wind, ascending into

a sky filled with bouldery black clouds. The *Fat Lady* climbed up and up until we were clear of land and flying over open water. This plane seemed to have more of an affinity with heaven than with earth.

Tiny's wire, his back-up fuel gauge, had stopped bobbing the moment land had disappeared from sight. He kissed the shrunken head every so often for luck; the head seemed morbidly alive in the glow from the Engine Fire Push warning button, which had come on again.

"She's rising like a homesick angel," he said. "Nothing ain't over till the *Fat Lady* falls apart."

I waited for the worst—for the engines to die, and then for my own death, a falling out of the sky, that rush, the cracking open, the heart giving a final finger to the wind. And then the bite of water, the blue sting.

In my mind, I heard the *Fat Lady* singing, "This is the End."

part four / tranquilandia

It is a sin to be surprised.

—Tranquilandian saying

chapter thirteen

Death Clinic, Heaven Valley State Facility for Women

> *If you are in the wrong place at the wrong time you are*
> *considered out of bounds without authorization and subject to*
> *disciplinary action. Running away from the prison or*
> *attempting to escape is strictly forbidden.*
> —*Inmate Information Handbook*

> *There is more hope on Death Row than in any*
> *place of similar size in the world.*
> — Stephen Levine, *Death Row: An Affirmation of Life*

I'm not here so they can teach me how to walk across a
room with a book on top of my head. Prison is not charm
school, I would have told my mother, if I'd hadn't run out

of space. I'm here because I'm *doing* the book. Right to the very last page, the page that's been ripped out so I don't even get to know how the mystery is going to end.

I'm reasonably sure it's going to go one of three ways. I've ruled out lethal injection and the firing-squad. Which leaves the gas chamber, hanging and the electric chair.

Rainy says I should be thankful I'm not in a concentration camp. She watched a documentary called *Heaven Commando* (the name for people who worked in the crematoria at Auschwitz), which showed women being tortured "to see how much they could take." One woman took the beatings, the immersion in a tank full of raw sewage, but still wouldn't give up the whereabouts of her child. In the end, they got so mad at her they threw her in a cell on top of a mattress that had been stuffed with barbed wire. "That would be the last straw," says Rainy. Definitely not the Ritz.

I ask Rainy if they ever found the child. Rainy says it was a trick; they knew she was dead all along. They showed the kid leaving her teddy bear on top of a pile of clothes at the entrance to the showers. They showed another prisoner stealing it, then trading it for an onion.

Right as Rainy. I mean, she's right—I have much to be grateful for, like a permanently positioned TV, operative (unless they're mad at you) from your house, access to books, recreation time for an hour once a week in the long, windy corridor atop the north block, where we can play dominoes or Sorry. By the time I am executed, I could be a qualified hairdresser, scuba-diving instructor, real-estate agent or undertaker. I should be grateful, too, for a permanent mailing address.

Frenchy used to go shopping, which would always make her cry, but she wouldn't call shopping or crying a hobby. A hobby was something you were supposed to enjoy doing, like tearing wings off butterflies, not standing in the middle of an aisle weeping over whether to buy one-ply toilet paper or two. She'd often wondered how many other women felt like weeping, too, but kept shopping instead, holding themselves together until they got home, where they could take it out on the kids. She thought maybe that's what set her apart from other people, that they could keep their tears inside even when they were mad at something and didn't know what it was. And that most people didn't lose hope the way she did.

As Frenchy says, hope rhymes with dope—you got any?

Frenchy doesn't have friends, only interests. Drug interests, mostly. Like the Mafia, but she's a one-woman mob. She claims drugs are what made her lose her nature before she came to prison and had to change her ways (by *ways* she means the ways she gets her drugs, the ways she gets high and so on). I haven't figured Frenchy out all the way yet, and I probably won't have time to, considering.

It just seems Frenchy never had *chances*. The women's group that is fighting my case, for instance—why don't they take up hers? I know why: because she's a poor, black, drug-addicted lesbian with an ugly spot, one who doesn't give a flying fuck what happens to her next.

Frenchy's been in and out of prison most of her life. Her relationship with Laverne ended like everything else in her life, when she was not in a position to do anything about it.

They pulled her out of noon count and told her, point-blank, "We just got the call your friend is dead."

"I've never been down on my knees in my life," Frenchy said, "but I was on my knees to Mrs. Christianson. Wasn't there any way I could get out for the day to make arrangements and attend her funeral? Mrs. Christianson said what the judge had told me—that Laverne had cancer at the time I committed the crime, and I should have considered that."

My father used to tell me, "Look your last on all things." The last time I got to look inside a punishment cell was the night my father died. I'd been on the Row for six years at that time. My counsellor said it was for my own protection, so that I didn't hurt myself. They probably expected me to throw some kind of fit, then they could have used tear gas to subdue me for my own good. I think I disappointed them, because when I was informed of his death, I asked if it was true that after you die your fingernails keep growing. I've been a nail-biter all my life. In death, I hope to have "to die for" fingernails.

Your hair keeps growing too. Frenchy insisted on getting a haircut the day before (the second time round), but the matron said no, last time her hair blunted the scissors. Frenchy said if her hair had been blonde, they would have shaved it. It's whatever you want, or don't want, in here that gives the authorities the power to break you before they finally kill off whatever's left.

A week before my father died, I was allowed to make a three-minute "condolences call." I could hardly hear my father's voice, it was so small; he asked when I was coming back. I cried and said I didn't know, and asked if he had forgiven me for everything I'd done to hurt them. I love you, I tried to say over the long distance, and then my mother came on the line. I knew my father couldn't speak because he had nothing left to say that would give me anything to hang on to.

Then the line went dead. And it was as if I had been left with no one.

Vernal writes that he's been seeing a psychiatrist. He pays her ninety-five dollars an hour to tell him he has trouble getting close to people. So far he has learned two things: that at every moment, whether we know it or not, we choose between having good things now and better things later; and that life is short and there may be no tomorrow, therefore it is pointless for him to continue to delay all forms of gratification.

Vernal has started drinking again, "just for today."

Officer Freedman told us another firing-squad joke. Arthur and Rose, a middle-aged Jewish-American couple, are touring South America. One day, Arthur unwittingly photographs a secret military installation and soldiers march the couple off to prison, where they are held and tortured in an effort to get them to divulge the name of their contacts in the CIA. Eventually, they are tried in a military court, charged with espionage and sentenced to death by firing-squad. The next day at dawn, they are taken out and made to stand against a wall, and the sergeant asks them if they have any last requests. Rose says she wants to call her daughter in Chicago. The sergeant says that's not possible and turns to Arthur. "This is crazy!" Arthur shouts. "We're not spies—we're tourists!"

"Arthur!" Rose cries. "Please! Don't make trouble!"

Most people say they've died and gone to heaven. For me, it's the other way around.

People make a lot of jokes about Heaven. Most of them are only funny if you haven't been there. You don't get many women here who live to say, about their experiences on death row, "Been there, done that."

"I've got a joke for you," I say to Frenchy. "What's black and knocking on the door?"

"Fuck that motherfucker and the train he rode in on," says Frenchy.

The right answer, I say, is "The future."

Frenchy doesn't get it. How can something that doesn't exist, like the future, be knocking on the door?

Rainy gets out her pencil, but then she can't think of anything to draw. The idea of the future doesn't inspire her at this time. I say we should all be concerned about the future because we have to spend the rest of our lives there, and I tell another joke, about Poland, where a curfew has been imposed. Two soldiers are leaning against a lamppost. It's seven-thirty at night and one of the soldiers suddenly jumps up, raises his rifle and fires, killing a young woman who is walking down the street. The second soldier is horrified. "Why did you do that? It's only seven-thirty— curfew's not until eight o'clock."

First soldier: "I know where she lives. She never would have made it home on time."

Dostoevsky maintained that at the moment of imprisonment, life, as you've known it, stops. You lose the use of your life, even as you go on living, and your mind must find a way to endure this knowledge.

Dostoevsky also said that two plus two was the beginning of death. When I asked Frenchy what she thought that meant, she told me for her it had always been one trick at a time, and only two choices: "A straight or a Frenchy." I learned two things: that Frenchy hadn't been reading Dostoevsky in her spare time, and how she got her name.

"What's two plus two?" I ask Officer Gluckman. Her eyes start bulging, even more than usual. Officer Gluckman's eyes are too big for the rest of her face, and instead of trying to correct this fault, she accentuates it. Looking into her glasses is like gazing into the eyes of some terrible deep-sea fish that has surfaced only long enough to know it doesn't belong anywhere but in the bleakest depths.

I ask her again if she knows the answer, and she tells me to shut my cake-hole. She suspects I am making a joke at her expense. Unlike the others, Officer Gluckman doesn't believe in humour—she finds sicker ways to harass us. For instance, she won't use our names, but she alludes to them all the time.

"You better walk between the rain drops, 'cause I'm gonna be watchin' real close," she said to Rainy. "And the first time you get wet, I'll come down on you." "Pardon my

French, ladies," she says whenever she descends into the vulgate.

When I drew her attention to the fact that all the women guards employed on the Row have male pronouns in their surnames—Officer Robin*son*, Officers Gluck*man* and Freed*man*, Officer *His*sick, Officer *Hen*nessy—she told me she'd had enough of my lipping off.

"What's she going to do, put you in jail?" Rainy says.

She found a way to get to me eventually. Guards are not descended from Planet Compassionate. We get them from earth.

Officer Gluckman brought a Talking Nano to work— one she must have taken away from her kids for an infraction of playroom conduct—a virtual pet you have to feed, put to sleep, wake up and otherwise look after. Officer Gluckman doesn't take care of it properly, on purpose, and when she walks by my house, I hear its plaintive voice: "Feed me. I'm sick." And there's nothing I can do, of course, no way I can save myself from having to dig up everything I regret, everything I'm ashamed of, everything I've buried. Every day I have to listen to the one tape I've tried, over and over again, to erase. "Feed me. I'm sick."

The worst part about guards is that their behaviour is unpredictable. For instance, ever since the firing-squad failed to kill Frenchy, we have been on lockdown and haven't been let out to take a shower. Once a week they bring a basin full of cold water and set it outside our cells. We have to sit on the floor and stick our arms through the bars to reach the basin if we want to have a whore's bath (what Rainy calls it when you wash yourself in the sink).

They don't allow us dental floss or our own deodorant. If you want deodorant, you have to stand by the door of your house, naked from the waist up, arms raised above your head, at five to eight every morning. At 8 a.m., a nurse walks down the row with a can of Right Guard and sprays your armpits.

We are allowed lipstick, even though none of us wears any. There's no point trying to figure out the way the guards think—why we can have lipstick, eyeliner and face powder, but no deodorant. No use trying to figure out where they get their ideas, or what they think about when they're alone, driving home after their shift, or if they *have* a worldview that doesn't come with bars around it. I know one thing for certain: guards are the only people who come to prison every day voluntarily. Their own unhappiness, I believe, causes them to behave even more cruelly towards others, as though cruelty could prove to them that they have a hold on life.

In victims, Pile, Jr. told my judge and jury, what starts out as a primitive urge for survival can turn into a fondness for one's captors. Psychologically, it is explained as a return to infancy, to the days when the human baby depends on others for food, warmth and comfort. When, as adults, we find ourselves in a similar state of dependency, as I had found myself when I had initially been taken hostage, we revert to the same tactics we used to please our mother to win over the person or persons who now hold over us the power of life and death. To all this add the fact that I was pregnant, and had my own baby to protect—didn't it make perfect sense that I would wish to befriend Consuelo de Corazón? All I had been trying to do, in fact, was to become, in the eyes of my captor, a human being.

The reporter from *Newsmakers* called Rainy "a cruel and heartless mother." Rainy says even though she now has a personal relationship with Jesus Christ, she still can't forgive herself for leaving her twins on those railway tracks. If she'd only left one of them, she would only feel half as bad, but she could never have afforded the operation.

Newsmakers had a picture of Rainy with her twins. They had been born joined at the hip and shoulder. They also shared the same brain. Rainy said they had screamed all the time because they were in constant pain, and she had to learn how to give them needles every four hours. She took to using the drugs herself, and that made her babies worse.

If she could turn back the clock, she would pick her babies off the tracks before the train turned them into a fine red mist and hug them to death (her words). She'd hug those kids so hard her arms would snap off like sugar peas.

How you feeling? I'd asked her one day when she was sitting with the photograph in her hands, staring somewhere beyond it.

"I used to think only good things hurt," Rainy said to me.

I say, next time someone asks her to compare being given the death penalty to being hit by a train, tell him this: no mother is so heartless and cruel as the society that executes her.

chapter fourteen

I dreamed I was trying to bury Angel again. His body was lowered into the earth. I woke up as one of the guards lit a cigarette, took a few drags, then tossed it in after the coffin.

Dawn coloured the eastern sky, and when I looked out my window, I got my first glimpse of the island that looked like an upside-down fish hook. I had pictured it as being flat, a speed bump above sea level, but Tranquilandia was bisected by a range of bottle green, black-ridged mountains.

We began our descent, flying south along the coastline, very spooky and piratical, with pelicans massing over the crags. Tiny Cattle circled a sheltered cove where Las Blancas moored its fleet—a sailboat, *Conejo Blanco*; a cruiser, *La Mordida*; a cigarette boat, *Pablito E*; and their most recent acquisition, a U.S. Coast Guard cutter.

The airport runway, on a thin spit of sand leading up to the edge of the dense forest, looked quiet—suspiciously so. "I'm going to give it a fly-by," Tiny said. "They didn't let me get in this close last time, so we may be in luck."

He took a low pass across the strip, buzzing the harbour. "*Basuco*," he said, pointing to the *Fat Lady*'s predecessor, a half-submerged Convair. "I got so addled that time, I must have missed the runway."

I closed my eyes, half expecting the same thing to happen now, but Tiny touched down and stood heavily on the brake pedal to bring the plane to a halt before the dirt strip ran out.

"Whoooooaaa little dowgie!" he cried, pumping harder and harder on the brakes. "Whooooooaaaa little dowgie," again, as we bumped up the runway.

Even after Tiny had shut down the plane's engines, the air continued to hum. I think the mosquitoes, which must have sensed fresh blood, would have broken down the door if Consuelo hadn't punched it open first.

A lone figure in a white suit strode towards us from the direction of the yacht basin. His hair was cropped short, making his head seem almost too big for the rest of his body. He carried a machete in a yellow holster.

Consuelo embraced the man, who looked as if he had just finished shaving—with the machete. El Chopo (the Gun) had applied little pieces of toilet paper to the places on his neck and cheeks where he had nicked himself. His suit was made of sharkskin, his designer cowboy boots from a couple of unlucky pythons. He had a blood-red orchid pinned to his lapel.

Consuelo pushed the man away, held him at arm's length so she could get a good look at him. "*Cómo estás, tío mío?*" she asked.

Her uncle said everything was "copacetic," a word, I learned, he used every chance he got, and asked if she liked his new suit, said he'd got it off a butcher in Baton Rouge who'd reneged on a loan. He lifted up the orchid to show two clean bullet holes, then grinned. El Chopo had Consuelo's lips, unusually red for a man, so thin they could have been razor-nicks that had never healed. When he grinned, which he did often and without provocation, the lips got even redder, as his cheeks pulled them tight.

Consuelo told him to get rid of the suit, that he looked like a pimp or a drug dealer in it. Looking back, with the objectivity I've since gained, I think, had I been on my jury, I would have concluded we were *all* criminals. El Chopo's sawed-off cowboy boots were as much a part of him as the .38 Consuelo carried tucked in the waistband of her army fatigues.

We left the plane, and I was led to the basin where the boats were moored, a bay ringed by ancient mango roots. The bare roots pointed out of the mud like bony fingers. Consuelo seemed impressed by the Coast Guard cutter, her uncle's new lodgings, which had anti-aircraft guns mounted on its foredeck and a swivelling M60 on its bridge. The warship's bridge house was decorated with symbols—four giant red marijuana leaves (each looked like the maple leaf on the Canadian flag), signifying that the ship had made four marijuana busts, and three white tear-shaped snowflakes, each representing a seizure of cocaine. These had been his sister's loads, El Chopo said, which is why she finally got fed up and ordered Las Blancas to apprehend the vessel, and why he had been appointed to guard the ship.

He showed us into the galley and told us to make ourselves at home. "Take a pew. Sit. Over there. Not on that," he said to Consuelo, pointing to a worn-out sofa. "It's falling apart. Everything around here's falling apart, present company included. That chair's still copacetic. Sit. *Siéntense.*"

Consuelo removed a gun holster and a box of vicious-looking knives that El Chopo said he had made "for therapy"; she told me to sit on the pile of newspapers on the chair. There were weapons everywhere, even hanging on the walls, along with a series of paintings, on velvet, of a woman looking bereaved. I could have been looking at Consuelo a few more years of suffering from now.

"The sister is always in mourning," El Chopo said when he saw me studying the paintings. "It is all she lives for, the death of others. That and making money." He paused and looked at me sideways. "She has an instinct about people. You know, she will tell you if your *nenito* will make a lot of money when he grows up or end up like his father in prison."

I said I hoped my child would have other choices.

El Chopo looked past me to where his sister, the Black Widow, wept tears of velvet from the wall. "*Tu eres inocente,*" he said. You are still innocent. And then, "It doesn't matter what you believe."

A true innocent is a person who doesn't know the meaning of the word. "It matters to me," I said.

"The two of you, you think too much," said Consuelo, making a dismissive gesture towards El Chopo, frowning at me. She opened a cupboard door, then closed it again. "At this moment, we do not need your philosophy of life, *tío grande*. We need food."

El Chopo tossed a handful of coffee grounds in a blue enamel pan and added water. "I live alone," he said. "I have time to think."

"*Amor*, stick to killing. It is what you do best," Consuelo said. Carmen had said the same thing about Consuelo. I wondered if these words applied to *everyone* in this family.

"My mother has always said my uncle is unkillable," Consuelo continued, as if for my benefit. "Time will tell. *Verdad?*"

El Chopo grinned, and set about frying a flying fish in coconut oil, preparing boiled yams spiced with ginger and red beans. I watched the way he worked, using his machete for slicing and chopping the ginger, and for flipping the fish, even for decapitating the bottle of coconut oil. Every so often, he would stop and stare at a blank space on the wall, or the floor, or out the window, as if he had forgotten where he was and had to descend into a trance to remember.

After this "small meal," he served figs from Buga, in southern Colombia, and licorice-flavoured *aguardiente*, and when Consuelo asked about her mother's deteriorating mind, he motioned me out of my chair and flipped through the pile of papers. El Chopo said his sister had become so irritated by the frequent raids the combined forces of the Drug Enforcement Administration and the United States

Coast Guard had attempted to make on the island ever since the cutter had been apprehended, she had threatened to cut off everyone who relied on her.

"She is fed up. She is paying bribes to the *campesinos*, to the army, the port authorities in La Ciudad, as well as to the DEA in Miami, customs and the Coast Guard, and they can all go to hell, she told them. They can all starve. Now look at the lies they are telling about her in the papers."

He spread the paper open on the table. "Black Widow Bites Back: Drug Baroness to Dump Chocolata's Paradise?" the headline read, followed by an article speculating on whether the Black Widow would soon be putting her whole operation on the market, and how this would effect "*la otra economía.*"

El Chopo pulled a crumpled pack of Pielrojas from his pocket and a box of tiny, waxy white matches. He lit a cigarette and blew smoke over his shoulder towards Tiny Cattle. While Consuelo and her uncle discussed whether the Black Widow had lost what was left of her faculties, I tried to read the rest of the article.

The Black Widow's paradise, Hacienda la Florida, was an eight-thousand-acre *finca*, big enough to encompass a small city within its borders. The Black Widow, who got her start flying 1,200-pound loads of marijuana from Colombia via Tranquilandia into Florida at fifty dollars a pound, and from there spread her operation west and north, had now acquired real estate all over the southern states, and carved landing strips in the swamp lands there the way she had in Colombia. On Tranquilandia she had built a network of roads, three artificial lakes, an airstrip with two hangars (inside which her planes could be loaded and unloaded), her large, sprawling country-style mansion, a cluster of thatched bungalows to house her staff and security guards, a clubhouse, restaurant, stable for her miniature pet ponies, and other outbuildings amid gardens filled with rare orchids and wild animals roaming at large, and aviaries filled with exotic birds.

The Black Widow had continued to control Tranquilandia, even if it was now from the shadows. People put up altars with her picture, and lit candles for her, all over the island. They believed she could perform miracles. No woman in their history, with the exception of Chocolata herself, had ever possessed a talent like hers for getting what she wanted out of her people.

There was an aerial photograph of the estate, including the mud-flats, the black fringe of mangrove swamp around the yacht basin and the remnants of a dark river wriggling out to the distant sea. El Río Negro flowed down from Nevada Chocolata and wound through the Black Widow's land. The first time the Hacienda la Florida got busted, the bodies of twelve soldiers killed by Las Blancas were pulled from the river. During the second bust, the raiding party dumped so much cocaine into the river that its once-clear waters turned white. Two file photographs pictured the dead soldiers on the riverbank and the drugs being dumped out of fifty-five-gallon drums into the river. "The river takes blood without changing colour—but not cocaine," the caption read.

Tiny had begun fanning the air, as if the smoke insulted him, and fiddling with the dial on the short-wave radio.

He wanted to get the weather; he asked Consuelo if he could have gas for the plane, because he had done what he'd been paid to do and wanted to get home to pick up his foot ointment at the pharmacy. He began scratching his feet, picking at the dead skin between his toes and letting it fall to the floor.

"Feet giving you problems? I cut off both feet for you," said El Chopo, chopping the air with his machete, exhaling more smoke in Tiny Cattle's direction.

Tiny repeated that he needed fuel, not surgery.

"Sure, we got gas." said El Chopo. "Lots of it." He could make something innocent sound sinister. It had to do with the way the words he spoke poked out at you, from the tip of his tongue into the slits of his lips.

Tiny turned red in the face. He stared at Consuelo, blowing air, then sucking it in again through his open mouth. El Chopo left the room and returned with a package the size of an airline pillow, wrapped in red cellophane and coded with symbols. He set it on the table and handed Tiny Cattle a small knife with a retractable blade. "Take a look for yourself. *Está muy puro.*"

Tiny slit open the package containing his *plata de polvo.* He broke off a piece of the flake—it came away like a chunk of shale—and crushed it in his hand. "There's too much glitter in this," he said, fingering the sample as he spoke. Cocaine began leaking from the slit he'd made, like an infection from under the scab of tape.

Consuelo, after touching some of the white flake to her fingers and tasting it, said, "*No, señor, es muy puro. Primera calidad.*"

Tiny made a face. "*Es bastante ordinario*," he said. He told Consuelo that the stuff was *basura*, garbage, and that snorting lines of this so-called primo-grade merchandise would be an insult to his nostrils.

"Then I will keep it for someone whose nostrils are not so easily offended," said Consuelo. The powder trickled from the package as she picked it up and turned it over in her hands. She scooped out a couple of rocks and put them in her pocket.

Tiny groaned, grabbed the package from her and turned it right side up again on the table. Then he went down on his hands and knees, trying to sweep up the trail of white powder that had spilled onto the floor, separating it from the flecks of dirt, the tiny particles of dust. He gave up finally, and strode out onto the deck.

"His father would not like to see him now," said Consuelo.

El Chopo too looked disgusted, and muttered something under his breath about unpleasant black people from the coast, before tossing back another shot of *aguardiente* and joining Tiny Cattle on the deck. The two men disappeared from sight.

At first I had been confused by Consuelo's attitude towards drugs. Now I was beginning to understand. Those who dealt drugs in large quantities looked down on people who used any substantial amounts. Users were referred to as "niggers" or by other racial epithets. You did not, as I often heard Consuelo say, sleep on your own poison.

Consuelo poured more *aguardiente* for herself, then turned to me. "When I was at school, my sisters and I used to chase the other girls to the wall—we had a wall around our school for security—and kiss them and marry them," she said. "Only the smart girls would let themselves be kissed. The stupid ones, and the beautiful ones, used to scream and get away.

"When I grew up I wanted to kiss someone, to marry someone, who could give me children. Someone like Angel."

Rule #3: Keep the hostage-taker talking; the more personal she gets, the better. "You must miss him," trying to sound as if I cared.

"Talk of love isn't for people like us," she said. She looked at me, hard. "You don't *miss* Angel. You remember him.

"*Recordar.* It means to remember, to pass again through the heart. *El corazón.*" She toasted one of her mother's pictures on the wall. "And Gustavo," she said, "and Mugre too. Even though he was a bad brother-in-law sometimes, I remember him."

She downed the shot, adding that *aguardiente* was not known as a women's drink, and that if I was ever seen drinking it in public, I would be assumed to be either an intellectual or a whore. Then she bit into a quarter section of lime that had been soaking in salt and chewed it until her eyes watered.

I had expected to hear the *Fat Lady*'s engines turning over and the plane idling on the runway, but I heard nothing. "Ten years ago, Señor Cattle got shot down in the jungle. He was captured and tortured by the Mujeres Armadas Revolucionarias de Colombia (the Armed Women

Revolutionaries of Colombia, the most powerful guerrilla group next to Las Blancas), who thought he worked for the CIA." She paused. "Do you want to know what they did to him, the Mujeres Armadas?"

She emptied her pocket on the table, took the knife Tiny Cattle had used to slit open the kilo and drew up a small amount of mother-of-pearl-like flake on the blade's flat side, then held it under her nose. I thought she was going to snort it, rocks and all, but then she lowered the knife, tapped the cocaine onto the table and began chopping it, cursing whenever one of the tiny crystal rocks jumped away.

"The revolutionaries, they did unnecessary things to Señor Cattle. They stripped him and tied him to the bed. They put a curling iron up inside him . . . like this," she demonstrated, making a circle with her finger and thumb, and poking the knife in and out through the centre of the hole. "Then they plugged in the iron. They left him like that all night."

She cut the coke into two thin lines. "They let him live, only so he could see what they did to his wife. They were amateurs. You saw their work? That ugly head?" She wrinkled her nose, as if to say these revolutionaries couldn't even shrink a head without destroying it.

She took a crisp hundred-dollar bill and rolled it into a thin straw. Bending her head low to the table, she vacuumed a line into her right nostril with a single snort. She shuddered, held her breath, jerked her neck back.

"Smuggling is like a drug to him now," she said. "It is his therapy, what gets him through the day."

She bent down to repeat the procedure through her other nostril, wiping up the leftover cocaine dust with her finger, massaging it into her gums, making a face.

"My uncle is right," she said. "Drugs are for the niggers."

chapter fifteen

The matron unlocked my handcuffs so I could bear down. She wore an apron with "Happi Flour: It Rises to the Occasion" printed on it, and there were dark smudges where her dirty fingers scratched continually at her groin. I saw rusty tongs on a red Formica counter, nests of lice under the matron's arms.

The doctor wore a black hood over his head. Two young guards stood outside the steel doors that kept opening and then slamming shut. One guard, off guard, caught his reflection in the mirror they'd placed between my legs so I could see the baby's head when it came out; he raised his rifle and took aim.

The baby wanted to stay deep inside me, attached to me, dressed in camouflaged fatigues, size 0.

I rolled over and stared at the ceiling. I lay that way for a long time, on the hard bunk in the dark cabin where I'd been left, afraid to go back to sleep because I knew the dream hadn't ended. I called for Consuelo, but she didn't come: now I felt the pain inside me, and brought my knees up to my chest and rocked my body from side to side, wondering what was going to happen to me, if I was going to lose my baby. I felt the nausea coming in waves, closed my eyes again and heard the open moan of the sea, the waves breaking on the reef beyond the lagoon, the wind wearing a sailor suit, a blouse with anchors, puffing and heaving towards me, her skirts blowing up over her face.

"Hey, hey, take it away! Get that ball and fight!" the greasy matron chanted. If my feet hadn't been in stirrups, I would have kicked her. The doctor told me to relax my shoulders, and gave me a shot in the hip. He said he wanted to get this over with because he had an appointment on death row.

The doctor had on a bloodstained baseball mitt. Without warning, he reached up inside me. "There's nothing in there," he said. I could hear his irritation, see his beady eyes through a slit in the hood.

"Fuck a priest, there's nothing in there."

Then I heard Angel say, "You shouldn't worry so much. Don't start worrying until they start shooting, and even then you shouldn't worry. Don't start worrying until they hit you, because then they might catch you." And I laughed because the doctor couldn't catch the baby, not even with the mitt.

The doctor put his hand on my stomach, punched it hard, and it started to go down. "Happi Flour. It Rises to the Occasion." The matron snapped the handcuffs back in place, breathing on me with her swampy breath. The doctor began rinsing off his mitt.

"The warden is going to hear about this," hissed the matron. The doctor removed his black hood and put it over my

own head, just as the guard pulled the trigger and all the lights went out.

I could write the rest of my story as if the hood they placed over my head has never been lifted, because that is the way it has seemed to me ever since.

I lay with my eyes wide open, still trying to push away the dream. The pain in my womb had subsided, but I felt scared. I curled back into a ball. Then I saw a light go on in the corridor. I called again for Consuelo, who came in her own time and unlocked the door, then led me back to the ship's galley. She seemed very uneasy, and asked me if I thought I was going to lose the baby. I said I didn't know, I was having what felt like bad menstrual cramps.

El Chopo, dressed in a skimpy pair of yellow bathing trunks and a black plastic apron, was frying another fish, and I could smell beans and rice mixed with the smell of gun oil. I doubled over and threw up a little black bile. Consuelo wiped the floor, saying she did not intend to nurse me for much longer.

El Chopo flipped the fish once in the frying pan, then slid it onto a serving plate. He was looking away out a porthole again. I was getting familiar with his trances, the way he'd stare forever at some fixed spot on the horizon, like an Easter Island statue on Thorazine.

Consuelo wiped her nose with the back of her hand. The pain had eased; I asked if I could go outside for air. She nodded but made a slapping gesture at her head to remind me of the mosquitoes. I didn't care, and pushed open the heavy door and let it close behind me. I wanted to be alone in the predawn stillness. The jungle sounds were already becoming familiar—the strange deep gurglings of the howler monkeys, like underwater sirens, whirling through the forest; the warning cries of birds; the constant mosquito drone; the occasional splash of a fish.

There was a shameless sensuality to Chocolata's island—the bold greens and blues I'd seen pulsating under the mid-morning sun when we'd arrived, the erotic reds and purples of the eggplant sunset I'd glimpsed through the ship's porthole. I could smell the salty female smell of the sea, the bittersweet clinging scent of rotting fruit and dying copra. Now, as the first grey and pink strokes of dawn daubed at the night sky, I could smell, too, the sultry odour of frangipani fading with the darkness as a flood-tide began sweeping an incessant stream of bobbing jungle growth back up the river—long strings of water hyacinths and tiny white orchids, their green leaves full of air bubbles to keep them afloat. Some of the strands caught onto the anchor chain of the *Conejo Blanco* and clung there as if they had grown weary of floating back and forth on the tides, waiting to be swept into the gulf.

Consuelo's voice calling me inside made the pain come on again, even worse than before; I sat down heavily at the table.

"I'd like the morning a whole lot better if it started a little later," Tiny Cattle said, getting up off the sofa where he'd been dozing and taking the bottle of *aguardiente* from the cupboard. He was complaining, still, about his feet, about getting home—how Consuelo had promised him one thing and now expected him to hang around until she was ready to do another.

Consuelo got up, took the bottle from him and emptied it in the sink. She poured him a large glass of water.

She forced me to drink water, too, but I knew I wouldn't keep it down. I heard the liquid travelling through my upper body and falling into my stomach. I closed my eyes as it started back up. Consuelo watched me gag and retch, then went over to the counter and cut a huge slab of papaya. She picked out a handful of black seeds and told me to chew them. I tried to do what she asked, but they were too bitter, so she crushed them and made me wash them down with a pink *gaseosa* called Colombiana. Then she took me back to my cabin, where I was sick again.

I heard her lock the door and check the lock twice. I pushed the strands of wet hair from my face, strands stuck together by vomit and tears. I kicked on the wall beside my bunk, but all I heard was laughter from up above, and the sound of my own panic, in darkness, tearing in my head.

I had not known, before Consuelo opened my cabin door again, tied my hands, then led me outside into the fierce heat of the day, that life could permit me so much pain. The sun had come out from behind clouds; the ship's deck was steaming. Consuelo seemed confused, one minute ordering me to move faster as I hobbled towards the waiting vehicle, the next ordering me to slow down.

She had been considerate enough to give me a cushion to lie on; the Jeep, although it looked new, lacked any system to absorb the shocks from the deeply cratered road. She untied my hands so I could hang on to the back of the passenger seat, where she sat on Tiny Cattle's lap. The door on the driver's side had been removed.

El Chopo kept asking Consuelo if everything was copacetic. At one point, Consuelo insisted I chew a handful of cardamom seeds that she produced from one of her bags—her "natural tranquillizer"—after which she tried to make me drink a whole bottle of water.

In Carmen's memoir, *Rescate*, she wrote about being tortured by the guerrillas. Torturers, she said, did not want you to die; if you died, you were beyond their realm of influence. To lose a victim could mean you might lose your livelihood.

I'd always thought that if tortured, I wouldn't resist, I'd reveal everything, that resistance meant unnecessary suffering. It hadn't occurred to me then that people tortured others for sport, or a sexual or psychological thrill, or simply to see another human being suffer. Carmen had withheld no secrets, was not an enemy or even a rival; she was simply a political prisoner. Yet her baby had been starved to death and Carmen had accepted his fate with a kind of stoicism I found unimaginable.

"There are good reasons for death" was as much as she'd had to say about it.

A pump shotgun and a box of shotgun shells lay on the floor, rolling from one side of the Jeep to the other as El Chopo negotiated the road's curves. Beside me on the floor I saw a vial of yellow pills, a hamburger with a bite taken out of it, a Coke tin someone had crushed in his hand. *Little Yellow Pills. Vial. Hamburger. Bite.* I said the words inside my head, as if they could be possible names for the baby that might any minute be shaken out of me.

I tried to sit up, taking the shallowest breaths I could to avoid inhaling the vehicle's exhaust. We were passing through a plumed forest of bamboo, with the occasional stand of goatwood or cedar trees opening onto a broad plain where ceibu cattle grazed. White egrets perched on their humps, taking refuge from the sun in the shade of crimson trees, the tips of every branch glowing with fiery cande-labra. Birds with foot-long ribbons for tails, and iridescent doves, landed on the red road in front of us, then flew up.

The road narrowed into a single track as we entered a valley of little wood and palm-thatch villages. Above us rose the steep and steamy bourbon-coloured Nevada Chocolata, fringed with wispy mists. Young girls in floral-print dresses with dishes of green plantains on their heads called out to us as we passed. Barefooted boys, their black feet swollen and ulcerated, ran along beside the Jeep, wav-ing packages of white cheese wrapped in banana leaves. We crossed a river where the grass was flooded and cattle fed on blue hyacinths and women scrubbed their children's thin bodies with lemons and mud.

My cramps had grown more infrequent. I shifted my position, propping myself up on one elbow so I could still see. I saw dusty greyish trees, scrub brush and the occasion-al pink-washed farmhouse smothered with scarlet bougainvillea.

I sat fully upright, this time to be sick into a plastic bag that smelled of cigarette butts and overripe fruit. I asked El Chopo to slow down, but he paid no attention.

We had reached the outskirts of the City of Orchids. The road wound through a hard-shell shantytown of bamboo huts with rusted tin roofs. El Chopo ploughed the Jeep though potholes and ruts filled with black scummy water, streets heady with fruit and vegetable debris, the cloying sweetness of decay, and stinking river mud like deposits around a clogged drain, everywhere you looked. A small boy, naked, with six inches of umbilical cord protruding from his distended belly, picked a drowned rat out of a puddle and hurled it onto our windshield.

Heat, a heat so lazy and intoxicating you feel as though you are always just waking from a wine-drugged nap: this is what I remember of the City of Orchids. Mud and rats and mosquitoes and flying cockroaches three inches long—I remember these, and feral children too, eating guava jelly with their hands at the side of the road, and old men with diseased feet, and young men who looked like assassins on every corner.

Driving through the balconied streets in the centre of town, where every ground-floor window was covered with ornate wrought-iron bars, everywhere I looked I saw funeral homes. I learned later, from Nidia, the maid at the Hotel Viper, that poor people always waited until a family member was on her deathbed before bringing her to the hospital, reinforcing their idea that a hospital was a place you went to die. Poor people did not own cars, so funeral parlours were positioned close to the hospital for convenience.

One *funeraria* offered cut-rate coffins for those who had lost their legs. Another specialized in thin boxes for the poor, thick hardwood ones for the rich and "designer coffins" for *los vivos*, those "full of life."

A graffiti-covered bus, whose windows had been removed, lurched up the street, listing like a boat about to discharge its cargo. El Chopo cursed and veered onto the curb, almost knocking down a flower vendor and his sign, *Flores Para Los Muertos*, at the entrance to the *mercado popular*. A bald, shirtless man spat at us from the back of the bus, as if the near accident had been our fault. Tiny Cattle said he believed they took the windows out of the local buses to make it easier for passengers to spit on people.

El Chopo parked in the No Parking Emergency Parking Only zone outside the hospital. A *mestizo* in bare feet hobbled up to the Jeep and tried to sell Tiny a pair of black-market sunglasses. When Consuelo helped me out, I almost tripped over a limbless man on a little plank with wheels.

"*Hay cigarillos?*" he asked. He nudged me and held up, between his teeth, an official-looking stamped document, complete with gruesome photographs, that showed his disability had been incurred in a bona fide accident when he was a young army recruit. Consuelo said the paper was most likely a forgery, but tossed him a package of Pielrojas anyway.

A bronze statue of an Indian, his naked legs and arms breaking free of his chains, stood at the entrance to El Hospital De Los Libres (the Hospital of the Freed). A man sat in a wheelchair next to the statue, smoking through a little hole in his neck.

Inside, a receptionist instructed Consuelo to take the elevator to the second floor. A nurse hurrying a bouquet of dead flowers out of a room that was being fumigated showed us where we could wait, in a cubicle partitioned off by thin wainscot panels topped with a grille of chicken-wire. A small newspaper clipping, in English, warned, "The Pill is a Killer." There was a sink with a dirty coffee cup in it, and beside the sink two white plastic containers, one labelled "Needles *Limpias?*", the other "Needles *Sucias?*" There was some question, it seemed, as to which needles needed sterilizing.

By the time a doctor came to examine me, the cramps had stopped but panic had set in again. The doctor prodded me on either side of my abdomen and said my severe pains were possibly caused by amoebas, unless it was my appendix.

I soon wondered if he had been to the same school of quackery as Consuelo. He wanted to do blood work, but I said I refused to allow him or anyone else in that hospital to stick one of their filthy needles in any of my veins. He shrugged and checked my blood pressure, then asked me to stick out my tongue. The morgue, he warned, was already overpopulated with people who had refused to co-operate.

Consuelo advised me to do what he asked, but when I stuck out my tongue, the doctor told Consuelo—in Spanish—that I had a very beautiful tongue and that he would like to arrange a bed for me in a "private part" of the hospital.

Consuelo thanked him but said that wouldn't be necessary. "She will be staying in a safe place," she told the doctor. If anyone asked, she said as she smoothed the creases out of a hundred-dollar bill, he had never laid eyes on me.

We got back in the Jeep and drove a short distance across town. El Chopo crossed himself as he parked outside a church presided over by a twenty-foot-high statue of

"Cristo Rey, Víctima." A half-naked Indian lay passed out on a stone bench at the statue's feet.

As we started across the *plaza*, which seemed to be a gathering place for vagrants, stray dogs and *gamines* who fired at one another with sticks for make-believe machine guns, we were accosted by three police officers. They asked to see my papers. There had been kidnappings in the area. Tiny Cattle lit the *jefe* a cigarette while the other two began rifling through my knapsack. Consuelo said my papers had been misplaced and gave the *jefe* a hundred-dollar bill "for his trouble." The *jefe* tipped his hat, and the three, plus Tiny Cattle, wandered across the square and disappeared through the steel door of a bar called El hígado no existe (The Liver Does Not Exist).

chapter sixteen

The Hotel Viper lay coiled on the shady side of the square, as if waiting for some hapless traveller to stumble into its fangs. It was high tide in the hotel's front garden, and the lobby was literally awash. The only light came from a dim bulb in a tiny plastic seashell fixed to the ceiling, with a thick layer of dead flies on the bottom. A dark, nervous little man smelling of hair cream and cheap cologne sat behind a desk reading a crime magazine. The cologne mixed with hair cream made me feel dizzy; I reached to grab hold of his desk so I wouldn't fall. Consuelo told him I was suffering from *soroche*, acute mountain sickness, which he didn't seem to question, even though the hotel appeared to be highly below sea level.

Consuelo asked to see *el viejo*, the old man, at which the clerk insisted we rest ourselves on a termite-infested sofa in the dining room. He brought *aguardiente* and a plate of cold fried eggs and guava jelly, the eggs redolent of his hair cream, and left us sitting beneath two eighteen-foot-long anaconda skins nailed to the wall.

The dining room was also home to a scarlet macaw, a green cockatoo and a bald parrot named Edgar, who had a neurotic habit of pulling his feathers out. He sidled up and down a beam under the dining-room roof, defecating and plucking. Suddenly, he swooped down and flew straight into a wall, lying stunned on the ground, screeching, "*Quiero una mujer!*" (I want a woman!).

The water continued to rise, and I started to shiver. Wet feet were unhealthy feet, Consuelo said; you only had to think of the feet of the men and women we'd seen along the road to know what happened if you spent your life without adequate drainage. She made me put my feet up on the sofa, and then covered me with a blanket that smelled of wet feathers.

I don't know if it was the bumpy ride from the south end of the island or the *aguardiente*, but I woke as it was growing dark, stretched out on the sofa with bugs crawling in my hair. I had dreamed I was travelling on a fast boat up the west coast of Vancouver Island with a load of cocaine. The landscape kept getting colder, icier. Birds were frozen in mid-flight and all the fish had frozen in silver arcs across an icy river.

There was no sign of Consuelo or El Chopo or the little man who had served us the drinks, but an equally mournful woman called Nidia, who said she was the maid, told me the termites were harmless unless I was made of wood.

I swung my legs over the side of the couch onto the floor and found the tide had receded. Nidia said she had prepared a meal for me, and took me down a musty passageway into a courtyard filled with pots of busy lizzie and morning glory the colour of licked bones. A balcony surrounded the courtyard, much like a catwalk around a prison range. A single table had been set for dinner under a shedding almond tree. I took the one chair, next to an old man with thin red lips and black, black eyes who told me he was dying, and about how much more interesting life had been during the war, and how this was a godforsaken island because you couldn't get good natural ices.

Nidia served us chicken necks, rice with gravel and warm Coca-Cola under a crackling bug-zapper; the scorched remains of flying insects fluttered down onto our food. When the old man asked for dessert, Nidia said the kitchen was closed. The man requested his brandy drink, but the bar, she said, was closed too. He told her he was going to take a stroll in the garden. "I don't have many nights left to squander."

Apart from the old gentleman, the hotel appeared to be deserted. I asked Nidia where everyone had gone, but either she didn't understand my question or she didn't want to answer it.

I tried my question another way: I asked her where were all the other guests who would be staying in the hotel that night.

She looked at me in surprise. "This is not that kind of a hotel," she said. "Guests do not stay here."

There are many ways of remembering, ways to forget. I have tried to forget my room in the Hotel Viper, my whitewashed cell with wooden floorboards that creaked, my sad bed, with a cross full of insect exit holes hanging above it. The ceiling, too, had been eaten away, dirty plastic and newspaper showing through, and wires leading to a single light bulb. Nidia told me not to worry about the little bits of plaster that kept falling; men were replacing part of the old roof, and she would sweep my bed every morning.

There were no curtains, and the iron fretwork over the window was *para seguridad*, Nidia said, the first security measure I was aware of, and one I suspected had more to do with keeping people in than keeping anyone out. I hadn't seen anything at the Hotel Viper worth stealing. I asked where the bathroom was, and Nidia pointed to a door in the wall, a section of the wall that had been cut away, so you had to pry it open. I convinced Nidia to leave the *baño* door ajar, asked for some soap, a toothbrush and a towel. Nidia shrugged. *Más tarde*. Later.

I remember Nidia leaving, and the despair I felt as I entered my walk-in *baño* (a quarter the size of my walk-in closet back home), where the heat and humidity had caused the one cupboard to split and break. Mosquitoes were lined up on the back of the toilet like jumbo jets waiting for take-off; a column of giant black ants marched across the wall. I undressed, hung my clothes on a wire hanger (hoping they wouldn't rust), and edged my way around the toilet into the shower-bath. There was no shower curtain and nowhere but a clogged hole in the corner of the room for the water to drain, which meant the water flooded my bedroom as I stood letting it trickle over my hair and face.

A roll of toilet paper that had been chewed by rats was all I had to dry myself with. I waded to my bed, still dripping wet; the pillow felt as small and hard as the kilo Consuelo had tried to give Tiny Cattle, the sheets thin and mournful as Nidia, who had made the bed, tucking the sheets in so tightly I had to fight to squeeze my body between them. I left the light on for comfort, but a colony of termites became attracted to the bulb hanging on a cord from the ceiling above the bedstead; they hurled themselves against it, shedding their wings, which then fell on me. I covered my head with one corner of a miserly sheet, but then I heard an explosion somewhere in the distance, and all the lights went out. Cockroaches kept me awake most of that night, skittering in the walls.

The next morning, I waited for my door to be unlocked or for someone to bring me food; I was hungry, and felt my baby's need too, which left me feeling even more desperate. My clothes were gone—the thought that someone could sneak in without waking me alarmed me. Two extra-large dresses—one grey, one pink—had been placed at the foot of my bed, along with two sets of underwear and a pair of *alparagatas*—sandals made of strands of coloured rope, the kind the *indígenas*, the local Indians, wore—that looked as if they were waiting to be stepped into, to walk me away from this life. With the sun hitting the tin roof, my room was like a steam bath; my arms and the backs of my legs were red and swollen with bites. I dressed, then tried the door, but it wouldn't open, and when I began banging on it, I managed only to arouse Edgar, who screeched that he wanted a woman, so I gave up and tried beating on the iron bars covering the window instead, hoping to catch the attention of the half-naked Indian still sleeping on the stone bench outside the church of Cristo Víctima.

The bench was directly opposite my window. I watched the Indian for a while, until he came all the way awake and began to stagger, in circles, around the fountain—I realized he'd never be able to save me. He wore a collection of battered tin cups around his waist on a piece of fraying rope. I watched him try to walk, then stop to catch his breath, undo the rope at his waist and set the tin cups in a row along the edge of the fountain. I counted nine of them. His goal seemed to be to try to fill each of the cups with water.

I watched as I waited for my door to be unlocked, watched the *gamines* waiting, often until the last moment, then darting in and knocking over one of the cups. When this happened, the Indian would pursue the fleeing boys, shouting at them and cursing as they fired their make-believe guns back at him.

It wasn't until mid-afternoon that Nidia arrived with food, a plate of *arepas*—a kind of primitive-looking corn-bread—and a slice off a massive roast called a *muchacho* (boy), which had been larded with pork fat and over-cooked. When Nidia left I pounded on the door, shouting at her to bring me something edible. Had I known how much worse my meals would get, I think I would have kicked down the door and begged for a quicker death.

"*Más tarde*," Nidia called back to me. Later. Everything was *más tarde*. I remembered Tiny Cattle saying the whole fucking Spanish day takes place *más tarde*. "*Tarde* means afternoon *or* it means evening *or* it means we're late." To Nidia it meant, always, never.

Day after day, I was kept prisoner in my room. Day after day, I watched the mad Indian lay his cups in a neat row on the fountain's edge, fill each one to the brim, and then, as he started to fill the last, wait for a *gamine* to dart in and knock the first two cups into the dust.

If I hadn't known better, I would have mistaken his routine for Zen practice—until the moment the old man grew angry, flailing his arms, yellow froth appearing at the edges of his mouth, pursuing the boys around and around the square. When he failed to catch them, the old man knelt below the statue of Cristo Víctima and prayed, while back at the fountain, water from the spilled cup trickled into the dirt and the boys resumed their torture of a crippled dog with blind eyes, and I watched. And waited.

My room was humid, a heat you couldn't escape from, exploding off the tin roof of the hotel, the iron fretwork over the window like a corrosive bloom. Whenever I did try to sleep, my dreams were interrupted by a demented rooster, which I heard but never saw, who crowed regardless of the hour. Every night, around midnight, the lights went out all over the City of Orchids. Nidia told me somewhere on the island a generator kept failing, and every night they were without power for seven, eight, sometimes nine hours at a time.

Always, right after blackout, Consuelo came to check on me. Some nights she would bring a lamp, and we would play chess with a crumbling set of black and red wooden pieces that often disintegrated in our hands. Playing against Consuelo was unsatisfying, for even when I won, which was half the time, I felt she had let me win, that she had cunningly set up positions where I couldn't avoid capturing her pieces, so I always ended up questioning my own strategies. One night, she accused me of cheating because *I* let *her* win. I told her she should learn to accept her victories, no matter how small, and she stood up—her eyes a deep darkness flaring in the lamplight—crumbled her queen into dust and walked out of my room into the dark. I watched her, through my open door, on the balcony, pointing her assault rifle at the stars— those million faint campfires illuminating the dark—and picking them off in her silence. I asked her once if she wasn't afraid the world might blow up in her hands.

"*Quién nos quita lo gozao?*" she said, lighting a cigarette. Who can take away the good times we've had?

I saw no one else but Nidia for days at a time, though the old man I'd met on my first night took great pleasure in sneaking into my room occasionally when I was sleeping, standing over my bed and pretending his arms were wings, swooping down over my head and belly and doing his bird imitations, so I woke up thinking I was being attacked by the deranged rooster with no sense of time. I awoke shrieking and shaking and covered in sweat, and then he would leave again, to smoke *mejoral*—a stimulant that you cut into tiny bits and mix with cobwebs, that "paralyzes you, like *basuco*," Nidia said.

Nidia brought food three times a day. After several months of being kept locked up, I began to record in my journal—another attempt to relieve the boredom—a list of the food I was given to eat, as if by describing each piece of greasy offal, each mouthful of rock-hard plantain, I could make the reality more palatable.

I know it is fashionable these days to include recipes in books, but I don't think anybody would covet my recipe for *mondongo*, a murky broth made from the lining of a cow's stomach, with a dish of coconut and cold potatoes on the side.

> *Day One: Breakfast:* Rice and noodles and hot (weak, mostly water) chocolate; *Lunch:* Rice topped with a mixture of pasta and chopped sardines, a glass of Coke (flat); *Dinner:* Rice and potatoes and a boiled chicken wing.

> *Day Two: Breakfast:* Stew of thick beef bones (no meat), a bowl of unsweetened milk; *Lunch:* Stew of potatoes and noodles, with a can of chopped fish (when I asked Nidia, "What type of fish?" she said, "*Tipo de atún*"; what, I wonder, is a tuna "type" fish?); *Dinner:* A greasy piece of fried cheese on a greasier piece of deep-fried bread.

> *Day Three: Breakfast:* A piece of refried white cheese; *Lunch:* A bowl of thin oatmeal (as far as I could tell) and pasta; *Dinner:* Lump of pork fat, fried plantains, boiled manioc.

Day Four: Breakfast: Pineapple stewed in cane syrup, fever grass tea; *Lunch:* Boiled fish, beans and rice; *Dinner:* A soup of sardines, pasta and potatoes—which I threw up later.

Day Five: Breakfast: Mondongo (cold); *Lunch:* Curried crayfish, rice with gravel, pumpkin pudding (no sugar); *Gourmet Dinner:* can of Del Monte pilchards in tomato sauce (Nidia says they are spoiling me!!!).

Day Six: Breakfast: Coffee and a corncake with sausage on top (which arrived ten minutes before lunch, so I didn't eat it); *Lunch:* Beans mixed with lentils in greyish water, a few bits of tough meat in puddles of grease, a spoonful of rice and a *gaseosa.* (When I showed Rainy my menu, she pointed out something that is true: I had a more varied diet when I was a hostage than I have here, on the Row.)

On Day Seven, I didn't eat. I made a list, instead, of everything I hated in the room, and didn't stop writing until I realized there was nothing I *didn't* hate, including my own list.

On Day Eleven, I gave up recording what I was expected to eat and watched the column of black ants still marching across my bathroom walls, wondered where they were coming from, where they were going, and then found where they disappeared into a crack in the cupboard, inside which they had rounded up a group of smaller red ants. Any time a red ant tried to escape the circle it was trapped in, a bigger black ant attacked it, biting it and squeezing it, and, after what seemed to me like prolonged torture, dismembering it and killing it. Feeling an immediate sympathy with the victim, I freed as many of the red ants as I could, brought them into my bedroom and let them eat whatever they wanted of the meals I barely touched. They still preferred my own flesh, and on Day Twenty-Eight I awoke to find myself covered with hundreds of itchy bites. I stripped my bed; if I had found any red ants, I would have taken them back to the *baño* and fed them to the black ones, feeler by feeler.

After Day Fifty-Five, because I'd taken to flushing most of my meals down the toilet, I woke every morning to find my pillow covered with strands of my hair, and, weeping, I collected the hair and wove it into a braid, adding to it every day, so that the braid grew thicker as the hair on my head thinned. Nidia must have spoken to Consuelo, because one afternoon Consuelo took the rope-braid away, saying she didn't want me hanging myself, and made Nidia stay with me while I tried washing down a plate full of *sobrebarriga* (hard, cheap meat) with a bowl of *agua panela*, a sweet drink made from sugar cane and served like coffee.

I knew Nidia must have a family to return to—a husband, children—but I was so desperate for company I was glad she had to stay. While I sucked on my dessert—a piece of gummy, sweet candy called *gelatina* (made from the bones of cows, I learned later)—she made herself busy, picking up the bits of plaster that had fallen from the ceiling during the day, saying she wished the men would stop this destruction. I told her I often prayed the whole ceiling would cave in on me, anything to get out of my deplorable situation. She looked shocked, but then whispered that a *bruja* could help me if I didn't want the baby. I said I wanted the baby, but not here in this airless prison, in the Hotel Viper, with no one to care. I worried that I had grown too weak and too unhappy to be a proper mother. Nidia said giving birth was very easy—you just lay down and the Fallen Virgin of Perpetual Suffering did the rest. As far as being a mother went, the Virgin of Miracles could be called upon at any hour of the day or night.

She said, too, that my room, no matter how much it felt like a prison to me, was "happier" than any room in the Hospital of the Freed: she knew because one of her daughters worked there as a nurse. Babies who were born in that hospital never came home. Their organs were transplanted into the bodies of the very rich, who came from as far away as Japan, Israel, England—many were *norteamericanos*. The body parts of children were the most desirable, her daughter had told her, because they were healthy, growing body parts, not yet contaminated by the excesses of life.

I thought Nidia was a child, a peasant, full of superstition and gossip, and a tendency to believe what she saw on television about the lifestyles of the rich. But when Nidia said she had eight grown children and three *angelitos*, I was shocked. I'd thought she was in her early twenties, but she said she was forty-three. Her husband was seldom home any longer, which was why she looked younger these days. He was a *cascarero*, like a travelling salesman: he sold nylon socks for men and a face powder, which, she confided in me, contained mostly flour. Nidia rubbed her own cheek, pursing her lips. "If only he would give *me* something," she said, "to soften my nights."

I asked if she still had children at home, and she sighed and said she hadn't seen any of her sons since they started working as *sicarios*. Anyone interested in a *trabajito*, could stop on any street corner and hire a child for an assassin nowadays. It was hard work with very little pay and not much future.

After she left I lay on the bed, amidst the little bits of plaster that continued falling on me, feeling the volume of my life bearing down on me. I lay listening to my heart, a lonely muscle, opening and closing in the darkness inside my body. When I fell asleep, eventually, I dreamed of a dark blue sea of babies rolling in the waves, being tossed ashore, sightless, into my arms, which could neither hold them, nor let them go.

part five / hotel viper

When that wall is erected within us as a safe place to hide from the misery of others, we become imprisoned in the delusion just as surely as those bound by suffering in the outside world.

—Tim Ward, What the Buddha Never Taught

chapter seventeen

Death Clinic, Heaven Valley State Facility for Women

*You are not allowed to pin on any safety pins or paper crips
[sic] on any part of the anatomy. Tatooting [sic] or changing
hairstyles or eyebrows in unusual forms is strictly forbidden.*
— *Inmate Information Handbook*

We are the prisoners of infinite choice.
— Derek Mahon

The HV executioners were profiled in this month's
Lifestyles magazine. The five *femmes fatales* could not be
photographed, but were middle-aged and Caucasian, the
writer said, except for "Leetia" who was in her late twenties
and African-American. All used aliases.

225

"Some people would make a hero out of you if they found out what you do to make ends meet," said "Wanda," in charge of the electric chair, who lived on a farm with her husband and their four foster kids. "To me it is just a job—all you're doing is pulling a switch. Before this I worked up the packing plant, hog kill. A pig is the hardest thing to kill. I done it so many times [the writer said that here she made a throat-slitting gesture] I got one arm bigger than the other as a result." He described her hands—one almost twice the size of the other.

"Cecile," the gas-chamber executioner, was a forty-year-old nurse who had wanted a career change; "Valerie," responsible for lethal injections, a former corrections officer. The hangwoman, "Leetia," owned a roadhouse. She was a vegetarian, a churchgoer, and had never married.

"Rejean," who "manned" (her word) the firing-squad, said that when it came to executing anyone, even "women of her own gender," she had learned to be philosophical. She had no misgivings about the death penalty. She compared a person's time on earth to a landlord-tenant relationship. "You trash the place, you don't pay the rent, you get evicted."

What made them want to work at Heaven Valley State Facility for Women? Rejean applied for the job because she needed money and "because somebody's got to do it." Leetia didn't have an answer. Valerie's reasons were complex: she had had a bad relationship with her mother, and said the job helped her heal "old wounds." Cecile said she liked the job because you met a lot of different people, but seldom the same one twice. Wanda had rewired her own toaster and become interested in "home electronics"; when she saw the position advertised, she'd thought it wouldn't be much of a leap.

The writer asked each of them if she felt capital punishment was a deterrent to crime, or just something to satisfy the public's need for revenge.

"I think some people are over-sensitive," Rejean said. "I've executed a lot of women. Do I look like I've been losing sleep?" Leetia said yes, in that a dead woman will never offend again. Valerie thought *deterrent* was a pretty big word, which probably meant she didn't understand it; Wanda said yes and no to both questions; Cecile wished there were a better way sometimes, but mostly she had no complaints and would go on doing the job until she had enough experience to get a better-paying one that didn't take up so much of her life.

Asked for survival tips, the women all said there was only one rule: Never establish eye contact with a person you were about to execute. Each one, except for Rejean, said she would sleep better if she hadn't had to look into a walking-dead woman's eyes before putting the trash out at night and turning off the lights.

Didn't they ever feel tainted? When you dealt in death every day, didn't you lose an important connection to life? the writer asked.

Valerie said no woman she'd ever executed was anything important. Cecile said if you're going to have mental problems about it, get another job. Wanda said yes and no, but that killing people had to rub off. "You can't shovel manure without getting shit on you."

I read this and felt only sadness. How is blindness cured by plucking out the eyes of the sightless?

The one other woman on death row who had been granted clemency, even though she didn't want it, was a serial killer whose cause had also been taken up by the Women's Empowerment Coalition. Her *modus operandi* was to gouge out men's eyes ("They could never see me, anyway, for who I was inside"). "Go ahead," she'd say to them. "Now let's see you fuck me blind."

Shortly after she was granted clemency (she was found too insane to be executed), she hanged herself in her cell.

Hanging used to be more popular than it is now. In the bestselling *Do-It-Yourself: The Science of Neck-Breaking* (I'm kidding, of course, about the bestseller and do-it-yourself parts, but because Rainy can't read, I make things up, just to see how much she'll swallow), you'll find one of the saddest stories you'll ever read, about a girl hanged in England in the early nineteenth century. She had been sentenced to death for trying to take her own life, which was a capital offence in those days. She slit her throat, and would have succeeded in bleeding to death if her father hadn't come home unexpectedly. He saved her life, a doctor stitched up her throat and then she was charged with trying to commit suicide. She pled guilty, got convicted. She was given the death penalty, and she chose hanging.

Her doctor pleaded for her life. He said that if they tried to hang his patient, her stitches would come undone and she would breathe through the aperture in her trachea, suffering unimaginable tortures that surely even a judge would not wish to inflict upon any human being, regardless of her sex, no matter how heinous a crime she had committed.

This girl was like me—she insisted on her right to choice, and she was hanged. As her doctor had predicted, her stitches came undone, and the hangman granted that the woman's suffering might be relieved, on humanitarian grounds, by the "medical person" in attendance at her execution. Permission was given to this medical person (the nineteenth-century equivalent of a corrections officer who has recently updated his CPR skills, no doubt) to clamp his hand over the aperture through which the woman breathed. But the fake croaker's hand wasn't big enough, and after the woman had danced, gasping and twisting, at the end of the rope for as long as anyone watching could bear, she was cut down and given clemency as a result of a "technicality."

Rainy, who had been listening closely as I relayed these details to Frenchy, had only one question. "Why did her father come home unexpectedly?"

Here's the thing: nothing is more predictable and more certain than death, yet nothing is less predictable and less certain.

"Whoopee fucking ding," says Rainy, a sign that she thinks I am thinking too much. It drives me when Rainy says, "Whoopee fucking ding."

Something I *have* always thought about: every year, from the day we're born, we pass the day on which we are going to die. We all know death is inevitable, but in most cases live in complete ignorance of its timing. Only two kinds of people are spared from continuing to live in this state of uncertainty: a) those who plan to take their own lives; and b) those who will be "put to death"—like Rainy and Frenchy and me.

When you live on the Row, you don't have a lot of opportunities to take your own life, even if you plan it that way. Our health and well-being are priorities here. If you catch lung cancer or wake up with a cold on the day of your execution, you'll get a rain check. They'll wait until you stop blowing your nose or coughing up blood before sending you on a trip to the stars.

Frenchy's a slasher; instead of getting jailhouse tattoos she mutilates herself, tattooing her rage on her skin. When she cuts deep enough it brings blood to the surface, so everybody can *see* her wounds.

But Frenchy's best-laid plans fail, over and over. She's made nine attempts at suicide since the first time she was given the death penalty. "Of course, I have to fail," she said. "I never, ever succeeded at anything I tried to do."

Rainy won't speak to Frenchy after she cuts herself. Stitches are one of her "issues": when she was eight years old, her father punished her for wetting the bed. "He thought if he sewed up my *chocha*, it'd teach me a lesson," she says.

Rainy went to school every day stinking and wet until a teacher reported her to the health nurse and they found out what her father had done. "He went to jail for it, but he never said he was sorry, and he never was. Sorry. He told the parole board he'd do the same thing again, if I didn't grow up."

Rainy says she's grown up a lot since then. "But I still pee the bed. Every night."

If the state decides to end your life for you, you don't, at first, get an *exact* DOD (date of departure); it could be any time within the next twenty years, depending on your trials (your guilt trials and your penalty trials), your appeals, public opinion, and the electoral and political processes. In states that employ the death penalty, judges are subject to re-election. We always know when there's an election coming up because the Row starts getting crowded, and then, one by one, the women are shifted to "death watch," a holding cell in the Health Alteration Unit (or the dancehall, as we all call it), a few feet away from the execution chambers. This means their execution is less than thirty days away.

When you get your "date certain," you know the date you're going out on, providing you don't get lucky and get cancer first. Some people argue that it's a cruel punishment, to be told you're going to get gassed on such-and-such a day. What murderer has ever told her victim, "I'm going to kill you. It may be a year, three years or even fifteen years from now, but I am going to kill you. Meanwhile, I am going to lock you up in a cage and torture you in small ways until I am ready to kill you."

In China, they spring it on you. Some say this is a more humane system, that in keeping a person uncertain of the date and time of her death, the state is preserving her status as a human being. You're in your cell, reflecting on the harm you have done to society and the terrible amount of money it costs taxpayers every year to keep you locked up, and suddenly there they are, at your door, calculating how much money they're going to make when they've got your vital organs in their hot little hands. You eat the remains of your breakfast, because failure to clean your plate is considered an infraction of prison conduct, subject to disciplinary action, then they take you outside and shoot you in the head.

Neither you nor any family member is notified beforehand, so there are no long goodbyes, no tearful partings. Just you, your bodyguards, a man with a gun and the croaker (who's supposed to make sure you are dead enough for him to start operating on). As a courtesy, to let them know you have finally paid your debt to society, your family will be sent the spent bullet casing afterwards. *And* they're required to pay for it.

There's one other way a woman can postpone her date certain (besides catching a terminal illness)—and that is by getting pregnant. Condemned women can "plead the belly" and get a stay, though a friend of Rainy's pled and nobody believed her. Even after two male orderlies and a male midwife examined her, they sent her to the Chair. Flames shot out of her head when they pulled the switch, and milk spouted from her breasts into the flames. At the autopsy, they found an eight-month-old "healthy" baby boy dead inside her.

Now when a woman pleads the belly, she's allowed to have an examination by a panel of *women* gynaecologists. We've come a long way, baby.

———

We *are* the prisoners of infinite choice. If you choose to be hanged, you next have to decide whether you wish to die from strangulation or from a broken neck. No drop at all, or a short one, usually results in strangulation—death from asphyxia, caused by stoppage of the windpipe, which causes convulsions (somewhere between the time it takes to drink a Starbuck's and the time it takes to finish an anniversary dinner with your ex), or from apoplexy, by pressure on the jugular vein. The long drop ends in a broken neck. Death is supposed to be instantaneous and painless, though as one woman said to the executioner before she fell, "How the fuck would you know?"

You'd think it would be straightforward after that—you choose the short drop or the long one, depending on how much suffering you feel you deserve—but it's not. After you make up your mind *how* you want to be hanged, you then have to choose the kind of rope you wish to be hanged with.

There are many different options—"No noose is good noose," as Officer Freedman says—and some of the descriptions make it sound like *haute couture*. The *Vogue* model turned chainsaw killer, for example, might opt for the soft, pliable, five-ply Italian silk hemp rope with a three-quarter-inch diameter.

Choices, says Rainy. Dead if you do, dead if you whoopee fucking don't. It's like being in a restaurant and finally making up your mind that you'll have the cheeseburger platter and the waitperson says, "Would you like Cheddar cheese or mozzarella on your cheeseburger?" and you go for the orange Cheddar. Then she says, "That comes with french fries, baked potato, or garden salad." You hum and haw, and then make a healthy choice, and say, "I'll take the garden salad." The waitperson says, "Will that be house dressing, oil and vinegar, french, thousand island or ranch?" You choose oil and vinegar, and then she says, "Will that be regular or lite?" It's a form of harassment, like Frenchy's train or guard humour. Why can't they just *bring you the fucken cheeseburger platter* without taking away your appetite? Why can't they just kill you without giving you so much choice?

It's because for years women didn't have options, my counsellor says. I don't bother pointing out to her that my question was hypothetical. A pro-choice state means taking responsibility for your life—and your death, she adds. As if.

The Science of Neck-Breaking uses mathematics to calculate the scientifically perfect drop for each person who might require one. There's an art to hanging, the author wrote, as well. What works for one woman doesn't necessarily work for the next. Her height and weight, age, whether she is physically fit or has spent a life horizontal on the couch eating Hostess Ding Dongs, and the length of the drop (controlled by the length of the rope)—these are the variables. The *Vogue* model will need less rope than a dwarf like Rainy to drop the same distance. Each person has a correct drop, and our drop is unique to each of us—like our DNA or our fingerprints. We can't pass it off as someone else's, or pretend it is not our own.

My mother says that before I got myself into this "bucket of hot water," she had been all in favour of a death penalty. "I think there would be a lot more people alive today if we had the death penalty in this country," she writes. But now she sees it would be a mistake to apply it in all cases. "What's sauce for the goose isn't necessarily sauce for the gander."

Frenchy is surprised by how many letters I write, and how many I receive. Prison for her, she says, is a place where you can't think of anything to say.

"What do you have to write about," she says, "when you're in a place where nothing happens to write about?"

I tell her I write about getting through another day.

The day before they hang you, you get weighed and sized. More technicalities. What is life but technicalities, details? "Don't sweat the small stuff," Frenchy says. But she's wrong. The small stuff is important, because a lot of small stuff can add up to something big. Two plus two is the beginning of death, and so on. I'm starting to catch on to what Dostoevsky meant.

The morning of your date, you put on your clean clothes, and you're taken out to the gallows, smelling like Bounce, Frenchy says. To the right of the gallows platform, in a room with walls seven feet high, three guards are seated on stools. In front of the guards is a shelf, across which there are three taut strings. Only one of these springs the trap that causes the execution. The other two are connected to buckets of sawdust—the equivalent of blanks in a gun—which fall through the floor along with the hanging body.

Each woman is armed with a sharp knife. She waits for the hangwoman's signal before cutting the string. It takes between eight and fifteen minutes before the heart stops beating, the legal time of death.

This time when Frenchy's last meal was brought to her, she kicked the tray high into the air, the undressed garden salad and the Diet Coke Rainy had ordered for her. "At least no one else will enjoy my leftovers when I'm gone," she said.

But she didn't go anywhere—except back to her cell. Something went wrong—or right, depending on your point of view—and the trap door wouldn't open. Frenchy survived—again. "Death is not just dying" was all she had to say about it.

A week later, an article in the local paper revealed that Frenchy's *femme* was not so *fatale* after all. Shortly after the publication of the article in *Lifestyles*, the hangwoman's roadhouse had been exposed as a notorious hang-out for cross-dressers, Leetia her/himself a female impersonator. She took early retirement. "I never liked to hang a woman," she said. "It always made me shiver like a leaf."

chapter eighteen

I don't know how many days, weeks or months went by. Sometimes I would be let out "for air," which meant a trip onto the balcony, but one evening I was taken down to the courtyard, where Consuelo sat on a partially submerged deck-chair, drinking *tinto* (strong, sweet black coffee) and eating *pandebono*, a kind of bread with cheese you bought on the street. She signalled for me to sit and help myself to her leftovers. Nidia, who said the power was still out in the kitchen, began frying zucchini strips on a charcoal griddle on top of an oil drum on the patio.

The old man—nobody had introduced us and he hadn't volunteered his name, so I'd nicknamed him Don Drano (he simply used people as a kind of sink, to push everything down)—had reappeared, and was complaining that communism had ruined this island, which was why you couldn't get decent natural ices. One other thing he didn't like about living here was the poverty, but you got used to it, he claimed, like the bad water and the noise and the unhealthy climate. He wanted to know what I thought of the squalid mess his daughter had left him to live in. The place was infested with every kind of living insect but fleas, and the only reason there were no fleas, he said, was that the bedbugs ate them.

His daughter? I sat watching his lips as he talked, realizing now why he looked so familiar. Consuelo, meanwhile, paid more attention to the dying almond tree than she did to her dying father. Someone had decorated the tree with milk cartons, split open down the sides, to make ornaments that spun in the wind (though in the protected courtyard, I never saw them spin).

When Nidia finally produced a meal, it was *sobrebarriga*, and other mysterious parts of a cow, and zucchini fried in an oil slick on the side. The food of the *indígenas*. I left my plate untouched.

El Chopo came back drunk from the North Pole Tropical Bar and Restaurant. *Perfectamente borracho*, he said: the manager had been aggressive and forced him to drink whisky. Nidia served *sabayon*, a milky drink made from *aguardiente*, instead of coffee, but I wasn't going to risk passing out from the effect of the potent liquor again. Consuelo told El Chopo she had business to take care of, and when she left El Chopo sat staring at the immobile milk cartons, then, after a drink that seemed to render him even more catatonic, passed out with his head down next to his cup.

Don Drano got up from his chair and asked if I would like to accompany him to the garden. It was the first time in many months I had been *asked* if I'd like to do anything, and for a moment I hesitated, not certain how to respond. This could be the moment, I realized slowly, to try to make my escape.

I looked to make sure no one was watching, then followed him, making myself as small as possible, out of the courtyard, over a weedy lawn, to a footpath that led to an iron gate and then through a walled garden of straggling fruit trees, big-leaved avocados and orchids with fleshy, tongue-shaped leaves. In the twilight I could make out only shapes and smells—the blousey ruffled lips, the fragrance of sweet, wet orchid blossoms, the enormous odour of the sea and the wind. Through the garden gate—which Don Drano locked behind me, proving to me he was more aware than he pretended to be—I could see the dark sea rolling in waves, moving further and further away from the shore, and the mouth of El Río Negro. I stood staring out to sea as, overhead, the sad pelicans flew south, hundreds of them. Don Drano told me this meant it was going to rain.

I have now read Chocolata's story in a book I found in the prison library. When she and her crew were hanged, their bodies had been gradually submerged by the swirling waters of the incoming tide. Three tides were allowed to pass over the women before their bodies were cut down and hung in chains in the port of the City of Orchids.

Don Drano told me when they cut Chocolata down and carried her ashore, her body was covered in white plumage. Some said her soul had become a pelican, and after that whenever a pelican flew south the rains would come; these were Chocolata's tears.

A green-grey mist rose off the glazed sea, where a fleet of banana boats drifted. The book, *The Pirate Queen*, said the executioner was almost as famous on the island as Chocolata herself. He had a club foot, and as she stood waiting to die on the gallows, the fierce woman pirate had cursed all male children born on the island by giving them bad legs so they would be doomed to be led by women.

The islanders worshipped their pirate queen. She was a hero to many, a goddess to some, Don Drano said; some islanders stole her body from the authorities and laid her to rest on a bed of orchids at the summit of Nevada Chocolata. The place was, to this day, known as Chocolata's Shrine.

"Virgin orchids," he said, "like these." He showed me the white, fragrant orchids, still favoured by the islanders, that grew wild along the Tranquilandian seacoast and were inhabited by biting fire ants. "You never pick them," he said. "They are not what they appear to be."

Consuelo was waiting for us in the courtyard. She scolded Don Drano for taking me away without her permission. The old man muttered his excuses and went to bed.

After my brief taste of freedom, I despaired of returning to my room and being locked in again. But Consuelo told me to sit as Nidia brought more food—frijoles, fried rice and guacamole. For a long time I sat gazing out at the ocean, listening to the screeching of the birds in the dining room, until Consuelo started an argument with Nidia over the best way to cook rice. When she seemed to be losing the argument, Consuelo broke a chair over the table and stormed off the terrace.

Nidia began wailing; she didn't want to lose her life on her night off. Consuelo soon returned—not, as Nidia had expected, with her .38, but with the keys to the Jeep. She told Nidia to take me upstairs to my room and lock my door properly before she went home for the evening.

When Nidia wouldn't stop sobbing, Consuelo picked up a piece of the chair she had broken and lifted it over her head. I thought she was going to kill the poor woman right there, and felt my arm reaching up, as if it were someone else's arm, and saw, out of the corner of my eye, Consuelo hurl the piece of wood over her shoulder. I saw the red stain of the bougainvillea.

Nidia rose to her feet and stumbled towards the stairs. I followed, as if she were the prisoner and I the one who could leave.

Once a week, a doctor began coming to "inspect" me. He was young, well-dressed, wearing a yellow silk mask that complemented his yellow waistcoat, and a tailored suit. At first I found it hard to take a hooded physician seriously, but he had a gentle manner, and as long as he was in the room with me, I felt oddly safe. He asked how I liked Tranquilandia, and I said I was enjoying myself immense-ly—I especially liked being locked in my room all day. I planned to devote a whole chapter to the island in *A Hostage's Guide to South America*, a book I was going to write just as soon as I escaped, and he smiled and said that was one book he would look forward to reading because he knew of no one who'd ever got away from Las Blancas, except in a coffin. I asked him if he considered it ethical to treat a woman, a *pregnant* woman at that, who was being held hostage without reporting it to the authorities. He replied that Consuelo de Corazón and her mother were the only authorities on Tranquilandia. He recommended I eat *helado con sabor de sangre* at least once a day—he claimed it was natural for women to lose hair when they were pregnant, and that blood-flavoured ice cream was one of the best sources of iron he could recommend. He asked me to be sure to look up some relations of his in Montreal if I ever made it back there.

Consuelo said the only place to get fresh *helado con sabor de sangre* was at the North Pole Tropical Bar and Restaurant. Even though I was almost too weak to walk, she made me get out of bed and go with her, then sit next to her in the Jeep and watch for assassins.

The break in my routine worried me. Even though I had come to believe I was in no physical harm—at least not until my baby was born—I didn't trust Consuelo. I was on my guard the moment I was in her presence. I remembered Angel's warning: "It is a sin to be surprised."

"*Aquí, se sube a pie y se baja en ambulancia*" (in this neighbourhood, you go in walking and come out in a ambulance), Consuelo said as she manoeuvred the Jeep through the narrow streets, where there were no road signs, no streetlights, not even any manhole covers left. I saw men and women wrapped in blankets made of rags, pigs and dogs rooting alongside them, through piles of garbage; some families had set up housekeeping in the twisted hulks of rust-eaten cars. The *olla* (literally, "the pot" or a dangerous place) had the feel of a battle camp back in the Dark Ages.

We parked beside the charred remains of a fire hydrant, and Consuelo gave a *gamine* a few centavos to guard the Jeep. We had started up the hill towards the *mercado* when a scrawny dog came snarling at me from the shadows and a small boy ran after it, beating it about the head with a thick piece of rope. Consuelo told me to ignore him and stay close to her, but then the boy appeared in front of me, asking for *un regalo*, a present, because he had saved my life. The boy's head was shaved, his eyes were drained pools. I said I had nothing, opened my empty hands.

"*Yo creo que tiene algo, señora. Deme un peaje,*" he said, and he raised the rope over his head as if he was going to strike me, the way he had the dog, which now stood cringing against a wall. I covered my belly, instinctively, and turned my body to protect my child.

"He believes everyone has to have *something*," Consuelo said, reaching into her pocket. "He expects us to pay his toll. He calls it a *peaje*, but it's not, it's a *rescate*, a ransom payment we are forced to pay just to be able to walk on our own streets. We are hostages to children in this city."

I thought she might shoot the snarling dog, but she filled the boy's palm with change instead, and he slipped into the shadows. "I am too tired to argue with him. We have bigger wars to fight, and all they can think of is their stomachs. Someone should get rid of him before he is old enough to make all of us pay in more unpleasant ways."

Where I come from, it is considered more hygienic and effective to kill guerrilleras while they are in the womb.

We turned a corner onto a street that took on a friendlier air. There were bars, fritanga stands, *juguerías* and *churrasquerías*, jewellery shops and, by local standards, fashionable clothing boutiques. Crouched in the doorway of Hot American-Style Fashions, a woman, covered from head to foot in newspapers and garbage bags, held out her begging bowl; Consuelo dropped a few coins in it, then continued on to a *juguería*, which sold juices made from fruits I'd never heard of—star apples, marmalade plums, tree tomatoes, honey berries. Consuelo ordered *zapote* (sapodilla) for herself, turnip-like on the outside but rich with orange flesh when you cut into it, and for me a *lulo*—bitter tasting, green—which, she said, would also help fortify my blood.

We walked on into the funeral-parlour district and cut through the *mercado popular*, which was beginning to empty. Consuelo led me through a maze of fragrant orchids beneath rows of yellow, blood-dripping entrails of cattle slaughtered that morning. No wonder the orchids hadn't sold, I said. Who would buy bloodstained flowers?

Consuelo said people expected orchids from the market to have blood on them; if the blood hadn't dried, you knew the orchids had been picked that morning. Once, she said, she'd bought a bouquet of nun's orchids because they looked fresh, like *sardinas*, young girls, but by the next morning they had become old crones, and she'd had to throw them out.

The heady scent of the orchids clung to me as we neared the back entrance to the market, where two *brujas* invited us to try their love charms: *legítimos polvos* to "dominate your man"; *polvos para las celosas*, sticky powders to ward off jealousy; tiny blue bottles in which to collect your tears. They could get anything we wanted, they cried after us: powerful *bilongos* to protect female warriors, emeralds from Muzo for fertility, dolls wrapped in grave cloth taken from ancient burial sites, dolls to protect you from insanity and the evil eye, fertility dolls, dolls to bewitch unwanted foetuses.

"*Brujas chimbas,*" Consuelo said disgustedly. Charlatans. Fakes. "There is only one real *bruja* left on Tranquilandia, and she does not come to the market to cheat and rob."

A single red geranium fought for its life amongst a holocaust of cigarette butts in a pot by the entrance to the North Pole Tropical Bar and Restaurant; a horseshoe and a piece of aloe vera hung over the only window for *buena suerte*. The sagging roof was made of corrugated iron and cardboard; shreds of last year's political posters flapped from the walls, which were painted with a blue wash.

The green door, bleached and flaked by the sun, was bolted, and when Consuelo knocked, an eye appeared in the judas hole. A man brandishing a handgun hastened to let us in.

Red- and blue-coloured light bulbs flashed over the bar, where a polar-bear rug had been nailed to the wall above a selection of alcoholic drinks. Another wall was taken up by a photo mural of the sun going down behind an igloo, a grinning Eskimo and a dogsled. *Música tropical* blared from two coffin-sized speakers nailed to the mural so that they appeared to be resting on a snowbank. I wondered if anyone who still lived in an igloo listened to *música tropical* or dreamed of getting sunburned in paradise. And I thought of the restaurant's counterparts up North, the wall-size photographs of white sand beaches, without a footprint to spoil the illusion, and thatched huts beside an ocean the colour of power-line insulators.

Young waitresses wearing white gloves, lace camisoles and white aprons over black leather skirts zipped their way from table to table taking customers' orders. I squinted through a fog bank of cigarette smoke mixed with *basuco* as Consuelo pointed me to an empty table at the back of the room. We were brought a clean ashtray and a bottle of dark rum called Ron Medellín. Consuelo sat with her back to the wall and ordered the fish fried in coconut oil, served with "plantain in temptation" and deep-fried Yucca for herself, the Mired Seafood, a non-alcoholic drink that came in a baby's bottle with a nipple, and a large bowl of blood-flavoured ice cream for me.

She lit an Indio and inhaled. "You never took up smoking?" she asked.

I shook my head.

"Bad habit," she said, then lifted and jutted out her chin to exhale the smoke through pursed red lips. She kept glancing around the room, and then over at the door: I think she lived her life in constant fear of being ambushed. As my eyes followed hers, I saw a tall, elegantly dressed woman enter the restaurant. Her gaze never landed on anyone in particular, but took in the whole crowd—the women leaning at the bar, or sitting on customers' knees, in tight red dresses slit up the side, knee-high boots or shiny black stilettos—*chulitas* who wore more eyeshadow than the night.

This beautiful woman looked as if she knew she didn't belong; she was hard to ignore, in her simple white silk dress that barely covered her knees. Her thick black hair fell in ringlets over her breasts, and her body had a carnal quality about it, her skin giving off an eerie, almost luminous glow. She wore a lot of expensive jewellery: the fingernails on her right hand, painted a moony, opalescent pearl, had been pierced and were linked together by a thread of gold chain, so when she spread her fingers wide her hands looked webbed.

It might have been her look, one of pity and sadness mixed, that made me avert my eyes from her full, pregnant belly and poke around in my Mired Seafood while Consuelo took her aside and said something I couldn't hear. She nodded and went away again, and Consuelo sat down and lit another cigarette.

"She used to work for us, for Las Blancas," she said, still watching the woman, who now stood speaking quietly to the triggerman at the door, "but she wanted to be independent."

Consuelo rubbed a hand over her face, leaned back in her chair and stretched. I watched the moon goddess leave the bar, alone. Consuelo shook her head. "You can't be independent," she said. "Only banks are independent."

Every evening, Consuelo took me to the North Pole Tropical Bar and Restaurant. When I continued to lose my hair, she accused me of not eating my ice cream but spitting it on the floor when she wasn't looking.

One night (I had long since given up keeping track of the days), as I lay on my bed with plaster dust falling down on me, thinking that even the Fallen Virgin of Perpetual Suffering must have grown tired of watching over me by now, I went into labour. After eating *ubre* (cow udder) for breakfast and a big piece of liver and *arepas* for lunch, I had snuffed a few red ants playing hide-and-go-seek in a fold of my sheet, then slept and dreamed of Angel again, and this time woke as the guards began shovelling earth in on top of him, and my water broke as the world outside turned to darkness. I pulled myself out of bed, hobbled to the door and began striking it with my fists. Nidia arrived, more quickly than usual; she looked at me and knew at once, and went to fetch Consuelo. When Consuelo came, she told me she had called the doctor but he wasn't answering his phone. He spent most of his evenings at the morgue, she said, conducting autopsies, and since my labour pains were now less than two minutes apart, that was where we would have to go.

chapter nineteen

A vast, corrupt energy filled the air as we sped into the scab-by outskirts of the *olla;* I exhaled and held my breath, as if by refusing to breathe I could prevent the corruption from enter-ing me. Consuelo began to drive faster, and seemed to aim for the potholes, as if the constant jarring might take my mind off the small earthquakes rocking my body on the inside.

I should have felt grateful to my baby: he was the one escape I had from the mindless birds tearing the air with their screeching, the fluttering presence of the old man, the biting ants, and my view of the madman with his cups chas-ing the young boys round and round the fountain. But I could not imagine a world, at that time, where I would feel grateful for anything.

We passed a scrapyard and a row of derelict buildings; I was beginning to contemplate giving birth on a bed of rotting vegetable matter, when I heard an explosion and Consuelo brought the Jeep to a sudden stop in the middle of the road. A crowd prevented us from passing. No one paid her the slightest attention as she leant on the horn and shouted at everyone to get out of her way. Just as I thought she was going to pull out her .38 and shoot her way through the mob, we heard another explosion.

Consuelo sprang from the Jeep, grabbed me out of my seat and began pulling me up the road. She shouted again for people to let us pass, but was once again ignored: we were sucked along with the crowd in the humid darkness. When we reached the bottom of the hill, a *gamine* came hobbling towards us out of his cardboard shelter to tell us a food concession had caught on fire and two cylinders of gas had exploded.

Consuelo, using me as a shield, pushed through the surge of bodies. My belly was being elbowed and bumped, and I tried to protect it with my hands. One minute my labour pains no longer seemed as intense, or as frequent, the next minute I wanted to lie down in the middle of the road and give birth where I lay. It was as if my baby, sensing what he was about to be born into, would think again. Perhaps my body was unconsciously giving him messages: *stay where you are; stay put; don't come out, whoever you are.*

I'd become expert at understanding the degree of danger I was in by the darkness in Consuelo's eyes. I could read her eyes the way some people read palms or sign language. Now, looking into her eyes was like looking into the smoking end of a double-barrelled shotgun. She steered me up the hill towards the North Pole, past the *churrasquerias*, where a group of shoeshine boys sat on their shoeboxes in a little circle, gnawing the gristle off bones people had tossed them. One, smaller than the rest, sat apart, trying to eat a bowl of grey, greasy broth with his fingers. I pleaded with Consuelo to let me rest, and she pulled me into the recessed doorway of the *joyería* next door to the *churrasquería*, where emerald rings, necklaces and bracelets were displayed draped over braided loaves of glazed French bread. I slumped against the barred windows, closed my eyes and began massaging my belly, only wanting to lie down.

"*Mire, mire, el fuego verde!*" Look at the green fire in it. Consuelo pointed to a gold-and-ivory, emerald-encrusted coke spoon and said someone should buy that spoon for the shoeshine boy so he'd know what it felt like to eat like a civilized human being.

I breathed—in through the nose, out through the mouth—feeling dizzy and nauseated by the sour, unwashed smells of the street. When I had caught my breath, we continued on up the hill towards the *mercado popular*. I saw myself giving birth beneath the great, bleeding slabs of beef, on a bed of bloodstained orchids, and told Consuelo I couldn't walk any further, she would have to leave me. Then I sat down.

She looked around and then made me crawl to where I wouldn't be seen, to the piss-smelling doorway of the Hot American-Style Fashion boutique; she told me to wait while she went to get the doctor. She took off up the hill as I sat doubled over in the doorway, panting and groaning.

"*Ayúdeme*," I whispered—help me—to the first person walking by who didn't look like a beggar or a thief. He was well dressed, I could see; he stopped, stooped to look at me, then reached into his pocket and threw a handful of coins in my face.

I curled up on my side and began to weep. I lay that way for what seemed a very long time, until I felt a firm, warm hand slip into my own. I pulled back, thinking it was a shoeshine boy asking for pesos, and begged him to go away.

"*Venga conmigo*," he said softly. Come with me. And then the doctor in the yellow silk mask lifted me from the doorway.

Candles burned in the hallway where he set me down; there was a strong chemical smell and a cloying scent of flowers. A series of Italian oil paintings depicting religious themes—the decapitation of John the Baptist, a saint having his intestines slowly unwound from his body on a reel—hung on the walls, alongside an old Spanish proverb carefully penned in Italic script: God Does Not Send Anything We Can't Bear.

The doctor took my arm, trying to keep me on my feet, as he steered me down the hall into a spacious, high-ceilinged room with rows of slabs in the centre of it. I heard a faint whirring sound, and as he lit a candelabrum, in the blackness I made out the jut of feet, the bulge of heads and bellies under the thin, yellowed sheets.

A nauseating wave of cold air hit my face; I recognized now the chemical smell of embalming fluid. At that moment, I felt a sharp kick in my side and a pain that buckled my knees. It was as if the smell of death surrounding me had given my child a new sense of urgency.

My teeth started to rattle, my body shook, my legs crumpled from under me and I collapsed to the ground. I fought to control both the contractions in my belly and my breathing. With each small breath I took, I felt as if my own intestines were being unwound on a reel, the tears icing over in my eyes before they had time to drop, like pebbles of frozen rain, onto my face.

I breathed through another contraction, saw the doctor leaning over me in his mask, then felt myself being lifted onto one of the mortuary slabs. I turned my head to one side, to avoid having to look at either Consuelo or the doctor, and saw, on the slab next to me, a woman's arm sticking out from under the sheet that covered her, the fingernails a moony, opalescent pearl, pierced and linked together by a thread of gold chain. A shunt protruded from her neck. The whirring sound came from a pump next to the slab, draining her blood.

Only banks are independent. Sitting where I am now, on the Row, I can see this was Consuelo's way of letting me know what happened to women who tried to go out on their own, women who didn't want to dedicate the rest of their lives to Las Blancas' cause. But I didn't think of her then, the moon goddess, or of what had become of her baby—everything in that place, even the reproduction of John the Baptist's decapitation, became part of my own pain. *God wouldn't send anything I couldn't bear.*

It was *more* than I could bear. But I would bear it, bear everything. I would bear this pain for my child; I would bear a son. But not for God: *God doesn't send anything.* My baby had not been sent; my child had come to me.

He came to me in that room smelling of embalming fluid, with orchid blades cutting shadows across the grim slabs. I lay on my back, hard against the marble where countless corpses had lain. I remember closing my eyes for a long time, then opening them and turning my head to one side to see a wreath of crucifix orchids in the middle of which a pair of baby boots sprouted miniature wings. Clipped to one of the wings in metal lettering, the one word: angel.

I could hear a baby crying, my baby. The doctor covered me with a sheet; I was exhausted and cold but felt a strong desire to hold my child, to comfort him.

I tried to sit up, get a glimpse of him, but the doctor stood in my way, urging me to rest: I could hear only the sounds my baby made wanting his mother. Consuelo, her back towards me, had him laid out on a slab. I barely stopped myself from rolling off onto the floor, trying to reach him.

"I wish his father could be here," Consuelo said finally. "Your *nenito* is everything he would have wanted."

She turned to face me, and lowered my baby into my arms. His legs kicked at air. He had his father's eyes, my very own pushed-in nose. He nuzzled my breast, groped with his mouth to find my nipple. He had made it this far. So far. A fighter. I counted: ten fingers, ten toes.

"He has a ponytail too," Consuelo said. I wanted to push her evil hands away as she smoothed the wet black hair on my baby's head, pulled a long, single strand straight up, as far as it would go. "And look." She indicated the depression in his chest. "Soon he will be taking women to bed and making them weep."

I rolled over on my side, put my baby on his back and pulled his arms away from the front of his body. He did, he had the same hollow place in his chest as his father. "*I was born with this . . .*" And I curled my hand into a fist and placed it in the little hollow, the way I'd done with Angel in the prison chapel, so many lives ago. "*My mother used to say it would fill up with the tears she would shed for me during her lifetime.*"

I kissed the hollow place, let the first of my tears fall into it. How long would the rest of my lifetime be? I loved him from that moment. I would never have done anything to harm him.

"Angel," I whispered. I spoke his name aloud, to the room, as if the gods that live within names could keep him from harm. Angel began to tremble, and I directed his mouth to my nipple again. My body, after giving birth, sagged like a puppet with no hand inside it.

Why couldn't my baby have been born in a hospital birthing room, under subdued lights, with Pachelbel's Canon piped in through speakers surrounded by welcoming bouquets of flowers: yellow and white roses, and tiny irises like little kingfishers, mixed with baby's breath? Angel began sucking angrily. His tiny hand opened and closed on air. I could feel the milk in my breasts trying to come in, and hated my own helplessness. I wished for sleep, for the gauze of home.

———

The world was dark when Consuelo led me back into it, the stars high in the sky and the moon chasing the wind. The doctor waited with me in the doorway while Consuelo went to get the Jeep and rouse El Chopo. She took Angel with her.

When they arrived back at the morgue, half an hour later, El Chopo—sweating *basuco* and *aguardiente*—said why couldn't women have babies at a more civilized hour of the night. Nidia, looking both sad and terrified, sat squeezed between Consuelo—who held Angel close, as if trying to decide whether she should give him back to me—and El Chopo. I knew better than to try to reach for my baby, even when he began to fuss, as if he sensed I was near.

Consuelo made Nidia get in the back of the Jeep, then told me to climb in beside her. She handed me my baby, who was dressed now in a nightgown and a pair of white knitted booties, and the doctor wished me *buena suerte* and reminded me to look up his cousins in Canada.

As we entered the plaza, the thought of being delivered back to my cell at the Hotel Viper filled me with gloom. I swept the stars with my eyes, the moon sinking over the empty square. The small boys had laid down their imaginary weapons and gone to sleep, and now there was nothing but fading moonlight on the stones, the slow splash of the fountain. The madman, if he had wanted to, could have filled each of his cups in the darkness, but that would have been too easy. Because then, having succeeded in what he'd spent a lifetime trying to achieve, this fullness, what would there have been left?

Consuelo got out at the entrance to the Hotel Viper, but told Nidia and me to stay in the Jeep. She instructed El Chopo to take us to the Hacienda la Florida. Nidia looked as if she would weep, but I thought only of Angel as we set off through that dirty city, loving him more with each bump, each swerve in the road; each second I spent with my son made me fall in love with my life and want it all, want everything. Even a future. For the first time since I had conceived this baby, I wanted both of us to live. But I was tired then, and allowed myself the luxury of hope. I sniffed Angel's silken hair, let him take my little finger in his hand, bury his face in between my breasts—each one bigger than his own head. How mountainous my breasts must have appeared in his eyes as he tried to nurse, the darkness rolling us away into the red dawn of another day. Nidia soon fell asleep, her head resting on my shoulder.

It was light by the time we reached the gates of the Black Widow's *finca*. Two heavily armed guards stood at attention beneath a cement pillar with a small airplane mounted on top, the plane that had flown the Black Widow's first load to America.

The guards opened the gates and waved us past. We drove through a landscape of man-made lakes and islands, and a maze of narrow roads overwhelmed by trees shedding their bright petals. I saw, too, what appeared to be a lion lying in the shade, tearing strips of meat off the remains of a gazelle. El Chopo said his sister collected animals from every part of the world and freed them on her land. She'd never been interested in protected species, but rather in species that protected themselves—lions, snakes, tigers, jaguars and, of course, human beings.

Beside a formal garden with a pergola and an aviary filled with birds of prey, we encountered a herd of miniature horses. At first sight, I thought they were rangy dogs. El Chopo pulled over and let the ponies, who seemed so loving and so trusting, snuffle and bunt the Jeep's door like affectionate puppies. I wondered how they survived, with tigers and lions roaming at large.

El Chopo drove on to the main house. I watched two jaguar kittens with oversized ears and whiskers romp in a flowerbed full of eye-searing poinsettias as Nidia helped me out of the Jeep, clutching my tiny bundle, who fought to keep from letting go of my nipple. A bronzed John Lennon, nude except for a pair of wire-rimmed glasses, a bullet hole the size of a man's fist through his chest and back, stared down at us from the top of a knoll in the centre of a walled garden full of statues. He looked hot and bewildered and far, far from home.

As we approached the house, a low-slung, sprawling country-style mansion with a red-tile roof, we passed a fountain where blood-coloured water issued from the core of a stone pineapple.

"La Fuente de Lágrimas—that's Consuelo's doing," El Chopo told me, seeing me recoil at this "fountain of tears." "She made the mistake of telling her mother, 'You can't get blood from a stone.' If I've learned one lesson in my life, it's never to tell the sister anything is impossible."

The pineapple, he said, was illuminated at night and also equipped with stereo speakers: after dark, "revolutionary tunes by Lennon himself" would issue from the lighted pineapple. I wondered if he was confusing Lennon with Lenin, and if they used the trusting horses' blood to supply the fountain. I shuddered, thinking, too, of the moon goddess on the slab next to me in the morgue, the shunt in her neck, her lifeblood draining away.

A black-haired Indian with a square, stocky body and sad night eyes let us into the house. He shook El Chopo's hand and Angel's baby finger. I don't know if I was supposed to be taken in by his manner, but it is hard not to feel kindly towards someone who takes an interest in your baby. He told me to call him Yepez and, pointing to a bench, to make myself at home, and then he began speaking to Angel in an Indian language while El Chopo conferred with two security guards. One of them, her jaw working overtime as she chewed a wad of gum, strolled over to examine my baby. She bent down, breathing cinnamon in his face, pulling his gown open with a buffed red fingernail so long it curled under at the end. She told me he was a very thin *bebé*, very homely and sickly looking. I felt like hitting her. Angel began to cry louder still, and Yepez gave him his little finger to suck. The woman frowned, as if she had never heard a baby cry, and offered him a piece of her chewing gum. I pushed her hand away.

Angel grew rigid in my arms—I didn't know a baby was capable of such fury. I stood up and began to walk with him, rocking him. Maybe he howled because he knew how I felt. I kissed the end of his nose, his perfect lips, drinking his tiny life. The only way I could stop his cries, I knew, was to put him back on my breast. He stopped screaming the moment I undid my dress and his mouth found what he had been missing.

El Chopo looked annoyed. The baby was a newborn, he said, almost apologetically, to one of the women, and hadn't learned how to behave. He told me and Nidia, who had started trembling the moment we set foot inside the house, to come with him, and we followed him down a wide corridor with doors opening to rooms on one side and a giant courtyard, with a swimming pool, tropical garden and waterfall, on the other. There was a library, a solarium, a private chapel and a bar, where a sign informed you to check your *pistolas* at the door. His sister's parties were famous, El Chopo said: something always *happened* when she entertained—like the time two French models and a German shepherd drowned in the pool. A tragedy was always an icebreaker, he told us. "It gets people talking."

We continued through the house and came out on a terrace overlooking fields that stretched to the horizon; this was where the old matriarch, the legend who controlled everything from the shadows, awaited us. She sat propped up in her wheelchair, her crumpled face fixed, in great sorrow, on the door; I recognized her at once from the velvet paintings. Her loose silk jacket was open to reveal the pistol she carried in a shoulder holster, her gold monogram inlaid in the mother-of-pearl handle.

She wore her long grey hair braided and coiled on top of her head like a nest of mating snakes. In her lap lay the carcass of a dead chicken. She had been plucking it with her teeth, and small white feathers stuck to her clothes, her hair, her face. Too frail to raise the bird as far as her lips, she lowered her face, took a feather between her teeth, pulled it out and began chewing. When El Chopo cleared his throat, she spat out a mouthful of white feathers and giggled, her small laughter like the ping of empty pop cans rolling away over stones.

A white rat with red eyes poked its head out of the Black Widow's armpit and sniffed the air. He slithered down her body and made for my leg. I clutched Angel, who refused to let go of my nipple, and took a step backwards, almost falling on Nidia, who hung back in the shadows, her eyes downcast, her body shaking harder than before.

El Chopo bent to retrieve the rat, then kissed the top of his sister's head. But she had noticed me and kept peering over his shoulder, and coughing, until finally she caught her breath and asked to see her daughter's baby, the one who had been born "with a full complement of limbs" (no way to correctly translate what she said, but it had sinister overtones). I thought she must have made a mistake in thinking my baby belonged to Consuelo, but I know now the old woman believed Angel had belonged to them right from the start. El Chopo told me to show her the child, but not to let her hold him. Her bones were so brittle they could break if anyone so much as hugged her.

She couldn't have reached for her gun even if she'd wanted to. This was the woman who lived for the death of others, and to make money. She was the one who would tell me if Angel would grow up to be wealthy or spend his life in jail. Or if he would grow up at all.

I took my nipple away from Angel, who went stiff in my arms. The old woman told El Chopo she wanted to see the baby's feet, and when I took off his little booties for her, she took a long time examining his toes. I put Angel to my breast again and his body relaxed. The Black Widow sighed, as if she were very pleased, and asked El Chopo where her daughter was. El Chopo said in La Ciudad, but that she would be coming to visit as soon as she could. The old woman asked where her son-in-law was, and why *he* never came to see her any more either.

"*En el norte,*" El Chopo replied. "*En canado. En Canadá.*"

"*Sí, cómo no,*" the Black Widow said sadly. Then she added how clumsy of Angel to end up in prison.

Clumsy? Unlucky, I thought, but clumsy? I could see how her mind worked, like Consuelo's. "*He couldn't have been paying attention, otherwise such a thing would not have happened.*"

The Black Widow closed her eyes, her chin dropped onto her chest and she began snoring. El Chopo reached to remove the feathers from the corners of her mouth. The white rat poked its head out from under her arm again, plucked a feather from El Chopo's hand and scuttled back into her dress. This was my first and last view of the Black Widow, though she continued to control my life from the shadowy kingdom of her failing mind.

chapter twenty

If my room at the Hotel Viper had been meant to demoralize me, break me down, my room at Hacienda la Florida softened me up, indulged me, prepared me for what I was to become—the person portrayed by the press, that is—a woman "seduced into a life of debauchery and drugs." La Reina de la Cocaína, La Madre Sin Corazón. I only know I did what I did in order to survive, and when you have nothing, sometimes you will take anything. Just to have anything—that can be enough.

If you deprive a person of beauty, lock her in a bug-infested cell, feed her sardines and pork gristle and then give her the opposite, wouldn't what I did be understandable? Not forgivable, maybe, but understandable? At Hacienda la Florida my vices were pampered so attentively they began to feel like virtues.

Pile, Jr. told the court when I arrived at the hacienda I was in shock, but shock was what I'd been in since the day I'd been taken hostage. This felt different. This felt true and clear and sweet—like love, when you're climbing the stairs, key in hand, and he or she is waiting for you in a room, before the night train comes stumbling past and you remember that love is the one lesson you never got right.

That afternoon it felt like love—the walls of my air-conditioned room the muted colours of corsages. Angel's cot stood in a sun-drenched window framed with flaming bougainvillea and overlooking a terraced garden.

Then there was *my* bed: an antique four-poster with linen sheets and a thick, lavender-smelling quilt for nights when the temperature dropped. Bowls of autumn-coloured orchids had been arranged on glass tables beneath black lampshades mounted on silver globes, next to chairs uphol-stered in purple velvet and treasures made of pre-Columbian gold in antique cases. I had a pitcher of purified water, and a bowl filled with papayas and mangoes. There was a bureau full of clean baby clothes, and a cupboard crammed with stylish dresses, hats, shoes and tasty lingerie, with shirred edging and tiny heart-shaped buttons of pure silk, for me.

I never believed love would last, but that first day in my beautiful room I didn't know what lay ahead of me; I just remember feeling . . . hopeful. One of the women who interviewed me when I was arrested asked if I'd ever known the meaning of hope. I didn't try to explain how my captors had given me hope, then taken it away, or how I was con-ditioned to find pleasure even more unbearable than pain.

My life took on shades of the film *Caligula*, in which any kind of tenderness was followed by a scene of such terrible mutilation you found yourself cringing whenever two people embraced, anticipating the hurt to come. As Frenchy would have said, hope rhymes with dope—you got any?

Nidia arrived with meals meant to tempt me—four, sometimes five times a day. She said I need only ask and whatever I wanted would be prepared for me. It is not true, as one of the tabloids reported, that I dined on the flesh of peasants (Nidia tried to force pheasant on me once, and wild peacock—the Black Widow's bodyguards, on their days off, cruised the island in their cars, spraying submachine gunfire at the peacocks in the bushes for target practice), nor that the Black Widow kept virgins chained in dungeons, fattened them on fermented mare's milk until they grew plump, then slit their veins and bathed in their blood to ensure eternal youth. I suppose people heard about the pineapple spouting blood and embellished the story.

Nidia worried that if I didn't eat, my milk would dry up, but Angel seemed happy enough as long as I didn't try to take my nipple away. I know I wasn't producing *enough* milk, but nothing else I did, other than nursing him, seemed to satisfy him. We played "This Little Piggie Went to Market" on the bed, and even then he cried until his face was red. We took baths (the first time Nidia showed me how to bathe him, I thought, I'll *never* get the hang of that!), and even after I stopped being afraid that I'd drop him and he'd drown, he still screamed. He was my life—it sounds strange, but I would have given up anything at that time just to make him smile. I would have given my own life, even then.

His crying was the only thing wrong with my life, other than the fact that I had no appetite and my hair hadn't grown back. That's how deluded I had become: I thought if Angel would only stop crying, my life would be . . . close to perfect.

One evening not long after I had arrived, Consuelo came with a gift: the emerald-encrusted coke spoon I'd seen in the window of the *joyería* in the City of Orchids. She said she wanted me to have it as a reminder of the night I'd given birth, but when I held it in my hand, all I could think of was the shoeshine boy eating thin soup with his fingers and the rich man throwing money in my face and the doctor's warm hand—the first warmth I'd felt in such a long time, before the morgue: God Sends Nothing We Can't Bear.

Consuelo fastened the spoon around my neck on a gold chain; it was the most garish piece of jewellery I'd ever worn next to my skin. She also gave me an envelope containing a hundred-dollar bill, an X-acto knife blade and a flap of paper. When I opened the paper (one hand was always busy holding Angel's head or wiping the sick away from his mouth, but I had got quite good at doing everything one-handed), a lot of the cocaine spilled into his hair.

I was horrified—I picked the larger flakes, the pure mother-of-pearl shale, out of his hair and blew the rest off his scalp. I felt I had contaminated something pure, someone innocent. When Consuelo left, I chopped up one of the larger flakes and snorted it through the rolled-up bill; I could smell his baby-scalp smell mixed in with the smell of money and drugs, and it made me feel afraid. Up until that moment, I had believed nothing could have been stronger than my new love for my child.

I stashed the flap of paper in a drawer, but I should have known from the days when Vernal and I had coke in the house: once you know it's there, you can never forget about it. When I couldn't get to sleep that night, I decided I'd cut myself another bump. Just a taste, a small one.

I don't know if anyone would have acted differently had they been in my place. It has been more than ten years since I've used cocaine, but even today, or whenever I think about it, my mouth waters and my palms start to sweat. Somewhere deep in my old brain there must be a memory stored from the first time I did a line and cocaine became my fate, my sweet annihilating angel. But you never understand the nature of the drug—you only understand the nature of the sorrow.

They say one line is too many, a kilo isn't enough; I took another whiff and, an hour later, one more, and then a couple of pick-me-ups when I began to come down. Angel was more restless than usual that night; when I nursed him, I thought I could hear his heart racing. I worried that the cocaine I'd snorted had passed into my milk, so I stopped feeding him, but that made him fuss all the more. In the end, I let him nurse until he fell asleep with his lips locked on my nipple.

Each day Consuelo brought another flap of paper, and I kept getting high; one night she cooked up some cocaine and handed me a glass pipe, and I had my first taste of *basuco*. Each time I inhaled, I rode a bicycle into the stars—then coasted in a paralytic state, plotting the exact coordinates of eternity, wondering where, along the way, I'd left my mind.

Somewhere in that universe of exploding stars and bicycle parts, I found my friend Daisy. She said she was from

Colombia (she said it like a warning), pronounced her name "Day-see," and wore cobra stilettos, which made her seem taller than she was, a red T-shirt and sprayed-on jeans. Daisy wanted to model my lingerie, and took off all her clothes, but even afterwards, when we were naked together, she kept those cobra heels strapped on.

It only happened once: I lay naked, except for the coke spoon around my neck, on the bed with Daisy, and Consuelo took photographs. Daisy could be sweet and rough, and I liked her touching me the way I needed to be touched. I didn't think anything of it until the prosecutor produced the photographs to show what kind of a mother I really was. A lesbian, crack-addicted one. All you could see of Angel was one arm, his little hand knotted into a fist, poking out of his cot. It is the only photograph of him I possess, and you can't even see his face, can't see whether he was crying. But he *wasn't* crying, I remember, because I wouldn't have been ignoring him if he'd needed my milk. Just for the record. Somehow, writing about it now, I sound defensive, but with Daisy back then, it wasn't anything warped or perverted, only a sort of tenderness and, I suppose, the drugs. When you smoke *basuco*, all you want to do is have your nipples and clit sucked. Well, that's not true. You *want* sex, but first you'd rather have one more toke. I *did* worry that the drug would contaminate my milk, not like the prosecutor said: she said I never gave it a thought.

My baby was not a drug addict. He was not neglected. As a mother, you know it at the time. You know if you are neglecting your child.

part six / annihilating angel

Cuándo se danza con diablo,
No se da un paso falso.

(When you're dancing with the devil,
Make sure you get the steps right.)

—*Popular song*

chapter twenty-one

Death Clinic, Heaven Valley State Facility for Women

You are not allowed to talk in a place where conversation is prohibited. You should not start rumours in order to put other inmates' or prison officials' minds into confusion.
—Inmate Information Handbook

When you're going through hell, keep going.
—Winston Churchill

After they failed to hang Frenchy, Rainy spent her days trying to make her *gain* weight: she wanted Frenchy to get so fat, she said, she wouldn't fit in the Chair. If she survives a third attempt on her life, Rainy is certain they will grant her a stay of execution. I wouldn't be so sure if I were Rainy. The state is pretty mad at Frenchy for not dying the first two times.

I tell my counsellor Frenchy deserves a break. Why does anyone have the right to put her through the ordeal all over again? Mrs. Dykstra just sucks in her cheeks, purses her lips and taps her finger on the *Inmate Information Handbook*. "One, it's in the book, that's why; and two, we follow the book, that's why." She looks at me, as if to say everything I need to know is in the book in front of me. In black. On white.

She glances at the clock. My time is up. I don't make a move to go. "And three," she says, beginning to sound exasperated, "because."

I sit there, staring at the Velcro fasteners on my shoes, thinking how long it's been—more than ten years, at least—since I've owned a pair of laces.

"Do I have to spell it for you?" she asks. "Because. B-E-C-O . . . " I leave before she has a chance to embarrass herself any further.

"I'll spell *because* for you," says Frenchy when I get back to my house. "B-E-C-A-U-S-E. Bitch Eats Candy Apple Until She Explodes."

Frenchy's chosen the Chair because she's running out of options. Her only other choices are lethal injection or the gas chamber. She says she picked the Chair because it's yellow, and yellow is the one colour that makes her feel alive. Rainy's seen the Chair and says it's not yellow any more—it's brown like a Teflon frying pan when the grease has been burned into it.

But Frenchy wants to fry, and once she's made up her mind, she shuts Rainy and me out every time we try to get close to her on the subject. Still, Rainy buys her zuzus and wham whams at the commissary, and Coke Classic; she hoards her dessert every night, her bread, cookies, Twinkies, whatever else she can scrounge, and saves it for her friend.

Frenchy started gaining weight, slowly at first, and then noticeably. She went from 110 pounds to 133 in less than three weeks. I didn't tell Rainy Frenchy'd have to weigh 250 for low before she'd be too fat for the Chair. Trying to make Frenchy gain back all the weight she'd lost trying to get so thin they wouldn't be able to hang her gave Rainy a goal, something to look forward to. She'd watch Frenchy step on the scales every day after her shower, a smile cutting her face in two when Frenchy stepped off again.

Rainy and I both saved our doughnuts for Frenchy. Frenchy is addicted to doughnuts; I've often heard her say she would kill for one. Then Rainy tells her to shut up, because they write down everything we say and it will go on her record. It won't look good for her in the future.

When Officer Gluckman chains me up to take me back to my house, and after a trusty has finished her search for drugs, I ask her a riddle. "How did the little moron break out of jail?"

Officer Gluckman says that if I expect a serious answer, I've got something else coming.

"He broke a doughnut in half. Two halves make a whole, and he crawled out the hole," I say anyway.

Officer Gluckman is probably still trying to figure out how I plan to escape through a doughnut hole. Apart from coming up with new ways to make my life miserable, she doesn't have a whole lot to think about.

I ask Rainy the same riddle. "What's a moron?" she says.

"It's what I do with the tomato sauce on my noodles," I go. "Put more on."   .

Every Wednesday we get spaghetti for lunch. I like lots (*lots*) of sauce on my noodles. Rainy puts the noodles in one section of her metal tray, sauce in another. She spoons on sauce, eats a couple of spoonfuls, puts more sauce on, eats a couple more spoonfuls, spoons more on . . . .

She says that's the right way to eat spaghetti. I say, "Well, I like a lot of sauce covering my noodles." She says, "But that's not the way to eat it." I say, "You eat your spaghetti the way you want, and I'll eat mine the way I want."

In the chow hall it seems Rainy and I always get into these life-or-death issues. Rainy argues that although she is accused of killing her twins, they were born joined, and as far as she is concerned, that is only killing one person.

The whole point is, she says, no one understands what she went through. To have these joined-together twins who screamed all the time because she couldn't afford to have them separated, to decide to put an end to their misery— did the jury think that was an *easy* thing for any mother to do? And then to walk away?

"What was I supposed to do?" she says. It's already been done, I tell her.

I think Rainy expected a medal at least, and her mug shot on the cover of *Parent and Child*. Instead, she got twin death sentences.

Rainy says she has profound feelings of love for me, and for Frenchy. But she never loved anyone else in her life, except for her twins, and she hates every one of the guards, right down to the squeak of their rubber-soled shoes. When Jesus said love thy neighbour, I don't think he was talking about people it is easy to love, I tell her. This must have hurt Rainy's feelings, because she never expressed her love for me again until the day Frenchy received her third date certain. Rainy says only one thing is certain: it'll be the hottest date Frenchy's ever going to go out on.

The announcement of Frenchy's impending death came, as it had done both times before, after her death warrant had been signed by the state governor. She greeted the news with a shrug. She was positive she was going to "get hers" this time—it would be third time lucky—and she had even written her own headline. She hoped it would be in every newspaper across the country.

She asked us to tell the reporters this: "Le Ethel Opaline Lafitte, Frenchy to those who give a shit, said goodbye to this cruel world, and to Laverne, whom she never stops missing, aged thirty-five years old, on April 1, 1998." She wanted this information to be published in the Obituaries section of her hometown paper. I say they probably won't print "shit" in a family newspaper.

"Then fuck them and the train they rode in on," Frenchy says.

I tell her, if she *is* turned off this time, she'll be front-page news, or at least front-page news in the Living section. She won't get stuck like the rest of the world in Classified Ads, Births and Deaths, or worse, in the Entertainment section, where I've seen a lot of celebrities end up. If I were a famous person, I'd be choked to find my death announce-ment next to an ad for a wet T-shirt contest at the cross-dressing hangwoman's roadhouse.

A death warrant is a single-page document bordered in black. Very final and official-looking, written in legalese so when you read it you won't understand a word of what is about to happen to you. They write it this way on pur-pose, because obscurity makes no emotional impact. Pile, Jr. can, in good conscience, have me sign a statement say-ing, "I hereby give and convey to you, all and singular, my estate and interest, right, title, claim and advantage of and in my life, together with all its blood, flesh, organs and parts hitherto undisclosed and all rights and advan-tages therein with full power to electrocute and otherwise to terminate the same by hanging, gassing, shooting or lethally injecting the same away with or without removal of said organs, anything hereinbefore or hereinafter," when what he is really saying is, "The state is going to kill you."

Frenchy has kept her previous death warrants as mementos. She sticks them on her wall with spitballs. Each bears the state seal and has been signed by the governor, whose signature is in turn witnessed by an official whose John Henry has become a straight line trailing off into a wisp from having to sign so many death warrants, day after day. He (or she) probably didn't even read any further than the first *whereas*, let alone the name of the person who had been sentenced to die. He was probably thinking about the lamb chop he was going to have for lunch. "WHEREAS Le

Ethel Opaline Lafitte, Frenchy to those who give a shit, did on the eighteenth day of September, 1982, murder Huey Troy Earl; WHEREAS *Le Ethel Opaline Lafitte* was found guilty of murder in the first degree and was sentenced to death on the eleventh day of March, 1984 . . ."

Once the warrant has been signed, the prison superintendent is notified and guards come to fetch Frenchy from her cell. The first couple of times she'd had no forewarning, but had been hauled to the warden of care and treatment's office, where the warrant had been read aloud. After this she'd been told she could phone a lawyer or a family member, if she had anyone left who would accept a collect call. Frenchy only had us, and we didn't have telephone privileges.

This time, Officers Robinson and Freedman come to get her, but Officer Robinson breaks down and starts crying before she's found the right key to unlock Frenchy's door. Frenchy knows right away why they've come for her.

She's never had any complaints about the dancehall, where she gets a new mattress and a pillow in a case, and the cell gets a fresh coat of paint before she arrives, two-tone—light grey over green, the line right at eye level when you are standing at attention beside your bed and they come to inspect it to see if you've folded the corners of your sheets properly. She gets a steel toilet and a steel sink, and everything stays very clean because her cell is swept and mopped every day. Every other day her floor gets a fresh coat of wax.

Frenchy asks if she can say goodbye to us this time before she goes, and this chokes Officer Freedman, too. I wonder if there will be tears when they come for Rainy, or for me? It is rare for a woman to survive what Frenchy has been through, and some of the guards feel, like us, that despite the rules, Frenchy should have been granted clemency.

Frenchy tries to comfort the guards, which makes it worse for them, because *they* are supposed to be in charge. Only Officer Gluckman remains unmoved. She walks by, dragging her Talking Nano along my bars to make sure I hear my baby crying for me. "I'm sick. Feed me." The voice gets more feeble every day, and I think if there is a merciful God, the batteries will croak and I won't have to listen to the voice I've buried deep inside. If he doesn't die soon, I think, I will kidnap him and put him out of his misery.

Officer Robinson and Officer Freedman aren't about to let Officer Gluckman know they are upset, or, in guard language, have lost control of the situation, so they take off, leaving Frenchy to dictate her obit and her famous headline: "Frenchy Fries."

My mother sends me a magazine article about a couple in India who took their crippled six-year-old daughter to a remote river and threw her in. No one would want a crippled bride, they said. They watched her struggle and finally drown, but felt she was better off. My mother says you'd never get away with anything like that in *this* country.

She says she sympathizes with the parents. "There were times I thought of leaving you in a snowbank, or on the beach, buried up to your neck in the sand. But then the mood would pass, and I was always glad I had decided to take you home. You were a baby, helpless, I could have done *anything*. I'm just glad I raised you before child abuse was invented."

Frenchy's previous death warrants were publicized by a news release issued shortly after the governor signed, and Frenchy has kept those clippings, also, stuck to her wall. Frenchy says seeing her name in the paper makes her feel "like somebody." Knowing that the whole country will be reading about her execution over their morning coffee almost makes dying worth it.

I tell Frenchy, the kind of person who can enjoy a cup of coffee while reading that justice has been done would spit his coffee out if he had to be there in person: the volts of electricity shooting through you, making your body leap and twitch; your eyeballs popping out of their sockets; your face, fingers, legs and toes left hideously distorted. Your brain temperature approaches the boiling point of water, and your body starts smouldering. In some cases, your skin even turns black. Frenchy hopes it *does* happen, so her "ugly spot" ends up the same colour as the rest of her body.

Frenchy says she's going to order stuffed olives, lobster salad, fried chicken, french fries, "killer" garlic bread and New York cheesecake for her last meal. She's going to ask for a second helping of everything on her plate before she goes so there'll be that much more shit for the guards to wipe up. But the guards don't clean anything—they make prisoners do the dirty work. That's how Rainy knows the Chair isn't yellow.

———

They took Frenchy out of her cell in the middle of the night. They didn't even give her a chance to say goodbye. Why? Rules, that's why. Or as Rainy says now, every time she gets the opportunity, "*Because*. Bitch Eats Candy Apple Until She Explodes."

Two days before she was executed, Frenchy sent a kite saying she'd been sent to a head-shrinker. He asked her if she had ever believed she was a secret agent of God, what century we were in and the name of the current president. She said she must have got all three questions right, because the shrink declared her sane enough to die. State law forbids the execution of a woman who is insane, and if a prisoner is determined to have become insane on death row, she is spared execution until such time as "mental health is restored."

Who among us is sane enough for execution?

Officer Gluckman says she saw Frenchy die, live, just after two. She was rebroadcast on the seven o'clock news, and again at ten o'clock and on the local news at eleven. Officer Gluckman says even the replays were hard to watch. She got tired just trying to imagine how the guard must have felt, the one who had to refasten the power lines to the Chair after the first surge of electricity, which seared Frenchy's flesh but didn't kill her.

I didn't see Rainy until the morning after. Frenchy had asked Rainy to be there "for immoral support." Frenchy said she knew what to expect. She told Rainy she would signal her if she found the ordeal worse than she had anticipated. She would make a fist.

Rainy wants me to write about Frenchy's execution as she remembers it, starting with the guard taking a long stick that looks like a lollipop with the word Ready on it and raising it to the back window of the chamber as a signal to the warden. At 2:00 the first jolt of electricity shoots through her body, which breaks from the straps that are holding her to the Chair. The electrode on the shaved part of her leg bursts from the strap holding it in place and catches on fire.

A cloud of greyish smoke and sparks pour out from under the hood covering her face. Her body straightens and quivers, and Rainy smells burnt clothing and flesh in the witness room and wishes she could open a window. She can even taste the smoke, like Frenchy's a T-bone on a barbecue and Rainy's standing too close. But there are no windows in this dancehall. The current stops, and Frenchy falls back in the Chair.

Two croakers go into chamber to pronounce her dead. One puts his stethoscope on her heart, turns around and nods to the warden and the witnesses, the usual sign that a person is dead. Rainy's eyes are still dry, and she's mad at herself for not crying because she knows it will go on her record: "Failure to react to friend's health alteration." But then it's okay that she isn't weeping, because the croaker is explaining that he meant the opposite—he has found a heartbeat. The second doctor examines Frenchy and confirms it. Frenchy is still alive.

A guard reattaches the electrode to Frenchy's leg and fixes the straps she's broken. This takes a bunch of time, Rainy says, and while he's making repairs and setting up the power lines again, Frenchy starts breathing. Her chest rises evenly. A gush of saliva oozes from her face, dribbles out from under the black hood. There's blood in the spit and it stains her white T-shirt, and Rainy says I should write how much the colour white suited Frenchy, even though she would never wear it by choice because she was prejudiced against it.

Her breathing comes slow and regular. But then a second jolt of current is sent into Frenchy's body. The stench of burning flesh causes one reporter to toss his cookies (another Rainyism), and more and more smoke shoots out of Frenchy's head and legs. Rainy sees Frenchy's hands gripping the Chair, and wonders if she is trying to make a fist to show that being electrocuted is worse than she'd expected it to be.

Again the croakers go in to examine her. Everything is out of control; the warden says something must be wrong with the generator and the guard's eyes are tearing and Rainy's shouting that they're all fucking killers, even though she knows it won't look good on her record. Frenchy's lawyer screams for clemency; Rainy says she's never heard a lawyer scream like that before, unless he hasn't been paid. "This is cruel and unusual punishment. Communicate that to the governor," he keeps raving.

But the governor won't interfere. He's mad because so much taxpayer's money has already been wasted trying to kill Frenchy he's afraid he won't get re-elected. Rainy says she's in tears now, and hopes her counsellor notices and writes it down in her report. Then she forgets all about her counsellor and gets ready for the third jolt, Frenchy's "third time lucky." And once again her head and leg boil, and the room fills up with smoke, and sparks shoot from her body like stars. This time the croakers stand gaping at Frenchy's charred and smouldering body, with her skin falling off her bones like a steamed chicken's. The time is 2:16 p.m. Rainy says she knew because the lights dimmed and the train was right on schedule. And Rainy knew Frenchy for sure must have rode the lightning over the wall this time, because when that train whistled she didn't even blink.

Prison time is chicken bones. Something to be sucked clean. That was Frenchy. More power to you, girl.

chapter twenty-two

The first time Daisy brought her son to my room, I thought he looked sadly ugly compared to my Angel. He was small for his age, and Daisy said he hadn't gained much weight since the day he'd come out of her, "fighting all the way."

She had named her baby after his father, with whom she'd played Space Invaders at the Hotel Bacata in Bogotá, and who'd shown her enough love to break her heart forever. She printed his name for me on the back of a cigarette package, as if a name, once written, was evidence of existence. When I called her baby Elijas (accent on the second syllable), she corrected me. The name, she said, was Alias.

I told Daisy I had named my son after his father too, but before I could explain Alias let out a high-pitched wail, which startled Angel; he began crying again. He hardly slept any more, and I had taken to doing lines all night to stay awake and keep him company.

After nursing her baby, Daisy put him in Angel's cot and said she hoped the two *nenitos* would make friends. It didn't seem as if babies needed friends, only—and always—their mothers. I told Daisy I wished Angel would develop other interests—interests other than me—and she laughed and said when that happened, I'd wish he was a baby again because a baby couldn't roll over, sit up, run away or talk back. A baby just sucked you dry.

When Alias continued to fuss, Daisy picked him up and scolded him for not working harder at making friends. Scolding him didn't stop him crying, so Daisy covered his tiny mouth with her hand. The screams oozed out between her fingers like bread dough when you try to close it in your fist. You can't contain a scream. I offered to hold him—this was the closest I ever came to seeing Daisy lose her temper—but when he turned his head towards my breast and began to grope, I quickly passed him back to his mother. Daisy fed him again, and then left the room with both boys and put them in the bath.

I stayed out of their sight, snorted a couple of rails, then cooked up the rest of the gram and smoked it. Daisy watched our babies while they splashed around making noises like newborn killer whales, and afterwards, when she'd dried them off and dressed them again, I had to argue with her about the clothes she'd chosen for Angel to wear. I never saw Alias in anything but layers of clothing—woollen sweaters and knee socks and booties that covered his tiny legs. I even accused her of having *bathed* him with his clothes on.

Daisy wanted to show me the walled garden, and went to find Yepez. Yepez, I could tell, was smitten with Daisy and the squeak of her cobra high heels. He offered her a piece of his chocolate bar, which was melting faster than he could eat it, before unlocking the gates to the Garden of Statues for us.

I stood for a moment, looking out over tangles of orchids and flitting clouds of blue and orange butterflies that filled the garden where Our Lady of Perpetual Help kept watch over the men and women, most of whom, with the exception of Lennon, had died for their country in the United States' war on drugs.

We laid our babies side by side on a carpet of tiny orange petals that had fallen from a *guaiac* tree, next to a clump of yellow orchids. A light breeze turned the orchids' physical similarity to bees into the frenetic appearance of a swarm, a mime show in motion. A swarm of real bees attacked the flowers repeatedly.

Daisy had brought along a textbook called *The King's English As She Is Spoken*. She wanted me to help her study English, because one day she hoped to visit *los Estados Unidos*. Yepez didn't leave the garden right away, but instead stood close by, pretending not to listen to us prac-tising *locuciones útiles* (useful phrases), such as "Over the hill to the poorhouse go I," and "I say, your skin is bone white, like an English teacup!" He was reading the plaques at the base of the statues that informed viewers how many bullets each victim had taken, and how "interested parties" would find the entry and exit wounds clearly marked on each body. Yepez kept making cow eyes at Daisy. After a while, Daisy closed her textbook and leaned back against the statue of Pablo Escobar Gavira, the Godfather, "who died trying to make the world a safer place for crime."

We sat quietly watching our babies, who spit up every so often and kicked their feet. When Alias kicked Angel in the shins, Daisy said her *berroquito* (courageous little one) was going to play soccer for the City of Orchids when he grew up, that he was "already practising." I thought Angel showed great restraint when he didn't kick him back.

Angel had a habit of balling his hands into fists and pummelling the air, a good sign, Daisy said—if you didn't fight back against life, it would quickly kill you. It would kill those who did fight, as well as the very good and the very gentle. If you were very bad, you could be sure it would kill you too, but it would be in no particular hurry.

"They take over your life if you let them," Daisy said. "*Los muertos.*"

Daisy had watched many people die. She thought maybe it was the death of others that made her own life seem so very long. She'd asked her old grandmother, who hadn't moved from her bed since the blackness had begun eating her, "When do you know you are ready to die?" "When you can no longer make a fist," her grandmother had said.

Daisy finally got up and went to speak to Yepez, and after that he scurried away, locking the gate behind him. Not long after, Nidia came with a tray, which she left outside the gate. We had to reach our hands through the iron bars if we wanted the drinks, sapodillas, and the *churros* (little doughnut sticks).

While we ate, and fed our babies again, I asked Daisy how long she planned to go on nursing Alias. I said Angel seemed to fuss more after he took my milk; I felt I wasn't producing enough to satisfy him. Daisy said she would breast-feed for as long as possible, because once Alias had been weaned, and if he wasn't still too sickly, he would be sent to La Ciudad, like all the other boys born to Las Blancas, to work as a *sicario*.

The freebase tokes were starting to wear off, so I already felt disconnected and edgy. When I said the thought of my tiny, innocent son growing up to become a teenage thug, assassinating people from the back of a motorcycle, was unthinkable, she laughed and said I didn't have anything to worry about because my baby would never become one of the *desechables*, the disposables, the born to be used once, then thrown away. Hadn't I seen the way Consuelo's face softened when she looked at him?

If I am honest with myself, I resented Consuelo's affection for my child; she treated him as if he were her own. On the other hand, I knew his survival depended upon her love, so found myself encouraging the bond forming between them.

We laid our babies down again—Angel fully naked and Alias dressed like a tiny Arctic explorer—their earnest limbs jerking in unison, as if they were practising running away. I asked Daisy if she stayed at the hacienda by choice, and she said she hadn't thought about it, but that she was treated better here than she would be treated anywhere

else. She had made so much money for Las Blancas, covering loads and never getting caught, that she now received
special favours, including freedom of the house, a place in
Consuelo's bed and the chance to make friends with
Consuelo's guests, like me. A place in Consuelo's bed? I
didn't question Daisy about this, but it answered a lot of my
own questions about Consuelo. I said I did not consider
myself a guest; guests were free to come and go as they
pleased, but a doctor in the City of Orchids had told me no
one ever got away from Las Blancas except in a coffin.

Daisy simply shrugged and said, "Why would anyone
want to get away from Las Blancas?" Alias had fallen asleep
with orange blossoms settling onto his face and in his hair,
and Daisy said this was his favourite spot in the garden,
here under the *guaiac* tree. Alias could spend hours watching the petals fall, would open his mouth as if trying to
catch one on the end of his tongue or bat them away with
his little hands until the game wore him out. She'd never
seen him as happy as when he slept under this tree, the
weight of blossoms on his sleeping eyes like coins.

Daisy knew the names of all the trees that grew at the
Hacienda la Florida—the scarlet *ceiba*, with its brilliant
japonica-like blooms, the yellow, daffodil-like *araguaney*.
She pointed to the far side of the walled garden, to a tree not
unlike one I'd noticed growing in the courtyard outside my
window—this was a very dangerous tree, she said, the *borrachio*, or "drunken" tree, the source of a drug that caused victims to lose their will and their memory, a voodoo powder
called *burundanga*, used in prophecy and witchcraft. I must
not go near that tree or else I might get *burundanguiando*. In

rural Colombia, she said, where she grew up, the tree was grown in every front yard as a warning.

When Yepez came to the gate and called Daisy's name, we trundled our babies back to the air-conditioned sanctuary of my room. Daisy repeated she didn't know *why* anyone would want to leave this life at Hacienda la Florida as she cut out four lines on the table, did two herself and left the others for me. She said the only thing she'd ever liked about cocaine was the smell of it; she didn't know why she bothered using it. She said she should have learned her lesson the first time she tried it and everything exploded in her face.

Daisy became talkative and outgoing when she got high. She told me that when was eleven years old, and her sister was eight, they'd been abducted from their parents' house in the country and taken to the city of Medellín, to a fortified mansion belonging to a famous drug lord. He had been kind to her—not like many of the other young girls, including her sister, who were killed and dumped at the side of the road when they were no longer useful—and had even paid for the operation when she was badly burned smoking the drugs (skin from her fleshy bum had to be used to rebuild her cheeks). "Now if you kiss my cheek, you kiss my ass," she liked to joke.

"I was one of the fortunate ones," she told me. "He took me back to my village [she pronounced it 'bee-lidge'] so they could return for me another time."

Her parents, she said, were given *basuco*—their reward for not protesting when their daughters were kidnapped. Now her whole community had collapsed as a result of *basuco* addiction. Livestock had starved, people killed each other, crops rotted on the vine. No one in her village lived for any other reason than the hope that their daughter would be abducted again and they'd get more drugs.

A year after she'd been returned to the village, she was taken again by the same drug lord. He had changed, she said, and now he wanted her to have sex with boys almost young enough to cut their gums on her body, and with old men whose gums bled when they sucked her breasts.

When the drug lord went away for a long time, to *el norte*, Consuelo liberated Daisy and set her up as a cover girl, posing as a tourist on a plane that was used to smuggle contraband. Meanwhile Daisy met her baby's father, who kept her in a hotel room, looking after her, even when she got pregnant. "Alias gave me a chance to make a new life for myself. I was very young to be starting out, and he didn't want me carrying in my *chocha* (where Consuelo had told her to stash the drugs) because I was *embarazada* (pregnant). That's the kind of man he was. We both ate a big meal of *bolas* (elongated condoms stuffed with cocaine) before we got on our plane. Alias said you carry it in your stomach— it's the one place they can't see into with their flashlights.

"We flew from Tranquilandia to Panama City. Alias said he liked that route because in Panama you didn't have to make payoffs at immigration; you could bribe the other, less corrupt officials. By the time we got to our hotel, one of the capsules had lodged itself at the entrance to his large intestine. He was in a lot of pain, and sent me to the *farmacia* for a *tónico*.

"I didn't go to the *farmacia*, I went to the bar. I had two choices: take him to the hospital, where they would have

X-rayed him and found the *bolas* and sent him to prison, or watch him die. I had to decide which would be the worse fate: losing the product or death. Las Blancas has a saying: 'If you succeed, send money. If you fail, don't come home.'"

When Daisy got back to the hotel room, Alias had made the decision for her. "He blew himself out through the stomach so no one would find the drugs and I wouldn't get into trouble. That's the kind of man he was."

Daisy went back alone, with the money she'd made from selling her share of the drugs, to face Consuelo. Consuelo gave her another chance. "I think she felt badly for the way her husband had used me," Daisy said.

"Her husband?" I asked. "The drug lord?"

"*El más famoso en el país*," said Daisy, who sounded surprised I didn't know. The most famous man in the country. "Angel Corazón Gaviria."

Alias had developed a rash and wouldn't eat. Daisy told me Consuelo was worried that he might have an amoeba in his intestines and had put him on a special diet. I told Daisy the rash might have more to do with the wool she dressed him in.

Consuelo had brought me another envelope after dinner, and I cut out four big lines—twice my usual amount— and snorted it. Then Daisy introduced me to the pleasures of smoking *mejoral*, and we became *paralizados* together.

After she left I cut out another line, even though, sensibly, I didn't need it, then sat in a chair by the window, with Angel in my arms, until the morning light began to fill the sky. There is nothing sensible about cocaine. I had a love-hate relationship with the drug: if there was any in the room I couldn't let it go unused, but the minute I'd done a line I wanted to be straight again, and then I'd do another line, and another, until it was all gone and I found some sort of peace in coming down. I realized, too, that I'd begun to think less and less about my captivity, that every line I snorted, every base toke I took, helped obliterate my life.

I kissed each of Angel's tiny, perfect toes, kissed his eyes, his earlobes, his fists, his soft baby-head. I lifted his nightgown and ran my fingers over the little hollow in the centre of his chest, stroking it, burying my nose in it. He made a gurgling sound, like the pineapple in the fountain when the blood gushed out of it.

That night I dreamed I stood once again inside the gates of the Mountjoy Cemetery, watching the guards in their fake-fur-trimmed jackets standing over Angel's grave, stamping their feet to keep warm. I picked up a handful of earth, threw it high into the air. And as the earth rained down on me, I buried Angel Corazón Gaviria for good.

chapter twenty-three

I must have dozed off watching the moon hike in the branches of the *borrachio* tree, because I dreamed Jesus and I were in bed together, having a threesome with the Virgin of Perpetual Help, who had wet black skin. From that dream I moved to another, where I climbed a sheer wet rock and kept slipping backwards. When I got to the top (I can't explain how I got there—it's the way dreams work), an old woman with a disembowelled goat was waiting for me. I panicked because I realized I'd dropped my baby somewhere on the mountain during my climb and couldn't remember how to get back down to him.

I had enough cocaine in my veins to make a vampire dizzy. My nerves had grown used to keeping odd hours, but that morning they had decided to go out dancing, and nothing I could do, except another line, would make them sit the next one out.

Daisy came with Alias around lunchtime and said she hadn't slept all night, that Alias had been coughing up more of the "black stuff." I saw fear in the corners of her mouth, a twitch in her cheek as she spoke of the trouble she had getting Alias to swallow the cow's udder Consuelo had prescribed for him.

I picked up Angel and tried to make him nurse, but my ears were ringing and the feel of his lips on my nipples made me tense; I told Daisy I might be getting sick too, that maybe I'd caught whatever Alias was suffering from. She didn't think so. "Two people don't get sick the same way," she said.

After she left, I finished off my gram and didn't move from my chair again, but sat gazing at my baby. He didn't cry as much any more, as if he was getting used to his life. I'd even swear I could see his whole body try to kick a smile onto his face whenever he saw me looking at him. I don't know why a mother should feel so flattered about being adored by her own child, but the way Angel smiled at me made me feel as if I were full of God. I bent and kissed him all over his tiny, serious body; I wanted to drink each minute of his life, to wrap my lips around the melting sweetness of each breath he took. For a moment, he was all the drug I needed. I breathed him in, I got so high sniffing him I felt I was talking to angels. I even worried I might overdose on the scent of him, that's how good it felt.

The next day Yepez let us out into the Garden of Statues so our babies could enjoy the sun. We walked down the Avenue of the Statues, across the stone bridge over the Brook of Tears, then sat on the bench in front of Our Lady of Perpetual Help. We laid Angel and Alias under the orange-flowering tree, and I told Daisy about my dreams: I was perplexed by the one about Jesus and the Virgin of Perpetual Help.

"Sometimes we are sent dreams to make us laugh at this life," Daisy said. Daisy said she would not take such a dream seriously—like all sex dreams, it was sent for pleasure, and pleasure, after it was over, usually meant you would suffer for having felt so good.

Daisy insisted the dream about my baby was the important one, and that I should pay attention to it. She told me I had to "clear my brain out," otherwise I might make the "wrong mistake" and lose my baby, or even my own life. The first thing I had to do was get rid of the drugs, and whenever Consuelo gave me more, I should get rid of those also. *Perico* (what she called cocaine) was a personality robber. "Get rid of your poison," Daisy said. "It is easier for Consuelo if you are like me, *trabado* [stoned] all your life."

Her words had little effect on me. Maybe the drug *had* taken me away from myself, from who I was, used to be, but I can't blame the drug, can I? My counsellor says it's convenient to blame drugs, but deep down we do what we want to do anyway.

I heard a pony whinnying in the distance, and the scream of a peacock and a howling in my brain caused by a single fly buzzing around my eyes. Daisy, who said my face looked bone white, "like an English teacup," watched Angel bat at an orange butterfly that kept swooping over his head. Daisy said the butterfly was a lost soul, fluttering about, looking for a new body to try on. She took a swipe at it herself, and this time it fell, stunned, onto the foot of a bullet-ridden statue. I cried out as it tried to escape from Daisy's fist, dragging its one torn wing.

"You will thank me for this," said Daisy, killing the butterfly, then flicking its dead body into the clump of bee orchids. "A wounded butterfly is very bad luck. The dead one can tell no stories."

When Consuelo learned I had twice taken Angel into the Garden of Statues, I thought I might not live to leave the house ever again. I had put his mortal soul in danger, she said; Daisy should have known better. The first outing after coming home from the hospital had to be to the church, to have the baby baptized. And if Angel died before he was baptized, she said, he wouldn't go to heaven or hell—he would remain forever in limbo.

I wanted to say that a walk in the garden hardly constituted an *outing*, besides which both our souls had been in limbo ever since she'd taken me hostage. But I let her speak, holding Angel close and trying to stroke his head, even though my hands were shaking. Consuelo was shaking, too, as she began rummaging through my closet, picking out a white silk dress for me (I tried not to think, at such times, of the moon goddess on the slab in the morgue, her fingernails, even in death, an opalescent pearl) and a creamy lace gown for Angel. She told me to be ready to leave for the church by the time she returned.

As soon as Consuelo left I did a line to calm myself, and then gave Angel another shot of my milk. He always watched me as he nursed, one eye on my face, the other on my breast. It intrigued me, the way his eyes could move independently of one another, each looking out for itself, leery of shadows, as if he had been trained, even before birth, to see movement. The curtain sighing in the slight breeze along the wall was enough to make him stop nursing and turn his head from my breast, as if he were listening to something I couldn't hear. *Nació de pie.* He was born on his feet, born all-knowing and street-wise; he could have picked a pocket or hot-wired a car with those newborn eyes. He grew bolder as he nursed, stretching his tiny limbs into each new morning, punching the air with his fists. That morning he seemed more eager than ever to fight, and he kicked his way out of the constricting baptismal robe Consuelo had chosen. When I tried to slip his feet into the pair of soft leather *botas,* he curled up his toes: I had to tickle his tiny soles to make him straighten his feet so I could lace them into the boots.

Nidia was late bringing breakfast, and this upset me more than it should have. I looked forward to her arrival every morning, with my *blanco y negro*—two big rails of cocaine and two tiny cups of *tinto.* An unshakeable daily routine was what, I think now, kept me sane. I didn't want anything to change. I wanted to cut out my sweet, white lines and drink my sweet, black coffee, and let the rest of my life, the world, float away. I wanted to feel the hum in my veins, the freeze creeping into my gums, the *nosola* burn, the bitter tang of cocaine mucus run down the back of my throat.

When Nidia finally arrived, I broke down in tears and couldn't eat. I left the coffee but snorted the rails, then gave

Angel, who had started to sniffle too, to Nidia. Nidia tried to comfort him while I changed out of my dressing gown into the white dress, fumbling with the pearl buttons the size of chick-peas up the front.

The house felt chilly that morning: only the fountain of blood pulsed with life. Yepez opened the back door of a white Mercedes that smelled like the inside of a coconut. Daisy, who sat with Alias, waiting for us, smiled when she saw my baby in his robe and said now he looked like a *real* angel.

Yepez, after a short argument with Consuelo—I'd yet to see anyone have any other kind of argument with her— took a back road through fields that were part pasture, part rock, and a few coffee bushes guarded by banana trees or shaded by the branches of the guamos. I saw women, many of them pregnant, with rifles strapped across their bent backs, on bended knees between rows of onions and potatoes intercropped with red-flowering poppies.

Beyond the pasture land lay the Río Negro. The dirt road we travelled followed the river, and in places the water had overflowed its banks. Consuelo cursed Yepez, calling him a *gordo maricón* (a fat queer) as he plowed the Mercedes over the muddy ruts. He didn't dare say it had been her idea to take this seldom-used road, but I could read it in his silence. If we got stuck, she said, he would have to get out and push us to the church. If we arrived too late, my baby would belong to the devil and we would have him to thank for that. He crossed himself, and the crease between his eyebrows grew deeper every time the car's wheels started spinning in another mudhole.

He should have turned around, Consuelo said, when he saw we were in danger. He was nothing but an ignorant peasant. I kissed Angel, covering his face with my hair, so that Consuelo wouldn't see his smirk. Perhaps I was projecting, but I think he had Consuelo pegged.

Daisy lit a cigarette, and when I rolled my window down for air, the car filled with a greasy heat that steamed from the jungle river. I rolled the window up again, just as the car came to a standstill.

None of Consuelo's curses moved the car, so we all got out and Yepez kicked a tire, splashing mud all over his uniform and Angel's gown. Consuelo told me to go and wash it off in the river: I was glad of the chance to get away from her. My last line of cocaine was beginning to wear off, and her mood, like the drug, worked its way under my skin and made me sweat from the outside in. Coming down, I felt numb. Daisy sat beside the dirty river, smoking while I tried to sponge off Angel's gown, which soon turned the colour of the yellow mud.

I could hear Yepez grunting and pushing, and Consuelo berating him even more; Angel's eyes had become fixed on a rock in the middle of the river. At first I thought I saw the rock move, and then I saw two naked boys, blacker than the rock, pointing at us and making faces. Something had died on the rock—I could see bones still partly covered with meat. One of the boys stood up and, with a stick, flicked a rib bone across the water in my direction.

The rib was so dry it floated on the river's oily surface. Daisy stood up, and for a moment I thought she was going to wade in, pick up the rib and throw it back at the boys, who slapped their thighs and thrust their loins towards her, mimicking lewd sexual gestures. Instead, she turned her back on them and strode to the car.

The boys had made a mistake by not blending in with the rock a while longer. Consuelo took her .38 out of her waistband and shouted at them to come and lie down on the road so we could use their bodies for planks. The boys jeered at this, but when she emptied her .38 into the rock, they struggled ashore and helped Yepez push the car out of the rut, crying and pleading for mercy. Consuelo made the boys run in front of the Mercedes on their twisted feet until the road turned away from the river and we were no longer in danger of getting mired.

The Church of Our Virgin of Mercy stood on a ridge at the foot of Nevada Chocolata. A parade of cars that looked as though they were only dusted off for weddings and funerals lined both sides of the steep access road. The fields surrounding the church were filled with more people, who had arrived either on foot or on one of the gaudy city buses parked at the bottom of the hill. Men and women sat gossiping in small groups, ignoring the service, which was being relayed to those outside the church through an ancient, very crackly, loudspeaker system hidden behind the ten-foot Virgin agonizing in white-and-blue plaster. Her long-suffering eyes were fixed on the ribbons of clouds spread out over the sky like little flags of truce.

A hearse, painted the same woozy colours as the buses and dedicated to *Mis Amorcitas, Olga y Elizabeth*, with a painting of two voluptuaries embracing across the hood, pulled up alongside the Virgin. It looked look more like an escort-service limo than a vehicle in which the dead took their final ride.

Consuelo walked over to the hearse, said a few words to her bodyguards, then disappeared into the packed church. I watched the coffin, white, pint-sized, being unloaded from the hearse. When Consuelo came to a *nenito*'s funeral, Daisy said, it made the pain much easier for a mother to bear. She picked at one of her peeling fingernails as she spoke. God sends nothing we can't bear, I thought, but if he does, he sends Consuelo to comfort us.

Consuelo emerged again, grabbed me by the arm, made sure her .38 was concealed under her jacket, nodded to Daisy and said, "We're going in," as if we were about to rob a bank. She began elbowing her way through the crowd, until we were inside the church, overflowing with babies and their mothers, and grandmothers, and great-grandmothers, aunts, sisters and cousins—all jockeying to be first in line, even though there was no line, only a swarming, a madness of mothers and their female relations. It didn't seem to matter who she trampled—the elderly or the infirm, a pregnant or nursing mother—Consuelo was determined to get to the front of the church, where a huge and bleeding Christ child hung crucified above the altar.

It was horrifying, in every baroque detail: the tears of blood, the tiny crown of thorns. Women bludgeoned each other for a chance to kiss his bleeding feet, while a harried-looking priest tried to keep order using a microphone. It was impossible to hear anything he said. I had never attended a church service where worshippers heckled the priest, or swore at him to get on with the blessing.

Consuelo wrenched Angel from my arms: he became the first of more than twenty babies that day to have holy water sprinkled on his head and the Salt of Life on his tongue. The baptism took less time than it takes to soft-boil an egg, and after he had been christened Angel Segundo Corazón Gaviria and we had fought our way *out* of the church, we had our picture taken beneath Our Virgin of Mercy, Consuelo declaring herself Angel's *madrina* and El Chopo, in absentia, the godfather.

I remember an interminable wait under the hot sky while, one by one, the remainder of the babies were baptized and photographed beneath the sorrowing Virgin. I could almost hear the misanthropic undergrowth surrounding the church gasping and straining for air as I stood, wanting only to return to the cool air of my room and to lie with Angel, nursing him, nursing our tiny, shared history. Daisy said that Angel looked different to her now he was baptized, that his face had softened, like a tomato held over a fire. To me he looked the same. He will always look the same.

When the baptisms were over, the priest prayed for the babies' souls. No one joined in his prayers—except to utter the odd "Amen," as if they wished he'd get it over with. There was a further wait while the funeral service was broadcast through the speakers. I wondered aloud where the baby's mother was, and Daisy whispered to me that she had known the woman, that she'd worked for Las Blancas but tried to go out on her own. "I think they buried her in a different place."

I saw, again, the moon goddess's arm sticking out from under the sheet in the morgue. Now I knew what had happened to the babies of women who wanted their independence.

When the small white coffin was carried from the church, silence fell. I watched the burial clouds that had appeared suddenly over the peak of the mountain, spreading in black masses across the sky, as Consuelo and five others shouldered the baby's coffin and walked with it up the mountainside, the men with their cursed feet, limping and stumbling behind. Daisy said she'd never seen Consuelo look more peaceful than when she carried a coffin up this hill, that a person could learn all she'd need to know about suffering just by watching her. As we reached the entrance to the graveyard, I felt Angel's small body shrink beneath his robe.

The Cementerio de Niños, with its endless rows of small, forsaken graves, sulked away up the mountain as far as the eye could see, to where the small white crosses became indistinguishable from the slopes of crucifix orchids. Most of the crosses, leaning at odd angles, gave nothing but the baby's name and dates. A few were blank; others bore plaintive inscriptions. In places the earth had cracked, as if those down below had moved over to make room for the new arrivals.

Angel's hungry mouth groped for something to comfort him, and I undid the top buttons on my dress. I felt a little milk coming in as he gummed my nipple, and I watched the coffin being lowered into the grave, and Consuelo throwing a handful of earth in after it. Daisy stood by herself, rocking Alias, until the grave was piled high. Consuelo thrust a cross into the mound, jamming it in hard, as if it were a stake meant to keep the baby down.

The priest asked us to help him pray. He mopped his head, looking around as if he expected to be punished for his part, as if the earth might open again and he would be sucked down into an unforgiving hell. He knelt beside the coffin, his hands folded together before his face, as if eating his own hands, in prayer.

Consuelo paid no attention to the priest; she glanced at her watch, then at her gum-chewing bodyguards, who never stopped looking wary, the way those paid to die first often do.

Daisy told me later that if Alias died, she would die of grief too. But she would want to be buried somewhere else, far away from this graveyard. That way, she would never have to hear her *angelito* cry.

chapter twenty-four

I lost track of the days—not hard when you are locked in a room with nothing to do but feed and bathe your baby, eat, sleep and get high. Here, on the Condemned Row, I keep track of the days by X-ing them off on the calendar. It's not as if I have anything to look forward to, though Freud maintained that death is our ultimate goal in life.

Nidia let me out of my room for a few hours a day; sometimes Angel and I sat by the pool, where just before dusk the garden filled with hundreds of doves. We'd sit beside the waterfall and watch Yepez shoo them up into the trees, until the branches appeared to be covered with feathery snow.

One afternoon, Yepez took me to the solarium to show me the Black Widow's prized orchids—orchids with wine-streaked lips and brilliant yellow throats; green and pink orchids hovering like a formation of helicopters. One had waxy orange petals that looked like wings; for a moment I mistook it for a butterfly, like the one Daisy had crushed in the garden. Yepez knew most of their names—the spice orchid, the jewel orchid, the Medusa's head orchid (with flowers more curious than beautiful and a scent, he said, that may be intoxicating or fetid, depending on the species). The two he himself would always recognize any-where were the Holy Ghost orchid, by its overpowering smell, and the goblin orchid, by its twisted shape. The Black Widow, though, could still tell you the difference between a scorpion orchid and a leopard orchid, blind-folded.

From what I had learned about Consuelo's mother, she was not much different from the orchids she raised—both were masters at making a host of creatures do their bidding to ensure their survival. In the orchid world, as in the Black Widow's, it was the survival of the most devious. Like her orchids, the Black Widow had evolved elaborate devices for luring hostages and pressing them into her service: one orchid enticed insects with the scent of food, another used sex as a lure, and a third variety drugged its prey.

Yepez said he was glad he wasn't an insect. They fell for the ruse, no matter how many times they had been deceived.

I had just finished bathing Angel, and we were lying naked on the bed, when Consuelo came by to drop off another flap, then rolled a fat joint—*maduro con queso* (tobacco and marijuana mixed together with *basuco*). She poured herself a glass of *aguardiente* and sat on a corner of the bed, looking at me while Angel rested with one eye open. I loved him so much I always wanted to wake him when he started to nod off, as if I couldn't afford a minute without him, as if we had so little time left.

Consuelo picked up Angel and kissed him. Her face always relaxed when he smiled at her. I had to allow myself to believe she actually cared for him then, and I've gone on believing—it makes life easier now.

"*Mi chinita adorada,*" Consuelo called him. My little angel. But her face changed as she squeezed his tiny, naked thigh between her thumb and her finger. "Maybe it is time you started weaning him. He is thin. Maybe he is getting sick from your drugs? When you are gone, he will not need a wet nurse; he will be looking for another connection."

When you are gone. It is interesting the words we choose to remember, the ones we forget. In court, the prosecutor used the word *connection* every time she got a chance. But she never mentioned my *real* connection to Angel, the connection that went far deeper than drugs or money or the fact that I smoked *basuco* and let Daisy do things to me I wouldn't have let her do if I hadn't been out there on a cocaine high.

They say every grave holds a reason. I try to imagine my son standing over my grave, wondering why I'm down there under the grass and he's up above, always looking for the connection that could make him feel so sweet and sad and good. Mrs. Dykstra, my counsellor, says these are morbid thoughts, ones I should banish from my mind.

Angel gave Consuelo the lazy eye, balled his hands into fists and took an equally lazy poke at the air. I know I sound like a mother speaking, but he had something, that baby. It made people reach for him, as if they hoped that by touching him, some of his grace, his way of being in the world, would rub off.

Outside, the sun had not yet cleared the *borrachio* tree, or sent its soothing rays to loosen the hold of the strangling creeper making its way around the tree's trunk. Outside is where I wanted to be, but I turned my back on the window and stayed inside the room, inside myself. Angel made cooing sounds, like a pigeon fluttering in a coop, and when Consuelo left, locking the door after her, I lay on the bed, nursing him as best I could. And as Angel seized hold of my nipple I prayed, I actually prayed: let the drug take his small, perfect body. Let the annihilating angel take his heart, his lungs, his kidneys, even his soul—so that as long as he lived he would live life without feeling pain.

When I next saw Consuelo, she said the words I had so longed to hear in the first interminable months of my captivity—that a plane would be leaving at the end of the week, and I would be on it. She believed I was a *berraco*, a person with courage, and because she did not feel any animosity towards me, she was prepared to help me.

My eyes were fixed on the two jaguar kittens outside my window; they were tearing apart one of the tiny horses' heads. I made myself turn away and went and stood by Angel's cot; I looked at him looking out for me, an expression on his face that seemed to say he would always be there if I needed him.

It would be a straightforward proposition, Consuelo said. Tiny would fly me directly into the States. But in case we ran into a problem, and were forced to make a controlled entry, I would accompany a coffin, pose as a bereaved mother. The papers were being prepared for me, a baby's birth and death certificates. How well I played the part would determine Angel's fate.

Without Angel, I wouldn't have to act. I would be grieving for my own, a fact Consuelo was counting on. I asked her what would happen to my son if I didn't make it through. For everyone's sake it was important, she said, that I thought only about success.

If you succeed, send money; if you fail, don't come home. But Consuelo didn't just want money this time. She wanted something even more valuable than my life.

"Angel belongs with me," she said. "He is family." She said she intended to raise my child like any other, to give him a normal life and prepare him for his future. She said that Las Blancas would benefit from his leadership one day, that Angel would have chosen this life for his only son.

A normal childhood? The chance to grow up to be a drug lord and go to prison, or get gunned down? I hadn't allowed myself to think of any kind of "normal" childhood for my son. The moment I could do my next line or take my next toke of *basuco*—that was what I'd come to see as *normal.* I had slept on my poison, and my poison had kept me sleeping.

And Daisy was right: it suited Consuelo to keep me this way. She gave me a bag with a rock in it the size of Angel's fist. The finest yet, she said; *una muestrica* (a sample) *de primera calidad:* pharmaceutical-strength cocaine. I would be covering a planeload of this same product as far as Los Angeles. She would let me take all I could carry *en la chocha.*

Now more than ever, my son depended on me, she said. If I did my job, delivered the load, stuck to my story and wrote about Las Blancas only in terms of its dedication to human rights, no harm would come to him. I would be free; I could go on with my life. "*Y cuándo tu estés triste, recuerda que Angelito existe,*" Consuelo said. And when you are sad, remember that Angel exists.

God does not send anything we can't bear.

That was a lie. He had sent Consuelo. He had sent fear and cruelty and heartbreak in a world more full of weeping than He could ever know. And Consuelo, I knew, would not think twice about killing my child if it suited her to believe I had betrayed her.

After she left, I felt so sick at heart I didn't know what else to do—I broke off a chunk of the rock and chopped it with my X-acto blade, and before I knew it I was talking to angels again and my own baby was demanding to be fed. For the past few days he had been spitting up my milk, and no longer cried out for it. In a lifeless way he would begin to fuss, and then I wouldn't feel like changing him or bathing him, or being a mother or eating the *arepas* Nidia brought me on a tray, with *tinto* and a plate of *maracuya* and papaya.

Nidia fussed too: I must eat more food and make myself stronger; I was *demasiado flaco*, too thin; I had to get healthy; what would Señor Angelito do if I got thin and passed away? Away sounded like the sort of place I wanted to go, but only as long as I could take Angel with me. I snorted the lines and felt thick-headed and confused again, and then shivered, not from the cold, but from the slab of light that hits you in a new day, when the sun smears itself all over your morning window. I remember watching Angel on the bed, the sun striking him like a backhand across the mouth, the frown on his forehead—I hadn't thought babies were old enough to have anything to frown about! That's how much I had learned, or how much innocence I had lost.

I smoothed his worried brow, kissed the hollow place in his chest. Then I held him tight in my arms and told him Consuelo was going to release me in a few days, but that I didn't want to be free if it meant having to leave him: what would I do with freedom?

Rainy asked me, one night, did I believe love was something you could stop and start? Did you have any control over it? Could you make yourself not love someone if loving that person hurt too much? I looked at Angel watching me with round eyes that seemed to say, don't ever stop believing in the goodness of this world. I felt, even as I stood there holding him in my arms, that he was the one holding me; his strength, like an undertow, pulling me down deep into a place where I could see myself as I must have appeared to him. Women don't have babies, I decided; babies give birth to *us*.

I held Angel next to my heart as I stood by the window watching the trembling bougainvillea and the drunken tree with the white creeper, which seemed always to be struggling with itself—whether to break free or love what kept it bound.

part seven / cover girl

And yet all we have is somehow
born in that murdering. Born in
the fire and born in the breaking.

—*Jack Gilbert*

chapter twenty-five

*All inmate correspondence shall be censored under the
supervision of the Warden of Care and Treatment. No
correspondence shall be approved which is critical of the
policies of the State Department of Corrections.*
—Inmate Information Handbook

*For a wound to heal, it has to close. Once it's
closed, you begin to forget. You bury the pain
and by the time a scar forms, you have
even forgotten what caused the pain.*
—May Browne

Mark Twain wrote that he had suffered a great many catas-
trophes in his life, but most of them had never happened.

Losing my child was one catastrophe that *did* happen, and I have suffered for it; forfeiting my life seems a small price. I feel almost as if I am being given a second chance at love, as if I might be going to meet my child on another, spiritual plane.

Rainy wants to know if I've ever seen a real angel. I tell her no, not in person; I've felt one, though. There was an angel in the room with me when my baby was born.

What proof do I have, Rainy says, if I haven't ever seen one in the flesh? I ask her, How much proof do you need?

"Any little thing," Rainy says. "A pair of wings would do."

The first victim of lethal gassing at Heaven was a pig. (Even "Wanda," the executioner, said pigs are the hardest things to kill.) If lethal gassing worked on a pig, the man who designed and built the gas chamber said, it's sure to work on a woman.

The pig was lowered into a wire cage that had been laid across the armrests of a stainless-steel chair inside the chamber. When the gas reached his snout, he jumped to his trotters, scrambled up the side of the cage as far as he could go and began bashing his head against the steel, trying to force his snout through the wire, beyond the reach of the choking fumes. Finally he fell to the floor, where he lay farting and grunting until the end.

A reporter for the state *Advocate* wrote, "If the mercy of nepenthe comes as slowly for the human body as it did for the little porker, then there will be terrible things done to women's souls and their tortured brains. . . ."

Rainy wishes he hadn't written that. There are already enough bloodthirsty people, she says; it will only encourage them. Within two days of the pig successfully dying in the gas chamber, more than three hundred people had put in their bids for ringside seats at the first killing of a woman in the gas chamber at Heaven.

The guards wished the girl luck, Rainy says, which was nice of them. One guard, who was bawling her eyes out, told her to "break a leg."

"Then they leave, and you're all on your sad and lonely." It's "Goodbye, cruel world," Rainy says, as they slam shut the steel door, giving the bright red handles on the wheel a final turn, sealing the chamber tight.

The warden is at her post, with the executioner and the attending croakers. Opposite them, on the other side of the chamber, are your witnesses and a TV crew. They stare at you through the thick glass, and you wonder if they're worrying about any of the lethal gas escaping while they concentrate on shooting you from the best angle.

The warden signals the executioner, who opens the valves, and sodium-cyanide pellets the size of pigeon eggs (manufactured by DuPont, they come in one-pound cans, Rainy tells me—trust her to find God in the details) fall into a pan filled with sulphuric acid beneath your chair. The poisonous gas begins to form, and your cell fills up with the sickening-sweet odour of bitter almond and peach blossoms.

You inhale the fumes, feel dizzy, strain against the straps. You breathe—you try not to breathe. Your head aches, your chest aches, you're slipping into unconsciousness. You can't hold your breath, you can't breathe. Your head jerks around a lot as your body fights, but it's a losing battle. You stop fighting. Your heart stops.

I ask Rainy how she knows all this; she wasn't even there. She says each time the cyanide fumes choke out a life in Heaven, they also seep into the total chemistry of human society.

A prison is no place to be, as Rainy frequently reminds me. There is no place noisier during the day, nowhere quieter at night. I have often woken up in the middle of the night since I've come to live on the Row, and I lie picturing the faces of the other condemned women glowing like the phosphorescence of tropical plants as they dream of a better place to be than in Heaven on their narrow cots. And I can hear my own heart beating, no matter how I try to block out the sound. I listen to the sound of my breathing, each breath fighting with the next to be let out, until the sandman begins to lean on me and I hear the rubber-soled squeak of Officer Gluckman's shoes as she huffs down the range with her nightstick (held by a black leather strap to her belt), and the dying Nano. She drags her nightstick across the bars and then stands in front of my house, but I can barely hear his voice any longer, crying out to me, "*I'm sick. Feed me.*" Officer Gluckman's the one who is sick, but a sickness like hers doesn't deserve to be fed, so I don't show any emotion as I brush my teeth or make my bed and then stand with my arms raised over my head, waiting for the angel of mercy to come with the Right Guard. You have to hide things to keep love—covering up, putting everything outside and crying on the inside. I keep all my tears inside, because when I left Angel behind my heart packed its bags and left home for good.

This evening Officer Freedman interrupts me in my house, where I am peacefully watching another live execution (the channel they now keep my television permanently tuned to).

"Heard the one about the gal who's going to be executed, they offer her a last cigarette? 'No thanks,' she says, 'I'm trying to quit.'"

I keep my eyes tuned to the screen, where a girl who shot and killed a taxi driver after robbing him of $4.36 and his Medic-Alert bracelet is now going to die in the gas chamber.

When Officer Freedman sees I have disappointed her again, that I am not going to die laughing, she turns her eyes to the TV too, because just as the girl finishes getting dressed in a new pair of jeans and a fresh white T-shirt without pockets (no underwear, no shoes, nothing where the gas can accumulate and kill the guards when they go in to untie her afterwards), she slices her tongue almost all the way off with a sliver of her personal mirror she has kept hidden in her mouth. She bleeds all over everything, especially her white T-shirt. Because her arms are slippery with blood, and because she can't weigh more than ninety pounds, she manages to slip out of the straps holding her in the chair just after the executioner lowers the cyanide into the vats of acid. She races around the chamber, beating her fists against the window, but soon after she gets her first whiff of the gas, she stops screaming.

"*Feed me. I'm sick.*" I turn from the horrible spectacle to another one—Officer Gluckman standing beside Officer Freedman, smiling at me. She dangles the dying Nano at the end of her leather strap and shakes her head. And when I say nothing, she decides to inspect my underwear; she's disappointed when I lower my sweats to reveal I am wearing the right colour. Am I interested in last week's *TV Guide*, she asks (she's nuts—no point taking it personally), and then complains a lot about her back, which needs replacing, and how she was up again till after midnight reading reports, and how this place is understaffed and nobody understands how important her job is and how seriously she takes her work, and how no one else could ever do her job for her. I want to tell her the graveyard is full of people who think they are indispensable, but I don't; I offer to trade places with her for a day instead.

"With my luck," she says, "I'd choose the day you go to get gassed."

I don't let this cruel remark phase me. "My luck too," I say, "because then I'd be doing *your* job for the rest of my life."

My mother writes that Vernal arrived in a taxi and "chauffeured her around town" so she could finally return the unreliable lamp. Vernal took her for lunch afterwards, and ordered her a Scotch while she waited for her soup to arrive. "The clam chowder was lovely," she writes, "but I had to give Vernal the Scotch. I told him, 'I wish I *could* drink whisky. I know it's *so* good for you.'"

I read an article in a magazine that says it becomes more difficult to love your parents the older you get, the same way it becomes harder to love your own children as they themselves grow older and begin to appreciate your love. I wish I could say I'd had the opportunity.

There's this to think about: If I hadn't had Angel, I could have lived my life without ever wanting anything enough to hurt over.

WHAT IF WE NEVER WANTED ANYTHING ENOUGH TO HURT OVER? I wrote this in big letters and stuck it on the wall in front of the table where I sit to write, and Rainy asked me if that was going to be the title of my book. No, I said, it was too many words.

She thought about that for a while. "Well," she said, "maybe I could use those words for the twins." Her twins shared a grave and she had always wanted them to have a marker, but hadn't been able to think of anything important enough to have carved in stone. But she liked *What if we never wanted anything enough to hurt over?* I told her it sounded like she was making an excuse for having to kill them, as if she'd loved them so much she *had* to leave them under a train, and she said finally someone got the picture.

She said this the night before she disappeared. I'll always remember how Rainy looked the last time I saw her—as if she had finally found some kind of peace in knowing she had wanted something enough to hurt over. Now, too, when I say, "I'll always remember . . ." I think of Rainy. "It's a pretty sure thing," she said. "You won't have time to forget." Rainy never stopped reminding me that here on the Row, "always" has an expiry date.

Rainy believed in reincarnation, that she would always be here on earth in one form or another. For that reason, she wanted the word *always* on her headstone. "Something simple, to make people think."

"Always *what?*" I asked.

"See, you're thinking."

I reminded Rainy Always was a brand of panty liners. Did she want people thinking about *that?*

"Even better," she said. "'*Always, with Wings.*'"

I can't let myself think too much about what happened to Rainy. I know she wanted to die on a Monday, not a Friday—because being turned off on a Friday would be a bad start to a weekend—and in the late evening, at bedtime, when she was ready for a good sleep. She didn't want to die in the morning, with the whole day ahead of her, because she might miss something, like spaghetti for lunch.

The fact that Rainy didn't have any good veins left didn't save her. She underwent a "cut-down": her arm was slit open—by corrections officers who had no experience as surgeons—searching for a usable blood vessel.

Rainy's was a high-profile case, and tickets to her execution had sold out the morning they'd gone on sale. Some people camped overnight to get the best seats in the house. That must have boosted Rainy's self-esteem.

One of the guards assigned to Rainy—to make sure she remained sane and healthy in the Health Alteration Unit during the days before her lethal injection—spoke to a reporter. "We give execution—lethal injection—at eleven in the morning, right after coffee. Usually it's a Friday, end of the week; you need a break after it. On Friday, around five a.m., I go upstairs and bring the individual down to the death cell, right next to the lethal-injection chamber. Then I sit with her until it's time to go.

"I drink coffee, play cards or watch television with the individual. Sometimes she just likes to talk, or she'll ask to see the chaplain. Whatever I do, I try to make her last hours memorable. My official title is Death Watch Officer, but really I'm just a glorified babysitter."

chapter twenty-six

I scarcely remember those last days with Angel on Tranquilandia. To say they are a blur would be as clear as I can get. I begged Consuelo to let me stay, or, if she had to send me away, to let me take Angel with me. Without him I had nothing to live for, I told her. "We don't choose our blessings or our curses, *mijita*" was all she would say.

Angel seemed to be growing more fragile every day. When babies are hungry they cry, but Angel was too weak now to make the one sound I so badly wanted to hear. The day before I was destined to fly away with a coffin that held the body of someone else's child, Consuelo came to say Daisy and I were to take Angel to see the one *bruja* she could trust, the one who lived on the mountain, at Chocolata's shrine.

The *bruja* would help Angel get strong again; Consuelo said she wanted me to understand what Angel had been born to, and how he had to survive and grow up to claim what was his own. Tranquilandia was his birthright; knowing this should make it easier for me to bear leaving my baby behind.

She opened my curtains to let in the day; during the night someone had planted, on the sharp end of a stake driven into the ground at the foot of the *borrachio* tree, the half-chewed head of the miniature horse. His tongue stuck out of a corner of his mouth, as if feeling around for a last taste of sweetness. A bib of flies tucked into his throat, feasting there. I asked Consuelo to close the curtains, and after she left, saying Yepez would be driving her to the city for the day, I climbed into bed with Angel and rocked him and tried to make him eat. He kept turning his head away from me, and I felt scared. If I hadn't had him, I could have lived my life without ever wanting anything enough to hurt over.

My mind was a mess, and now was the moment I needed a base toke, another hit of the intoxicating *mejoral*, a long line of Bolivian marching powder to make my brain cells come to attention, fall in line, shoulder their rifles, beat their drums. I felt flat, lifeless. I got out of bed and broke another piece off the rock from the *muestra* Consuelo had left me, crushed it into smaller rocks and made a *bola* to carry with me. Then I broke off a bigger chunk and cooked up a toke.

Angel started complaining again, but stopped fighting the minute I began dressing him; he didn't even resist as I slipped his feet into his little boots, tickling his sole out of habit to make him straighten his toes. When Daisy came, a while later, she found me staring at the closed curtains. She told me Alias had stopped breathing during the night; she had shaken him and now he was feeling better, but sometimes he still had trouble catching his breath. Consuelo had taken him to the hospital in the City of Orchids, "to see the best doctor money could buy." I told her I felt there was little hope left for any of us.

"You only learn to know hope when everything in you is dead," Daisy said. At the time I didn't understand what she meant, but now I do. There is more hope here on death row than in any other place in the universe.

I told Daisy Consuelo's plan for me. I didn't think I could leave my son behind. As I said these words out loud, and pictured myself walking anywhere in the world without Angel's small body nestled up against my breast, I began to weep; my tears fell onto his face, rolled off into his ears and down his neck to the hollow place in his chest, and collected there.

The fields surrounding the Church of Our Virgin of Mercy were deserted, except for a solitary old man, in a loose-fitting shirt and baggy trousers, turning the earth with a broken spade. He didn't look up as we parked. El Chopo, whom I hadn't seen since the morning he delivered me to the Hacienda la Florida, said he would wait with the car. Even before we started our climb I felt the hot, wet air on my skin. The trail looked steep, the mountaintop, Chocolata's shrine, far away in the sky.

A vulture kept an eye on us, higher than the clouds that hovered, whitely, like the corpses of angels. As we passed the Cementerio de Niños, a look of sadness scudded across Angel's face. Daisy said it was a pity there was no shade in that place, only, day after day, the sun, and always the *angelitos* moaning for their mothers.

She kept quickening our pace, and once we got beyond the graveyard, where the rough road narrowed into an even rougher trail, I had difficulty keeping up to her. A long line of rifles had been thrust into the earth like fenceposts to mark the trail, which might otherwise have been indistinguishable through the fields of crucifix orchids. The few trees that had been left standing grew straight and white, topped by bunches of leaves that reached for the sky like zapped hairdos.

Propped against one of the rifles was a sign: "If You're Going to Make a Start, Keep on Going—If You Know What You're Doing. But If I Were You, I'd think it Over."

"It's to discourage people from going to the shrine for the wrong reasons," Daisy said when she saw my worried look. "It is not meant for people like us."

For people like us. What had I become?

I had made a start, I would keep on going.

Yellow storm clouds had begun gathering to the north, over the City of Orchids, while above us the vultures continued to make their slow rounds in the sky. The Buddhists were right, I thought: desire was the cause of all suffering. The desire to live, and for my child to live with me—to grow up whole and be allowed to hear the wild music of the world, to stumble from his dreams and to hear the humming of wild bees, know the taste of rainwater on his tongue or the smell of a campfire burning out at dawn—I had never felt desire so strong.

I suffered as I climbed, a kind of sickness that I am beyond suffering now, sitting here in a cell the size of a rich person's coffin. I hope I never desire anything again. Or even *want* anything. To want is to be weak, vulnerable. Prey for the wolves. Pray for them. As Frenchy once said, "'The Lord is my shepherd, I shall not want.' I don't get it. If he's my fucking shepherd, why shouldn't I fucking want him? That's the trouble with the Bible. It fucks you up."

But that day on Nevada Chocolata, I felt desire. The desire to hold and be held, to take Angel home with me, to smell mock orange drifting through a June window at the Walled-Off Astoria while I drink jasmine tea sweetened with wildflower honey, leaning against pillows part drifting cloud, part daydream. I desired my child, who needed me. I kissed his face as I climbed, kissed his name over and over again in my head, each beloved letter of his name, as I followed the cold line of rifles up into the higher, cooler air, stopping every so often to look down on the cemetery embedded in the hillside, to remind myself of the reasons to keep going. *"When you are sad, remember that Angel exists."* It took all my resolve to pick my way around the stabbing rocks and large, meaty-leafed plants, and go on.

At a sudden point, the stark upland scenery softened and became an almost subtropical forest, a haven for an innumerable variety of orchids growing on tree trunks, on branches and along the ground. Some rose up on erect flower stalks into lurid, contorted shapes; others jumped out at you, big enough to steal your jewellery. Even the air was filled with spidery green, jewel-like blossoms, scarcely larger than the heads of pins, drifting down from the trees.

We made slow progress up the trail onto the last of the high ridges that trapped the clouds and barred the sun. Tiny cold streams cut down the mountain's face. Even now, when the sun shone on the rest of the valley, the top of the mountain, a grim heath of yellowish bog grass and stunted *frailjones*, was blanketed by swirling cloud and horizontal rain.

When we reached open, swampy ground, where only small clumps of grass and mosses grew, I thought I could smell a fire burning, the smut of cooking. We continued upwards until the ground levelled off again, and there in a huddle of rocky outcrops I saw a crude shelter constructed of wooden beams and different kinds of palm bound together with vines. Daisy stopped and called the *bruja*'s name.

An unusually tall, black-skinned woman with a halo of wild red hair came to greet us. She hugged Daisy, her eyes fixed, all the while, on Angel, eyes the colour of Mejool dates, so soft and brown they made you want to bite into them and suck the sweetness from their centres.

The *bruja* said she'd been expecting us—she'd seen us in a dream. We followed her into the hut, which offered little shelter from the elements; when my eyes adjusted to the darkness, I saw dismembered bits of goat hanging from iron hooks suspended at different heights over a low fire. Lumps of meat, and maize and cabbage slices, floated in a watery broth that simmered in a pot, moon-shaped wedges of onion undulating through the greyish foam.

The *bruja* prepared thin slices of black bread spread with thick layers of sweet guava jam, and Daisy began to tell her the reason for our visit. The *bruja* held up her hand. She already knew why we had come.

The odour of death simmered on the fire. The *bruja* filled a blackened kettle with water from a jug and set it over the flames. She added more logs to the fire, and Angel started to cough as the room filled with smoke. I felt sleepy and relaxed one minute, wide awake and edgy the next.

When the water boiled, the *bruja* made coca tea, which she said would help clear my head—the air on the mountain was something you became acclimatized to. She prepared a glass bottle with a nipple on it for Angel too (she'd had to bottle-feed her baby goats after their mother died, she said), saying the coca tea would take away his hunger and make him very calm. She said *la coca te cuida el cuerpo*, takes care of the body, and Angel drank it all down without pushing the bottle away even once.

The wind round the hut made a sound like a baby getting ready to cry, but Angel himself looked more contented than ever. Unlike me: every time I thought of the cocaine I had in my pocket, my palms started to sweat. The *bruja* must have recognized the desire in my eyes—there were black holes in my aura, she said, and where there were holes, there was *mucho sudor, mucho peligro* (lots of sweat and danger). She sighed, as if expelling the grief of the world that had suddenly burdened her.

I drank another cup of tea when she offered it. It gave me an excuse to go outside to relieve myself and do a line. I have to admit, there's no point at *this* hour of my life pretending I had any control left. Around the back of the hut, out of the wind, I reached into my pocket for the *bola*, opened it and crushed one of the rocks between my thumb and forefinger. After I'd snorted as much as I could, I promised myself, again, I would get rid of my poison. Quit cocaine. Forever. Again.

When I went back inside, the *bruja* asked if I was ready to visit the shrine; she said I should wrap my baby well, because the four winds could be very cold on the mountain and his body was very thin. She said she always paid attention to the different voices of the wind: the angry voice, like words being raked over a gutted road; the low, soft voice that speaks of the wet undersides of leaves; the complaining wind, like the sound of worn shoes dragging along wet pavement in autumn; the sensual wind that wafts towards your face carrying the scent of bruised guavas.

Today, she said, it was a bitter wind that blew, and I heard the rasp of it through the green bamboo.

We left the sound of the wind behind and climbed a path that wound up through a forest of clouds, beneath thin silver waterfalls and black, hanging orchids that looked like executioner's hoods, and blue butterflies the size of bats. A fountain of water gushed out from a crack in the crown of a massive boulder, spilled over and flowed down the sides of the rock, surrounding the cave that sheltered Chocolata's shrine like a moat. The cave, which had been carved by the wind and rain, and the constant waterfall of tears, was now sealed off from the elements by a roughly hewn door studded with iron nails.

The *bruja* took three white candles from her pocket, saying she had to bring new ones each time she came to the shrine because the *anti-sociales* stole any she left, even the partially burned ones. In the old days, she'd kept a box of them in the cave so the true pilgrims didn't have to knock on her window and ask for her *velas*.

I'd read of pilgrims who walked seven times between a volcanic monotony of hills, fulfilling a private quest, and of those who left behind tiny silver images of their ailing body parts, which they had rubbed in medicinal earth, and of the penitents who sought transcendence through fire-walking or piercing their bodies with iron hooks then hanging from scaffolds wheeled to the shrine. But what had *I* expected to find? Hope? Something that would make sense of all that had happened to me since I'd been taken hostage and arrived on Tranquilandia? The *bruja* lit one of the thin white candles. In the yellow darkness the flame gave off a green light, making the cave feel like a crypt.

I hadn't expected a coffin, let alone one overflowing with offerings from those who had made the trek to Chocolata's shrine to have their bullets or money or crops blessed—passport photographs; plastic Diet Coke bottles marked "Holy Water, Do Not Consume"; three Miami telephone directories and a worn copy of Che Guevara's handbook on guerrilla warfare; *Soldier of Fortune* magazines and *Penthouse* centrefolds; cigar cutters; rosaries; tins of sardines; empty bottles of *aguardiente*. The coffin was set in a recess in the cave wall, and as I stood taking inventory, I saw the red, burning eyes of a white rat as he scuttled back into the darker chambers.

I heard him squeal as he shuffled away, heard his frantic

rustling sounds, and then only the wind, wheezing for breath, at the mouth of the cave.

The *bruja* lit the other candles and set them on the stone ledge next to the coffin. Even when she was a *jovencita*, she said, she remembered coming here to view what was left of the pirate's remains. In recent years people had taken away *recuerdos*, had worn the pieces of her body like amulets around their necks so that they might inherit the pirate's female power.

The *bruja* said she remembered a time on Tranquilandia when the crops were bountiful and the bullets Chocolata blessed always hit the targets they were intended for. There was money for hospitals, a soccer field in the City of Orchids. Planes touched down on the island every day, and boats, laden to the gunwales with their white cargo, sailed away. The law kept its distance, well offshore. But as Chocolata's body disappeared, so did the good times, the prosperity.

Orphanages and schools closed down because the drug barons could no longer afford their endowments. The soccer field had become a place where addicts smoked *basuco*. Hospital wards became haunted by the ghosts of the *angelitos*. For many years, the islanders had prayed for a boy to be born with strong legs and feet: only one such as this could break Chocolata's curse and restore prosperity and happiness to Tranquilandia.

"He is the one," said the *bruja*, smiling at Angel, "El Narcosanto is what the people are already calling him." There was no hope, as I'd said to Daisy earlier, for any of us; the *bruja*, like Consuelo and the Black Widow, believed my baby was fated to become Tranquilandia's Big Narco Saint.

As the *bruja* turned to leave the cave, I saw the rat's red eyes again, his skin whiter than a winding sheet, humping out of the darkness towards the coffin. I gripped Angel tight; then, as I backed away, the rat knocked over one of the candles and began gnawing the end of it.

I watched, unable to take my eyes off his teeth. A quarter of the way through, he abandoned the candle, knocked down a second one and began chewing *it*.

I remember my father comparing rats to bad land developers, how they eat up everything in sight. Their greed is selfish and goes beyond basic survival: rather than eating one apple or one potato, a rat will take a bite out of every potato or apple in the basket, spoiling the rest for everyone else.

If the rat knocked over the one remaining candle, Angel and I would be left in darkness. I reached in my pocket and hurled the *bola* at the rat. He didn't blink, as if he was used to having high-octane cocaine thrown his way. He raised his pointed nose and sniffed the air, then he scooped the condom up between his paws and disappeared into the back of the cave again.

I knew that in "controlled" experiments (as if *anyone* can control her cocaine use after a while), rats will keep doing the drug until it kills them. Cocaine is their drug of choice, and their death of choice also.

Mine too, before I came to the Row and had to make another kind of choice, an ultimate one. I wonder if anyone will notice how, as I get closer to the end, more and more of my life on the Row seems to be imposing itself on my narrative? I suppose it's because "the end" is what got me here in the beginning.

The prosecutor said I killed my child rather than leave him in Consuelo's hands. What mother, she said, wouldn't do what she thinks best for her child? The prosecutor didn't know how to open her mouth without sneering. In asking for the death penalty, she even quoted Oscar Wilde: "Each man kills the thing he loves, and so he has to die."

When Oscar Wilde wrote that, he wasn't talking about infanticide. The line wouldn't have worked if he'd written, "Each mother kills the thing she loves," not in my case any-way, though maybe in Rainy's. Wilde wasn't even necessar-ily talking about killing *people,* but I'm losing my train again, getting away from that day on Chocolata's mountain.

We waded through the moat, back the way we came. The water in the pot had boiled away to nothing but a frothy sludge, and the *bruja* ladled a piece of kidney for each of us into a porous clay bowl.

She gave Daisy a supply of coca leaves, told her how to make the tea and how much Angel would need. For me she had made a *polvo* out of the pollen of wild orchids: a *legíti-mo polvo* to help me make my way. If I applied the powder underneath my tongue, she said I would have an unevent-ful journey.

Angel settled in Daisy's arms as we started down the mountain and suddenly I felt dispensable, like the moon goddess, like the *sicarios* on the streets of the City of Orchids or the people of Tranquilandia itself, *like Dixie Cups—use them once, then throw them away.* I looked back briefly at the *bruja,* most of her blending in with the dark-ness of the doorway, except for the volatile lipstick, the emergency of red hair flaming from her head.

When we passed the graveyard, I felt the grief of the wind, the same grief the earth must feel, year after year, admitting its dead. And I remember thinking, then, how full life was of moments that should have gone differently.

chapter twenty-seven

The keys dangled in the ignition. El Chopo sat slumped over the wheel, his face turned from the mountain as if he preferred a view of the valley. Daisy opened the rear door on the passenger side and climbed in. When El Chopo didn't stir, Daisy tapped him on the shoulder. He didn't move. She tapped him again, harder, and his body shifted, enough that we could see the blood on the side of his neck and in his hair, and that the top of his head had a hole in it the size of a Campbell's Tomato Soup tin. When I described this to Rainy, she said Campbell's could sue me for using their name if it made you think about a person with his brains blown out. Rainy thought it would be okay to use Campbell's if I said a tin of chicken noodle soup, not tomato.

At the time it was tomato soup I thought of, and I told

her I couldn't see the connection between a hole in a person's head and chicken noodle soup.

"Use your noodle," Rainy said. "Hasn't anyone ever told you to use your noodle?"

She was right, and I revise my story in Rainy's memory: the hole in El Chopo's head was the size of a tin of Campbell's Chicken Noodle Soup. I stood dazed in the dry dust of the parking lot, and I remember Daisy shaking me and telling me to hurry, we had to get back to the hacienda.

It took much manoeuvring for the two of us to slide El Chopo's dead weight over into the passenger's seat. Daisy held Angel as I drove, trying not to think about the sounds arising from El Chopo's body, or about his blood, pooled and dark on the floor at my feet. I drove without thinking about the quiet man in the field below the church, what he must have heard or seen and how he went on turning the earth, trying to dig the sun into the soil so that its shining would not be wasted.

Mucho sudor, mucho peligro. Everything inside me wept, but I fought to look composed. Until I got to my room and remembered I was to leave the next morning, and Angel wouldn't be going with me. When I imagined Angel not being with me when I needed him, I felt a familiar panic in my body, starting in the pit of my stomach and lodging in my throat, so that by the time Nidia brought my evening meal, I couldn't eat. She said I looked sadder than a monkey in a clump of *cajica* grass—that meant very, very sad. I said I didn't want to leave my baby behind, and Nidia said, "*Sí, sí,*" as if she understood. Those last hours at the Hacienda la

Florida took something from me. When I gave Angel up, I lost a part of myself that has felt dispossessed ever since.

I was sitting in my chair, staring into the darkness, when Daisy pounded on my door. She begged me to come quickly, but my door was locked. I began shouting for Nidia, who, when she finally came, told me, through her weeping, that Daisy had lost Señor Alias. I ran with her to the chapel, where the Holy Ghost orchids choked my nostrils with their scent. Four tapered white candles burned—two at the head of the coffin and two at the foot. Daisy knelt beside the small white coffin, rocking back and forth, moaning.

His heart stopped beating, Nidia said, and not even the doctor could revive him. She opened his gown and showed me the enormous incision in the centre of Alias's chest— the inside a brown-red pulp, like guava paste, blackening around the edges—where the doctor had inserted his hands and tried to massage his heart. It must have suited Daisy to believe her child had died naturally, the same way she believed the butterfly was better off crushed. Whether he died of natural causes or not, I knew it suited Consuelo to have him dead: she needed a body for me to take home in a coffin. I made a fist without even knowing it, and drove it softly through the thin crust of this world. Angel trembled in my arms, opened his lips, then closed them again and let out a sigh. The scent of the orchids reminded me of the night he had come into the world.

I looked down at Alias again; this was the first time I'd seen him without his many layers of clothing, including his knee-high socks and knitted booties. I saw now that he would never have made any soccer team: one of his small legs ended in a stump, with miniature cauliflowers of flesh where his toes should have been. I looked away, and tried to turn Angel's head away too, as if we hadn't come face to face with that hard wall, the one with no handholds, the one we couldn't climb.

Nidia began washing Alias's tiny body, his skin the colour of sour milk under the blue light bulb in the lamp beside the coffin that gave us all, I saw now, a terrifying pallor. When she had dried him and dressed him in a long white gown, she laid a cradle orchid beside his head and placed another in his hand. I helped her gather up every orchid in the room, and we arranged them around Alias's body, then I undid the clasp of the emerald-encrusted coke spoon Consuelo had given me and put the chain around his neck. I wanted him to have something beautiful, something the other *angelitos* would envy. I hadn't thought of it as symbolic, as a burial of my way of life. That's the way Pile, Jr. presented it to the jury. He said the moment I gave up the coke spoon, I had turned my back on "the life." The truth is I gave Alias the coke spoon because it was worth a pile of money, and I thought Daisy would appreciate that.

Daisy, her eyes gulping back pain, stroked her baby's head, pushed his hair out of his face, kissed his neck and buried her nose in his flesh, as if she could catch a last breath of her child and never let it go.

That night I didn't sleep, but lay guarding Angel. I held him close and tried to explain how I would never stop loving him. When I said that, he seemed to grow lighter in my arms, as if he understood. He had always been such an ancient person. Some babies are born old, others never grow up—it takes all kinds, as Rainy always said. Rainy had a way of making everything seem simple, with her twerpy philosophy of life.

What I did, I did out of love, because I wanted Angel to live. I chose life for my baby. It wasn't like the prosecutor said—that I had only one thought in mind: drugs.

In the drug world most of the jury had seen on television or read about in the papers, women smuggled drugs inside their babies' diapers, their bottles, their plush toys—in one case, a dead baby had been gutted and stuffed with cocaine. A passenger sitting next to the mother became suspicious when the plane was delayed for several hours and the baby didn't wake up.

This jury had seen and heard it all, and I don't think it occurred to any of them that I might consider it immoral to use a child in such a way. They had a dead baby, an airplane and twenty-five green army bags, each one containing ten of Consuelo's "children" (kilos of cocaine). I had cocaine in my blood, in my vagina, on my mind and in my brain: what more evidence did they need?

When Nidia came with Daisy in the morning I lay unable to move on my bed, and when Nidia asked me if I hadn't slept well I could hardly get the words out—my throat felt as if I had swallowed a roll of quarters. Nidia promised she would help Daisy look after Angel; nothing was forever, she said—how could I begin to think I would never see Señor Angelito again? I said as long as Consuelo lived, there was no chance of Angel and I being together.

"Consuelo won't live forever," Daisy said. She reminded me of what happened to El Chopo. "Even the unkillable have to die."

And then Daisy said, "I am a Colombian. I will always know where to find you."

Daisy assured me, as she'd done many times before, she would care for Angel "as if he were her own." I wanted to trust her, I *needed* to, but I'd seen what had happened to her own. I went to my stash and set out two big rocks on the bathroom counter.

I know I'd promised myself I'd quit, but these were to be my last lines, because I knew things would be different when I got home. At home I wouldn't have this terrible need. Looking at me now, people don't see how desperate I'd become. The tears and sweat and the dirt you pick up just walking around in your life, these all wash off. But you can't wash your heart.

I went to the place where I kept my pipe and my X-acto blade, and they were gone. Or else I'd put them somewhere different and forgotten where. Sometimes I even hid my stash, to test my memory, as a kind of game. I looked in all the obvious places, and then in the places where I'd only hide something if I was really boxed and not thinking straight. My pipe, my blade, my journal, *Contigo Soy Feliz*, had gone. All I had left were my drugs, the hundred-dollar bill, the photograph of my baby. Of Daisy and me and my baby, that is. And for the moment, I had Angel.

I was crazed over Angel, and I wasn't even parted from him yet. I crushed the rocks and snorted the lines, then washed my face and body, as if I could wash his memory from my skin and the tears from my face, which was swollen and looked frightening. Such a face might be an asset, if I ended up having to pretend I was a grieving mother going through immigration. But I almost looked *too* sad. There is sadness and there is beyond sadness. I had to be dignified in my grief, passionate but not over the line. I walked a fine line, and the fine lines in my brain had helped put me back on the right side of the road again. The road going on forever, the way in which we are led away from the self. I dried myself, feeling my body all over, as if my hands were detached. Then I sealed the cocaine inside a condom, inserted it deep in my vagina.

Daisy helped me slip on the white silk dress I'd worn to Angel's christening. She told me the Hotel Viper had burned to the ground during the night, and that Consuelo's father had died in the fire. Consuelo believed it was the Drug Enforcement Administration, retaliating for Las Blancas having captured the Coast Guard cutter, that had killed El Chopo and her father; now she was forced to step up security all over the island.

Nidia hugged me hard, and cried as she told me she'd seen Yepez and two men carrying Alias's coffin out of the chapel to the car early this morning. She left the room; she wouldn't say goodbye to me, because she knew she would see me again "in a better place."

I flattened my hundred-dollar bill and put it in my shoe with Angel's picture, and I'd rinsed my face and smoothed my hair when Consuelo arrived to take Angel away from me. On the day following my arrest, my hair would be described as "torrential" on the front page of every newspaper in North America (it had rained that morning, and a muttersome wind had followed me from the detention centre to the courthouse), my skirt "slit up the side" (it had torn getting into the police van) and my face "expressionless." My face expressionless? It was just that I had no other way left to look.

La Madre Sin Corazón. The Mother without a Heart. The mother who had sinned in her heart, and so become heartless. The truth was Angel had taken a bite out of my heart, and grief had eaten the rest.

Consuelo repeated her warning: no harm would come to him as long as I played my part. She poured me a glass of *aguardiente*, "for courage," she said. I now believe I was *burundunguiado*, that Consuelo slipped the voodoo-powder *burundanga* into my drink, just as she might have slipped it into the *basuco* I'd smoked on other occasions, and even the cocaine I'd inhaled. I have read the reports, the ones Pile, Jr. submitted as evidence. "The victim may have no memory of the event, or may remember the event as a dream. Memories of events while on this drug may come into consciousness many years later. The CIA/FBI/DEA and most police departments know about this drug. It is used by security forces to 'make people forget'; this tasteless and odourless substance can be given by liquid, cigarette or inhalant. Victims of this drug often report distorted vision, especially things being made wide and small, of things starting to stretch."

Things starting to stretch, beginning with the truth, the prosecutor said. How convenient to forget or to have no memory of the event when life and death and millions of dollars are at stake.

I remember some things—the fountain being dry when we passed it, the stone pineapple the colour of rust. And outside, everywhere, guards dressed in army fatigues. Consuelo had enlisted the army to protect her mother's hacienda, Yepez said. Especially against *norteamericanos* and their leader, El Presidente, who believed that by killing people, they could stop all *negocios blancos* on Tranquilandia. I don't know, now, whether I remembered Yepez saying that at the time, or if memories of the events have recently, after I began writing this, flooded back into my mind.

Everything about that day, and my journey, is far from clear, especially my motivation. The Mercedes idled in front of the house. I remember Yepez haranguing a soldier who had gone out hunting peacocks and brought one home alive, wrapped in his leather jacket. No one made a move to free the bird from its suffocating prison. Yepez told me to get into the car, and we sped away, my last view of the hacienda being of the crying leather jacket in the middle of the road.

That and a wounded butterfly clinging to our windscreen. I asked Yepez to stop so I could free the butterfly, but he said there wasn't enough time to kill anything; he had orders to get me to the airstrip, or else *he* would lose his life.

Yepez was rattled. He nosed his way through the herd of miniature ponies that had gathered on the road. No amount of honking or cursing on Yepez's part could make them budge. He started sweating and looking at his watch, then pounding the steering wheel. I thought he was going to run over one of the ponies, which refused to stand up, as if by laying down its life it could prevent me from laying down my own. I should have paid attention—but I needed another line, and the only drugs I had were stashed inside me.

Yepez drove around the pony, onto the swampy grass. For a moment I thought he was stuck—permanently, this time—but he manoeuvred the car back onto the pavement as if nothing had happened, as if the sweat falling off his face could be blamed on the humidity. The wounded butterfly flapped against the windscreen—"*looking for a new body to try on*," Daisy had said—then fluttered, finally, to the ground as the sentries at the gate waved us through and we drove south from the hacienda, along the road I'd taken another lifetime ago, on my way north to the City of Orchids with Angel safely inside me. Within minutes we were headed down the dirt road past the basin where El Chopo's ship was moored. Yepez approached the runway, looking more worried than ever, telling me to lie down on the back seat in case there was a problem.

Soon I heard a vehicle approaching. Yepez got out of the car—I heard him greeting someone—and then he poked his head in the window to tell me it was safe. When I sat up and looked around, I saw the plane that would carry me away from Tranquilandia; it was in much better condition than the one I'd arrived in, though I can't say the same about Tiny Cattle. I hadn't expected to see him ever again, but when he climbed out of the Jeep, straw hat minus the crown, same dark glasses, I felt a mixture of relief and fear. Fear that he had been holed up at The Liver Does Not Exist since I last saw him, and relief to see a familiar face. His hands were shaking, and Yepez didn't look much steadier after guzzling from the bottle Tiny produced from his coat pocket. As they loaded the coffin containing the remains of Daisy's child, I smelled *basuco* and figured Tiny Cattle had probably been smoking all night, and was now levelling out by drinking.

I felt both drowsy (the *burundanga?*) and pumped up, the high-grade cocaine humming in my veins, making my brain crave more, to stay alive, high, numb, dancing on the head of a pin, through the eye of a needle. Dancing all alone, except with my thoughts of Angel, my invisible dancing partner, as if by dancing into the unknown I could avoid inhabiting the menacing space of each present moment.

I climbed aboard the plane, which was filled with orchids, the scent as rich and numbing as the smell inside the Black Widow's solarium. Each orchid was wet, as if it had been picked weeping. There were orchids with flushed lips and slashed purple throats; orchids with white beards and bloodshot eyes. I even recognized one—"*with flowers more curious than beautiful, and a scent,*" Yepez had said, "*that may be intoxicating or fetid, depending on the species.*" I squeezed past the coffin on its bed of crushed virgin orchids, releasing their strong smell of sex and death. The scent made me want to take off my clothes and roll around in them, let their beautiful sensuous tongues lick off some of the hurt.

I felt as if the orchids were alive—human, alert presences on board the plane—as if they had me under surveillance, each with their own version of my story to tell. How she got here. Why she stayed. What she planned to do with the rest of her life. When the rest of her life would begin. What her death would feel like. What the sweet hereafter would bring. I wondered, too, as I buckled myself in next to Tiny Cattle, whether the plane itself wasn't a coffin meant for me—if we would drop into the sea, and I would cling to the wreckage in an ocean alive with orchids, before sinking forever into an orchid darkness.

Flores para los muertos. Thinking of that journey makes me almost too sad to go on telling this story. I want to shut everything down, close the book on it. Stop the images, like the one where my womb is an orchid and Angel is wrapped in it, struggling to get free.

And then there's the image of the plane being diverted to Panama, and the one of me deciding to flush the rest of my cocaine. Or the image of me being locked in a room at the airport, snorting as much as I could. A room with no view. A room with only one door to leave by, a door that opened inward.

It was in Panama where it all began to go wrong. Now I remember. But I am jumping ahead of myself. The way love jumped away, jumped out of me.

I looked down over Chocolata's island as Tiny Cattle drove the plane up into the air. I almost felt homesick, leaving that world of nightmares and dreaming. Having as much cocaine as I wanted, and having my baby in my arms whenever he needed comforting, had become home to me, familiar and routine. What lay ahead were different dreams, new nightmares.

Why would anyone want to get away from Las Blancas? I wondered what Angel was doing at this moment, if Daisy was feeding him coca tea. I wondered what kind of life, by leaving him behind, I had sentenced my child to.

Tiny Cattle was unusually silent. He chewed a wad of coca leaves; his jaw creaked when he chewed, as if it were opening and closing on rusty hinges. I looked down on Las Blancas' fleet—at the warship where El Chopo had spent his last months, making knives for therapy. I didn't know then what I know too well now: that memories are all we have. We remember what we have survived, which gives us hope for the future. Through memories, we make our peace with time.

While Tiny Cattle poured the last of the *aguardiente* down his throat, I looked over my shoulder at the coffin, as if making another kind of memory. The smell of the orchids was like a drug itself, and the scent made me think again of the moment Angel was born, how full of death his small life had been, how I would like to think he would go on living. I know one thing is true: I loved that baby, and I would have done anything for him if I thought it would spare him pain. I said this to the jury and they took it literally, not just as a way of speaking. They were supposed to be a jury of my peers, twelve well-intentioned men and women. Not one of them, not one American, when it came right down to it, could understand that there is a fate worse than death. I believed, I *still* believe, there is a fate far better than life.

All moot points now, as Pile, Jr. would say. Moot and mute. I heard the radio crackle, and Tiny reached for his radio phone and began to sweat harder as other voices filled the cabin.

"We're going to be doing some sightseeing," he said. I couldn't follow the instructions being issued from the radio. "We're taking the scenic route."

I could feel the cocaine I'd stashed inside me, as if it was about to come out prematurely, sliding slickly and whitely into this world.

Tiny Cattle didn't look at me. "It's Panama. I'm supposed to have a window. Nothing to worry about."

Nothing to worry about, he repeated, as long as I kept my story straight. "You need backup, I got this."

He patted his jacket, reached inside, and then said, "Take it and keep it next to you. Just in case."

But when I didn't reach for the weapon, he placed it in my lap. "Tec-9. Semi-automatic. Reputable kill rate." He looked over his shoulder, as if to make sure no one else was listening. "I wouldn't leave home without one. It's the ideal holiday gun."

chapter twenty-eight

Tiny Cattle grew more talkative as we broke through a bank of thick, grey cloud and circled that bleak no man's land that surrounds every airport I've ever been to. He prattled on like a tour guide, pointing out ships lined up at sea to enter the canal, vultures over the Hilton "where there were the best pickings" and off the coast, in the distance, the paradise island of Contadora (where the shah of Iran had stayed while in exile). Tiny said he'd lived "somewhere down there" with a Costa Rican beauty. He could always find his way back to their apartment because there was a bust of Einstein in a little traffic island across from his building's main entrance. "Alfred Einstein. You know, the genius."

As we came in for a landing, I saw bunches of green bananas hanging on clotheslines and a pack of dogs scratching at a mound of dirt. Tiny Cattle tucked our small aircraft in under the wing of an Avianca jet, as if the jet were a mother hen. I half expected to be surrounded by loudspeaker-toting police officers with their Uzis trained on us, but instead we sat, with the engines shut down, watching other peoples' luggage being loaded onto the jet.

After a while, a thin, harried-looking man holding a clipboard came out of the building, and Tiny opened the door of the plane and lowered the steps so he could climb aboard. The little man glanced at the coffin, crossed himself, then asked to see my passport, which he held upside down: either he didn't know how to read, or he couldn't be bothered. He flipped through, saw no entry or exit stamps and frowned. He questioned Tiny Cattle about our point of departure, and Tiny said they didn't have authorities on Tranquilandia; the official said he knew—every time he visited his brother on that island he got taken in by someone pretending to be an authority, some *gordo maricón*. Tiny said thieves were a problemo everywhere these days, which was one good reason for staying home, where the only surprises you got were the ones on television.

"*Sí, cómo no,*" the man said wearily, and he wrote on his clipboard and pulled at his chin as if he didn't know what to do next. He asked Tiny where we lived and the purpose of our visit to Tranquilandia, and Tiny said I was a tourist. The little man glanced at the coffin; Tiny began whispering, as if I wasn't supposed to hear, "the señora, *qué lástima,*" and jerked his head to indicate the coffin.

"*Claro, qué lástima,*" the official said, but he didn't sound as if he thought it was clearly very sad. He asked

what had happened, and Tiny Cattle said we were sightseeing and there had been an accident. The señora was taking
the body home to Los Angeles—"her *niño querido.*" My
beloved boy.

The official shook his head and said he wouldn't detain
us much longer; he just had to make sure my papers were in
order. As he probably knew, there were many *problemas*
these days: planes loaded with contraband, *narcotráfico.*
What was worse, he added, as if his feelings had been hurt,
many of the *narcotraficantes* had tried to cut the
Panamanians out. They weren't receiving their fair share,
their *mordidas.*

He pointed to a group of baggage handlers hunched
together with two men dressed as pilots, all of them sharing
a cigarette under the wing of the Avianca jet. "You see that?
They are smoking drugs. That plane was supposed to have
left an hour ago. The pilot gets drugs and steers his plane
into the Andes? No problem. They find another pilot.
Every *hijo de puta* is a pilot." He went on to recommend that
Tiny Cattle do his *negocios blancos* with the police. "They
get everything for nothing, so they can sell it cheap." He
had a brother-in-law on the police force, he said, if Tiny
was ever interested in making an honest connection.

Tiny Cattle thanked him, opened his wallet and gave
the man his *mordida.*

"*Sí, hay muchos problemas,*" said the official. He said he
didn't go looking for trouble, but problems always seemed
to find him.

Tiny Cattle then asked if he would like me to open the
coffin, so that he could inspect the remains. It had been a

messy accident, he said. The official looked at the coffin and scratched his face again. No, he said, he did not think it would be necessary to open the coffin. Out of respect, he said, looking at me sideways, for the señora.

He bent down to sniff one of the orchids. He touched it, and then sprang back and began wildly shaking his hand and shouting, as if in terrible pain. I looked closer at the orchids to see what could have hurt him: the official had been bitten by a fire ant.

I remembered Don Drano, in the garden at the Hotel Viper: *"Virgin orchids,"* he'd said, *"Never pick them. They are not what they appear to be."*

The shaken official told us to come with him at once to the terminal. Another problem had found him.

I saw posters on every wall as we made our way through an underground tunnel into the terminal building. "Missing," they said, a word summing up a lifetime. And, underneath the word missing, the smiling, gap-toothed photograph of some four- or five-year-old who was probably, by now, turning seven in an unmarked grave: "Have You Seen This Child?" I wanted to turn and run back to the plane, fly back to Tranquilandia, take Angel in my arms and never let him out of my sight ever again.

Inside the building, Tiny Cattle disappeared with the official and I was left to wait in a room with a chain-smoking American who wore a loose, oatmeal linen suit, a cowboy hat and a T-shirt that said "I Scored." He had missed one flight already because of these people's incompetence, he said. An American passport was supposed to open doors, and it did everywhere else in the world, but not in Panama. "As far as Latin Americans are concerned," he said, "fuck them all but six, and leave those for pallbearers."

A Panamanian businessman, who'd also been detained, offered to buy us both a whisky once they had returned his wallet.

When half an hour had gone by and Tiny Cattle hadn't returned, I decided to find a washroom. I wanted a pick-me-up, and I thought if I could get to a bathroom I would take out the cocaine I'd stashed, do a little bit, then stash it back inside.

The only nearby washroom in this secured area was closed, "for inspection." I tried the door, but it was locked, and when I backed away, as if to give myself a run at the door before kicking it down, I saw a young policeman, holding an oily lunch bag, watching me. He wore his white gun-belt aslant, cowboy-style, and he strolled over and asked if he could help me. I said I was looking for a *lavabo*.

"*Está enferma?*" he asked. He reached into his bag and pulled out a fistful of pork scratchings, popped them between his greasy lips. His mouth reminded me of the hole in the floor of my *baño* at the Hotel Viper.

I told him no, I was not sick. I didn't think I should be required to give him a reason for wanting to go to the bathroom. He munched on his *chicharrones* for a while, trying to look important, and then asked to see my papers.

I explained that my passport had been taken from me. He asked where I was born, and I said Canada.

"You are very far from home. Your husband is not with you?" He stuffed his bag of pork rinds in his trouser pocket as an older policeman, who seemed to be in charge, headed our way. The young officer asked his *jefe* for permission to search my bag; the chief smiled, showing two teeth rimmed with gold.

I gave up my bag to the young officer. "*Hay una problema?*" I asked the *jefe*. He patted his revolver. It wasn't the answer I'd been hoping for.

I felt cold all of a sudden, and for the first time I noticed the bad smell in the terminal, half-diesel, half-human. By the door a *campesina* was selling oranges she had built up into a little pyramid. The *jefe* walked over and helped himself to one, peeled it, then broke it into pieces. He sucked the juice from each moon-shaped section, spit out the seeds and dropped the rind on the floor.

At that moment, the young policeman found Tiny's "ideal holiday gun." The *jefe* told him to check to see if it was loaded, and it was.

"She is not a tourist," I heard the *jefe* say to the young police officer.

The official who had boarded our plane alerted security. The *jefe* showed him the gun they'd found in my purse, and said he wanted me detained for questioning. When I protested, and started shouting that I wouldn't say anything until I had spoken to a lawyer, the *jefe* suggested the official put me in "the small room" where I could rest, and that he should call a doctor to "investigate" me.

When the *jefe* left, I tried to calm myself down; I told the official I didn't need to be put in any room—I would answer whatever questions they he had for me now, on the spot. Tiny Cattle said nothing, but mopped his brow with a handkerchief and mumbled about killer humidity and needing to get the show on the road as soon as possible. I felt, suddenly, that I had dried up inside, the way a river dies in a time of drought. I said my baby's name, I said *Angel*, and it was then that the dried-up places inside me began to crack. The fissures widened, so that whichever way I turned I was doomed to fall.

The official laid a hand on my arm. "*Por favor, señora*," he said. *Por favor*. There was something so hopeless about his words, so resigned to sorrow, at least when I allow myself to think back over that day. It was almost as if he would have saved me if he could.

He led me away to a windowless cell with a hard, narrow bed, a single (stained) sheet, no air conditioning. I had a sink, a toilet. The room was bigger than my prison cell is now, but it felt small to me then, and less hospitable. A dead-end room, the first of many. No way out but the future.

Before he left, I did what I had seen Consuelo and Tiny Cattle do. I took off my shoe and offered the official my mad money, "for his trouble." The official turned it over in his hand, and then smiled and shook his head sadly, as if I had insulted him. It was a *billete chimbo*, he said: Pamananians were not *estúpidos* who accepted fake bills passed off on them by greedy *norteamericanos*.

He took the counterfeit money anyway and left, locking the door behind him. Time closed in on me; I felt as though I hadn't slept for days. How long would I have to wait? I thought of Angel, the way he reached for me. I banged on the heavy door, using my fists and then my head. "*Señor, por favor, ayúdeme.*" Help me. Please help me.

I had no watch, no clock, nothing but the slow ticking to death of time inside my rib cage. One bright light bulb, surrounded by a wire cage, burned down on me. I sat on the toilet and pushed out the condom of cocaine I'd been saving.

I had nothing to chop it with, no X-acto blade, no hundred-dollar bill with which to suck the coke up into my nostrils. I took a pinch and snorted it straight from my hand, inhaled as much as I could, then blew my nose into a piece of waxy brown toilet paper. My nose was full of blood, and now my head began to sing and spin, but it didn't go numb the way it used to, or was supposed to, and everything felt too clear. I slipped the cocaine into my shoe and crawled under the sheet, trying to stop the racing of my heart, the congested feeling in my head and chest.

I had to flush the rest of my stash down the toilet. Once it was gone I could confess, explain to the official that I was a hostage trying to make her way to freedom, a woman who'd been forced to leave her baby behind. But then Consuelo's words came into my head: how well I played the part would determine Angel's fate.

I took the remaining cocaine out of my shoe and poured it (most of it) down the toilet, where it dissolved slowly into a white river before I flushed it away.

A while later the official came back with a bologna sandwich (no butter) and a plastic glass of fake orange juice. I didn't have an appetite. I asked to make a phone call, to contact my husband, but he said to make a call you needed a "message slip." I asked if he could find one for me. He didn't think so.

He informed me that a doctor would be coming to examine me. He wouldn't look me in the eye as he spoke, as if he was embarrassed for me. He toyed with his clipboard. I think he might have been afraid of the desperation he saw in my eyes.

He didn't return that night. I didn't *know* it was night, of course, it was only a guess. The cocaine I'd snorted before flushing most of it away kept me from feeling hungry, so I didn't care when nobody brought breakfast. I'd slept very little—it's hard to sleep under a burning light bulb with only a thin sheet to cover your head—but I decided to come fully awake by doing a line, knowing that whatever I had to face in the new day would probably not be pleasant.

I still had the coke in my shoe. I fished it out. The humidity, and the fact that I hadn't had time to seal it properly, had turned the fine white flake into a grey, mucousy pulp, like something I might have blown out of my nose after a night of excess. I would like to be able to say I flushed the rest of it down the toilet—all but a rock or two, which I decided to try to save—I would like to say I flushed it for the *right* reason (to get rid of it, to show I had power over it), but I didn't. I kept it, even though it was useless to me now. The only way I might have been able to save it would have been to dry it out under a heat lamp.

That's when the bulb went on in my mind. I could save what I had left of the sample by drying it under the bright light burning down on me.

I was standing on my bed, which I'd pushed into the centre of the room, my hands reaching towards the light, when the official, the *jefe* and two other men—undercover agents who had DEA written all over their pressed Levi's, black T-shirts, mirrored sunglasses and shoulder holsters— burst through the door. I remember thinking, Why didn't they just unlock it? They owned the keys.

"When you find yourself listening to their keys, and owning none, you will come close to understanding the white terror of the soul . . . " The white terror of the soul had been, for me, the prospect of living without cocaine. Maybe if I hadn't held on to that last small bit, my testimony would have had more credibility. I was caught, red-handed, as they say, with an ounce of what had once been pure flake. They exaggerated: it wasn't an ounce—it was, at the most, a couple of grams. But it didn't matter in the end, because they opened the plane's luggage compartment and found two hundred kilos.

I had no bargaining power. Tiny Cattle had disputed my story, turning on me and telling a whole different version to the Panamanian officials, so that by the time the combined forces of the DEA and DAS were called in, I didn't stand a chance.

Frenchy said my mistake was cornering a rat, that he had to do what he did in order to save himself. I see that now. All I could think of at the time was what would happen to Angel. A good mother wants what's best for her kids, Rainy always says. At least Rainy knows *her* kids are in a better place than this one.

The following is the scenario as told to the Panamanian

authorities by Tiny Cattle. He had been hired to fly me to the States with a deceased infant. He'd been around a long time, and one of the reasons was that he knew better than to get mixed up in any drug dealings with Las Blancas. He signed a deposition saying I had planned to sell the drugs for personal gain when I got to Los Angeles.

It isn't written anywhere, but I know Tiny Cattle bribed the Panamanians, paid them to back up his story. Tiny Cattle turned state's evidence in exchange for immunity.

Frenchy said, "Don't blame yourself. You got kidnapped; they got you doped up. They stole your baby, and they set you up." I should have had Frenchy for a lawyer. Whatever else she might screw up, she wouldn't assassinate my character.

I was the missing link, the police maintained. Las Blancas had been under surveillance in what they called Operation Orchid, for five years. While they couldn't touch Consuelo or the Black Widow as long as they stayed on Tranquilandia, they had her people in Panama and Los Angeles. And they had me.

I was under arrest for murder. I tried to stay calm, even when a doctor came and told me to take off my clothes; I told him they had already found everything I had. Two soldiers helped him strip me and strap me to the bed. The doctor took my temperature, rectally, then conducted his oily rape. "There's nothing in there," he said. I could hear his irritation, his little eyes like slits in the birthmark covering his face. It seemed to me he kept his fingers inside me for much longer than was necessary, but when you're arrested you lose all your rights—you're banished from commerce with mankind.

The doctor tested me for venereal disease. He asked when I had lost my virginity. If my feet hadn't been restrained I would have kicked him. The soldiers snickered. I heard Angel saying, "*You shouldn't worry so much. Don't start worrying until they start shooting, and even then you shouldn't worry. Don't start worrying until they hit you, because then they might catch you.*"

I had been caught. The doctor told me to get dressed, to wait. Then one of the DEA agents came back with the photographs.

Before he led me out of that room, in leg-irons and with a chain wrapped around my body, the agent asked if I had any requests. I asked him to give back the picture of my baby, the one they'd taken from my shoe, and he did. This small act of kindness was more than I could bear. After they had restrained me, and jammed a needle in my arm, I sat quietly, between two Drug Enforcement Administration officers, on a U.S. military plane bound for Los Angeles and tried to sleep. Everything that could not be finished by weeping or enduring seemed to brush past me into the night, taking flight towards the next world that awaited me.

chapter twenty-nine

Death Clinic, Heaven Valley State Facility for Women

> *Religion can be a significant influence in a person's life,*
> *especially during imprisonment, when more time for*
> *thought and reflection is available.*
> *—Inmate Information Handbook*

> *There are no peoples, however primitive, without religion*
> *and magic; neither are there peoples so civilized that they*
> *are devoid of magic. All people turn to magic when*
> *knowledge, technology, and experience fail.*
> *— Bruno Malinowski*

If childhood is a time when we allow the creation of gods,
adulthood is bound to be a disappointment. The damage is
that in writing, you may recall what you've tried to erase,

you dig up what you buried, then *phhtt*—a flying cockroach hits the bug-zapper—the moment you find out what it is you don't want to know about yourself. Then it's over. Your ringing, shining life.

The photographs of Daisy and me in bed were exhibits for the prosecution, numbers 3 to 10. They had been found in the coffin, along with my journal, my pipe for smoking *basuco* and my X-acto blade. Even in court, the sight of the pipe and the blade made my mouth start to water.

The photographs of the baby wearing the coke spoon I had around my neck when I was in bed with Daisy were exhibits for the prosecution, numbers 11 through 21. When I first saw them, I wasn't prepared for the colour transparencies. Somehow I'd always pictured death as being in black and white, as if all the colour drained out of you along the way. Most of the pictures you see of dead bodies are in black and white, after all, as if there's no point in wasting colour film when there isn't a heartbeat. I'd even accepted that dead people's *blood* was black.

This time they'd spared no expense and used Kodachrome, so the blood looked real and the baby's skin the colour of the cocaine paste I'd been holding under the light when the authorities came through the door.

The American coroner testified that the baby had not died from natural causes. His chest had been split open and his heart removed. All his vital organs, in fact, were missing. The coroner said there was evidence the organs had been removed while the baby was still living.

Some of the jurors got sick looking at those photographs. One, who was pregnant, started crying, and the judge let everybody go home for the rest of the day. Everyone except me.

In the photographs, the baby is lying on a porcelain slab; I think that's what affected me more than anything else. If I have had a moment in my life that mattered, it was the moment Angel was born, and I looked up and saw the wreath of crucifix orchids and the baby boots sprouting, from their heels, a pair of newborn wings.

This morning I am served with a copy of the State Execution Guidelines (by Officer Gluckman, who else?). I sit in my house as she leans on my bars and complains about how she sometimes wonders if all the people who expect normal, productive, reasonable, cheerful, effective behaviour from her every day have ever gone through the kind of pain and anguish that she has over the past months because of her back.

There is a moment, though, when she looks at me and I think she might possess some empathy. But the moment passes, and she asks if I want anything; I say, "A cup of hot tea would be appreciated," and she goes away and comes back half an hour later with a lukewarm coffee.

The State Execution Guidelines give me an idea of what I can look forward to. Next will come the reading of the death warrant. I'll be moved to Death Watch and isolated from other Death Clinic inmates. With Rainy and Frenchy gone, I'm used to living alone.

When Phase I of Death Watch begins, all my "personal items" will be taken away, including my wedding ring, which I've asked to be returned to Vernal. The only books I'll be allowed are "religious tracts, maximum possession ten (10)." I'll be given tobacco, though I don't smoke, and couldn't smoke even if I wanted to: the dance-hall has been designated a smoke-free environment, and their policy is one of zero tolerance. The state legislators have gone even further: they decided to air-condition the death chambers at Heaven Valley "to make it more comfortable for everyone."

Once Death Watch begins, all visits with "outsiders" will be "non-contact." Legal visits may continue to be of the "contact" type, up until one week before the execution, when Phase II of Death Watch begins. It won't make any difference in my case. All my visits with Pile, Jr. have been non-contact, even when we've sat side by side sharing a soft drink in the visiting park. Non-contact in every sense—with Pile, Jr. being utterly beyond reach.

With Phase II of Death Watch, whatever property you have left is taken from you, except for a few "comfort items": "one (1) TV (located outside the cell), one (1) deck of cards, one (1) Bible." Very specific day-by-day regulations go into effect as the countdown to D-Day begins, starting with "Execution Day Minus Five (5)," when your executioner, wearing a black hood over her head, comes to introduce herself. On "Execution Day Minus Four (4)," testing of the equipment to be used for the execution begins. This is the day, too, when you take an inventory of the property they have taken from you and make a list of who gets what. You also write down what you hope will be your funeral arrangements, and get measured for the clothes in which you will be executed.

I have asked that my remains be sent home for burial. Vernal is supposed to be looking after this. He still can't forget about Angel. "I would have looked after him, you know. You only had to ask."

Vernal says we need to talk about "practical matters," like a last will and testament and where I'd like to be "put." I tell him, "in the same place as Dad," and that I don't want Mum ordering anything like "Rest in Peace" for my head-stone. I never was, and I never will be. At peace with any-one or anything. Except Angel.

Another practicality is the dog. Brutus has been diag-nosed with Canine Cognitive Dysfunction Syndrome. "It is difficult to watch your dog age," Vernal writes, with a P.S. from Brutus to show me how far the disease has progressed. "I used to remember where I buried every bone, but now I can't even remember how to bite."

He wanders aimlessly, sleeps more during the day and makes mistakes on the carpet, Vernal says. His pet-care provider recommends a new drug that is supposed to give old dogs a new lease on life, but there are side-effects.

"I'd give him a choice between lethal injection and the firing-squad," I write. But Vernal never sees the humour in anything I say.

On "Execution Day Minus Three (3)," you get the day off. A guard will be posted to sit outside your cell to record, every fifteen minutes, what you are doing—probably as close as most of them will ever get to creative writing.

On "Execution Day Minus Two (2)," the equipment is tested again, and there's an execution-squad drill. If they really wanted to get your underwear in a knot, they'd make you sit in the Chair, or stand on the gallows, as a kind of dress rehearsal. I'm not going to suggest this to Officer Gluckman, though. She'd bring it up for discussion at the next guard meeting and wouldn't even credit me with having thought of the idea.

"Execution Day Minus One (1)" is the day the kitchen takes your last-meal order. Unless you are like Frenchy, who always got her order in early.

Your last meal is served on a paper plate, and your only utensil is a plastic spoon. If you request a steak, the cook has to cut it into bite-sized bits for you, then reassemble it to look like a steak.

I haven't thought about what I will order, but I know it won't be anything I have to chew. I don't think I could lift the plastic spoon as far as my mouth either, so I won't start with soup.

The Aztecs called on priests to perform their sacrifices, and each one sat disguised as a god. Chanters came forward and began to dance with the prisoners and encourage them to sing.

The only ones dancing and chanting around here are the death-penalty proponents who wait outside the prison gates with their placards, cheering and hooting when the power dims or they catch a whiff of the deadly gas spewing from a T-shaped exhaust pipe high atop the dancehall.

Inside the prison no one is celebrating. Sometime around midnight you are allowed a one-hour contact visit with a clergy person, if you want one. At four in the morning you are served your last meal, and no later than 5:30 a.m. the official witnesses to the execution, thirteen in number, meet at the prison gate and push their way to the front of the mob. If you are the person being executed, you are allowed to designate the thirteenth witness (in Frenchy's case it was Rainy, but Rainy didn't ask me—she said she wouldn't even ask Jesus to get out of bed for her at that ungodly hour). I miss Rainy more than I had thought I would. I miss her Rainyisms—the dead if you dos, dead if you don'ts; the whoopee fucking dings. I almost miss her interrupting me all the time with her dumb but honest questions.

The twelve witness seats are sold on a first-come, first-served basis. As I've already said, they have no trouble filling the seats; people would pay to watch if there were standing-room-only, but fire regulations don't allow it.

At 6 a.m. the media witnesses arrive, also thirteen in number, and everyone is escorted to the Witness Viewing Park, where they are seated. Your execution team assembles in the death chamber. Somewhere behind this scene you are allowed to shower, change into your last new clothes. The superintendent reads your death warrant to you one final time. Only the prison chaplain will be allowed to accompany you as far as the death chamber.

The Aztecs led their victims, one by one, to the sacrificial stone. Each was given a drink of divine wine and shown how to defend himself. Some preferred to throw themselves on the altar and get it over with, some tried to fight; but it was all the same in the end. The heart was torn out, held up, offered to the sun, then sealed in a jar.

The state never shows much interest in the bodies of executed criminals. As soon as you are pronounced dead, you are taken to a waiting ambulance and transported to a medical examiner's office. An autopsy is performed, as if there can be any doubt about what killed you! I once read an interview with a coroner who said that even in death, no two bodies are alike, none is unremarkable. Sometimes in suicides you find advanced liver cancer, impending appendicitis, right-sided hearts; in the bodies of women who have been executed you might find a heart with a hole in it, as if an average-sized fist had slammed right through her body and out the other side.

Your remains are returned to your family, if your family will accept you. A mortician will prepare your body so you look natural, covering the cyanide rash on your leg with make-up, forcing your tongue back into your mouth. If no one claims your body, you'll be sent out for cremation. Then you're brought back to prison in a jar.

Rainy followed Frenchy to the Hill—you get a view of it from the chow-hall window—which is where they bury the ashes of all unclaimed Death Clinic inmates. She got a Styrofoam urn, and her inmate number on a slab of white-painted wood. The dead in prison don't even get their names back.

For most women, it's a pretty sad way to end up. I mean, each of those women was somebody's baby once. A mother, like me, nursed each one and loved her—even if it was just for a little while.

———

Having looked at it from both sides, I have come to believe that the death penalty is another symptom of the confusion in our society. Capital punishment does no more to deter crime than the Aztec human sacrifices did to keep the sun burning in the sky. Capital punishment, in our present-day state, could be described as an institutionalized "spiritual" response to a problem in modern life when our knowledge and technology fails. The right-wing religious groups *like* this magical solution. Their advocacy of capital punishment is a symptom of their own disease, their need to focus their hatred on those among us in society who are already most diminished.

The criminal has become the enemy, the only person left to hate now that we are expected to love our neighbour, no matter what his race, religion or sexual persuasion. The criminal is the Jew being chugged away to Auschwitz, the nigger on the chain gang, the queer in the closet, the spic, the wop, the wog; the criminal is a stranger, a monster, Female Evil incarnate. Through our hatred, criminals become something much bigger, more frightening, than what they really are. Men. Women. Like me. Like you.

I've seen enough here to know that nothing is certain, certainly not death, but I can't say I was prepared for Pile, Jr.'s latest letter.

"Do you think you are a good risk to be let back into society?" my classification officer asks.

A good risk? Well, I tell her, I won't invade Kosovo.

She says this isn't the answer she is hoping for. What am I supposed to say?

Pile, Jr.'s letter explained that as a result of the Women's Empowerment Coalition's latest efforts, I have won a new hearing. The coalition received an affidavit from a woman in Tranquilandia, casting a new light on the prosecution's version of the events in my case. And because of the passage of time and the difficulty of reassembling witnesses and evidence, the state might be willing to make a deal. The result would be a sentence under which I would be eligible for parole. If I accept the deal, Pile, Jr. said, I would be the first woman in history ever to become eligible for parole from a life sentence while still being held under a sentence of death.

A hearing would mean going through the whole process all over again. Many woman have had their sentences commuted or reduced by the Supreme Court who seem eager, these days, to overturn a death verdict; Pile seems to think I've got a real chance at Life.

I recalled Daisy's warning: she was Colombian—she'd always know where to find me. She wrote to me also, in her best King's English, saying she was married now, had two healthy boys of her own and worked at Hacienda la Florida as a drug-rehabilitation counsellor. The hacienda had been raided again not long after I left, she said, and was now (she drew a happy face) under new management. "There is no one left from the old days, except I."

No word of the Black Widow. Or Consuelo. Nothing about my boy. Daisy, though, had finally come to accept the truth about how her first son, Alias, had died.

Inside the card was a pressed butterfly. "The dead one can tell no stories," she wrote. "But for my son's sake, for Angel's, it is time I tell yours."

The night I received her letter, I dreamed I died. I found Angel alive and woke up in Heaven, believing we could both live forever.

In this world there is an unending supply of sorrow, and the heart has always to make room for more.

acknowledgments

Grateful acknowledgment is made to the following for permission to reprint previously published material:

Excerpt from *American Psycho* by Bret Easton Ellis. Reprinted by permission of Vintage Books.

Excerpt from *The Dwarf* by Pär Lagerkvist, translated by Alexandra Dick. Translation copyright © 1945 by Hill and Wang, translation copyright renewed 1973 by Farrar, Straus and Giroux, Inc. Reprinted by permission of Hill and Wang, a division of Farrar, Straus and Giroux, LLC.

Excerpt from *The Prince of Tides* by Pat Conroy. Copyright © 1986 by Pat Conroy. Reprinted by permission of Houghton Mifflin Company. All rights reserved.

Every effort has been made to source the quote used as an epigraph to part two. Any information regarding its authorship would be welcome and may be sent care of the publisher.

A version of chapter 7, entitled "Valentine's Day in Jail," was published in *Fever: Sensual Stories by Women Writers*, edited by Michelle Slung, and in *The Best American Erotica*, 1995, edited by Susie Bright.

The same story was optioned by Back Alley Film Productions to be developed into a television series called "Desire" for Showcase.

Selections from the death-row sequences have been published in *Monday* magazine.

My thanks to Diane Martin for being my editor, and to Stephen for all the years he saw me through.

Susan Musgrave is the award-winning author of two previous novels, *The Charcoal Burners* and *The Dancing Chicken*, as well as many acclaimed works of poetry, most recently *Things That Keep and Do Not Change* and *What the Small Day Cannot Hold: Collected Poems 1970–1985*. She lives near Sidney, British Columbia.